IF

BEFORE I WAKE

The Better Off Dead Series Vol. 2

TALES OF SUPERNATURAL HORROR

IF I DIE
BEFORE I WAKE

The Better Off Dead Series Vol. 2

TALES OF SUPERNATURAL HORROR

EDITED BY R.E. SARGENT
AND STEVEN PAJAK

Published by Sinister Smile Press
P.O. Box 637
Newberg, OR 97132

Trade Paperback ISBN – 978-1-953112-03-3

"The boundaries which divide Life from Death are at best shadowy and vague. Who shall say where the one ends, and where the other begins?"

-Edgar Allen Poe, The Premature Burial

Contents

AT THE CORE LIES DARKNESS

Steven Pajak

1

THE EXAMINING ROOM WAS COLD, sterile. White walls and cabinetry; the only color in the room the blue plastic chair and the faux leather examining table beneath the protective paper covering that stuck to the backs of your legs each time you moved. Dr. Hoey entered the room after nearly twenty minutes, and by then, Nick's nerves were raw with anticipation. He immediately looked at the woman, measuring her expression. He wished he hadn't; this was going to be bad.

Dr. Hoey rolled the white stool in front of Nick and sat with her legs together, hands on her knees. She was a thin woman in her forties, of Korean heritage. Her dark hair was pulled into a ponytail, and the horn-rimmed glasses slid slightly down the bridge of her nose. When she spoke, she had a slight accent.

"Mr. Sawyer, can you confirm how long you've experienced your symptoms?"

Nick considered the question for a moment. "For a while

now, I guess. I mean, the stomach pain and the difficulty swallowing. And the diarrhea. The blood in my vomit, that's new."

"I see. How long since you noticed the blood?"

"Last week. No, two weeks ago. Just a little at first."

"How often do you regurgitate?"

Nick thought again. "Almost daily."

"And the blood? Daily?"

Nick nodded.

Dr. Hoey looked at Nick for a moment. "I see."

She stood and guided the stool back to the cubby beneath the desk. Standing, she began typing on the computer keyboard, and an image appeared on the wall-mounted monitor beside her. Facing Nick, Dr. Hoey said, "This is the CT scan of your abdominal and torso regions, Mr. Sawyer."

Nick stood beside Dr. Hoey now, his eyes fixated on the monitor.

Dr. Hoey pointed at the onscreen image. "This is your stomach, here your liver, here your pancreas. Here is the large intestine. The dark lesions on these organs are carcinoids. Cancer, Mr. Sawyer."

Nick was quiet. After a moment, "But…all those areas are almost entirely black."

"Yes. I'm afraid the cancer has metastasized aggressively beyond the stomach and into almost all the surrounding organs and tissue."

"My God." Nick's hand went to his mouth. He stared at the scan; his eyes were drawn to the dark masses that covered almost his entire midsection.

"This is a lot to take in, Mr. Sawyer."

"What…how…can we treat this?"

Dr. Hoey's eyes were sad. "Your cancer is quite rare and extremely advanced, Mr. Sawyer."

"Okay, but there…must be something we can do, right?"

"Stage four is the most advanced form of the disease."

He waited. When she did not continue, he said, "I don't know what that means."

"There are no treatments, Mr. Sawyer."

"That's…that can't be right. What about surgery? Chemo?"

Dr. Hoey was quiet.

"There must be something we can do."

"Mr. Sawyer, is there someone we can call? Someone who can be with you right now?"

"No." Nick looked at Dr. Hoey. "Am I going to die?"

Dr. Hoey only looked at him with sad eyes.

"But I'm only twenty-six. I'm too young to die."

She continued to look upon him with sorrow.

"There must be something. Anything."

Dr. Hoey took Nick's hand. "I'm sorry, Mr. Sawyer."

Nick's legs felt weak. He squeezed Dr. Hoey's hand. "How long?"

Dr. Hoey hesitated. "Two or three months. We can give you medication to manage the pain and help with the nausea…"

A sort of numbness washed over Nick. Everything around him blurred, faded into the background. He stopped listening, tuned everything else out. He focused on the CT scan, his eyes searching desperately for areas where the awful disease had not taken hold. God, there were so few. Impossibly few.

2

NICK RUSHED TO his desk, pulling off his coat as he went, draping it over the back of his chair haphazardly. He plopped into the chair and looked at his watch.

"You're *so* late," Aimee said. She peered over her computer monitor. "Dan is looking for you. He already came by twice."

"I had a…was he pissed?"

Aimee's eyes said, *dumb question*. "What do you think?"

"Should I tell him I'm here?"

Aimee hesitated, and her eyes disappeared behind her monitor. "I wouldn't wait for him to come back again."

Nick turned on his computer so it would boot and then stood up. He confirmed his shirt was tucked in and his tie was straight before walking through the maze of desks to his supervisor's office. Phones rang in the background, and he felt everyone's eyes on him, as though he were a man being escorted down death row. He gulped as he approached. The door stood open, and Nick paused at the threshold for a moment before he knocked on the door frame.

"Hold on a sec," Dan said and pressed the mute button on the phone. The irritation in his voice made Nick's stomach flitter. "Jesus Christ, Nick. Nice of you to finally show up at…"—he consulted his Rolex—"…nine-freaking-thirty. You're an hour late."

"Sorry, I had a doctor's appointment."

"Yeah, don't we all?" Sarcasm and condescension oozed easily from Dan's lips, like they were his first languages. "You could have called, let us know you were running late."

"I'm sorry, I didn't expect it to take so long. I thought—"

"Jesus, you have an excuse for everything, don't you, Nick?"

Nick looked at the floor, not sure what to say. It was best not to say anything.

"You know we're already backed up with our invoices this month. Freaking Donna's out on maternity leave, and you pull this shit?"

Nick continued to stare at the floor, hoping this would be over soon. His stomach clenched, and he thought he could literally feel the darkness consuming his flesh from the inside. It seemed to burn.

"I've got clients calling me asking me about their orders— like this asshole on the line right now—and I'm due upstairs for a conference with senior management in fifteen minutes, but here I am listening to your excuses. You're freaking killing me here, Nick."

"I'm sorry," Nick said again. "I'll call next time."

"How about you just don't be late? Huh? How about that,

Nick?"

Nick nodded. His throat burned when he swallowed.

"Quit standing in my doorway with your dopey face and get some freaking work done."

Nick walked back to his desk, shoulders slumped, head down. Behind him, Dan yelled, "And you stay late to make up your time! Can you at least do that, Nick? Or is that too much to ask? Christ!"

At his desk, Nick pulled folders from his inbox and started to sort through them, feeling the awkward weight of his coworker's eyes on his back. Aimee peered at him over her monitor.

"That sucked. You okay?"

Nick didn't answer. He stood up and walked quickly—trying urgently not to run—through the office maze to the men's restroom. He stepped into an open stall, secured the latch, then pressed his back against the door. He was sweating and starting to hyperventilate. His stomach lurched and he fell to his knees and leaned forward just in time, retching into the bowl. Fortunately, he had not eaten breakfast this morning—or most mornings anymore—and expelled only a foul-smelling, pale-yellow liquid. Ribbons of bloody mucous corkscrewed through his vomit.

"Oh, God," he croaked.

With his head resting on his forearm over the commode, Nick broke down. He sobbed; his body hitched and shuddered. He pulled his knees up against his stomach, which sometimes helped alleviate the horrible pain in his belly, but not always. Nothing seemed to help his burning esophagus and horrible heartburn. He even felt the heat inside radiating inside his ears.

The bathroom door opened, and sneakers shushed across the tile and stopped outside the stall. Nick's eyes slid toward the door—he was too weak, in too much pain, to move his head. He recognized the sneakers even before he heard her voice.

"Nick, are you okay? You don't sound good."

"Go away, Aimee."

She hesitated. "You didn't look too good, either. You look…sick."

His voice sounded phlegmy, nasally. "Please, just let me be."

Aimee hesitated again. "I just want to help."

"Please, just go away."

He retched again, purging yellowish bile ringed with ribbons of mucousy blood. After a brief coughing jag that made his head pound and his throat feel like he swallowed fire, he heard Aimee leave. Sweat drenched his face. He hugged the toilet bowl, his face resting against the unsanitary seat where who knew who set their sweaty asses. Nick didn't care. He'd be dead soon, anyway.

3

HE WIPED MOISTURE from the steam-silvered mirror and didn't recognize the man staring back; dark bags under his eyes, red, flaky skin, patchy stubble, gaunt face. According to his bathroom scale, he'd lost nine pounds since Dr. Hoey had diagnosed his cancer two weeks ago. He held up a hand and covered the stranger's face that looked back at him. He hated looking at that other version of himself; that face was a constant reminder of impending death.

Acutely aware of the time and not wanting to get reamed out again by Dan, Nick quickly dressed and headed into work. He skipped breakfast and didn't bother making lunch, because he knew it would remain uneaten, sitting in the communal refrigerator until it molded and someone finally tossed it into the trash.

Arriving several minutes early, Nick hung his coat over the back of the chair and sank into it. He was winded just walking from his car. He flipped on his computer, feeling like he was moving in slow motion, every movement sluggish, exaggerated. While the computer booted, he started to sort his inbox and prioritize.

Aimee peered over her monitor. "You look…horrible."

"I'm okay." He didn't look at her.

She stared at him, considering what to say. "You really don't look okay, Nick."

He stapled two sheets of paper together and moved them to his outbox before realizing that was a mistake. He moved them back to his inbox. Aimee was still looking at him.

"I'm really worried about you."

Now he looked at her. Her strawberry-blonde hair was tied into a bun. He couldn't ever remember seeing her style it another way. Her eyes were blue behind the lenses of her designer glasses. He saw genuine concern in her gaze.

"Just a flu or something, that's all. Has me feeling a bit worn."

He couldn't see her mouth behind the monitor, but he knew she was biting her lip. It was her thing. Her nervous habit. It was cute.

She disappeared behind the monitor. "I hope you feel better."

During lunch hour, he went to his car to be alone. He couldn't bear to sit in the lunchroom, thinking of ways to lie to his coworkers about his weight loss or why he wasn't eating. So, instead, he sat in his car, throwing up yellow bile and bloody mucous into an empty coffee ground tub that he kept on the floor behind the passenger seat.

After he purged, he rested his head against the steering wheel, breathing deeply, waiting for the throbbing in his head and behind his eyes to fade. The fire in his throat and the cramps in his stomach were a constant. Swallowing his own saliva made him tear up from pain. He wondered if it would continue this way until…the end.

What if it gets worse?

The thought shook him.

Nick knew it probably would. He remembered the CT scan on Dr. Hoey's monitor. So much darkness eating away at him from his core, spreading its fearsome dark tentacles like vines of destruction, consuming everything. Perhaps the malignant tentacles had reached his heart by now. Maybe working their way up his spine to his brain even.

Nick found himself parked outside St. Michael's Church, uncertain how he'd gotten there. He didn't remember starting the car or driving it out of the work parking lot. He switched off the ignition and pocketed the keys. His hands gripped the steering wheel; he was completely unnerved.

He'd passed the church every day on his way to work and again when he headed home each evening. Nick hadn't set foot in St. Michael's for many years. He'd been raised a Catholic; he'd been baptized, had his first communion, and confirmation at St. Michael's. He'd also attended St. Michael's for grammar school before attending Notre Dame High School for Boys. Nick lost touch with his faith after his parents passed away during his first year at college. Given his current diagnosis, Nick believed that unconsciously driving to St. Michael's was a sign he could not overlook. Some larger force was at work here.

The church was empty this time of day between morning and evening weekday masses. Nick crossed himself with holy water and then stopped at a pew midway down. He knelt and made the sign of the cross before sliding into the pew. The wood was cold beneath his backside. The smell of what he thought of as Catholic Essence—Frankincense and Myrrh—floated pleasantly upon the air. He turned down the kneeler and prayed, his hands clasped in front of him, arms resting against the pew-back in front of him.

Nick started with the Lord's prayer then Hail Mary, those prayers that he easily remembered. He soon realized the prayers he'd learned in his youth were ingrained in his memory, and being here suddenly brought them all rushing back. He recited the Apostles' Creed, Hail Holy Queen and the Nicene Creed from heart. He lost track of time, losing himself in fevered prayer.

"Hello, son."

The priest stood beside Nick. A small Bible was clutched between his hands; a dark brown rosary—the color of well-oiled leather—was intertwined between his fingers. He wore a black shirt and white clerical collar. Wisps of fading black hair were slicked back high on his mostly balding head. He looked at Nick with pale green eyes.

"Hello, Father."

"May I sit with you?"

Nick hesitated. "Yes."

He slid over, making room for the priest.

"I'm Father May."

"Nick Sawyer." He shook Father May's offered hand.

"My apologies for disturbing your prayer."

Nick nodded.

"Something is weighing heavy on you."

Again, Nick nodded.

"Perhaps I can help."

Nick shrugged.

Father May set down his Bible but kept his rosary in hand. "Try me."

Nick sat back in the pew. He turned slightly to face Father May.

"I'm sick…"

Father May nodded and watched Nick with sympathetic eyes, encouraging him to continue.

"Stage four cancer. It's in my stomach…all over my body."

"What is your prognosis, Mr. Sawyer?"

Nick locked eyes with Father May. His voice waivered.

"Two months. Maybe three." After a moment, tears welled in his eyes. "Father, I don't want to die."

Father May nodded. The corners of his mouth turned down slightly. "It's natural to fear death. To fear the unknown."

"I'm not ready…to move on. There's so much more I want to do…*need* to do, Father."

Father May was quiet. After a moment, he knelt. He offered his hand to Nick.

"Let's pray for guidance, Mr. Sawyer."

Nick took the priest's hand and knelt. Together they prayed.

4

NICK WAS EXTREMELY tired; he felt exhausted down to his bones—deep in his marrow. The malignancy spreading around him claimed every ounce of his energy, every drop of his will. Kneeling beside his bed, he looked at the clock on his nightstand. Only eight in the evening, yet he was beyond fatigued.

His discussion with Father May that afternoon left him feeling at ease. Prayer and immersing himself within his faith after a long hiatus gave him a deep sense of hope. He certainly did not think that praying would cure him; he was not that naïve, but knowing that his faith would bring him closer to God, who would greet him on the other side with open arms to receive him, brought him great spiritual comfort.

On his knees, Nick retrieved the rosary from his nightstand drawer. It was his confirmation rosary, blessed by the archbishop. He found it in a box high up on the closet shelf, and he was relieved he'd kept it all these years. Now, holding the crucifix between the thumb and forefinger of his left hand, he made the sign of the cross with his right and began to pray the Apostles' Creed. When he finished his prayer, he got into bed. Though he knew it must be wishful thinking, the pain in his stomach and throat seemed muted. He realized he hadn't vomited in more than three hours. Feeling hopeful, Nick closed his eyes and prayed for a miracle.

He woke sometime later, not sure what disturbed his sleep. He sat up and pushed himself against the headboard and looked around the room. A small orb of light the size of a quarter appeared in the doorway, floating in the air about three feet off the floor. As he watched, the orb glided toward him, growing as it drew closer, until it was the size of a basketball hovering at the foot of his bed. At its center, it was white-hot, blinding, and it dimmed ever so slightly around the corona.

As Nick gaped at the orb, it began to increase in size slowly, like a balloon being inflated by a steady stream of air. When it grew to a circumference of nearly three feet, the sphere suddenly went supernova, exploding into a brilliant light that enveloped the room, extinguishing all darkness. The divine radiance infiltrated the room in its entirety, until only the radiant refulgence existed.

Nick raised his hand, shielding his eyes against the blazing luminosity. He could not see his hand in front of him. He looked down, expecting to see his body upon the bed, but he was awash in a sea of light. The light itself seemed to ripple, pulse, as though it were alive. He felt the glow emanating against his skin, tickling his flesh. He could not see, but he knew every hair on his body was standing on end, as if raised by an electrical current. A complete sense of peace swept over him, and he felt as though he were afloat, weightless.

When the voice of the divine light spoke, it was from within his mind. The being spoke Enochian, the language of angels. Nick somehow understood the words, his mind in some way translating the celestial tongue.

I AM RAPHAEL

Nick internally recognized this was merely a dream, brought on by his visit to St. Michael's that afternoon, the hope he felt his return to faith had sparked.

Speaking without words, Nick said, *I have cancer. I'm dying…*

The light came closer, warming Nick's skin. He felt his cheeks flush.

Save me, Nick thought. *Please, save me. I beg of you.*

I WILL ANSWER YOUR PRAYER

Raphael, the being, the energy, whatever it was, drew upon him, the white-hot center of the all-encompassing brilliance hovering above him now. Nick could not move; he was completely paralyzed. An appendage separated itself from the brilliance, and Nick felt it—an intense heat like a scorched tip of a brand—upon his stomach, felt it push through his flesh, through the wall of his abdomen, and into his gut.

Nick screamed, but not with his voice. The light somehow grew brighter as the entity scraped at the demon-cancer, trying to separate it from his body. He felt it being pulled from him, but the cancer held to him with its malignant tentacles. The light now became blinding, and he felt the heat of it begin to singe his flesh. The pain was excruciating, like none he'd ever experienced. As the horrible agony grew to a crescendo, Nick felt the dark mass give up its grip, and finally, there was only blessed darkness.

5

HE WOKE WITH a scream in his throat. He sprung up, pushing himself into a seated position. Gasping, he kicked free of his blankets and pawed at his shirt with his hands, pulling it up to reveal his stomach. He expected to see a bloody hole where the entity had reached within him. His stomach was unmarred, just pale flesh and a fuzz of thin navel hair.

Nick fell against the headboard and let out a shuddered sigh of relief. He wiped sweat from his brow as he focused on slowing his breathing. The dream was so vivid, had seemed so real. Even now, as the warm sunlight filtered in through the slats of the window blinds, he could not shake the idea that it was no dream. He laughed shakily, feeling silly. It was foolish to believe an angel had visited him during the night and removed the cancer from his stomach.

He frowned suddenly. He was still going to die. The cancer was still inside him, every day spreading, permeating deep into his organs, his tissue, his cells, bringing him one step closer to a painful end. He had only two months to live—three if he was lucky—and yet he had done nothing to get his affairs in order, had made no final arrangements.

Nick had an insurance plan—one of the few good things about the company that employed him—that would pay out one and half times his annual salary upon his death. However, Nick had no beneficiary named. He had no immediate family, no close relatives. He remembered an uncle on his mother's side in California, though he'd met him only once when he was a young boy. He couldn't remember anything about him other than his name was Richard.

He made a mental note to add Father May from St. Michael's Church as his beneficiary. In fact, later this afternoon, he'd go to Human Resources to draw up that paperwork. And later in the evening, he'd visit his attorney to draw up his will and instruction for his interment. Nick already had a plot—bought and paid for—at Queen of Heavens cemetery, where he'd buried his parents. His final resting place would be nestled between Mom and Dad.

He still had work ahead of him. He needed to get through the morning first. He swung his legs out of bed and stuffed his feet into his awaiting slippers. He reached for his cellphone on the nightstand. His hand came away slick; a dark, sludgy substance clung to the side of his hand. He looked at the nightstand, and his breath caught in his throat.

The blackish, malformed shape sat in a small puddle of the sludgy black goo that made him think of burnt motor oil. The object was about three inches in circumference and felt spongy when he prodded it with his finger. He dropped to his knees and bent closer to examine it but recoiled quickly when he inhaled the foul stench of it. He turned on the lamp with one trembling hand.

Although Nick's stunned mind wouldn't believe it, he knew that somehow, he was looking at his cancer tumor, the one that had first sprouted within his belly and eventually should have spread throughout, consuming him like an evil plague.

6

NICK SAT IN the same pew as he had the afternoon before, when he'd driven to St. Michael's on autopilot. He prayed while he waited for Father May, enthusiastic to tell the priest of his dream. Surely, what happened to him was a miracle, and Father May would help him understand, guide him through this holy wonder.

"You look much better today, Mr. Sawyer," Father May said when he finally came to Nick.

"I am better, Father."

Father May sat beside him. "I'm happy you returned. Can I pray with you again?"

"Yes. But first…I have something I have to share with you."

Father May raised an eyebrow. "Oh?"

Nick told Father May about his dream, describing the orb with great excitement and detail, the brilliant light, the voice that spoke from within his head. He became somber when he recounted how the entity reached into him, pulling the cancer from him. When Nick finished, Father May stared at him.

After considering his remarks, Father May spoke. His voice was soft and understanding.

"Mr. Sawyer, it is not unusual for someone suffering from a prognosis such as yours to have such dreams of being healed."

"But it wasn't a dream, Father."

"I am a man of great faith, Mr. Sawyer. I believe in miracles. I believe that God works in mysterious ways, sometimes through men and women like doctors who perform miraculous surgeries or through scientists who discover or create cures to incurable diseases."

Father May paused, again considering his words. "This dream you had, Mr. Sawyer, was not literal. It should be interpreted as a sign from God that he has accepted you and will receive you, not that he's healed you."

Father May placed a hand on Nick's shoulder. "I don't want you to lose your faith, Mr. Sawyer. But you have to understand that what you witnessed was just a dream."

Nick looked at Father May and frowned. He'd been so sure that, if anyone, Father May would believe.

"I want to show you something," Nick said.

He rummaged into his bag and lifted out a repurposed mayonnaise jar and held it out in front of him. Father May's appeared repulsed by the contents.

"I don't understand. What is this?"

"My cancer."

Father May's eyes shifted from the disgusting malignancy to Nick, then back to the tumor.

"When I woke, this was on the nightstand beside my bed."

Father May was silent. He continued to stare at the tumor.

"This is a miracle, Father. You must believe me."

Father May could not seem to take his eyes off the specimen in the jar. Finally, he looked at Nick. "I need to pray and seek guidance, Mr. Sawyer. Will you pray with me?"

Nick set the jar down between them, watching Father May's eyes again slide toward the dark flesh before he finally knelt, made the sign of the cross, and began to pray silently.

7

DR. HOEY WAS dumbfounded. She used her fingers to enlarge the CT scan on the iPad, zooming in on the stomach where the largest concentration of tumors had been. After a moment, she looked up, started to say something, stopped, then started again.

"I don't understand. I don't…know how this is possible."

"It's gone, isn't it? All of it?"

Dr. Hoey looked back down at the scan. She shook her head in disbelief. "Yes."

"You're sure?"

She stood and used her iPad to cast the current CT image onto the large monitor mounted to the wall where Nick's previous CT scan was already displayed. The new image on the right showed absolutely no dark spots, no masses, no lesions. All of his organs and tissue looked completely normal.

"I don't understand," Dr. Hoey said again.

Nick looked at Dr. Hoey. She pushed her glasses up the bridge of her nose. She looked back at him, at a loss for words.

"This is not a mistake?"

Dr. Hoey shook her head.

"And the first CT scan…that was not a mistake?"

"How could it be? You presented with symptoms. Were your symptoms not real?"

Nick remembered the pain, the vomiting, the bloody mucous.

"They were real."

Dr. Hoey looked at Nick again. "Do you have pain now?"

"No."

"Vomiting?"

Nick shook his head.

"No symptoms at all?"

"No."

"For how long?"

Nick thought about it. Two weeks had passed since the angel visited him. "Two weeks."

Dr. Hoey looked at the two images. "I can't explain it."

8

NICK ROLLED OUT of bed, feeling better than he'd felt in a long time. He felt rested. He'd slept through the night without pain or vomiting, which hadn't happened in many months. He showered, shaved, and dressed. In the kitchen, he made breakfast. He actually had an appetite, which made him happy.

After eating, Nick checked the calendar on the refrigerator door and realized he had the next two weeks off. He'd forgotten he'd requested vacation time; he didn't have plans when he'd scheduled the days earlier in the year. He'd only requested the time off so he wouldn't lose the benefit; just getting away from the office and Dan for two weeks was Nick's idea of paradise.

Fed and feeling good, Nick changed into joggers and a sweater and started to do some work around the condo, which he'd been putting off for a while due to his health. He spent the morning and afternoon doing odds and ends and even stopped to take lunch. He ordered from his favorite sandwich shop and couldn't stop smiling the whole time as he ate the toasted submarine.

Later, he decided he wanted to get out of the house for some fresh air. After checking his social media, he learned the folks from the office were meeting for drinks at a local pub. Normally not one to socialize, Nick was in good spirits and decided he needed a night out. He arrived at the pub around six, realizing he was a bit early when he didn't spy anyone from the office. He was about to leave when Aimee spotted him and called out. She'd been in the ladies' room when he first entered.

She hugged him. He stiffened a bit, unaccustomed to the contact, then recovered and returned the embrace.

"This is unexpected. I missed you at work today."

"Vacation," he explained.

"What is *that?*" Aimee joked. Although paid vacation was one of their benefits, Supervisor Dan frowned when anyone from the team actually wanted to use their time off.

"I don't think I've ever seen you outside of the office."

Nick smiled. "You have now."

Aimee laughed and touched his arm. "Let's get drinks. The others should be here soon."

She led them to a booth at the back. Nick scooted in, and Aimee slid in next to him. Holding her drink, she sipped it from a tiny straw. "You look…well."

"I feel well." His drink sat in front of him on the table, and he sipped it. The Jack and Coke warmed his belly.

Aimee stared at him and stirred her drink playfully. Nick noticed her hair was down and fell just below her shoulders. Her hair framed her face in way he'd not seen before, and for the first time in the three years he'd worked across from her, he realized she was attractive.

"Your hair…it looks nice that way."

Aimee blushed. "Thank you."

"And you have pretty eyes. I don't think I ever told you that."

She smiled coyly. "You finally noticed."

Nick felt his earlobes get warm, and he drank more of his cocktail.

Aimee examined him for a moment over her own drink. Her tongue played at the tip of the straw, unconsciously flirting.

"You're different outside of work."

Nick raised an eyebrow.

She touched his arm. "In a good way, of course."

"It's nice to see you without a monitor in front of you."

He groaned inside. He sucked at small talk.

"You like what you see?"

The heat in his earlobes spread into his cheeks.

"Yes, very much so."

Aimee finished her drink, her eyes never leaving Nick.

"You better catch up."

Nick lifted his drink to his lips and took a swig.

Aimee stared at him then said, "I'm just gonna say it. I have a crush on you."

Nick sputtered and coughed as Jack and Coke went down the wrong pipe.

Aimee laughed. She handed him a napkin, and he wiped his chin and dabbed tears from the corners of his eyes.

"Sorry, just wanted to put that out there. In case you were wondering. Now you don't have to. Wonder, I mean."

Nick recovered and kept his cool. "Good to know."

He remembered the day Dr. Hoey diagnosed his cancer. He'd broken down in the bathroom at work, and Aimee had come to check on him. He thought of other times that she'd shown interest in him or tried to engage him into deeper conversation at the office. Not obvious signs that she liked him, but certainly signs, nevertheless. And he'd been oblivious.

After a brief silence, Aimee got up from the booth.

"Well, I'm…uh…going to get another drink. You want in?"

He slid out of the booth. "I'll join you."

At the bar, Nick ordered the drinks. Aimee sat at an open stool and patted the one beside her. Nick sat. Their drinks arrived, and they remained at the bar getting to know each other beyond their shared time at the office. Their coworkers began to filter in over the next hour, but Nick and Aimee stayed at the bar. For Nick, only Aimee existed in the here and now.

How did I not notice how pretty she was before? Nick wondered. *Or how cool and funny she was?* He realized he'd been missing out on someone wonderful who sat just the other side of his monitor this whole time. If he'd still had the cancer in his belly, he would have missed out on this moment.

Two hours passed in the blink of an eye. Aimee suggested they get some fresh air. She excused herself and ran to the restroom while Nick settled the tab. Outside the pub, Aimee took Nick's hand as they walked toward the pier. They found an empty spot overlooking the calm lake.

"Look at all those stars. You can't see them from the city."

Nick looked up, following Aimee's gaze. Millions of stars dotted the sky. He'd never seen so many at once. It was breathtaking.

When he looked back, Aimee was staring at him.

"You look cold," he said.

He took off his cardigan and slipped it around her shoulders. Aimee leaned forward on her tiptoes and kissed him. Her lips were warm. The kiss lingered for a several seconds before they parted. They stared into each other's eyes. Nick kissed her again, this time longer. She put her arms around his waist, and he returned her embrace.

NICK WOKE, STARTLED, but quickly relaxed when he realized where he was. His bedroom was dark. The sheets were cool against his nude body, yet his skin was damp with sweat. Aimee lay naked beside him, the sheet covering the lower half of her body. One hand was tucked under her chin and the other draped over his waist. Several loose strands of her reddish-blonde hair lay across her cheek and stuck to her slightly parted lips. He touched a finger to his own lips; he could still taste her lip balm.

He watched her sleep for a while. She was so pretty, beautiful even. Three years they'd worked together, her desk across from him, separated by thirty-inch computer monitors, yet he never noticed her attractiveness. They'd sat at the same table in the breakroom during lunch, chatted about books or movies on occasion, yet he failed to notice her true personality; she was funny, spontaneous, and flirty.

Aimee was also *really* good in bed. They'd both been a bit tipsy and caught up in the passion of the moment when she'd kissed him at the pier. When Aimee breathlessly suggested they go to his place, Nick never expected they'd end up in his bed. They made out in the Uber and then more heavy petting on his sofa before Aimee took his hand and led him to the bedroom.

Nick smiled, remembering the deeds of their encounter, recalling the supple curvature of Aimee's breasts, the flare of her hips, and the way she moaned softly as she writhed on top of him, her hands pressing against his chest and her soft, warm breath caressing his face with each exhale.

As the light of early dawn started to chase away the shadows, Nick sat up and slid his feet into his slippers. When he stood, his stomach clenched, and a tight knot of pain made him double over in agony. He clamped his teeth together and wrapped his arms across his abdomen, hurrying to the bathroom. He managed to close the door behind him and turn on the vent before he vomited in the vanity sink. Yellow bile and ribbons of blood. He gagged and retched again, purging more of the disgusting vomit into the basin.

He leaned over the sink, hands gripping the vanity tightly. He breathed desperately through his nose and out his mouth in an attempt to control his gorge. He blinked away tears and stared at the mess of bile. Dread radiated through his body; the cancer was back. Somehow, it was back.

9

FATHER MAY REMOVED his reading glasses from the bridge of his nose and set them on his desk. On the iPad in front of him were Nick's three CT scans. The third scan, which Dr. Hoey had scheduled several days ago, confirmed the cancer was back. The mass was small and confined to his abdomen. It had not yet metastasized or spread, though he knew it would.

"And you are sure this second image is not a mistake?"

Nick shook his head vehemently. "Even if it was, look at the difference between the first and third."

Father May put his glasses on again and looked.

"Maybe this means the second image was a mistake, and the third images shows the cancer is regressing."

Nick sighed. He'd played the same devil's advocate with Dr. Hoey. "That wouldn't be possible without treatment."

Father May focused his attention on Nick. "Then how do you explain the second image?"

Frustrated, Nick took the iPad, put it to sleep, and slipped it into his shoulder bag. "I already told you how."

Crossing his hands in front of him, Father May's expression was sympathetic. "You truly believe you were visited by a divine light that cured you of your cancer?"

"An angel."

Father May nodded once. "Yes, right, the angel Raphael."

"I believe that, with all my heart."

"Then why do you think the cancer returned?"

Nick hung his head. When he spoke, his voice was almost inaudible. "That's what I don't know." He looked up now, fixing Father May with his wide eyes. "Maybe there is something I was supposed to do…something required of me that I failed to do."

Father May frowned. "I don't believe that's how miracles work."

"So, you believe it was a miracle?"

"That's not what I am saying, Mr. Sawyer, but if indeed God sent Raphael—his healing angel—to remove your…ailment…it would be because of something you'd already done, something that deserved to be rewarded by divine intervention. There would be no conditions. Certainly no take-backsies."

Nick considered this a moment, after which he shook his head. "There must have been something…something…"

Patiently, Father May opened his desk drawer and retrieved

his rosary. He wound it around his right hand. "I don't know that we will find the answers, but we could pray on it. Would that be okay?"

Nick was quiet, doing his best to remember the encounter with the glowing orb and the entity that spoke inside his head. *Angel,* he corrected himself. *It was an angel, Raphael.*

But he must have missed something. He must have. It occurred to him that Raphael had visited him the evening after praying with Father May at St. Michael's and then after his own prayers before turning in for the night. Perhaps prayer was the answer. He had nothing to lose.

10

THE MONDAY HE was supposed to return to work, Nick called off, too sick to leave the house. He spent the whole day in pain, vomiting everything that he put in his stomach. He saw several missed calls and unanswered texts on his phone from Aimee. He wanted to respond, but he didn't know what to say.

No, I'm fine, just took the day off because I'm dying.

Hi, sorry, no, we can't go out to dinner because I have cancer and I'll vomit all over the place.

No, I can't make love to you, because my stomach hurts so bad and I may have a case of explosive diarrhea in the middle of climax.

He was miserable, depressed. If this was how the rest of his days were going to be, then there was no point in living them out.

Why spend my last days suffering? Why not just end it now?

But he knew he didn't have the balls to take his own life. Besides, it was the ultimate sin for a Catholic. Truthfully, Aimee was the reason he wanted to keep going. Aimee was the best thing that had happened to him in…well, forever. He was happiest when he was around her.

Aimee made him feel a sense of the familiar and a sense of comfort whenever he was around her. She made him feel breathless with wonder and curiosity. Each moment he was with her, it was as though time had suspended, making the whole world seem still except for the two of them. So, if he had to suffer through the horrible pain until the very end, he would cherish each and every moment he was privileged enough to spend with her.

After another cycle of vomiting and diarrhea sent him running to the bathroom, the pain finally subsided for the moment. Exhausted beyond belief, Nick curled up in his bed and prayed that God would take away his suffering as he went to sleep.

11

THE BLAZE OF the divine light woke him. The angel, *his angel of light*, had again returned. Nick lay still, paralyzed, awash in pulses of gloriously pure energy that flowed over him, through him, enveloping him until he'd become part of the awesome light-energy.

Raphael hovered over Nick, his voice soothing. Soon, the tentacle of light separated from the core of the angel. The light flared and pulsed, blinding, and then the tentacle disappeared deep within Nick's belly. The fire came, then the excruciating pain, followed by blessed darkness.

12

THE MALIGNANT FLESH was there on the bedside table, just as he'd hoped it would be. He breathed a deep sigh of relief, and his whole body seemed to relax; the horrible, evil thing inside of him had once again been excised. Nick Sawyer had been given another chance.

Nick eyed the rancid, putrid tumor. The viscous, black liquid had begun to ooze down the side of the nightstand. He retrieved a Tupperware container from the kitchen and used a spoon to push the disgusting demon-cancer inside before sealing the lid. After he cleaned the remaining mess with Clorox wipes, he sat at the edge of the bed, considering his next course of action.

He thought back to the visit the night before. The angel Raphael told him that the cancer was a demon, and therefore could not be killed or destroyed, but that it could be passed on to another. His options were significantly limited. Either give the cancer to someone else or wait for it to once again grow inside of him—causing him to suffer until he died. Neither were ideal options.

As he considered each scenario, he couldn't believe he was actually doing so. Was he really sitting there wondering if he could knowingly pass the demon-cancer to someone? That would be a death sentence, and he could not stomach being the cause of someone's death, not from such a horrible disease. He simply could not give cancer to someone else for his own sake. It was unethical, unconscionable, and immoral.

Would it not be a sin?

He could not understand why Raphael would even give him the option if it were.

Nick vaguely remembered reading in the old testament about how God tested Job's patience, Shadrach, Meshach, and Abednego's faith, and Peter's love. Was this choice a test? Did the divine entity expect him to choose between living a longer life or damning himself for all eternity?

Nick needed guidance, and there was only one place he could go for help. After calling in sick to work for the second time that week, he drove to St. Michael's Church.

13

NICK SET THE container with the demon-cancer on Father May's desk. He watched the priest's reaction. Father May slid the container toward him and tilted it slightly so he could see the tumor without removing the lid.

Father May shifted his eyes to Nick. He asked the question, though he already knew the answer. "Is this the same…cancer that you showed me before?"

Nick shook his head.

"You've had the dream again?"

Nick nodded.

"It was the same?"

Nick leaned forward. "Yes and no. It was the same in that Raphael appeared and he removed"—Nick pointed to the container—"*that.*"

"And how was it different?"

Nick told him about the message from Raphael; he had to pass along the cancer; it was the only way he could truly be cured.

Father May sat back in his chair, his face wrinkled with concern.

"I should have seen this before. There are great forces at work here, Mr. Sawyer, that are beyond yours or my understanding. We must tread carefully."

"I don't understand."

"I do not believe you were visited by the angel Raphael or any divine entity, but instead by something…malevolent. Evil, Mr. Sawyer. No creature of God would put your soul in jeopardy by asking you to poison another."

"You're saying I was visited by…"

"A temptation from the devil, cloaked as an angel of light."

Nick shook his head, completely confused.

"What you described is characteristic of the evil angel, who takes on the appearance of an angel of light. He performs perceived miracles with hidden objectives and deceits that mask his evil intentions."

Father May leaned forward. "Darkness and light are metaphors for evil and good, Mr. Sawyer. If a man sees an angel of light, he will automatically assume he is being visited by a good being, for the correlation of evil with darkness, and of good with light, is a powerful archetype in human history. In the Bible, light is a spiritual metaphor for truth and God's unchanging nature. Light is the place where love dwells and is comfortable. God has created light, dwells in the light, and puts the light in human hearts so that we can see and know Him and understand truth.

"So, when 2 Corinthians 11:14 tells us that 'Satan disguises himself as an angel of light,' it means that Satan capitalizes on our love of the light in order to deceive. He wants us to think that he is good, truthful, loving, and powerful—all the things that God is. To portray himself as a dark, devilish being with horns would not be very appealing to the majority of people. Most people are not drawn to darkness, but to light. Therefore, Satan appears as a creature of light to draw us to himself and his lies."

"How can you be sure it wasn't an angel of light…a true angel?"

Father May shook his head. "As I said, no angel of light would make a condition of your cure—your miracle—to give that malignancy to another child of God. You must see that is what Satan wants you to believe. By masquerading as an angel of light, and performing a perceived miracle, he is deceiving you to believe that he is good, when he is truly poisoning your soul by asking you to sin in return."

Nick sat silently. He stared at the darkness within the container, more confused—and frightened—than before.

"Mr. Sawyer, you must listen to me carefully. You are locked in a battle for your eternal soul and must not take this lightly."

"What should I do, Father?"

Father May again shook his head. "This is beyond my depth, and I must seek guidance. I will speak to my superiors. In the meantime, Mr. Sawyer, do not do anything with…the contents of that container. Do not be tempted."

14

NICK POURED TWO fingers of Jack Daniel's Old No. 7 into a tumbler and then knocked it back quickly. He wiped at his mouth as the heat spread in his belly, and then he poured more whiskey.

On his laptop, he had several tabs of websites open, his research about the Bible's Old Testament. Not that he didn't believe what Father May told him about the devil masquerading as an angel, but Nick needed to learn more, absorb every detail from every possible source he could locate on the subject. He needed to understand exactly what was happening so that he could decide what he would do next.

Nick swallowed more bourbon. He shouldn't even be thinking about this. Whether the entity was an angel or devil in disguise, there really was no decision to make here, right? He couldn't pass this demon-cancer along to anyone. Putting aside religion, putting aside faith, putting aside whether or not good or evil forces were locked in a battle over the fate of his soul, he couldn't live with himself knowing he'd condemned another. He just couldn't.

The doorbell rang. Nick started. He wasn't expecting anyone. He quickly closed the laptop lid. He replaced the bottle of Jack Daniel's into the cupboard and the empty tumbler in the sink before answering the door. He was surprised to see Aimee, though he should have expected she would show up.

As soon as he opened the door, Aimee hugged him. Her scent was intoxicating. After a moment, she pushed him out to arm's length.

"Are you okay? You weren't at work yesterday or today. You haven't answered my texts or calls."

"Sorry. I just haven't been feeling well. Been sleeping a lot."

"Well, you could have just told me that. You had me really worried."

"Sorry." He sounded like a broken record now.

Aimee stared at him. Her brow was creased. Finally, she said, "You really don't look so good."

"Come inside."

Nick closed the door behind her. Aimee put her purse on the kitchen table and draped her coat over one of the chairs.

"Nick, have you been drinking?"

Nick swallowed. He knew she must have smelled it on his breath.

"I had a swig. Was hoping it would help me sleep."

Aimee touched his forehead, then took his face in her hands. "I'll take care of you now. Have you eaten anything?"

Nick shook his head. Even though he was actually feeling okay at the moment, the booze was sitting heavy in his stomach.

"Go lie down and I'll make some soup or something."

"You don't have to do that. I'm not really hungry now."

She looked disappointed.

He took her hand. "Come lie down with me on the sofa. We'll watch a movie or something."

"Oh, Netflix and chill, huh?"

Nick smiled. "But emphasis on the chill."

Aimee smiled. "Okay, but whether you feel better tonight or not, I'm gonna jump you."

Nick wouldn't argue with that.

15

PALE LIGHT FROM the moon slipped into the dark room through the blinds, leaving shadows across the carpet. Nick felt warm and kicked off the sheets, then sat up. Aimee was asleep beside him, laying on her stomach, facing away from him. Looking at her, he was overcome by emotion.

He was falling in love with Aimee. They'd only been dating for a short time, but she was special. Something amazing and profound was developing between them, and it saddened him that he would not be around long enough to see their relationship blossom into something extraordinary.

Nick had not told her about the cancer; he lacked the courage to tell her. Truthfully, he was afraid of how she might react, and he was not yet ready to let go of this happiness. She had to know, though, and if she felt the same way about him as he felt about her, she would stay. She would stay with him until the end. That was a lot to ask, he knew, but he desperately wanted her to stay. He wanted her face to be the last thing he saw before he slipped away.

After a while, Nick slipped quietly out of bed. He stood

naked, looking at the nightstand for several minutes before opening the drawer. His hand trembled slightly when he touched the container that enclosed the demon-cancer; it felt warm to his touch. He carried it with him to the bathroom and closed the door. He set the container on the vanity and sat on the closed lid of the toilet.

In the dark, the tumor appeared to pulsate. He stared at it, trying to determine if it had gotten smaller. He thought maybe it had, which meant he did not have much time left. As the demon-cancer shrunk, the tumor inside of him would grow and metastasize until it claimed him entirely.

16

THE NEXT FEW days were the best days of Nick's life. He and Aimee spent all of their time together. She stayed every night at his place. They had dinner together and then watched television for a while before moving on to some heavy petting that then led them to the bedroom. They made love every night.

In the mornings, they had breakfast together, then they'd each head into work in their respective cars. They both agreed to keep their relationship on the downlow at the office, because Dan frowned on employee fraternization, and Dan was the type of asshole that would fire them because he was secretly jealous of their happiness. So, they flirted over their monitors, held hands in the breakroom under the table, and sometimes snuck a kiss near the water cooler alcove when no one was around.

Nick had not yet told Aimee about the cancer. He felt horrible guilt over hiding the truth about the mortal disease, but he did not want to ruin things between them, at least not yet; not until he had to. He was so happy, so fulfilled, for the first time in his life.

That Thursday afternoon, the reality of his world came crashing back at him. After lunch with Aimee, Nick was at his desk reading an email Aimee sent him describing explicit acts she'd like to perform on him later that evening, when he felt a twitch of pain in his stomach and his bowels suddenly started to loosen. He ran for the bathroom and made it just in time. As he sat on the toilet, holding his stomach and squirting his bowels into the porcelain bowl, he started to cry.

17

BEADS OF PERSPIRATION formed on Nick's temples. He approached Dan's office and paused to rap his knuckles against the frame before stepping inside. Dan was playing a game on his iPhone. He glanced up quickly, then reverted his attention to his phone.

"What do you want, Nick? Can't you see I'm busy?"

Nick's stomach cramped, and he felt acid reflux burning in his chest and throat. "I'm not feeling well. I'd like to leave for the day."

Dan checked his Rolex. "Christ, Nick. There's only three hours left in the day. Suck it up and tough it out, for shit's sake."

"I'm sorry, I can't. I'm really sick, Dan."

Dan dropped his phone onto his desk in disgust. "You always pull this shit, Nick. If you're not calling in sick, you're coming in late or you're leaving early. Honestly, it's no wonder we're always behind on work around here."

Nick squeezed his eyes shut and gritted his teeth. Pain pushed through his intestines with a vengeance. Sweat beaded on his forehead; his face flushed, and his ears grew hot.

"You're not just hurting me when you do this, Nick, but you're hurting the team. You're hurting everyone out there. You make us all look bad; hell, you make me look bad. You understand I have people upstairs that I have to account to, right?"

Nick swallowed hard. He felt the sickness in his belly, churning with vengeance.

"I'm not getting fired because of you, Nick. So, go take a minute in the bathroom, get yourself together, then suck it up and finish the rest of the day. Then you can go be sick on your own time."

He returned to his desk and shrugged into his jacket.

"Nick, what's wrong?"

"I have to go. I'll call you later."

He shouldered his bag and headed for the exit. Dan was standing in his doorway, yelling something, but Nick tuned it out. There would be hell to pay tomorrow, but Nick would worry about paying that debt when it came due.

Aimee caught up to him at the elevators.

"Nick, what's happening? Dan's going ballistic back there."

"I can't talk about it right now."

Aimee grabbed his arm and turned him toward her. He locked eyes with her. "Let me help you. Something's wrong, so why won't you let me help?"

"You can't do anything. No one can do anything. Just go back to work before you get in trouble. Please."

The elevator arrived. Nick got on and pushed the door-close button. He couldn't bring himself to look at Aimee as the doors slid shut.

On the drive home, Nick had to pull over. He pawed frantically for his coffee can on the floor and then vomited sickly, yellow-red bile into it. His stomach clenched, and he gritted his teeth as sharp pain tore into his midriff. After a while, when the pain was tolerable, he drove through it, in a hurry to get home.

18

NICK RUSHED INTO the condo and barely made it to the sink. He rinsed the yellow-red-mucousy vomit down the drain and then used a damp dishtowel to clean his chin. He sat at the kitchen table to catch his breath. His phone vibrated in his pocket. It was Aimee again. She was blowing up his phone, calling non-stop since he rushed out of the office.

He dug the phone out and set it on the table. Fourteen missed calls and four frantic text message notifications appeared on the screen. He needed to set Aimee's mind at ease; he knew if he didn't, she would show up in a few hours, after her shift was over. He would not allow her to see him like this. Not before he could explain everything.

Using the Google voice app, Nick dictated a text message to Aimee, explaining that he didn't feel well after lunch, that what he ate did not agree with him, and that he was going straight to bed. He swallowed, pushing the burning reflux back down into the pit of his stomach, then added a second message.

I should feel better tomorrow. Thanks for worrying over me. You're very sweet. I miss you more than you know. <3

After sending the completely inadequate text, Nick went to his room to lay down. He wasn't lying about that in his text message. When the pain was this awful, the best thing to do was sleep. His level of pain was greater than it had been in the past, though. The rest of the evening and well into the night, his stomach throbbed fiercely. He lost count of how many times he rushed into the bathroom to vomit or shit liquefied bile from his burning ass.

Whenever the pain pulled him from sleep, he stared at the container on his nightstand, convinced that he could actually see the putrid tumor shrinking. The container had become a macabre hourglass, the oozing mess measuring the passing of each second left on his death clock. The dark mess mocked him, taunted him. Nick Sawyer was running out of time. Morning couldn't come soon enough.

19

THE NEXT MORNING, Nick struggled to get out of bed. The lack of sleep and the symptoms of the cancer made even mundane tasks a herculean effort. He left his condo an hour earlier than usual, because he had an important stop to make before work. It was a matter of life or death, so to speak. It was not a decision he'd taken lightly; he spent the sleepless night searching his soul for the right answer.

Aimee was waiting for him when he got off the elevator. She threw her arms around him and hugged him before he stepped off.

"You had me so worried." She stepped back to look at him. "You really don't look well, Nick. You should go see a doctor."

"Been there, done that. Got some medicine. I'll be feeling fine in no time."

She looked at the box of pastries tucked under his arm. She smiled. "Jelly doughnuts are the cure?"

Nick smiled back, a real smile that he didn't have to work at. "Not just any doughnuts. The best in town. Dan's favorite."

Aimee grew concerned. "I don't know if pastries will be enough to smooth things over with Dan. He was really pissed about you walking out like that. He slammed his door and didn't come out for the rest of the day."

"Then we better get inside before we're late and we both have hell to pay."

After kicking his messenger bag under his desk and struggling out of his jacket, Nick looked up and saw Dan watching him from the doorway of his office. Dan consulted his Rolex and then angrily beckoned Nick to his office before turning curtly and retreating inside.

Nick picked up the box of pastries. There were two jelly-filled pastries in the stiff white box. He was not concerned that Dan might share these with anyone. Dan was a selfish prick.

"I'm going in. Wish me luck."

"Luck."

Looking at Aimee's cute smile, her blue eyes behind the chunky-framed glasses, her hair tied back, he again assured himself he was doing the right thing. Again, he marveled over the fact that the woman of his dreams had been in front of him all this time and he'd never really noticed her. He could have had so much more time with her; he couldn't help but wonder where they'd be in their relationship now, if they'd gotten together sooner.

There's still time, he reminded himself. *This isn't over yet.*

Seconds later, Nick stood in Dan's doorway. He expected to

be nervous; instead, a soothing calm had fallen over him. Nick stepped inside and stopped a few feet in front of his boss's desk.

"Before you say anything, I want to apologize. What happened yesterday, the way I handled it, was very disrespectful to you. I let you down, I let the team down, and I let myself down. There is no excuse for my behavior, and I promise you here and now, I will never act in that manner again and will not let you down again."

He'd rehearsed this apology on the ride to work, tweaking it in his mind until he was confident it was exactly what the man would want to hear. Nick felt foolish and self-deprecated by playing lip service to an asshole like Dan, but he understood it was necessary.

Dan stared at him for several uncomfortable seconds.

Finally, Dan motioned to the box. "What is that?"

"Oh, this is for you." Nick set the box on Dan's desk. "Just a token of my appreciation for all that you do for me…and the team."

Dan pawed the box toward him. "Are these from Finkel's?"

Nick smiled. "They are. I got your favorites. Fig and Cherry."

"So, what? Am I supposed to thank you?"

"No. This is me thanking *you*."

"You know, I could fire your ass for insubordination?"

"I do. Again, I am very sorry for my behavior."

Dan looked at the box; he eyed the fruit-filled pastries greedily through the clear plastic window.

"Don't think this…box of junk is going to buy you any favor."

"I wouldn't think of it."

"I'm going to be watching you, Nick. I've been very tolerant of your behavior over the years, but I've had enough. Just one more screw up, just one more…anything, and I'm sending your ass packing. You understand me?"

"Yes, completely."

Dan opened the box.

"I don't know why I'm even giving you another chance."

He poked his finger at one of the desserts, then brought the tip to his mouth and sucked at the crystals of sugar. Nick's breath caught for a moment, expecting Dan to cringe at the smell of the liquified demon-cancer Nick had injected into the treat with an eye dropper. Dan licked his lips, and Nick relaxed again.

"I wear my heart on my sleeve, that's why. I'm a sucker when it comes to giving people second chances."

Dan retrieved a napkin from one of his desk drawers, then plucked one of the pastries out of the box. Holding it up in front of him, he looked at Nick.

"Don't make me regret this, Nick."

"You won't. I promise."

"Since you're making amends, get me a cup of coffee."

"You got it."

"And then get to work. You're going to stay late today to make up for yesterday, right?"

"Yes, of course. Nothing would make me happier."

Dan bit into the fig-filled pastry, sugary crumbs sticking to his lips. A sound of pleasure escaped him as he took another bite.

Nick left Dan's office, a smile spreading across his face. He was feeling so much better already. He took a deep breath and sighed, feeling the burden of fate lifted off his shoulders. He had the rest of his life ahead of him, and it was time to start living.

DEAD PICS

Gerald Dean Rice

HE TWO MEXICAN PRISONERS WERE shirtless, hands bound behind their backs, squinting their eyes against the pounding sun. Mike marveled at how calmly the thin, older one spoke when he had to have known he was about to be executed in moments. His companion, a chubby, younger man, his head roughly shaven, sat watching him. Two soldiers stood to either side partially out of frame, only their lower bodies visible. Mike guessed they were military by their fatigues, and perhaps the two prisoners were from some drug cartel. The video skipped, and the two men were suddenly sitting with their backs against a brick wall. One soldier yanked on the cord of a chainsaw once, twice, and the small engine roared to life. He held the tool up for the camera's view, giving it three quick revs before approaching the thinner man. To Mike's surprise, the prisoner seemed calm despite his impending gruesome death. Mike would have imagined trying to escape, to get away from the chainsaw before it could carve into him, but the man waited, almost expectantly. What indignities must these two have endured before getting to this point?

The chainsaw was lowered and slowly, carefully, tapped the throat of the skinny man, blood spurting at his feet. The soldier backed away as if admiring his handiwork, and the chubby prisoner watched with apparent mild interest. He didn't scream in terror or plead for mercy or even beg for the soldiers to end his compatriot's life quickly. The soldier came back in with the chainsaw as cautiously as before, going for the man's neck again. The skinny man grimaced one last time, the life not quite drained out of him, but instead of backing away, the soldier continued until the prisoner's head flopped backward and his body slumped against the wall. The remaining prisoner scooched away a few inches, but not to get away from him. He seemed to be trying to get a better look.

His staring was short-lived as the second soldier stepped forward with a thick, curved knife. He palmed the top of the chubby prisoner's head, placing the knife to his throat. The chubby man tucked his chin, but it was too late; the soldier began sawing into his flesh, and a moment later came a hollow sound like a novice blowing into a flute.

The video ended, and Mike smiled. This one was a keeper. He right clicked on the screen, scrolled down the pop-up menu, and selected "Save As." He named the file "Twins" even though the two condemned men looked nothing alike. They weren't even the same shade of brown.

Mike sat back, closing his eyes to mentally savor what he'd just seen. It wasn't just the gore. Sure, that was his favorite part, but the resounding look of acceptance, of abject deflation, like every drop of fear had been squeezed out of them. Mike had never seen that before. He made a mental note to see what more he could find on these two later.

Mike had gotten his first picture when he was twelve but wouldn't have actually called himself a collector until he'd turned twenty.

Back when he was a budding teenager, the photograph of a dead, half-naked woman who'd appeared to have been stabbed to death had fascinated him. He didn't remember the magazine he'd seen it in, just that he had torn it out, folded it up, and pocketed the picture. Out of the three hundred–plus days he'd had it in his possession, Mike had taken it out almost every day and studied it as if the act of looking would reveal something new. Many times, it had, although most times he was simply revisiting all the old lines, curves, and jagged, bloody edges.

By the time Mother had found that picture and a few others—mostly animals—under his pillow, that picture had been well-worn, white-line creases from the many times he had folded and refolded it to the point of tearing. She had chastised him, paraded those pictures in front of everyone in the family as she berated him, called him an animal and any number of choice words, before she'd burned them. He hadn't been angry, knowing even then that having those pictures wasn't normal, wasn't right. He'd already committed every piece of that black-and-white photograph to memory and could recall it even now. From the slash through her palm that had nearly severed her pinky finger, to her splayed limbs. Every wound, the wrist bent at an impossible angle, her ragged fingernails. Even the passive look of what he later reminisced upon as quiet defeat on the woman's face. He hadn't known her story, hadn't cared, but guessed she'd given whoever her murderer had been the fight of his life before he'd taken hers.

Mother had ordered his father to take him to the garage and beat him. Weepy-eyed, Father had taken him out and, just before he'd begun with that thick, black belt of his, had said that this would hurt him more than it would Mike. Mike had doubted that but, in his terror, kept his tongue in check rather than offering to beat his father to spare him the pain. Then the belt had come off, as old and as creased as that photo had been. Afterward, Father had hugged him for a long time and pled with Mike to never do such a thing again. He asked him where he'd gotten such a sick thing but begged off before Mike could answer. Then he promised that if Mike tried really hard and never did such a thing again that he would buy him his first car in a few years. Mike liked that, but the only thing the incident had taught him was the necessity of secrecy. He'd vowed back then to rebuild his collection and make sure he hid it someplace where no one could find it.

Mike opened the folder to view the files on his flash drive. He had numerous folders, all with actual, legitimate purposes that he used on a regular basis, though these were only dummy copies taken from another flash drive. He navigated through sub-folder after sub-folder until coming to one titled A-1. This was the flash drive's true purpose; the rest were a mask in case the file ever fell into anyone else's hands.

"Mike?" his wife called from upstairs.

"Yes, honey?" He'd just opened a JPEG of a corpse that appeared to have been partially eaten by dogs. He snatched out the flash drive, and the window closed immediately. He minimized all the windows just before she walked into the kitchen.

"What are you doing, honey?"

"Nothing, Hun. I was about to go over the budget again." She gave him a knowing smile.

"Mike. The budget? Come on, you know the budget doesn't need to be tinkered with. You are always on top of bills." That was true. Mike was a planner. That had partially grown out of his secret being discovered as a child. He hadn't been afraid of the consequences after being found, but a fundamental need to insulate himself from anything unexpected had become paramount. Mike had begun to plan everything and found wild personal success. He did financial planning as a side job, and it more than made up for any budgetary shortcomings from their primary jobs. If things kept going well, he was thinking of going into business for himself. Since he didn't have any clients at the moment, he couldn't tell his wife he was doing someone else's budget.

"I wanted to take a look at it is all," he said.

"So, if I check your browsing history, I won't find any porn?"

Mike laughed. Sure, he did like a few dirty websites every now and then, but that wasn't an issue between them. At least as far as

Lyssa was concerned. She liked the smutty stuff more than he did and actually thought he was a little prudish. It wasn't like she would have been mad about it had she caught him with it. Lyssa wasn't like that. If anything, she wished he did have a fetish of some sort. Too bad she would never know he really did.

"Baby, I want you to take me out to dinner." Mike made a show of looking around.

"You mean to tell me you haven't made anything? Woman!" He reared his hand back, and Lyssa ducked her head, giggling as she covered her face with her hands.

"Seriously, I want to go out tonight. We need to celebrate."

"Celebrate?" He searched her face. "What for?"

"The bruises are all gone," she said and raised her hands in the air victoriously. Mike rolled his eyes. His wife was a jokester and sometimes went overboard. Whenever things got serious, she tended to go in the other direction. Her great uncle's funeral had been painfully embarrassing.

He gave her a squeeze to bring her back to the subject at hand.

"Come on now—what's up? What should we be celebrating?" For the moment his flash drive and A-1 were forgotten. This was Lyssa's typical M.O., to be coy when she wanted all of his attention. And Mike was to blame for a great deal of that. He tended to zone out, to be completely unreachable. He allowed her to draw him in, prepared for her to go into another routine of some sort, but then she planted her hands on his shoulders, all pretense dropped from her face.

"I'm pregnant."

"You're what?" His response was more reflexive than inquisitive. He wrapped his arms around her still-petite frame and drew her in. This time he did squeeze hard and meant it, tears springing to his eyes. "When—how do you know? Are you for sure?" Another rhetorical question, but he couldn't do anything about the words coming out of his mouth at that particular moment.

"Yes," Lyssa said, prying her husband off. "And it was just this morning. I was late last week, and I took a test…"

"You knew last week?" He hugged her again, lifting her off her feet and spinning her around in the air. "Yes, yes, *yes*!"

They were gone for dinner in less than three minutes. Lyssa had orange juice while Mike had three glasses of pinot noir. This time, it was his turn to be publicly unbearable as it was all she could do to keep him from toasting the whole restaurant. They spent three hours talking about names, renovations that needed to be done to the house before the baby came, and anything else in preparation. They'd set a plan before they were married for the first ten years. The house, the business, *then* two children back-to-back. Lyssa's announcement had thrown everything up in the air, but Mike didn't care. It felt spontaneous and reckless, but this child was all he wanted now.

Only one person took open offense to Mike's loud half of their conversation. "Hey, pal, could you pipe down?" a big man said at a nearby table. "My kid just made all A's on his report card, but you don't see me making a parade out of it." He was sitting at a table with a woman and a boy who looked about twelve, both of them looking anywhere except in Mike's direction.

Perhaps Mike was on the obnoxious side and he could have been more considerate of the other patrons; something in the man's tone bothered him, though. Fueled on alcohol, Mike stood out of his chair, knocking it over. The man's eyes widened, and he responded in kind, being more careful with his considerably bulkier frame and rising slowly out of his chair.

"Roger," the woman, presumably his wife, said with a warning tone. Roger held a hand up to his wife. "For God's sake, Marty, don't look." She wrapped a flabby arm around the boy's head, masking his eyes with her fingers as she mashed the boy's head into her overflowing bosom. The boy had eyes only for what was happening and gave no indication that he had heard his mother or had any intention to obey her instruction. Roger had at least fifteen years on Mike and several inches and a hundred pounds or so of mostly muscle.

The man moved with the lionish grace of a former athlete, and Mike knew he was in over his head. Fear, though, never entered into the equation for him. Many years ago, Mike had incorporated from his uncle the notion that fear was the absence of true emotion. While logically he knew he was about to lose whatever conflict was about to occur, he was too far past the point of no return to simply stop and attempt to extricate himself from this situation. He could act or not act with a clear, steady mind. Being afraid could only cause him to slip into a reaction that more than likely would make the situation worse.

Mike had also adopted an expression of his uncle's. "Everything is perfectly fine. Until it isn't," the man had often said. In fact, he had said that very thing to Mike as they were eating ice cream, just before walking in front of an oncoming steamroller.

His eyes drew back to Mrs. Roger. She looked familiar. And then he realized. It was in her hands and the set of her eyes. The slope of her shoulders and long, goose-like neck. She was at least thirty pounds heavier and had dirty blonde hair, but she could have been a sibling of the woman from his first picture, the woman who had fought her murderer. But that had been twenty years ago, and the picture had looked old even then. Mrs. Roger would have to be her daughter or niece.

Mike said *something*. He immediately forgot what, and whatever it was caused Lyssa to stop her nervous laughter and begin tugging at his shirt sleeve to get him to sit back down. Mike doubted sitting would have done more than embolden old Roger. Something about the look in those eyes, round as dinner plates and fiery like Christmas logs, and Mrs. Rogers' plaintive tone gave him the impression the bigger man was used to using his fists to get his way. Muscles bulged on Roger that Mike didn't even know existed on the human form, cords standing out in his neck like his head was some meaty appliance requiring multiple outlets to run. Mike raised a finger, tapped it on his nose twice, and pointed at the much bigger man.

This apparently struck a final nerve, and Roger charged, which really only consisted of him taking a small step forward while rearing back a mighty paw to strike Mike in the face.

Mike didn't exactly lose consciousness, more or less browned out, coming to on the floor with someone gently patting him on the face when he felt fully moored to his body again.

Surprisingly, it was Roger himself.

"Oh, geesh, I'm sorry, man. Really. I don't know what happened." From the look on Roger's mustachioed face, he felt worse than Mike did. "Look, I'm really, really sorry. I don't know what—"

"It's okay," Mike said. "Everything's fine, perfectly fine." Other than a little tenderness above his eyebrow, Mike felt none the worse. He'd sensed that there was something stressful going on with Roger but had no interest in hearing about it. Somewhere in the back of his mind, it clicked that that murdered woman from the picture so many years ago had been struck down by her husband's hand. Maybe he had been just as brutish as Roger or maybe as meek as Mike himself. Mike recalled the old marks that had looked like smudges to his young eyes way back then, but now appeared to be old, healing bruises. He had never bothered reading the article; perhaps her killer had been caught, or perhaps the crime that had taken her life had not been solved.

Mike grasped Roger's meaty hand and the man yanked him to his feet. Anger was the world's second most useless emotion, and when Mike found he could stand and even jump under his own power, he didn't care anymore. He considered Roger through the filter of his new insight, then over to the big man's wife and son.

Everything *was* fine.

After verifying for herself that her husband hadn't sustained brain damage, Lyssa had launched herself at Roger but peppered him with flaming English instead of enraged fists. Mike had to pull her away while Roger had the balls to look sheepish, taking a double earful from the manager of the restaurant who was eagerly throwing both parties out, *posthaste*.

Once outside, Lyssa looked at him with an expression he had never seen before. Those meaty, tough guy types had always been a turn-off to her, but this looked like the opposite.

"Why did you say that to that woman?" Lyssa asked.

"Say what?"

Mike pressed, but Lyssa wouldn't repeat it. She shook her head. "Just don't say anything like that ever again."

A chill went through Mike. This was the closest he'd come to fear in more than twenty years. He had to admit the notion of his wife finding out about his hobby gave him a definite sense of unease. He wanted his son or daughter to have every possible advantage, and his wife leaving him because she thought he was some sort of ghoul was a step in the wrong direction.

They'd talked about the "fight" all the way home. She'd driven because she said he was still a little tipsy, although the more likely reason was her concern after he'd had his eggs scrambled and bread toasted. Although ten minutes after they'd gotten on the road, she'd slid a hand into his lap and found him warm and waiting. They attacked each other with a ferocity of uncoordinated urgency as they came into the house, fumbling their way through the kitchen and falling upstairs, peeling out of their clothes along the way.

Mike awoke. There was no grogginess, no yawning, no sense of disconnection, no searching mentally to locate where he was and how he'd gotten there. He was naked in his bed with his wife, and he'd been asleep for only a few hours. There was no one in his house, although there was something that needed protecting.

The flash drive. He'd left it on the kitchen counter, right next to the laptop. Lyssa was a light sleeper, but tonight he had a feeling she would sleep a little heavier. It wasn't ego telling him that; he just knew his wife and the meaning of the sounds she made while sleeping. No matter how vigorous tonight's physical activities had been, she would rise early like always. Even though he knew it was ninety-nine percent impossible for her to find A-1, he had to get that flash drive and hide it before she started sifting through it over her bagel and coffee.

Mike slid out of bed, slipped on some boxers and his microfiber robe, then snuck out of the room, making his way down the hall and downstairs like a burglar in reverse. He found the laptop and flash drive right where he'd carelessly left them. Mike touched a key, and the laptop whispered to life again. He was about to shut everything down and go upstairs to the sleeping, soon-to-be-mother before remembering he'd been interrupted earlier.

Hadn't he put in a sufficient amount of time with her, though? Was it so wrong to take maybe five minutes for even the quickest of peeks?

The JPEG of the half-eaten corpse was waiting for him. That wouldn't have gone well had Lyssa seen it, and Mike wondered how he might have tried explaining. One pic could have been plausible—he just stumbled across it online or something like that. Maybe he could have laughed it off. Unless she demanded he tell her the truth. Had she done that, despite his better senses, he would have wilted under that laser-sharp, soul-filleting stare and cat-o-nine tails tongue that had sufficiently cowed a man more than twice her size. Lyssa was Mike's weakness, and it was near impossible to resist her.

Mike sat, and as he plugged in the flash drive once again and waited for the pop-up window to open the folder, a thought occurred to him: maybe he *wanted* to be caught. Maybe his recklessness stemmed from an absence of fear and a desire to feel it again. He dismissed the thought as best he could and quickly went to A-1 again, the thumbnails of all his JPEGs, GIFs, PNGs, lining up in neat rows. He had Kurt Cobain, R. Budd Dwyer, Yitzhak Rabin, and countless other famous photographs and videos, but he wasn't some celebrity whore. He also had files of the same sort for everyday joes. Pictures of murder scenes, car accidents, cell phone pics of corpses found in ditches or in the middle of the street after hurricanes and tornadoes, autopsy photos, electric chair executions, beheadings, public (and private) hangings, shredded torsos from animal attacks, and even ashen remains of self-immolators. Mike was surprised by how many of that last kind he'd found. Many were Chinese, though surprisingly, many were not. By last count, Mike had four thousand, three hundred thirty-seven. Rather than scroll through them all, he opened the sub-folder "Current Hits."

The first file he opened was titled "robbud," a thirty-three second MPEG of Pennsylvania State Treasurer R. Budd Dwyer's final seconds. He was holding a long .357 Magnum in his hand.

"—ease leave the room if this will…if this will affect you," came the semi-tinny baritone voice. Several others in the room rose, and a man in a light-colored sport jacket stepped into frame a moment. Dwyer held a hand out, urging him to stand back. "Don't, don't, don't—this will hurt someone." More voices clamored, and Dwyer quickly turned the barrel of the gun up, so it was pointing toward the roof of his mouth. He opened wide and put a hand over the trigger guard with his free hand, his mouth a wide "O."

Half an instant later, his body jerked imperceptibly with the muffled boom of the gun, then fell behind the podium, red magically appearing on the wall behind him, a waterfall of blood pouring from his nose. People screamed, and the blur of someone running past the camera came next, but what was that just before Dwyer had pulled the trigger? Mike clicked on the double arrows to rewind, and everyone did a quick backward ballet until he lifted his finger.

"—omeone," Dwyer said and lifted the gun same as before. He seemed to wait a beat or two before putting it to his mouth.

"What the hell?" Mike said, pausing the MPEG. The image of R. Budd Dwyer quivered on screen as if stuck between two frames. He hadn't seen anything like that since the days of VHS. This wasn't supposed to happen on a computer file. He went back to "Current Hits" and clicked on a GIF of Leslie Loren, a heavyset woman who'd hung herself in what appeared to be a basement. It was about eight frames looped end-to-end of her swinging from a noose tied around a beam, so she was in constant motion.

At first, it appeared as always, her limp body in a flower dress with a short-sleeved dark sweater unbuttoned, short black hair obscuring her downturned face. But then her head shook. Maybe it was only two or three frames, but it hadn't been there before.

Mike's eyes danced between the still-quivering image of Dwyer then to Loren, her head shaking faintly. He'd watched this video at least a hundred times, and she'd never done that before.

He pulled back from the screen, rubbing his knuckles into his eyes. He had to be tired and probably a little tipsy still. Of course, he couldn't trust what he was seeing. The thing was he didn't *feel* tired. He felt as refreshed as on any Saturday when he slept in to ten o'clock. And drunk? He'd certainly been well en route to sober on the drive home from dinner more than five hours ago, according to the time on the microwave, and he and Lyssa's extracurricular activities as soon as they'd gotten through the door had certainly burned off the remaining effects of the alcohol before he'd gone to sleep. No, what he was seeing right now was there. He toyed with the idea of Leslie Loren's moving head being some new detail he hadn't noticed before. Surely, her swinging feet attracted the most attention. And the not-quite-paused Dwyer had to be the result of Windows Media Player not loading properly or something.

He closed both files and clicked on the picture titled "TShakur." The black-and-white photo of the slain rapper, post autopsy, pre sewing-up came on screen. All the near-white strips of flesh were internal parts of him, bulking him out in a manner that was completely unnatural to a living human body, making him look like some kind of discarded meat puppet.

This picture was wrong too, though. Shakur's arm was hanging off the autopsy table. Both arms were supposed to be *on* the table.

Mike frowned. Maybe he was remembering things wrong, but this was spoiling things for him. Perhaps this was a physical manifestation of the stress he must have been under at the thought of becoming a father. That didn't feel true, though when it came to things subconscious, it was anyone's guess. Parenthood was coming ahead of their timetable, and he was feeling unprepared. Weren't they ready now, though? Mike had always thought a certain amount of time needed to pass, but there would be no heavy strain to fit a new child into their lives financially, emotionally, or physically. Husband and wife, future father and mother, were as well off as could reasonably be expected at their respective ages.

So, if he could consider that ruled out, what was it? Then the thought came to him that did fill him with a minor amount of dread. Perhaps he was outgrowing A-1. He'd given thought to it on more than one occasion and actually deleted all of his files twice before. But the craving had always returned, and he restarted his collection. Perhaps this was his mind's way of telling him it was time to give it up again, this time for good.

Mike rolled that thought around in his head, sitting back again. He didn't want to give up A-1, at least not consciously. He would have to give this more consideration.

But what better way to consider than to continue looking? If these files revolted him in some fashion, it would be a simple step to just "Ctrl-A" and delete them all goodbye.

The thought of doing that, though, didn't sit well with him, and for that reason alone, at least on the surface, he knew he shouldn't get rid of them. He considered making one of those pros and cons lists, then thought better of it.

Mike sat up and scrolled to a random file. He double-clicked a thumbnail of a severely thin man lying in bed propped up. The man was half covered in an even thinner bed sheet that did nothing to hide his pronounced skeleton showing beneath near-translucent skin.

Mike knew this man only as Miller and assumed he was emaciated from the ravages of some disease. This picture was wrong too, though. Instead of being made to look comfortable, his hands folded gently over his sunken chest, mouth and eyes closed, the thin man's legs were positioned haphazardly at his sides, his almost nonexistent lips peeled back as if he'd died screaming. His eyes were half-lidded, staring dully into the camera.

Staring at *Mike*.

Mike closed the file, a chill passing through him. What was happening? Was this Lyssa playing an elaborate joke on him? It couldn't have been. He would know if she knew. She would have been repulsed to see the contents of A-1 and wouldn't have kept her disgust to herself.

Mike could understand why. The only why he had no answer for was why these pictures appealed to him. He was normal in every other way he could think of. He watched TV, had friends, had had only two jobs since graduating college, and it went without saying that he all but worshipped his wife. He kept in contact with family and visited his parents every other year in Florida, the original picture incident a ghost of a memory. Lyssa had volunteered him to help in a soup kitchen, and he'd felt a huge sense of accomplishment. Mike was even registered to donate bone marrow. In short, he couldn't have been described as someone having sociopathic tendencies. A-1 was only a fetish and not a sign of anything more that would denote any serious deficiency of character.

He sat there for several moments in the chill morning air of the downstairs. He hit "Ctrl-A" on the laptop's keyboard and selected all the files. He held a finger over the delete key, willing himself to press it. It was difficult, but he did it. A small window popped up, asking him if he was sure he wanted to delete his files. The options were simple enough, "yes" or "no." Mike arrowed over to "yes" and hovered. A shiver ran through him in a way that had nothing to do with the temperature. He didn't want to lose A-1; he realized he would miss it. They were special to him, treasured. He didn't know why and supposed he didn't need any more reason than grown men who still collected comic books or women who were sitting on Beanie Baby collections years after their popularity had evaporated. And hadn't he been careful all this time? Was there purpose in thinking otherwise? Not once had Lyssa seen them; not once had she even suspected anything. There was no reason he couldn't go many more years enjoying them. And if the day came when he did get tired of them, then it would be simple to delete these files and destroy this flash drive. The risk of being found out was almost nearly nil.

After clicking "no," Mike double-clicked the MPEG for Marty Grantham. Marty had been the subject of a news story in Kansas and had been showing the reporter around the house he was renting when he walked past a gas line that had been leaking right as he was lighting a cigarette. The gas immediately caught fire, turning into a torch and setting Marty and his curly orange afro ablaze. Even though he rolled, and the reporter and cameraman eventually tried to help, he burned to death over the course of the next ninety-seven seconds.

That was what was supposed to happen anyway.

Instead, Marty tucked his lighter into his back pocket and went on talking about his leaky pipes or whatever deficiency there was at the rear of his rented home. The pretty young reporter with her poofy eighties hair went on nodding in her light gray shoulder-padded skirt suit. He even heard the cameraman say something about smelling gas.

Mike closed the MPEG as they'd begun making a hasty retreat.

This was definitely wrong. Nobody knew about A-1, so this couldn't have been some sort of joke. And blackmail made even less sense. Mike wanted to rip out the flash drive and fling it across the room. But he was always annoyed by those scenes in movies when the guy shoved everything off his desk or toppled over the bookshelf. Someone had to clean that up, but the movies never showed that part. Here in real life, the flash drive would have shattered into a hundred little pieces and the one shard he wouldn't have swept up would have waited for a bare foot to step on it. It would have been just his luck for a piece to have been big enough to be recognizable as part of a flash drive, and what would the explanation have been that followed had that been Lyssa pulling the piece of plastic out of her foot?

No, he held his spiking temper in check and tried to reason out a solution. But he was interrupted before one came.

"Let us go," a baritone voice fit for radio said. That was *the* R. Budd Dwyer, although Mike had no file of any kind where the man had said that, and he certainly hadn't opened the lone file he had where Dwyer had spoken.

"Excuse me?"

At first there was no answer. Then came a low scratching, followed by what sounded like someone patting the business end of a working microphone.

"Is this on? Can he hear me?" It sounded like the voice had moved away. Mike looked around as several voices mumbled in response. It sounded as though they were in the room with him but filtered like they were on an intercom.

A voice cleared and then said, "Let us go!" The voice that could have doubled for any number of anchormen or radio hosts boomed. Mike jumped in his chair then quickly scrolled over to "robbud" again.

He opened it, and instead of a man a few dozen seconds away from tickling the roof of his mouth with the barrel of a high-caliber firearm, Dwyer was looking at him.

No, not at him. Into one of the cameras recording the press conference. That hadn't happened, though. Dwyer was like any seasoned politician—he worked the cameras while simultaneously ignoring them. Even with the loaded gun waiting inside an envelope that he'd placed there to take his own life, Dwyer had been the epitome of experienced, although a bit disconnected.

This Dwyer wore the haggard face of a man on the brink of exhaustion rather than mental collapse. His eyes were bloodshot, his lips dry, his face somehow older. He looked closer to sixty-seven than forty-seven. He combed at his forehead like a teenager with a shock of hair in his eyes even though his hair had retreated and thinned.

"If you can hear me, whoever you are, let us go. Give us

peace."

Mike's mouth hung open. Dwyer wasn't talking directly to him, but to an external, faceless *someone*.

And somehow, he was aware.

Dwyer went on staring into the camera, inches away from it. The video was still only thirty-three seconds, and it timed out while he was still in front of the camera. Mike backed it up ten seconds.

"We're tired, we're so very tired. Please, stop. Just sto—"

Mike closed the Dwyer MPEG and opened "koolaid" or James Jay Jackson. "Big Jim" Jackson was a morbidly obese man who'd somehow managed to get out of his apartment, up seven flights of stairs, and onto the roof. At the time when someone had begun recording, he was already at the ledge.

It had to have been someone's camcorder because the shot had begun shaky, like someone had just run and grabbed it. Then the shot steadied and zoomed in on Jackson, a bed sheet wrapped around his lower body, his floppy man-breasts exposed. The amateur cameraman was supposed to stay in tight on the man all the way down until he exploded on contact with the mostly concrete sidewalk below. Jackson only stood there, though— something that was somewhere between a slouch and a squat.

Actually, he was doing something else with his hands. Mike looked closer at Big Jim, who was faced in the direction of the camera that had to have been across the street in another building several stories below by the angle.

Jackson was flipping the bird. Both birds.

By this point in the video, Jackson was supposed to have already plummeted to his death, so seeing him up there still, giving Mike (?) middle fingers, was a shock. But Mike quickly went on the offensive.

"What's he doing?" the woman holding the camera said. Mike muted the media player.

"Do it," he said. "Do it, you fat bastard. Do it *now*." His voice was an angry growl, almost unrecognizable to his own ears.

Jackson wobbled like he'd been nudged from behind, his

arms pitching out from his sides like he was suddenly atop a tight rope. The expression on his face was too far away to make out clearly, but Mike believed he saw hate in those eyes and thought that was an odd emotion for a man to have who was about to take his own life.

Jackson fell over, his arm lashing out at the last second and catching the lip of the building. His considerable bulk easily peeled away his grip, sending him cartwheeling end over end. The camera followed him down before he landed on his head, his body accordioning as his insides became his outsides.

"Oh yeah," Mike said. The way his body had erupted had reminded him of the Kool-Aid Man and how he'd always come bursting through walls in those commercials. Except Jackson was the wall and his Kool-Aid had come bursting out of him at least a dozen feet in every direction.

This was an unwelcome yet manageable twist. They were trying to not do what they'd been doing all this time. Mike didn't understand how; some of these files he'd had for years, some only a few weeks. He spent the next ten minutes opening and closing files at random and finding subtle but noticeable changes with each. Like how most of them had gotten slightly closer to the video cam, as if they were trying to sneak up on him.

He opened "robbud" again, and the man had moved away from the camera some and was standing between it and the podium where his .357 was bulking in a manila envelope. He'd removed his suit jacket and rolled up his sleeves and seemed to be making a case for something.

Mike unmuted the media player to listen.

"—that if you fail to meet our conditions, we will be forced to take action."

"Wait a minute, what was that?" Mike said.

Dwyer narrowed his eyes and jabbed a finger at Mike.

"If you do not comply, we will kill you and your whore over and over again."

Mike had never been the type of person to accept threats.

When his first bully had swatted his sandwich out of his hands and stomped on it in the cafeteria, Mike, who was two years younger and six inches and twenty pounds smaller than the other boy, had promptly punched him in the balls and proceeded to ram his face into the linoleum until the boy's front teeth had been shattered. His second bully had spent four weeks in traction in the hospital.

This threat he'd have to be more creative about. Deleting them was what they wanted. Watching them either die or seeing them after they were dead was what he wanted.

He rewound the video to the beginning before the Senator spoke. "I understand, Senator Dwyer, but we're going to have to agree to disagree. If there is some way for you to come out here, I'll kill *you*. Until then, why don't you take out that gun and blow your brains out?"

Dwyer's mouth opened, and he made a sound almost like he was about to say something. He took a step back and looked behind him, then fixed his stare back on Mike.

"No!" Dwyer said, sliding the big manila envelope out from behind the podium. "You'll pay!" He took the gun out, and the audience gasped. He managed to aim it at the camera, but with a nod, Mike made him turn it around on himself. "You'll pay!" he managed to say around the barrel, right before he pulled the trigger.

"What do you know? I shaved off six seconds," Mike said.

There was a sound in the basement. Mike didn't know how to describe it other than to say it was a sound. He went to the basement door and opened it. At the bottom of the stairs was the corpse of Kurt Cobain. He wasn't moving, but there he was, being dead.

Marie turned onto the stairway and looked up at him. He didn't know her real name and had picked one that had seemed fitting. She must have been drenched in gasoline, the smell of it wafting up from the basement. The way she walked up the stairs reminded him of a spider's slow crawl. The notion of him being afraid of her, had it occurred to him, would have been ridiculous. Mike had seen Marie die no fewer than five hundred times. How could he be afraid of her? He took a step back and opened the mudroom door. Inside was a sink next to the washing machine. Mike turned on the cold water and grabbed the little spray hose next to the faucet. He waited until Marie was about halfway up before spraying her in the face.

She gasped, her face whitening with shock.

"What's the matter, Marie? You look like you could use a shower." Mike wished he could have chased her down the stairs, but the hose didn't stretch more than two feet. He let it retract back into the sink and stepped back to the basement stairs.

Marie vanished, her sobs echoing after she was gone. Leslie Loren's noose swayed empty to the side of his nook table. A quick glance up showed him it was hanging in mid-air. The big woman emerged from the family room a moment later, complete with bulging eyes and lolling tongue. She was about six inches taller than Mike and at least a hundred pounds heavier. He couldn't punch her in the nads, although there was something that would probably be equally debilitating.

She reached for him with both hands like a zombie. Mike smiled. This was just too much.

"You're working too hard, Leslie." He quickly stepped under her thick-fingered hands, slipping an index into the neck of her dress, making sure to hook the slip beneath before ripping the whole works right off her.

Leslie's eyes bulged even wider, and she clapped her hands over the mound of hair at the apex of her tree-trunk thighs, shaking her long, pendulous breasts in his face in the process.

Mike gave her a small shove as she huddled around her massive girth, dissolving in mid-retreat.

Ken Esther appeared next, peering at him over the couch. Mike loved this guy. His *solumoristosis*, or butt face, was undoubtedly why he'd killed himself. God had played the cruelest of jokes on him, but Kenny had to have been in on it; he'd shot and killed himself right between the cheeks. Corey Hughes took one hand away from the stinking intestines draping out of him and reached for Mike. Mike elbowed him aside, taking a wet loop of entrail with him and stuffing it down Ken's pants.

Bill Morris was waiting for him at the stairs like they would walk up together. Mike got the implied threat: that they would do something to Lyssa if they didn't get what they wanted.

"This is the total opposite of cool, man." The man's complexion was ghostly even in the dark. He'd poisoned himself after being convicted of embezzlement and was already dying at his sentencing hearing. So, this one wanted to attack with some sort of reason. Mike punched him in the stomach. Not particularly hard, but hard enough to let him know Mike knew where to hurt him. The man doubled over and dissolved before he hit the floor.

"This is old already," Mike said. "Where's Dwyer?"

Andre LaBelle hooked an arm under Mike's and lifted him off Morris. LaBelle had the distinction of being the only other person Mike had video of committing suicide by gunshot. He had done it in front of his camcorder at the kitchen table. There been a plate with crumbs on it and a fork smeared with what looked like chocolate icing. Mike had guessed he'd had himself a slice of cake before doing the deed.

Andre "The Truth" LaBelle had been a professional boxer, a junior middleweight. At five foot eight, he would have been eye-to-eye with Mike in life, with the build of a Greek god. He clipped Mike on the chin with a flash of a right hook that sent him staggering but, surprisingly, not unconscious. Out of a career that had spanned twenty-three wins, two losses, and one no-decision, The Truth had successfully knocked down every opponent save one, and that included a minor title holder. Mike was surprised that he was only stunned. He had become a fan of The Truth, postmortem, and had looked up many of his fights and interviews on YouTube. Opponents who had simply stood in front of him and tried to duke it out were always dispatched within a few rounds. He had been a southpaw who was described as one of those fighters who had "power in both hands."

Either Mike had a much better chin than he would have

guessed or the ghostly representation of The Truth was nowhere near as strong as the real thing.

Before he could test the theory, many more bodies appeared. Some of them were just that, bodies lying on the floor, though many more walked or crawled toward him. Out of the faces, he could recognize the more active ones were from videos. The ones from pics were more lethargic or zombie-like. Mike quickly retreated for higher ground, jumping on the couch and kicking at the ones nearest him.

"Enough of this already," he said. "Where the hell is Dwyer?" They grabbed at him, and he squeezed hands until bird-thin bones broke, gouged eyes or empty sockets, shoved thick bodies as full as sponges with brackish goo, kicked out legs as thin as kindling until he was dragged off the couch. They weren't particularly strong; they overwhelmed him with numbers. Mike ripped Angus Smith's chest open, which had the consistency of papier-mâché, and was reaching into the man's chest to squeeze that weak heart when he was grabbed from behind. Mike didn't know who it was but got his legs under him and shoved backward. He crushed whoever it was against the door and felt the body sag, then fade. They were fighting at a near stalemate, but Mike knew his strength wouldn't last long. There had to be more than fifty in here. He had to end this now.

"We can either do this all night or you can get Dwyer out here now." He kept his voice calm and managed to control his breathing. They hesitated a moment as if gathering their collective breath, not seeming to want what he'd done to the others to happen to them. Mike threw his hands out, and several of them jumped back, a few vanishing. Then the rest began to come at him again.

"No, that's enough." Dwyer appeared at the head of the crowd, gun in hand. "I won't let you hurt us anymore." He took a step forward and aimed at Mike's head.

"What are you going to do with that?" Mike said. "Kill me? I think you already know that you're not as strong as me. What if that gun doesn't work? Or one of those bullets just bounces off me? Will that make me even stronger than you? Let's say you do kill me. What happens after that? Do you think this then goes away for you? Someone will eventually find that folder and find all of you. You'll be even more of a novelty than you are now. Killing me won't help you get watched less; you'll be sensationalized as part of the freaky collection of the guy who was somehow shot to death even though there's no gun in the house and no sign of a break in."

"I'll just leave this gun here," Dwyer said. "Right next to your head. People will think you killed yourself."

Mike shook his head. "Let me call your bluff right now. You put that gun down and it disappears. If you think what passes for your lives is a nightmare now, wait 'til I'm gone."

Dwyer combed at his bald head with the crook of his index, the gun quavering in his other hand.

"I-I mean it." He cocked the hammer back on the .357. Mike folded his arms and shifted to one foot. "We could go upstairs and show your wife what you've been doing."

"And I could upload you on YouTube."

"What's…what's YouTube?" He licked his lips. Several others, more recent, Mike noted, evaporated.

Dwyer's image shivered like a monitor being Degaussed. Many began vanishing. A moment later, it was only the two of them.

"Let us go. *Please.*" Dwyer's gun arm shook with the last word.

"No." Mike thought a moment. Maybe the time was coming for him to give them up. It would be on *his* terms, though. "Tell you what. We'll do a gradual transition. Maybe over the next four or five years." Mike figured his son or daughter would be taking up a great deal of his time, and those little ones were such mavens of technology and natural snoops that A-1 could finally find its way into the wrong hands. He didn't want his child following in Daddy's footsteps.

Well, at least he didn't think so.

Dwyer plead with his eyes. "We can't. They won't—"

"You're a politician. You'll find a way to sell it."

Dwyer let his arm drop and his head hang. He turned and began shuffling away.

"Uh, hold on a second," Mike said. The dead senator peered over his shoulder at him. "Since you're here…"

Dwyer's eyes went wide.

"No!" he said in a low voice. "Not *here*. Leave me with some dignity!"

Mike raised his eyebrows. "Go on. Do it."

"You dick." R. Budd Dwyer hesitated a moment before his gun arm curled up to point the .357 toward the roof of his mouth and he gripped the trigger guard with his other hand. Tears were streaming down his face as he resumed the last eight seconds of his recording, opening wide. "Burn in hell," he said around a mouthful of barrel.

Perhaps it took a second longer, perhaps it didn't, but when he squeezed the trigger, the report was deafeningly loud. Mike flinched in surprise, and a moment later, he heard Lyssa upstairs.

"Mike, what was that?" She sounded alarmed but still groggy. Dwyer lay slumped against the wall, a spray of red like an exclamation point above him. Blood poured like a faucet from his nose.

"Nothing, honey. I just dropped a plate." He watched the dead state senator slowly dissolve. "Go back to bed. I'm gonna sweep up and I'll be right up."

He heard her lingering by the door. She might not have believed him, but his wife was even more afraid of coming downstairs at night. He let go of a huge breath of air when the door gently closed.

Cleanup consisted of watching the remains of his visitors vanish. Mike had the feeling that if he turned the lights on, they would be instantly gone, so with the lights off, he enjoyed the digitized bits of skin, bone, and blood float away and disappear like ashes in a fire. It was a little disturbing that the bullet had left a pin-sized hole in the wall. He'd have to get to that first thing in the morning. He heard sobbing from the table and made his way back to his laptop. On screen was a video he'd almost forgotten about. There was a young woman onscreen who looked like she was lying on her bed in front of her own laptop. He wondered a moment who'd recorded this and with whom she'd been speaking to have reduced her to tears. Of course, this hadn't been the original recording; this girl was probably reacting to Mike not letting them go. She quickly got back on script, pushed off her belly and onto her knees, climbing off the bed before running and jumping out of her window. He felt the tiniest pang of the third most useless emotion: guilt.

Then Mike smiled.

He shut down his computer and went upstairs.

THE BABY WOKE up at night often. In Hannah's first three months, he preferred to get up with her. Not just because Lyssa had done so much, he actually liked having the alone time with his daughter. And it wasn't like he needed to get up for work anymore. Mike's financial planning business had taken off and he'd been able to quit his full-time job. It was so successful he'd bought a new SUV for the baby, and they were planning an addition for the house in the spring.

Now Hannah was a little more solid. As much as he'd loved her as a newborn, he was enjoying his time with her even more now.

He'd begun using the flash drive for another clandestine purpose, one he had every intention of sharing with Lyssa. They were planning a visit to her parents; her father had fallen ill before Hannah had been born and they all wanted to see each other. But there was a place in Puerto Rico he wanted to take her after. It was going to be the honeymoon they couldn't afford when they'd first gotten married.

Lyssa had assumed they would never go anywhere outside of the contiguous United States because Mike was a "money vulture," as she so lovingly liked to put it. She was kidding, per usual, but Mike was certain at the kernel of that oft-used joke was truth. He'd always rebutted that he was "chintzy" and laughed it off, all the while planning this particular escape.

Mike opened his laptop and turned it on. The machine quietly hummed to life before the logon screen popped up. He typed in his username and password one-handed, cradling his four-month-old daughter in one arm. After checking on all the accommodations and reservations, Mike took out his flash drive. It had been a few weeks since he'd seen A-1 (even though he almost always carried it in his pocket out of a feeling akin to superstition); the baby and the new business kept him very busy. He plugged in the flash drive and went back to the stove to check on the baby's milk. He checked it against his wrist and, once he was satisfied, gave it to fussy Hannah, who promptly quieted and began drinking.

Mike navigated to A-1 and hovered over the first file. He wasn't sure he had to delete this folder. He hadn't had a problem with keeping it hidden, and that thing a little over a year ago had actually worked to his benefit. Now that he knew they were alive or whatever they were between two-dimensional representations of people who had died and actually being alive, he could make them do so much more. He could make Leslie Loren hang herself with an extension cord or Myron Davies pose dead with his arms away from his face or Kelsey Hammond turn so he could see exactly how much was left of her shattered head after colliding with the steering wheel at a hundred twenty miles an hour in the Porsche 911 Carrera her parents had bought her for her sixteenth birthday. The immolated monk was now crispy critter *and* contortionist.

R. Budd Dwyer had built up a pretty good twenty-seven

second stand-up routine before blowing his brains out.

It might even be an interesting side job if he could figure out how to monetize it. He could make the income Hannah's college tuition, although he wasn't holding his breath. Besides, he already had investments in place for that.

His daughter finished with the bottle, and he sat her up. She promptly burped, and then he sat her in his lap, facing the screen. Why not? She was too young to remember anyway. He picked a file at random and opened it.

This one started with a woman screaming. She had a pleading in her eyes for the camera, much like all of them did nowadays. She hadn't screamed like that in any of the previous views, though, and that was just fine by Mike. And the look in her eyes...the *despair.* *That* he could do something with.

Everything was fine.

Perfectly fine.

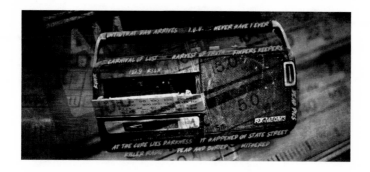

FINDERS KEEPERS

Jane Alvey Harris

"BUT MOMMY, PLEASE! THAT'S NOT FAIR…"

"Don't you think you're being a little hard on him, Abbs? It's his birthday."

"Oh, so we should teach our son that it's perfectly fine to behave like an entitled little demon on special occasions?" I glare at my husband.

"Not at all." Jason lowers his voice and moves closer. "But babe, how can we teach him anything if we punish him while we're emotional?"

My irritation spikes. He said "we," but I know he thinks he's a better parent than me. And I resent that he acts like he has to handle me with kid gloves because of my "issues." His stupid line is straight from the "Parenting with Love and Logic" workbook our family counselor gave us last month.

"We made this rule together, *Daddy*, remember?" My voice is sugar-sweet, but he flinches at the snarl on my lips.

Ike whimpers, and I turn in time to see a huge crocodile tear slip from the corner of his eye.

"He just turned six years old, Abby, for Christ's sake! Everybody deserves a second chance."

"Ike, tell Daddy how many chances Mommy has given you." I kneel down in front of our son and lift his downturned chin, but he refuses to look at me.

"I've used up all my strikes." His lip trembles. His narrow shoulders crowd his little ears and his eyebrows are bunched in the middle of his forehead like tiny storm clouds. He's doing the same thing I do when I'm struggling to be brave: trying not to cry. My resolve wavers.

Jesus. Why do his lashes have to be so long? And now they're all stuck together with unshed tears, pressed against the little-boy curve of his cheek. *Be strong, Abby,* I tell myself. *Remember what Dr. Thomas says: "Parenting isn't easy, but rules and boundaries are what's best for him in the long run."*

Jason lets out a frustrated sigh. His disapproving stare beats against my back in waves, but he doesn't say anything. I'm grateful we're a united front, but why do I always have to be the bad cop?

"Listen, Ike," I say, pulling his tension-tight body into my arms. I don't want this to be the way he remembers his birthday. "Daddy's right. Everybody deserves a second chance, so…"

Ike's shoulders relax an inch, but he stands stock-still, no doubt wary of this unexpected mercy. Good grief. My son thinks I'm a monster.

"…*if* you're on your best behavior, and *if* you promise you won't leave it out again, just this once, you can have your new tablet back on Sunday after church." The dark mood that's settled around me lifts with every word I utter. This is what it means to be a good parent: tough but fair. Firm but not unyielding. Ike will grow up respecting me and trusting…

"That's. Not. FAIR!" Ike straight-arms himself out of my beatific embrace, indignant anger bright in his petulant eyes.

The force of his childish shove barely knocks me off balance, but I lean back away in confusion, my butt landing hard on the family room floor's woven rug.

"Hey, buddy, listen, okay?" In a split second, Jason is there, crouching down and pulling Ike onto his knee. "Buddy, you shouldn't push Mommy, okay? She said you can have your new tablet back if…"

"But I didn't leave it out! I put it away before we started eating cake! I didn't want it to get any frosting on it!" He wiggles out of Jason's arm and stomps his foot, his chest heaving beneath the top of his mismatched Marvel Universe pajamas.

"Go to your room. NOW," I command.

"Abbs, come on…"

"No way, Jason. I'm done. I was ready to compromise. I was going to let him earn it back with good behavior. But now he's lying, too? I won't put up with this."

I focus all my parental authority at my sullen offspring and point down the hallway leading to his room. "March, mister!"

Ike treats me to a glare of pure animosity and stomps off out of the living room, his bare feet slapping deliberately against the hardwood in the hall. When he reaches his door, he turns and flings a martyr's, "You're so mean! I HATE YOU," straight at my face.

But I'm ready for the onslaught, thanks to Dr. Thomas. I deflect his attack with ease. He doesn't mean it, and I won't make the mistake of taking it personally and doubting myself.

Except.

Except what if he really did mean it? What if he really hates me? Maybe it's my fault that he chose to lie so defiantly like that, right to my face? He's never done that before. I mean, he must think I'm stupid if he thinks I'll believe such a blatant lie. Dishonesty is learned behavior—didn't Dr. Thomas say something like that? Have I failed at parenting already?

"Abbs," Jason says quietly, coming up behind me. He doesn't put his arms around me—probably because he's half-afraid I'll rip his head off if he touches me. And honestly, I might. "It's been a long day, babe. Just take a deep breath, okay? You know he didn't mean that."

Thank God for Jason. Those are exactly the words I needed

to hear right now, and he knew it. I turn around and wrap my arms tight around him, dissolving in his strength and warmth.

"Come here." His lips move against my hair before he pulls back and kisses my forehead. Taking my hand, he leads me to the couch and sits down. I curl up against him immediately.

"How did that even happen?" I ask. "I was trying to fix it."

"I know, I know. I'm proud of you, Abbs. You're making progress."

Automatically, I stiffen. He's parenting me. But then I sigh and take a deep breath, consciously unclenching. *Just listen to him,* I tell myself. *Remember, he's on your side. You're on the same team.*

"Tell me how I could have handled that better," I ask, sincerely wanting to know. Now that I've calmed down, guilt and regret swiftly move in, filling the empty spaces that departing anger has left in its wake. My heart breaks at the memory of betrayal on Ike's face.

"I'm not saying you were wrong to take away his tablet or to send him to his room, Abby…" Jason begins, then hesitates.

"But?"

"Well, it was really crazy here this afternoon. There were at least two dozen kids and adults coming in and out of the house. Isn't it possible that someone else picked up his tablet and brought it out of his room? Hell, it could have been your mom, wanting to show Sarah what she'd gotten her grandson for his birthday."

"Oh my gosh, Jason, you're right!" I sit up straight, my mouth falling open in horror. "Shit. I'm such a terrible mother," I cry, collapsing back against his chest.

He tightens his arms around me. "You are *not* a terrible mother. Ike knows you love him. And we kind of knew this would come up eventually, didn't we?"

"We did?" I'm mystified.

"Well, yeah. I mean, what happened with Sarah at the mall that time when you guys were little, remember? And how old were you when Maple ran away?"

"Six," I whisper, bewildered that I hadn't made the

connection myself.

"And do you remember what Dr. Thomas said?" Jason asks. "He said it's very common to be triggered by an event when something similar comes up, especially if it happens to someone who is around the same age you were when your trauma happened. He told us to watch for something around Ike's sixth birthday."

I sit up again, eyes saucer-wide, scooching across the couch until my back hits the opposite armrest. Is this early onset dementia? How had I forgotten what Dr. Thomas said only last month?

Jason chuckles and scooches after me, closing the space between us. He smooths my hair back from my face. "It's going to be okay, babe, I promise."

But I'm spooked. "Grandpa gave Maple to us on our sixth birthday without even asking my parents first." My voice is a hushed monotone as the memory wells in my mind and the story spills from my mouth. "Mom and Dad were pissed, but Sarah and I begged them to let us keep her. We promised we'd take care of her, that we'd feed her and walk her and clean up after her if she made any messes."

"I know, babe," Jason soothes.

His expression is so compassionate, it breaks my heart. How did I get so lucky to marry such a wonderful man? He's been so patient with me, so understanding. He could have told me to sit down and shut up, could have taken Ike's side and…

Oh no. Ike.

I'm on my feet in an instant, practically sprinting toward the hallway and Ike's door.

"Wait a sec, Abbs." Jason grabs my arm and steers me back to the couch.

"No!" I sob, yanking my arm free from his grasp. "Jason, our baby must think I'm the wicked witch! You've got to let me apologize to him. I've got to make this right."

Desperate, I knock on Ike's door. "Ike, baby? It's Mommy. Can I talk to you?"

No answer, but I can hear his muffled cries coming from under his Thomas the Tank Engine comforter, and my lungs squeeze with self-reproach.

"Honey?" I rap again with my knuckles, then try the doorknob. Locked. "Will you please open the door, honey? Mommy made an awful mistake, and she wants to say she's sorry."

"Go away!"

My knees sag at the sorrow soaking his voice. I turn and lean my back against his door, closing my eyes. My poor Ike. The one person he should trust most in the world has betrayed him. Called him a liar. Banished him to his room on his birthday, and for what? For nothing.

"I was wrong, Ike. I'm so sorry. I should have believed you."

No answer.

On my tiptoes, I reach up, feeling backward along the top of the door frame for the key.

"Abby, wait." Jason has been observing from the family room, but now he joins me in the hall. "I know you feel awful, babe, but maybe we should respect his boundaries and give him some privacy for a while?"

I nod, repentant. I'm in no position to question his judgment right now. As Dr. Thomas would say, "Nothing good ever comes from emotional parenting." Instead, I slide my back down the door until I'm sitting crisscross applesauce on the hardwood floor.

"It's okay, Ike," I say, just loud enough that I hope he can hear me from beneath his blankets. "I'm not coming in. But I'm right here for you in the hall, okay? In case you change your mind and will let me make it up to you."

Silence.

"You can't sit here all night, Abby," Jason says, offering me his hand. "Come to bed. You'll both feel better after a good night's sleep. You can talk to him in the morning."

What was that sound?

I hold up my hand to quiet Jason. Putting a finger to my lips, I press my ear against the door. Ike has stopped crying. And then

I hear the back-and-forth creak of the old rocking chair.

On the black-curtained stage of my mind, the time-worn rocking chair comes into focus. The rocker had occupied the corner of the room I'd shared with Sarah until we were ten years old. It's probably the only piece of furniture I still have from childhood. It'd traveled with me through college and graduate school, survived two moves since then, and was the sole remaining relic Ike had allowed to survive the transition from his nursery to his big boy room.

Jason can't understand why I've kept it so long. He's offered to buy me a new one dozens of times, but Ike loves the long creaking groan of the gliders against the wood floor as much as I do. I nursed him and rocked him to sleep in that chair. When he was younger, Ike read to his stuffed animals in that chair on days it was too cold or wet to play outside in his sandbox. My grandfather carved and joined it himself, gifting it to Mom when Sarah and I were born. Sure, the varnish has long since cracked and peeled, but the maple arm buttons are glossy-smooth from decades' worth of different-sized hands running up and down their length.

Jason hears the rocking, too, and smiles. "See? He's fine, babe. Just give him a little time. He'll forgive you and you can use this as a way to teach him that adults make mistakes, too. You can model personal responsibility and humility. This'll be a parenting win!"

But Jason's words are distant and tinny. Was that a rasping cough I just heard? Yes, there it is again. A low wheezing cough, followed by a dry, humorless laugh.

That doesn't sound like Ike. And yet, it's somehow familiar...

The persistent brittle creak of the rails elongates, stretching and growing louder until it scrapes through my inner ears. Dread coils around me as if lowered from the ceiling shadows by a sinister hand. With each reticulated creak, a noose of fear descends in loop after infinite loop, slowly constricting my chest as a long-buried image resolves into sharp focus in my mind.

An old man sits stiff in the rocker, staring straight ahead.

Weak light from the single lamp on the nightstand illuminates his stark white face in shocking profile against the playful Lego posters hanging on the wall above Ike's bed. His tall, wraith-thin body folds at tight angles to fit the chair, but its wrists extend beyond the curling armrests, poking out of crisp, old-fashioned shirt sleeves. Bony fingers bend at impossible angles, wrapping around the curved wood in a bloodless grip. He could be a wax sculpture…only his feet in their pointed leather shoes press back and forth, back and forth, while the thin wool of his ancient socks sag low around his knobby ankles.

Ike lays huddled under his fleece blanket and comforter, hating me, betrayed by me, completely unaware of the evil presence only feet away…

I'm on my feet in an instant.

"Abby?"

I slam my shoulder against the door, but the joist barely registers any force. Frantic, I back up and slam again. "Ike, open the door!"

"Abby!"

The key! I forgot about the key. Desperate, I fumble above the door casing with quaking hands. Finally, my fingers close around the small brass key. Shakily, I jam it into the lock, but the knob won't turn.

A low cackle snakes out from between the wooden leaf and the threshold. With the snapping of ancient joints, the man turns his head until his eyes bore into mine from behind the closed door.

"Abby, you need to breathe. Abby, look at me!"

"Jason!" I cry. "Help me, Jason, please! He's in there, Jason. Can't you hear him? He's going to take our son!"

My fists flail uselessly against the door, bloodying my knuckles. Pinprick panic stipples my mouth as dread constricts the oxygen from my lungs. The scream clawing up my throat lodges in my narrowing airways, choking me.

I'm lifted off my feet, the nightmare image swimming in my mind…

…chalky, white skin…

…bulging, dilated eyes…

…painted red lips pulled tight over rotting, barbed-wire teeth…

"I said I'd come back, little Abigail." The stench of fetid death rolls off his heavy black tongue. *"Did you really forget about me?"*

"Abby, dammit, answer me!"

My head snaps violently on my neck, jarring me back to reality. "Ow! Why are you shaking me?" I yell.

"I'm sorry, babe." Jason's nose is only an inch from mine. Relief floods his face as I rub the back of my neck. "Shit, I thought you were in some kind of trance! You were just sitting there with your hands over your ears, rocking back and forth and muttering, 'He's back, he's back, he's back.' I've never seen you act this way before."

Sitting?

I'm still sitting on the floor in the hall with my back against Ike's door.

Dazed, I stare at my husband. "I wasn't beating the door…?" I trail off. "You didn't hear anything else?" I ask tentatively. "No laughing or anything? Coming from Ike's room?"

"Laughing? Why would Ike be laughing after what just happened?" It's Jason's turn to be confused, but he doesn't give me a chance to answer. "Jeez, Abbs. You really freaked me out. I thought you were having a stroke or something."

My lungs finally expand, as if they'd just thawed after being kept frozen and buried deep inside my chest. I can breathe. I realize I've unconsciously been clenching my fists, digging half-moons into my palms with my nails. I wilt against Jason's chest.

None of it had happened. None of it had been real. No bloody knuckles. Ike is safe in his room just on the other side of his door. There's no one else in there.

The question is: am *I* okay? Definitely not. The image of an ancient, demonic man—his grating voice, the stench of rot and decay—the whole thing had been so vivid. It had felt so real.

But it couldn't be. Could it?

Of course not. Demons aren't real. They don't exist. Maybe I'd seen a scary movie or had a nightmare about him when I was young?

I make a mental note to call Mom tomorrow and ask if she remembers me mentioning anything like that when I was little. Taking Jason's hand, I let him help me to my feet and lead me farther down the hall to our room.

Even with my new resolve, a numb, gnawing terror lingers around the edges of my peripheral vision while I wash my face and brush my teeth. I almost don't recognize the pale, frightened woman gazing back at me from the mirror. She looks so young, so vulnerable. Behind her, inky shapes collude in the shadows, reaching dark fingers toward me from the wavy-warped glass of the shower, creeping furtively from corners where the light doesn't reach, sliding up the cabinets and twining between my toes on the cold marble floor.

Just breathe, Abby, I tell myself over and over.

IN BED, JASON'S warmth curls around me. I tuck against him—his little spoon—pulling his arm back around me when he shifts in his sleep. I'm safe here, with his breath in my hair and his chest pressed against my spine. I match my inhalations to his and close my eyes, grateful that the haunting images have dissipated for now.

I offer a silent prayer, something I hadn't done since I was a child. *Please watch over my baby while he sleeps. Please let Ike feel my love. Bless him with good dreams tonight.*

In my mind, I drag the rocking chair out of Ike's room and into the southern chill of a mid-January morning. As I drift off to sleep, the fire I've set devours the dry kindling between the gliders. Crackling tongues of flame lap up the spindled legs until the entire thing is ablaze beneath a bleak gray sky.

SOMBER LIGHT STEALS between the plantation shutters, waking me from a dream in which Sarah and I were trying to teach our new puppy, Maple, how to fetch and roll over. I smile at the memory of Maple's rambunctious puppy energy, the way her silk-soft ears fell forward over her face as she pounced repeatedly at her squeaky chew toy…

I sit straight up in bed, memories of the horror from last night crashing in around me. Jason groans, shushes me, and turns over on his side. It's early. I pull on some fuzzy socks and tiptoe from the room, closing the door quietly behind me.

Turning on the coffee pot, I open the kitchen blinds before grabbing a notepad and pencil off the catchall corner of the counter. Outside Ike's room, I plant myself on the floor. I can hear his muffled voice chatting amiably on the other side, probably reading one of his Pokémon books to Ellie, his stuffed elephant. He sounds sweet and happy, and my heart wells with relief. My little boy still believes the world is a good place.

Without making a sound, I write a note in big letters:

Ike, I'm sorry :(

I love you so much <3

What would you like for breakfast?

Quietly, I tear the page from the pad and fold it once. On the outside I write:

To: Ike

From: Mommy

…and slip it under his door.

"Good morning, Ike," I whisper, just loud enough for him to hear me. "I wrote you a note, buddy. Will you write me one back, please?"

Sliding notes to each other under doors is my favorite game Ike and I play together. It started a few years ago when I was sick in bed. Jason, who was working from home so I could rest, told Ike that under no circumstances was he to bother Mommy. I woke to the din of a nearly hushed skirmish in the hall, with Ike insisting that he "didn't disturb her, I promise!" and that his drawing "would make her get better." And he was one hundred percent correct. The colorful stick figure drawing—complete with sticky pancake-syrup fingerprints along the edges—is tucked neatly away in the top drawer of my nightstand. I pull it out whenever I'm feeling down, and it cheers me up. Ever since that day, I've kept several pads of paper and a 64-count box of Crayola's on the kid-sized desk in his room for this very purpose.

A short, one-sided conversation takes place behind the door—Ike is consulting his stuffies—and I lean my head back on the wall, smiling as I hear his bare feet land on the rug and then patter across the wood floor to his desk.

I honestly hadn't anticipated situations like this when Jason and I decided to get pregnant. How could I have? Motherhood has brought up so many things from my past I could never have imagined…things I hadn't even remembered. Right now, I'm just happy for forgiveness and second chances. Happy for Jason's love and patience. Overwhelmed at the buoyant love for the precious, perfect little human we had created together. In this fresh new day, it's easy to dismiss the abject terror of last night as an over-reaction due to stress and hormones. Of course, I'm not going to burn the rocking chair my grandfather made in celebration of his twin granddaughters' birth.

Rustling on the other side of the door pulls me out of my musings and back to the present. My ears perk up as I listen to his knees crack as he crouches down and pushes a piece of folded construction paper under the door. I'm already smiling as I pick it up. Today he's written in block letters with a red gel pen:

TO: MOMMY

"I haven't seen you write like this before, Ike," I exclaim.

"You're growing up so fast!"

As I unfold the paper, a low, wheezing cackle floats up to me. Dread spreads icy fingers across my shoulders and up my neck as I scan the words hard-pressed into the thick paper:

DO YOU REMEMBER HOW YOU LOST
MAPLE WHEN YOU WERE A LITTLE GIRL?
I DO.

This isn't Ike's handwriting.

The paper trembles in my hands. "Ike?" I call, but my voice is barely above a whisper. The rocking chair begins a slow, dry creak inside the room.

"Ike," I say, louder this time. I'm up on my knees, frantically twisting the doorknob, but it's locked. "Ike, open the door for Mommy, honey!"

Prickles of alarm spike my blood pressure.

Another unnerving cackle, farther back in the room this time, but I distinctly hear the sound of rasping breath on the other side of the door as another note slips through to the hall:

YOU TOLD YOUR MOMMY AND DADDY
THAT SHE'D CHEWED THROUGH HER LEASH.
BUT YOU LIED.
YOU FORGOT TO TIE HER UP THAT NIGHT
AND SHE RAN INTO THE ROAD.

Beneath the angry red scrawl is a crude but realistic drawing of a dead puppy, with X's for eyes and a pink tongue lolling out.

Bile floods my mouth. I'd never told a single soul the truth about what happened to Maple. No one. Not even Sarah. I'd firmly pushed the guilt of her disappearance and my lie to the bottom-most crevasse in my body and buried it under layers and layers of denial.

The doorknob rattles in my hand. My fists pound on the door. I'm way past pretending to keep my cool.

"Ike, sweetheart! Open up. This isn't funny, Ike. You need to let Mommy in, right NOW."

Another note:

YOU KNOW THE RULE, DON'T YOU, ABIGAIL?
FINDERS KEEPERS.

I drop to my belly, pressing my eye against the crack between the floor and the door. Inside the room, the rocking chair tips forward and back, forward and back. Ike's little feet dangle and kick off the seat. He's singing a little song, "…finders keepers, losers weepers…"

An eye.

A gruesome, bloodshot eye, set deep inside a cadaver-white face, stares unblinking back at me.

All the blood trickles from my head, leaving behind a thunderous crash of waves in my ears. For a moment, my heart refuses to beat. I'm acutely aware of my ventricles, bunched in contraction, squeezing tighter and smaller, radiating pain from my sternum up my neck…

"Breathe, Abby!" Every molecule of motherly instinct shouts in unison, louder than the rush in my ears. *"Ike needs you. NOW."*

An image of a chalky, dead hand touching Ike forms in my mind, eclipsing every other thought. Finally, my heart drops a beat. My head spins, but I lurch instantly to my feet and aim a kick dead-center at the door.

The frame shakes. The white-painted wood splinters.

A hideous cackle responds.

Gulping a huge lungful of air, I steady myself and back up against the wall opposite the door, aiming for the spot with the splinters, and…

"Abby! What the fuck are you doing?"

Jason's rock-solid arms wrap me in a bear hug. The cruel cackle behind the door mocks me as I struggle in his arms, but he's much stronger than me, and I'm too frantic and dizzy. He lowers me to the ground.

"Abby, stop fighting me. Please, just breathe. You're hyperventilating. Breathe, and tell me what's happening."

It's the helpless worry in his voice that quiets my limbs. As the adrenaline seeps away, shuddering, terrified sobs wrack my body.

"Daddy?"

A small, confused voice stops the sobs in my throat. I strain my neck around Jason's shoulder to see our son standing in his doorway, clutching his silky blanket and rubbing sleep from his eyes.

Jason relaxes his grip on me, rising first to his knees and then to his feet before offering his hand and pulling me up beside him. "Hey, good morning, buddy," he says to Ike, tousling his curly brown hair.

"Something loud was banging on my door," Ike complains. "It woke me up."

Instead of answering, Jason reaches down to grab Ike's hand. "Come on, buddy. Wanna help me make pancakes?"

"Chocolate chip?" Ike asks, pulling Jason down the hall toward the kitchen.

"Yes, sir," Jason says, with a concerned backward glance at me. "And whipped cream!"

As soon as they round the corner, I push the splintered door open and step into Ike's room. His bed is rumpled, and some of his stuffed animals have fallen to the floor, but nothing else seems amiss.

Only, do I detect a faint whiff of sulfur in the air?

Almost reluctantly, I approach the rocking chair, running my finger along the faded stain of the back support. What's wrong with me? It's a chair. A simple, handmade rocking chair, constructed in celebration of my arrival in the world. A keepsake. An heirloom. Not some haunted, menacing object.

Yet, I can't bring myself to sit in it.

What the fuck, Abby? I ask myself, sinking onto Ike's bed. *You'd better snap out of it before Jason has you committed.*

In slow circles, I massage a dull ache that's been building behind my temples for days. I don't know how to explain what's happening. It couldn't be stress or tiredness—I'd slept almost eight full hours—and I'd been happy at the thought of making things right with Ike when I woke.

But sitting here now, it's like a great weighted blanket of exhaustion envelops me. My limbs feel heavy, sluggish.

A flicker of fear spasms in my chest; this isn't normal. How I'm behaving isn't normal. Something's wrong with me.

No. There's nothing wrong with you, a reasonable voice speaks in my head. *There's a legitimate reason you're behaving this way. Think, Abby. Focus. Remember.*

Thick fog clouds my brain, and I whimper. It takes monumental effort to get the gears in my head spinning in reverse. What had set me off…?

…it was the notes! The not-Ike note that had slipped beneath the door into the hall!

Instantly, I'm on my feet and at the door. I bend down to grab the folded-up pieces of paper, triumphant. Jason will have to believe me now. I had every reason in the world to kick the door in. Some nightmare had locked himself in the room with our little boy!

My hands shake with vindication and relief as I rush to the kitchen, stumbling and off-kilter in my hurry to not only wipe the worry from Jason's mind, but to make a plan to protect our son, together. Nothing—not even bloodthirsty demons—stand a chance against Jason and me when we're united. He's my rock. He'll know what to do.

"Read these!"

Jason wipes pancake batter from his hands on a kitchen towel before taking the notes I've thrust at him. The curiosity deepens between his brow as he opens each one and reads them.

"What are these?" he asks, handing them back to me, one eyebrow raised. "I don't get it."

"They're the notes!" I whisper-shout, barely able to control the volume of my voice. I don't want to frighten Ike, who's sitting on a barstool whisking newly cracked eggs into the batter. "The notes from that…that monster who was cackling in Ike's room last night and this morning, too."

"Honey, just sit down," Jason says. He sounds almost defeated. "Breakfast will be ready soon. And I texted your mom. She's coming over with Sarah."

I search his face, shocked by his reaction. "Please, Abbs." He steers me to the table and pulls out a chair for me. "Just rest, okay? Can I get you some Advil or something? You look like you've got a headache. I'm sorry if you didn't sleep well." His lips brush against my forehead as I sit down, woodenly.

"No, I'm fine," I say, numb. I'm staring down at the creased papers in my hands. They all say the same thing:

To: Ike"

From: Mommy

That's it. I turn them over, but all the other sides are blank.

They're all from me.

Silent tears slip down my cheeks. How can I be a mother and a wife if I'm losing my mind? Who will take care of my baby? What if the person he needs protection from is me?

Peremptory rapping at the back door startles me. I hastily wipe my eyes. It has to be Mom and Sarah. Sheesh. They certainly didn't waste any time getting here. Briefly, I wonder what, exactly, Jason said before realizing the truth is plenty enough to alarm them.

I'm standing as they let themselves in. All Mom's attention is focused on me. As she wraps me in a maternal hug, Sarah and Jason exchange a loaded look.

"Oh, sweetheart," Mom says, squeezing me tight. "I'm so sorry this is happening." She steps back to hold me at arms' length, examining me from head to toe. Keeping hold of me, she turns and shoots a nod at Jason, who scoops up a giggling Ike and flies him like an airplane out to the couch in the living room. When Ike's landed, Jason tucks a blanket around him and turns on an episode of *Ninjago*.

Since when did everyone start speaking in a secret language of furtive glances about me behind my back?

With her hands on my shoulders, Mom guides me into my

chair exactly like she thinks I'll break to pieces if I move too fast. It strikes me as very odd that, while she seems *concerned* that she's been summoned here early on a Saturday morning to deal with me, she doesn't seem *surprised*. It makes me wonder just how long the people in my life have been expecting me to have a mental breakdown.

Mom sits down next to me and grasps my hand. Sarah pulls out a chair opposite us. She hasn't spoken a word to anyone since she came in. She just gazes at me with a look of twin-sisterly compassion.

What the fuck is going on?

"Tell me exactly what happened, sweetheart," Mom says. "Try not to leave anything out."

Jason returns to the kitchen. He takes the empty griddle off the stove and turns off the flame before sitting down next to me and taking my other hand.

"It's nothing," I start. "I guess I just got confused or something. I've been stressed lately…"

"You were stressed, so you tried to kick down Ike's door?" Sarah's inflection is flat, disbelieving. I stare at the table, avoiding her eyes. Why does she always have to call me on my bullshit?

"Listen. I don't know what else you guys want me to say, all right? I thought I heard someone in Ike's room last night. It freaked me out. And then I thought I heard him again this morning…"

"Him?" Mom asks, but am I crazy for thinking it's not really a question? "Him, who?"

"Why does it matter?" I shrug, defensive. "There was obviously no one in there."

"Sweetheart." Mom takes a steadying breath. I can see her searching for the right words. "We're not interrogating you…"

"It sure feels that way," I say.

"Have you called Dr. Thomas?" Sarah asks Jason.

"No." He shakes his head. "I wasn't sure if I should on a Saturday morning."

Mom sighs. I watch all this like I'm floating outside of my

body, like it's happening to someone else on some stupid Netflix Original melodrama.

Through more silent communication conducted in the air over my head, I watch Jason, Mom, and Sarah come to some sort of agreement. Mom is somehow elected Supreme Leader by completely tacit vote in their surreal Olympic Telepathy Team.

"Abby," Mom begins. "Can you tell me what you heard? It's important, honey."

But I'm done with whatever stupid game they're playing. "Why are you guys doing this?" I yank my hands away from Mom and Jason and slide my chair back away from the table. "What's going on? Why won't you just tell me what you're thinking? Because it's obvious that you're all in on something that you're not telling me!"

"Daddy?" Ike calls from the other room. "Is Mommy okay?"

"Everything's fine, buddy," he calls back. "Watch another episode of *Ninjago*, okay? Breakfast will be ready soon."

"I'm sorry it seems that way, Abby," Mom placates. "I'm trying to find out how much you remember."

"Remember of what?" I ask, still angry, and hurt, but quieter now. "I told you. I thought I heard someone…or something…in Ike's room. But obviously I was wrong. What? Am I the only person in the world who's ever thought they heard something they haven't?" It feels like I'm under a microscope, with them all poking at me to see what I'll do and say reflexively. And it's starting to feel like they've been examining me quietly for a long time. I dash the stupid tears from my face with a balled-up fist and then entwine my hands together in my lap.

"That's not what your mom's talking about, babe." Jason coaxes one of my hands from my lap and smooths it out between his fingers. He traces the lines on my palm gently—something he often does while we're driving in the car together—and it reminds me: these people love me. They aren't my enemies.

"I'm sorry," I mumble as more shameful tears fall. "I don't know what's gotten into me."

"Don't be sorry, Abbs," Sarah says. "We all love you."

I nod, gratefully, and finally meet her eyes.

"This is something we've talked about with Dr. Thomas, babe. It's just that, he said you might not remember…" He stops midsentence, like he's unsure how to finish, and I'm bewildered.

"He said I might not remember what we talked about, or something else?"

"Both," Jason says. "And he told us—your mom and Sarah and me—to be careful what we say because it might bring up things you aren't ready to process."

"Wait." I'm even more confused. "He told 'us' that? As in you guys have been meeting with Dr. Thomas behind my back?"

"Abbs…" Sarah begins. Mom and Jason shoot her a sharp look, but she stares them both down. "I don't care if Dr. Thomas says she'll remember when she's ready. Can't you see this is hurting her? For God's sake, Jason, she almost kicked down Ike's door this morning. What if he'd been standing too close?"

Sarah fixes her eyes on mine and continues. "Do you remember when we were little, Abbs? Whenever we went anywhere in public, we had a rule…"

"Of course I remember." I nod impatiently. "We were always supposed to hold each other's hand, so we wouldn't get lost."

"Right. And do you remember who made that rule?"

"No." I shake my head in frustration. "Why would that matter?"

She doesn't answer my question. "Do you remember the time we went to the mall and we let go of hands because I wanted to go in the candy store, but you didn't?"

"Yes." I don't know what any of this has to do with Ike. "We were supposed to stay where we were by the bathroom and wait."

"That's right. You were always a rule follower."

"And you were a rule-breaker. So what?" Why is she bringing this up now?

"Well, do you remember what happened after that?"

That's strange. I actually don't remember. I look at her

blankly.

"Your sister got lost," Mom says quietly. "Only for a few minutes, but you were very upset, Abigail. When Grandpa brought you two home, Sarah was fine, but you were hysterical. We couldn't calm you down. Eventually we gave you some Benadryl, and you slept for almost two days straight."

"You don't remember telling Dr. Thomas any of this in your EMDR session?" Jason asks.

I shiver. Why can't I remember?

"I sat with you while you slept," Mom says. "I was so worried. You tossed and turned, and you kept saying, 'Finders, keepers,' over and over again."

Goosebumps climb my legs and march across my arms to congregate on the skin over my solar plexus like a murder of crows.

"That's what I heard," I whisper, eyes wide as saucers. "In Ike's room last night. And this morning…! The rocking chair was creaking, and a voice was singing, 'Finders keepers, losers weepers.' But it must have been Ike…"

How could it have been Ike? I question myself. *He'd just woken up when he opened the door.*

"I thought I heard someone else in there with him, though," I insist, aware that I sound defensive again but unable to stop. "There had to have been someone else in there with Ike!"

"Who, Abigail?" Mom asks.

"I don't know! I can't remember…"

But I do. I remember. I remember every gruesome detail of the gruesome, ancient man.

"Try, Abby," Jason pleads. "It's important."

Just tell them, Abby! I yell at myself. *They're trying to help you!*

"Fine!" I say and plow ahead, letting everything spill out in a rush. "I thought I heard a creepy old man, okay? I don't know who he was, but I…I saw him, under the door. He was staring back at me with a horrible eye, and a red, red mouth. His tongue was black, and he smelled like death…"

One of Jason's hands is rubbing my back just above my

tailbone, and I suddenly realize I'm hunched and shaking, holding onto his other hand for dear life.

"That's okay, sweetheart. You're doing fine," Mom says. "You're going to be okay. We can stop now…"

"No, we can't, Mom," Sarah says. "Do you have any idea how hard it's been to watch her suffer and not even know what was going on myself for so long? It's like she turned into a completely different person when Grandpa Blake died. I felt like I'd lost my best friend!"

Is Sarah crying? Shock clamps tight around my esophagus, and suddenly I can't swallow. I've never seen my twin sister cry before. She's always been so strong and defiant, almost protective…

…suddenly I'm six years old, standing petrified in front of an open casket set up on the gold shag carpet in the front room of the house we grew up in. Every instinct in my body screams at me to run, to hide, but I'm frozen, unable to move a single muscle. The chalky, bloodless face framed by white satin holds me captive. I'm transfixed by the paper-thinness of his skin, of the thick, coiled veins on either side of his temples. They're still faintly blue…did they pulse…?

"It was Grandpa Blake…" I breathe.

Jason has pulled me against his chest now. He's rocking me slowly like a baby. Mom's hands have replaced his, rubbing along my shoulder blades. She's making shushing noises with her mouth.

"Abigail," Sarah says, leaning across the table and reaching out her hand. "It's taken me a long time to understand that Grandpa Blake was not a bad person. He didn't mean to hurt you or scare you…"

"He was sick, Abbigail," Mom interrupts. "His dementia changed him."

"Grandpa hurt me," I whisper. I squeeze my eyes shut tight, but it doesn't stop the avalanche of images and memories from crashing down over my head:

Grandpa dragging Maple back from the street, his hand

bloody from the knife he'd plunged into her heart.

Grandpa, glaring at me from hollow eyes, watching from the entry to the men's bathroom at the mall after I'd let go of Sarah's hand.

Grandpa yanking me around to make me watch as he pulled down Sarah's skirt in front of the candy store and spanked her until livid welts rose on her bare skin.

Waking in a cold sweat to see Grandpa's furious face hovering over my bed—creaking slowly back and forth in the rocking chair he'd pulled close—his breath snarling hot and sour on my face: "Finders keepers, Abbigail."

I can't breathe. My hands claw at my sweatshirt; it's too tight. Frantic, I push away from the hands rubbing me, holding me…there are too many hands…I need to find some air. But my legs won't support me. I take one wobbling step before tipping clumsily forward against the table. As I right myself, the bile that's been rising in my throat all day floods my mouth, and I vomit violently.

The last thing I see before blackness overtakes me is my son clutching his blanket, staring at me in abject fear.

…A stinging pinch in the back of my hand…

…A lurching jolt—like a shopping cart wheel jammed on a pebble—jars my teeth against each other. But why would I be in a shopping cart…?

…The wail of sirens seems to come from right inside my head, so close…too close…a constant blaring howl that doesn't recede, doesn't diminish. And the stink…the same smell of sulfur I'd detected in Ike's room this morning…something is burning. "Jason, is something burning, babe? I smell sulfur." But my words are trapped on my lips; something tight presses down around my mouth…

…claustrophobic blackness closes in around me. *What is blacker than black, though?* My wide-open eyes search and fail to find any light. A black tunnel. A black hole. Is this what death is? *There's supposed to be a light at the end of the tunnel!* the voices in my mind scream, but even they are drowned out by the omnipresent mechanical buzz that seems to saturate my soul…

…blackness fades in and out. Am I asleep? Awake? Dead? I have the disorienting sensation of losing time. It's loud, chaotic. Snatches of heated conversations drift in and out of my ears and my consciousness like a drafty campfire. The wobbling squeal of rubber wheels syncs with the movement of fluorescent lighting and paneled ceiling tiles above me. I'm on my back, staring up, blinking against the cold, impersonal light.

…*Is this the light at the end of the tunnel?* I ask myself. The harsh scent of ammonia mingles with the sulfur in my nose…

…what are the voices saying? *Focus, Abby!* I scold myself. *Wake up. This is important! They're talking about you…!*

"…in a perfect storm. The CAT scans show the tumor is pressing against the…which would explain…memory loss, mood swings…as vomiting and…"

"…hallucinations, too, Doctor? She was talking about voices and said…the smell of sulfur…"

That was Jason's voice! "Jason," I shout, "Jason, what happened? Where's Ike, Jason? Where are we going?" But no sound comes out. Tears crowd my eyes as my lips remain infuriatingly closed.

"…kind of hallucination isn't actually something I'm familiar with…the optic nerve…usually blurry…you described. But stress and emotional trauma can absolutely combine with physiological…makes sense, actually that the two would converge…"

I'm fully conscious now, but the stupid squeaky wheels and the beeping of a million monitors makes it impossible for me to hear any more than snatches of the conversation Jason is having with whoever the doctor is. Inside, I'm thrashing and yelling to get their attention, but on the stretcher, my body is completely inert.

But I've heard enough to understand that there's a tumor in my brain. Is it possible that my repressed memories, combined with a brain tumor, could have caused me to imagine everything last night and this morning? The horrible face; the reek of death; the ugly, threatening words? Could Ike's birthday—losing his tablet like I lost Sarah and Maple—could that have triggered such a terrifying chain of events?

Relief sputters erratically in time with the cold electric light from above. It doesn't embrace me, only hovers over me, just out of reach. The full implication of the unseen doctor's words are beginning to sink in with devastating certainty: I have a brain tumor.

What's going to happen to me?

My pulse is loud and slow in my ear, the ominous footfall of grim mortality drawing inexorably near. *Kick, dammit!* I scream at my feet, but they're leaden, weighed down by memories of my grandfather and the cruel realization of how fleeting life is.

The oxygen mask is too tight; the bands dig into my skin. I want to rip it from my face, but my hands are strapped down. The air in my lungs fights with the oxygen in my mouth. *Do something!* But I'm completely helpless. I can't do anything, nothing at all.

Tears wet my face, running down my cheeks and mixing with my sweat-damp hair. What if this is the end? What if I never get to kiss my husband again? What if I don't get the chance to hold my son close and tell him I love him? What if I spend my last waking hours tortured by the trauma of my childhood and unable to communicate with my family?

What if Ike's last memories of me are when I tried to kick down his door or when he saw me vomit and pass out in the kitchen?

"She's crying! Stop, Doctor, she's awake!"

At the sound of Jason's voice, my eyes fly to his. Oh, thank you, God! Thank you, thank you, thank you!

The gurney stops in the middle of a paneled ceiling tile, and the doctor peers into my eyes with a dazzling penlight.

"Abby, can you hear me?" Jason's words are urgent.

I still can't find my voice, and I'm trying not to freak out that I can't move my head enough to nod. But I can blink at him, and

I do, furiously.

"Nurse, is there a room we can use?" the doctor asks over his shoulder. "Let's let Mrs. Hernandez have a moment with her family before taking her to pre-op." I watch him with grateful eyes as he turns back to Jason and asks, "Is your son still here?"

The ceiling tiles begin to pass overhead again as we wheel toward a room. My stomach squeezes with anticipation.

"Yes, he's in the waiting area with my mother and sister-in-law. Will they be able to see her as well?"

"Of course. But this will be brief. The surgeon is scrubbing up now. I'll send someone for them."

Relief finally embraces me. Ike is here. I'll get to see him, to make sure he knows how much I love him. To tell him I'm sorry for yelling at him last night, for scaring him this morning.

Maybe it was panic that had held me frozen, unable to move, because by the time we reach the small space partitioned off by curtains that slide open and shut on a metal rod, I've stopped fighting the oxygen and I can wiggle my fingers and toes.

I try my voice. "Jason?" It's muffled under the mask, but he hears me.

"Hey, babe," he whispers, smoothing some loose hair back from my face and tucking it behind my ear. I can tell he's putting on a brave face, but there are tears in his eyes. "You gave us quite a scare, Abby."

Slowly, and with infinite effort, I raise my hands to my face and pull the mask to the side. No one tries to stop me, and I can't decide if that means I'm definitely going to die so it doesn't really matter or that I'm doing much better and I don't need it anymore. Either way, it's easier to breathe without it mashed around my mouth.

"Jason," I say quietly, reaching for his hand. "Do I look okay? I mean, I know I don't, but will you help me sit up a little? I don't want Ike to see me this way."

A tear rolls down his strong, angular face, and it breaks my heart.

"Shhh, shhh, don't cry, baby," I whisper. "We've got to be strong for Ike."

He smiles. "Everything's going to be fine, Abby, I promise. I'm just so glad you're awake. I didn't want to send you back there without talking to you, without telling you I love you." He leans his head down to rest it against my chest. The stubble from his chin tickles.

"You're so brave, Abby. When I think about everything you've been going through…I had no idea. You must have been scared out of your mind!"

"Do you really think I'll be okay, though?" I whisper into his neck.

He stands up and strokes my face. "I know you will. The doctor said it's a good thing all this other stuff came up now—I don't mean good, it's awful—but he thinks the stress made your symptoms worse. If you hadn't passed out and we hadn't brought you to the ER, you wouldn't have had a CT scan, and they might not have detected the tumor until it was too late. It's still small, Abby. They can remove it. And I've already talked to Trevor. I can work from home as long as I need until you recover."

The love and certainty in his eyes are a balm to my high-alert nerves. I breathe a shaky sigh of relief.

"Mommy?"

My heart. He's here, standing at the edge of the curtain. "Ike," I say, stretching out my arms. I've never been so happy to see anything or anyone in my life. But I have to keep my emotions in check. He's witnessed enough drama in the past twenty-four hours, and I've experienced firsthand how childhood trauma can impact you as an adult.

He lets go of his grandma's hand and scampers over to me. I'm slightly surprised at the uncomplicated joy beaming from his big brown eyes. "Mommy!" he says again, right up close to my face. He puts one of his little hands in mine. "Mommy, is that a needle in your hand?" His voice is full of wonder as he tentatively touches the tube running from my IV. "Does it hurt?"

"Nope," I say in response, ruffling his dark, curly hair. I'm so grateful he seems okay. I can't detect any confusion or mistrust or unease from last night or this morning. His energy is bright and innocent and loving.

I glance up to thank Mom and Sarah, but they're congregating just at the edge of the open curtain, talking to a surgeon in blue scrubs.

"Are you having a good time with Aunt Sarah and Grandma?" I ask.

"Mmmhmm." He nods. "We're going to go have lunch at McDonald's, and then guess what? We're going to the pet store to look at puppies!"

"Puppies?" I laugh, tickling under his chin. "But you don't even like puppies!"

"Mommy, yes I DO!" He giggles. "Daddy said if I find one I really, really like, I can bring her home!"

"He did, did he?" I grin.

"Yep! I'm going to name her Molasses."

"Molasses? What a funny name." I scrunch up my nose. "Where did you hear that?"

"That's what you make syrup out of," he patiently explains. "Maple and Molasses."

I blink. The surf of distant waves crashes in my ears.

It has to be a coincidence.

"Did you help your grandma make syrup this morning, buddy?" I struggle to keep my voice steady.

"Nope. But Grandpa Blake said you used to help him make syrup when you were a little girl and that you had a puppy named Maple. So, we decided my puppy would be Molasses. They'd be like twin sisters, like you and Aunt Sarah!"

All the arteries leading to my heart spasm in panic. "Ike. Your grandpa Blake is dead." My voice trembles. I clutch at Ike's hand.

"It's okay, Mommy," my little boy soothes. "Grandpa said he's sorry that he scared you. He said it was just a joke…"

"No, Ike, no!" One of the monitors attached to my chest

starts beeping manically.

"Abby?" Concern fills Mom's voice.

Ike leans closer. "Don't be afraid, Mommy." He pats my head. "Grandpa Blake says we'll all be together soon. You, and me, and him, and Maple and Molasses. He says that we'll be waiting for you."

My pulse is loud, in my throat, in my hands—racing, stinging. Behind Ike, the curtains twist and spin.

"Nurse, I need the anesthesiologist," the doctor calls, parting the curtain. "Blood pressure 180/120."

"What's going on?" Jason shouts, pushing to get close to me, but the surgeon and a nurse hold him back.

"Dr. Tanaka, we have a Code Blue, floor three," I hear over the PA system. "I repeat, Code Blue, floor three."

Is that for me? Am I a Code Blue?

"Don't worry, Mommy," Ike says as a nurse pulls him back away from me. "Just close your eyes. We'll be waiting for you when you wake up."

I swat a swarm of hands and fingers away from my face, but they keep coming. The stretcher is lowered flat and someone replaces the oxygen mask. They're wheeling me from the room.

Frantic, I crane my neck around, desperate to see Ike, my mom, Sarah. Why isn't Jason coming with me?

There's Ike, smiling encouragingly at me, safe in my mother's arms. But as I raise my eyes to meet her gaze, my heart stops cold. It isn't my mother's arms around Ike.

Dimly, I hear someone telling me to count backward from one hundred, but all my attention is fixed in terror on the dead-black eyes staring back at me from deep inside a chalk-white face.

Grandpa Blake.

His ghoulish red lips split open in a grin over his crooked, rotting teeth. His cadaver hands rest on the shoulders of my little boy.

"IKE!" I scream. But no sound escapes my lips. The stench of death rolls from the mask into my nostrils, choking me. I gag as inky darkness slides across my vision…

CARNIVAL OF LUST

Mike Duke

OVE MAY FADE WITH TIME, but a man's lusts burn bright all the days of his life."

Joey's big sister, Linda, dropped him off at the carnival around 8 pm.

"I'll be back to pick you up at eleven o'clock, okay?" she confirmed. "Meet me right here in the Armory parking lot."

"Yup, Sis," Joey answered. "WillI. do."

"Go find yourself some hot little girl, killer," Linda's best friend Jenny taunted him. "Get your lip-lock on!"

She pursed her lips and blew him a kiss. Joey watched her out of the corner of his eye, trying to play it cool as he got out of the car.

"Jenny! What the hell?" Linda chastised her friend. "You're gonna give him a complex, for God's sake."

Joey shut the door without looking back and walked away, trying to look like a big boy—spine erect, chest held high, moving at a leisurely pace with just the right amount of swagger in his gait. Inside, though, he was dying to find his friend Robbie. He reached in his jeans-jacket pocket, making sure for the tenth time he had the stack of tickets his mom had picked up for him earlier in the day as well as the twenty dollars he had earned mowing four of his neighbors' yards during the week, each afternoon.

He was lucky the carnival arrived during early September. The grass was still growing some. There might only be one or two more times to cut it and earn some cash.

The lady working the booth was heavy-set and too old looking for her age. Sagging jowls matched the Salem cigarette sagging down from between her wrinkled, ochre-colored lips.

"Cash only, kid," she informed him, looking down her nose.

Joey pulled out the tickets, looked at the sign that read, "5 tickets to enter," tore off five from his roll, and handed them to the lady.

The lady gave him the stink-eye, a suspicious, scrutinizing look. She squinted with one eye while a painted eyebrow rose high on her forehead above the other.

"My mom stopped by and bought them for me earlier today," Joey volunteered, feeling the woman's doubts as to how he obtained the tickets.

"How old are you, son?"

Joey cocked a real eyebrow and got a little smart.

"Thirteen, lady. And I ain't your son."

The lady recoiled in surprise. She took a deep drag off her cigarette, held the smoke in for a couple of seconds, then leaned forward and blew it in Joey's face. He coughed and waved his hand in front of his mouth and nose to clear the air.

"Little big for yer britches there, kid," she said but took his tickets as she looked him up and down then stared at his face, assessing him somehow. "You got a girlfriend to go with all that machismo, sport?"

Joey was caught off guard by the question and by her calling him "sport." It was Déjà vu for sure.

"Ummm…" He struggled to find an appropriate answer but couldn't come up with anything in time.

"That'd be a big 'ole 'no,' now wouldn't it?" the lady challenged him, blunt as a hammer.

Joey looked down at his feet.

"That's all right," the lady consoled him, her attitude seeming to soften. "Thirteen is a fine age to find your first real puppy love."

Joey looked up at her, his eyes pinched into a death-beam glare.

"Ah, c'mon, kid. I'm serious." She held up one hand and placed the other over her heart. "Now, c'mere. Give me your right hand. I'm gonna mark you with my good luck stamp—the one that draws the ladies like flies to honey, or at least draws the right one for you."

Joey didn't believe a damn bit of this gypsy bullshit she was spouting, but he held out his hand anyway. The lady took his in one of hers, rolled the rubber template across a pad of red ink, and stamped the back of his hand. Joey's flesh quivered suddenly at the lady's touch, and where she had marked him felt warm and wet immediately.

The lady whispered something in another language, the cigarette still in her mouth, but Joey was oblivious. She released his hand, and he pulled it back to look down at a red image of a smiling horned devil with a tail, holding a pitchfork, the red image imprinted on his skin. It was a female devil, though, and she possessed all the right curves, he noticed. He stared at the image, and its face seemed to fix him with a sensual leer, almost vulgar.

Joey liked it.

"Aight, boy. Skedaddle," she ordered. "And behave inside, ya hear?"

"Yes, ma'am," Joey said while giving a mock salute.

He started to turn and walk inside the carnival but had to do a double take over his shoulder. He would have sworn on a stack of Bibles the lady's eyes glowed red for a moment and her skin looked young and smooth out of the corner of his eye. But when he looked square at her, she looked no different than before. Joey blinked his eyes as he turned forward and made his way inside the carnival.

The cotton candy stand waited for him just past the entrance, and Joey made a beeline for it. The line wasn't too long. While he waited his turn, he scanned the people walking by for Robbie's face but didn't see him. A father with two children handed a small cotton candy to each of them, red for the boy and pink for his daughter. After the man moved out of the way, Joey approached the counter and placed his order with the older gentleman who manned the booth. He was dressed in a large, white apron that stretched across his rather rounded belly. A black bow tie and a white soda-jerk hat with a red pinstripe completed the image.

"A large blue one," Joey said, pointing at the menu with one hand while holding out two dollar bills as payment. He could never tell whether it was supposed to be some blue raspberry or blueberry, but it was his favorite artificial flavor.

Joey watched as the man twirled the paper cone, weaving layer after layer of the sugary webbing into a huge fluffy mass before handing it to him.

"Enjoy, kid," the man said with a smile that caused the tips of his gray handlebar mustache to arc upward. His face was a portrait of mindless satisfaction, but Joey paid no attention.

Joey walked off toward the rides, eating his cotton candy and looking around for Robbie. It was a Friday night, and the carnival was hopping with teenagers. Pretty girls roamed about in packs, prancing along in tight, faded blue jeans while young boys ogled, most of them too scared to speak. Some of the jocks had their girlfriends in tow, playing game after game to win a big stuffed bear or something similar, the primary motive being to prove their prowess at throwing balls, shooting hoops, or knocking down ducks and various other animal forms with a BB gun.

He looked down at the stamp on his hand.

Gypsy bullshit, Joey thought then gave himself a quick reality check. *Don't let it get your hopes up, Joey. Ain't no girls looking at you with lust in their eyes.*

Joey stopped in front of the strong man game—the one

where you swung the mallet and tried to ring the bell. A man wearing a tuxedo with tails and a top hat stood there, mic in hand, calling to all the men to step on up and prove how strong they were.

"Hit the mark! Ring the bell! Impress our vixen beauty, here," the man declared then stepped aside to reveal a lady exiting from behind a black curtain. "The lovely Mia Kerenski, all the way from the deep, dark woods of Bulgaria."

Joey stared at Mia, forgetting to breathe for several seconds. A black one piece with red frills and lace drew his eyes in, but it was her long legs, olive complexion, and spiraling jet-black hair that hung halfway down her back that trapped his attention and lured him into admiring her for some time.

She picked up the handle of the huge mallet, hands on the end, arms straight, hips tilted to invite any man up to the platform.

"Is there anyone here who wants to take a swing and try to impress the young lady?" the man inquired. "Hmmm? Show us your strength, your physical prowess, and perhaps the lady might want to walk about the carnival arm and arm with you later tonight."

The man paused and waited for any takers from the gathering crowd. He didn't have to wait long. A fit, blond-haired man in his early twenties bounded up the steps to the platform where the challenge awaited. Mia smiled at him and curtsied before passing the mallet handle to him. He was muscular, but Joey noted the man didn't take up a very good stance, and he choked up on the mallet handle instead of getting the full force out it. He swung the mallet and struck the target. The metal weight slid up the pole but lost momentum well before it reached the bell, falling back to earth with a dull thump.

"I'm sorry, sir," Mr. Top Hat said, "but great Hercules did not shine his gaze upon you this night." He patted the disappointed man on the shoulders as he began his walk of shame down the steps.

"Anyone else?" he called out.

Joey watched as a couple more men gave it a shot, unsuccessfully. Then a man raised his hand in the crowd.

Holy hell, Joey thought as the man ascended the stairs at a plodding pace. *This dude is huge!*

The man was easily six foot five and over three hundred pounds. He wore jean overalls and was obviously a good old farm boy. His hands were more like bear paws or catcher's mitts. He picked up the hammer and swung it down hard, ringing the bell with ease.

"My, my, my!" Mr. Top Hat exclaimed. "We have a winner! A truly incredible specimen of a man!"

They allowed him to choose from the giant stuffed animal selection or a T-shirt declaring him to be a true strong man. Joey finished the last of his cotton candy, threw the paper roll away, and walked up the steps to the platform.

"Well, well, well, folks. What do we have here?" Mr. Top Hat called out. "You're a rather young competitor, lad. You really think you can do this?" The man looked at him without revealing his disdain.

"Probably not, mister," Joey admitted, "but I'll give it every lick of effort I got in me, plus I'll probably have better technique than some of these other guys. I've been chopping wood all summer for my dad."

Joey smiled big and proud then looked at Mia, who grinned big and winked at him as she gave him the mallet handle.

"Good luck," she whispered. Joey felt a slight warmth on his hand but was so distracted by both Mia and the challenge before him it didn't register.

The mallet was quite heavy. Joey took up a more than shoulder-width stance a few feet from his target, holding the mallet by the very end of the handle to get maximum leverage. He raised it above his head, letting the wooden mallet fall back in between his shoulders. Joey inhaled deep and then tightened his whole body, bringing the hammer overhead and down with one explosive movement while dropping his weight at the same time. The impact caused the metal weight to climb and climb, stopping just shy of the bell, before falling back to the ground.

Although defeated, Joey felt it was a good showing for his age and grinned with pride. Mia smiled big and clapped for him. His hand grew even warmer, and he rubbed it with the other only to feel a strange heat against his fingers. He looked down and saw that the female devil stamp had a gentle red glow about it. It possessed a leering face and a seductive smile.

Pretty hot for a cartoon character, he thought to himself, then something drew his eyes upward. He could not explain why, nor did his mind really dwell on it long enough to question it. But as he glanced up, he saw Mia staring at him. For a moment, he thought he saw some lecherous grin cross her face. Joey rubbed his eyes then looked again. She was smiling like any beautiful teenage girl would who seemed impressed with a potential suitor, attracted to him even, perhaps. But Joey wasn't totally sure. He didn't have enough experience with these things.

The announcer lamented Joey's lack of success and asked him if he wanted to try again.

Joey declined but decided to go stand nearby for a bit. There, he ogled at Mia further as well as some of the girls who passed by, all the while idly rubbing his hand and feeling more and more aroused at the parade of beautiful flesh passing before his eyes. They might not look at him with lust, but he sure was going to look at them with it. A lot of it.

He knew now what those pretty girls looked like under their clothes, and it was a thing of pure beauty and fantastic splendor. His buddy Robbie's dad had a massive collection of *Hustler*, *Penthouse*, and *Playboy* magazines. Robbie knew where they were stashed and had led Joey to what might as well have been the treasures of the golden city Eldorado. If someone had offered him a choice between money for comic books and records or another chance at thumbing through those pages of glorious copper-skinned beauties with their perky breasts and tan-line free pelvises leading to luscious thighs, Joey knew what he would choose. Hands down. Zero doubts.

But better than magazines would be the real thing. His mind wandered to Jenny MacCreedy, his sister's best friend.

Ever since the first time his eyes beheld those glorious images inside those magazines, he had wanted to see exactly what Jenny had under those clothes of hers. She came over to his house all the time to hang out with his sister. She liked Daisy Duke shorts and midriff muscle shirts that showed off her firm abs and defined shoulders along with the crack of her ass. She was a sixteen-year-old goddess.

And just earlier this evening, he got the look he'd been dying for.

He heard her say she was going to go change into something else in Linda's room. Linda was making popcorn for the movie they were planning on watching before she had to drive Joey to the carnival. Joey hurried into Linda's room and hid in the wardrobe, leaving the door open just a crack so he could see out.

Jenny came in and shut the door, then kicked off her shoes and rolled back onto Linda's bed to pull off her jeans, revealing skimpy pink-lace underwear. Joey felt his privates tingle with excitement. Jenny stood back up, reached under her shirt, undid her bra, and pulled it out of one of the sleeves. Joey gulped hard and salivated. Jenny began to lift her shirt up, one of her full breasts dropping into view. Joey leaned forward in suspense, causing the door to move open, just a fraction of an inch, but enough for Jenny to notice. She pulled her shirt back down and eyed the wardrobe. A mischievous smile spread across her face. She stepped forward, grabbed the door, and threw it wide.

"Got you!" she exclaimed, but in a quiet voice. "Trying to get you an eyeful of my goods, huh, Joey?"

Joey's mouth dropped open, and he couldn't find words to speak, only stared at Jenny, then glanced down at her pink panties. It was as if they were lined with magnets for his eyes.

"What's the matter, Joey? Pussycat got your tongue?" she asked, letting a hand drift down to her pubic bone.

Joey stared at the sensuous mound above her "pussycat," unable to tear his eyes away. He finally managed to speak.

"Are you going to tell Linda and my mom?" His eyes pleaded for mercy, big and full of dread.

"Hmmmmm…" Jenny let the moment drag out, keeping him in suspense. "I tell ya what, Joey. Because I think you're cute, I'm going to make a deal with you."

"Okay," Joey said, hoping it was a good deal that involved keeping his secret.

"I'll show you mine if you show me yours. Chest for chest. Nether region for nether region." Jenny gave him a sinfully delicious smile. Joey's jaw fell wide open and put a sign up inviting flies to come on down and buy real estate. "Whaddaya say, champ? You brave enough?"

She cocked an eyebrow at him and tilted her hips. She posted her free hand at her waist and snaked her index finger under her panties, tugging the corner down a couple of inches to reveal her hip bone.

No tan lines! Joey's mind cried out.

He gulped big, closing his mouth, then dared to speak.

"Yes. Yes!" he assured her, then without waiting took off his shirt and flexed his pecs. He was thin, but it was all muscle and bone. Wiry and strong from all the yard work and odd jobs he did to earn spending money.

"Whoa," Jenny said, nodding her head in approval. "I knew you had some muscles. Lean but still muscular. The girls are going to eat you up in a few years." Joey blushed at the compliment.

"Now it's your turn," he managed to say without stuttering.

"Well, sport, I guess it is."

Jenny made a slight show of lifting one side of her shirt at a time until each voluptuous breast fell into view. Joey scrutinized every detail, committing it to memory—the way they hung, the line of demarcation where the bulge swelled in all its glory, the beautiful areolas surrounding her perfectly firm nipples.

Jenny lowered the curtain, ending the upper body show.

"All right. Drop those shorts," she commanded and smiled.

Joey felt a little self-conscious but, after considering the rewards, quickly unbuttoned his pants then shoved them and his underwear down to his knees. He stood there, fully erect.

"Whoa!" Jenny said and gave a mock salute. "Attention! You like what you see...I see." She let out a little giggle. "And, I must say, for your age, you are certainly packing some better than average heat. Impressive."

Joey didn't pull his pants back up as he informed Jenny, "Your turn."

Jenny hooked both thumbs in her underwear and, tilting her hips back and forth while pulling down one side at a time, bit by bit she revealed her "pussycat" to Joey. Her well-manicured thatch of jet-black hair led his eyes down to her lips. They glistened and beckoned him to come inside, or at least that's what he fantasized.

"You like that, Joey?" Jenny teased him. "I bet you do, don't you?" She licked her lips and then her finger before reaching down to spread around the moisture. Before Joey could muster up the courage to ask her if he could touch it, she pulled her underwear back up.

"Well, I think that's enough for now. Get back in the closet and hide until I leave. I'll keep your sister distracted long enough for you to sneak out of here. And remember, this is our little secret."

Jenny put her index finger to his lips, emphasizing the secret part, then palmed his face and pushed him into the wardrobe, shutting the door. Moments later, she had pulled on her Daisy Duke shorts and was headed out. Joey snuck out in a hurry and stayed in his room the whole movie, watching cartoons and trying to recover.

Robbie's gonna freakin' flip his lid over this, Joey had thought.

Joey's mind returned to the present, just in time to see Robbie approaching him. Robbie was sixteen years old but enjoyed hanging out with Joey. They had similar interests—riding bikes, reading comic books, playing Dungeons and Dragons and, of course, looking at naked women.

Joey couldn't contain his excitement. Rushing up to Robbie, he began spilling every detail of his sordid youthful adventure.

"You got to be shittin' me, man! No way!" Robbie exclaimed when Joey spilled the beans about him and Jenny striking the deal. He ate up every sultry bit, and when Joey relayed his first time seeing a woman's vagina in person, Robbie teased him in jest.

"I bet you wanted to touch that pretty thing with your cock something terrible, didn't you?"

Joey nodded vigorously then rolled his eyes.

"Oh God, yes!" he said.

"Well, buddy," Robbie put his arm around Joey's shoulders and pulled him close, "you've just cleared second base on the way to popping your cherry. You'll get there before you know it!"

Robbie clapped him on the back.

"Now," Robbie turned to look at Joey, "let's go ride some rides!"

"Hell yeah!" Joey answered. "How 'bout we hit the Octopus first? It's right over there."

Joey pointed on the other side of a large, inflatable slide, wide enough for eight people to come down at once and over two stories tall.

"Or…" Joey offered, "slide first, then the Octopus."

THEY HIT SEVERAL rides back-to-back. First, they cackled while shooting down the slide side-by-side headfirst. Next, the Octopus, which was one of Joey's favorite rides. The central core spun around while the cars at the end of each "tentacle" spun independently, creating brief whips of centrifugal force every few seconds or so. After a minute, the arms extended, shifting their cars into a vertical spin. Joey hollered in delight, pinned to the side of his seat. The arms lowered back down to their original angled position and then began slowing until the ride ended.

Joey probably would have skipped The Bullet, but Robbie browbeat him into it. A bullet-shaped car attached to each end of two long metal girders rotated around a central axle, swung high, crested at the top, then plummeted down toward the ground before it curved inches away, barely avoiding impact before heading up high again. Every time their car fell toward the earth, Joey wailed like a siren in the night.

The Zipper kept both Robbie and Joey gripping the lap bar for dear life as the ride spun on its axis, cars moving around it like the tracks on a tank, each car spinning and rocking all about. It was insane, but Joey loved it.

As they exited the Zipper, Joey noticed a pattern among the rides, in fact around the whole carnival. Apart from Mr. Top Hat and the cotton candy man, all the male workers were quite homely and, in fact, rather quiet. They sat at rides, taking tickets, eyes cast down, or went about pulling levers, checking safety latches and harnesses on rides, or walking around picking up trash with a simple stick and nail, but never engaging with the customers in the least. It was mostly older women like the lady at the entrance who were speaking to people over the sound system, working the booths and generally interacting with everyone attending the carnival.

He and Robbie approached a line of booths with various contests. Duck shoot, basketball hoop throws, whack-a-mole, the ring toss, balloon dart throw, and the milk bottle baseball throw. At each booth, a beautifully dressed woman stood, enticing every man and boy passing by to wage battle and win a prize. They all wore the same clothing: a one-piece, burlesque-style corset. Black and red vertical stripes were highlighted with red frills and lace along the bustline and groin. An enormous tuft of red feathers, all tipped in black, emerged from the top of their glutes, draped down almost to the back of their knees and wrapped around their hips. Each one also wore a satin, red rose tied in their flowing black hair.

They were gorgeous beyond measure. The *Penthouse* and *Hustler* women didn't seem to hold a candle to these gypsy ladies. Robbie was drawn like a moth to a flame, hemming and hawing left and right, unable to decide for several seconds which lady was the most beautiful to him. After much deliberation, he locked eyes with the woman manning the Balloon Dart Throw booth and made a beeline toward the counter.

"Hi," Robbie said and felt his tongue go numb. He opened his mouth to speak but felt mute. He looked down at his feet, not used to feeling self-conscious around the female species, but this girl was utterly out of his league. He finally managed to look up and make his mouth work at last, almost stuttering, but forcing the words past his lips without hesitation.

"You're incredibly beautiful. Did you know that?" He paused long enough to dig a dollar from his pocket and lay it on the countertop. "I'd like to play your game," he declared.

The girl's hand slipped out, smooth as butter, and retrieved the bill, making it disappear to where neither Joey nor Robbie could follow. Robbie didn't even try. His gaze never left the balloon girl's face except to stare at her breasts with a level of fascination that only teenage boys could pull off.

"Here you go, Robin Hood," the girl said with a bewitching tone that challenged and aroused at the same time as she slid the five darts across the counter to Robbie.

"Do you think you…can pop them for me?" Her body language was agonizingly seductive. Head turned slightly, eyes narrowing with a sensuous intensity as she began to speak, her tongue pushing unusually far forward with the word "think." With the word "you," she touched Robbie's hand, her electric flesh in contact with his. After a dramatic pause, her lips curled in before parting with an audible noise of separation as she said the word "pop." Her gaze alone was enough to suggest she was beginning to devour him already.

Robbie was undone now. A bird caught in a snare, an arrow piercing his liver. A net entangled his heart. One he was unable to escape. One, in fact, he did not wish to escape. Freedom was an ideal he desired no longer. He would do anything to secure this woman's affection and hold onto it for life.

His focus was laser sharp now. The world of lust he breathed every day had finally found its ultimate object of desire. He took a step closer, his hips pressing against the counter now as he slid his fingers beneath hers and gripped the darts in his left hand.

"You're damn straight I can pop them," he stated boldly to the girl.

"That's my tiger," she said and scratched the back of his hand before stepping back and out of the way. Joey noticed at that moment that Robbie also had the red lady devil stamp on his left hand. His, too, seemed to be aglow.

"Let me see what my man can do," the girl encouraged him.

Robbie moved the first dart into his right hand and took a big step backward. He wasted little time in aiming. It was a natural act to him. He threw darts all the time. But tonight, his body burned with an uncanny strength. He was precise but whipped the dart with a power he had never possessed before. His arm snapped forward like a pitcher slinging a fastball. The plastic feathers whizzed through the air. The dart skewered the first balloon, making it pop, despite it being underinflated, a typical carnival trick to make success more elusive.

The girl squealed with pleasure.

"What strong arms you have, tiger!" she exclaimed. "Do it again…for me."

Her smile was intoxicating to Joey, and it wasn't even fixated on him. To Robbie, it was the source of an incredible high. A feeling of being desired intensely beyond measure, beyond anything he had ever dreamed of. She wanted Robbie with all her being. He could tell. And it made him feel fulfilled and satisfied like nothing else he had ever experienced.

He threw the next four darts in rapid succession, busting a balloon with every one of them.

The girl clapped and cheered and bounced up and down.

Robbie beamed with pride at his accomplishment and with anticipation for his prize.

"So, beautiful," he asked, "what do I win?"

She pointed to a sign up high and to the far right of the booth. Neither Joey nor Robbie could remember seeing it there before, but Robbie didn't even care. It said, "FIRST PRIZE: Escort for the Night."

"You get me, tiger," she stated with a large smile, her whole body twitching with excitement.

For a moment, her whole countenance changed, becoming stern. She turned and looked toward the back right corner of the booth, out of sight.

"Peter!" she shouted. A young man with a large frame lumbered into view. "Pick up the darts and close the booth. I'm done for the night. Understood?"

The man nodded his head with reverential respect and responded with an acute level of excitement. "Yes, mah lady," he said before grabbing the darts one by one, as instructed.

The girl turned back to Robbie, eyes alight with the fire of young love or at least young lust. Robbie was infatuated, but Joey somehow couldn't take his eyes off the man gathering darts. He went about his job with a fond fervor, glad to serve, whistling while he worked. As he plucked the last dart from the plywood backstop, Joey saw the red lady devil stamp on the man's hand, except it didn't look like a stamp at all. More like a tattoo. But it glowed faintly.

"My name is Ruby," the girl introduced herself.

"I'm Robbie," he declared, as if he were no doubt a knight in shining armor, come to her rescue.

"Well, Robbie," Ruby said, slipping her arm in his and hugging her body snuggly against his, "let's take a walk about the carnival, shall we?"

Robbie nodded vigorously and began walking, following her lead. "Yes, mah lady," he said without thinking.

Joey looked away from the man in the booth to see Robbie

walking away with nary a word spoken to him.

"Robbie!" Joey called out and began walking toward him and Ruby. Robbie didn't answer.

"Robbie?" Joey called out, the confusion in his voice forming a question with his tone. Still no response from Robbie. He walked and laughed at whatever the girl, Ruby, was saying to him.

"What the hell, Robbie?" he shouted. "What's wrong with you?"

Ruby turned around then.

"Young man, be happy for your friend because he is happy." Ruby's voice had changed. Before, she enunciated every word with a perfect typical American accent, but now it was different. Eastern European or Russian perhaps, Joey thought, based on TV shows he had watched. "Go. Go now," she shooed him. "Go back to Mia and you can be happy, too."

With that, she turned around and walked off with Robbie, neither of them ever looking back.

Joey stood still, staring after them until they disappeared into the crowd, perplexed by what had transpired. It was beyond unusual. It was categorically bizarre.

And how the fuck did she know my name? he thought.

"Fuck this," Joey said aloud and moved over to the Whack-a-Mole booth. The girl there was just as beautiful as Ruby. Joey approached the counter, dollars in hand, but the girl leaned on the back wall, ignoring him.

What the hell? What the fuck is wrong here? What's wrong with me?

Joey could think of no reason why the girl should be completely ignoring him. He stared at the woman, frustration turning to anger.

For fuck's sake, I'm a goddamn paying customer. Why won't she serve me?

The girl's head snapped up in his direction. Almost as if she heard his thoughts.

"I am not for you," she said in the same accent as Ruby. "Go. You go to Mia. She is for you. You are for her. Go now and you can be happy, like your friend."

Joey stood there dumbfounded, utterly confused by this development. The girl waited a few seconds before furrowing her brow and actively shooing him away with both hands.

Joey took the hint and left.

I guess I'll go see Mia again.

On his way back to Mr. Top Hat and Mia, he passed more male workers, all joyfully performing their duties. Joey actively looked at the back of each one's left hand. The red devil lady was on every one of their hands. With each additional one he observed, the hairs on Joey's arms and the back of his neck stood erect. A chill moved through his spine, and his stomach felt like it was hanging over a chasm.

At last, he walked up to the platform where Mr. Top Hat and Mia stood. Her gaze embraced him this time. Intentional. Primal. Mystifying. With one look, she sprung the trap. Joey felt his will succumb to hers. Felt every desire for sex, belonging and being desired and satisfied in that one look. The way one corner of her mouth turned up in happiness made his world shine brightly as the sun at noonday. Contentment filled his being. She was everything he wanted. Everything he could ever possibly long for. She was the great treasure at the end of an adventure. An all-encompassing peace to immunize his heart against worry or anxiety of any kind. She was home. She was the night. She was a universe full of stars, the alpha and omega of his happiness. The end of emptiness. The place where he would forever belong.

Mr. Top Hat tipped his head, touching the brim of his hat with his left hand. Joey saw it but didn't process it—the red devil lady tattoo, all aglow.

Mia descended the steps, one foot at a time, in slow motion, her eyes never leaving Joey's. She read him like a book, his simple lusts laid bare before her natural instincts, the gift of her kind discerning his fantasies and dreams while simultaneously enslaving his will, preparing to bind him to her.

Joey was paralyzed, captivated with joy at the sight of Mia, at the thought of her desire for him, of how he would fulfill her every need and her his. They were perfect for each other.

Mia stood in front of him now. The fragrance of her perfume, the natural aroma of her silken skin, it was overwhelming to Joey. He was overcome with desire for Mia. His arousal was clearly visible.

Mia blushed as she slipped her fingers behind his head and through his hair. She leaned close and breathed exhilaration in his ear, a titillating promise of euphoria evermore that only her kind could keep. Her words whispered a Succubi lullaby filling his soul with hope. He shivered. A deliriously delightful high rushed through his every nerve fiber. Her voice. Her breath. Her touch. There was nothing else in the world to live for. To work for. She tugged against his head, and he bowed to her will. She kissed him, long and deep, her dark magic binding him to her, marking him as the object of her possession from henceforth. His hand burned and sizzled along the line of the devil lady stamp, making permanent what had been temporary. Joey didn't even feel the pain. There was no pain while in Mia's embrace. As Mia completed the kiss and began to pull away, a wisp of some smoke-like substance stretched between them for a moment before Mia inhaled and sucked the mist inside her lungs. Joey gasped in pleasure and opened his eyes, his face a portrait of mindless satisfaction.

"Come with me, my little bear. My first. You will always hold a special place in my heart. Let us go now and consummate our bond and sign the contract of your thralldom with your lusts fulfilled."

Mia slipped her arm inside Joey's and began to lead him away.

"Joey!" a female voice shouted from a distance. Joey didn't acknowledge it, didn't break stride.

"Joey! What the hell, man? You were supposed to meet us outside half an hour ago."

It was his sister, Linda, but he didn't care.

"Hey, Joey!" A different female voice. Jenny's.

For a fraction of a second, there was a twinge at the remembrance of Jenny's body and their playful show and tell, but she was nothing compared to Mia. Mia completed him in every way. He would never betray her. Never fail her. Never leave or forsake her.

Joey didn't even turn around to say goodbye to his sister or Jenny. He just squeezed Mia's arm and continued to follow her lead.

"What the hell?" Linda sputtered to Jenny, completely confounded by Joey's actions. "And who the hell is that chick he's with?"

"I have no idea," Jenny offered. "But don't let him get out of our sight. C'mon!"

Jenny took off at a trot with Linda on her heels. They could see Joey for a bit but couldn't seem to gain on him despite the fact he never sped up. It was closing time now, and more people were headed for the front gate. Joey and the girl disappeared amongst the other park attendees, there one moment and gone the next. Linda and Jenny ran ahead, darting in between the crowd, scanning for Joey, but to no avail. They made their way toward the exit gate to search the parking lot. As they passed the ticket box shack, an old, heavy set lady smoking a Salem cigarette called out to them.

"Y'all have a good night, you hear?"

Linda and Jenny didn't even spare the woman a glance, just ignored her. She grinned a big lopsided grin, cigarette still in her mouth. Her eyes glowed red in the moonlight, twinkling brightly for a moment then fading back to normal.

"Oh yes. You both have a good night," she mumbled. "Mia take good care of your brother. Hahaha. He in good hands."

The old lady took a deep puff off her cigarette, held it in, then blew out smoke into the night.

3 DAYS LATER

JENNY AND LINDA were just finishing stapling up Missing Person posters with both Joey and Robbie's pictures on them, "HAVE YOU SEEN ME?" in block letters across the top. Linda cried. Jenny hugged her in what she suspected was a hopeless sign of support. She didn't believe either boy would ever be found.

Two states away, the Carnival had come to town. Joey and Robbie both were happier than they had ever been in their lives. Robbie picked up darts for Ruby all day long, content just to remain in her presence. Joey helped set up the strong man game and carried the mallet out to the platform. During the day, he walked around the platform and out into the audience area picking up trash, but his eyes always returned to Mia at every opportunity. His passion…his lust.

I.O.U.

Kayla Krantz

1

THE SCRAPE OF THE BAG moving over the grass was soothing to Mason, the whispery sound like a lullaby out of a nightmare. This was his sixth victim. As he moved, he thought back through the night he had shared with her, from the very first moment he had spotted her at the bar, to the second the light had disappeared from her brown eyes. When he closed his own eyes, he could picture her face, see the expression on it a second before he grabbed her. Usually, he didn't like to risk making his captures in the middle of the city. There were witnesses, cameras, *obstacles,* but this girl had so perfectly matched what he sought out in a victim—long brown hair and a pretty face.

He didn't know what it was about brown hair that stirred him up. Maybe it had something to do with the sister he had a falling out with a decade before or maybe it was because of his mother, he wasn't sure. But with this girl, all he had wanted to do was brush her hair over and over until it fluffed up. Of course, that had been *before* he took her scalp off, keeping the beautiful locks as a trophy, along with the other five he had gathered.

Mason hardly thought about that now as he worked at digging a pit formidable enough to hold his dark secrets. The summer night made the work harder, and his pudgy hands sweated more than usual, making the handle of the shovel slippery. He cursed every time he lost his hold and the old handle presented him with a new splinter. He wanted to buy a new shovel so badly, but in his line of business, he feared that it would be used to track him for his crimes.

An owl hooted in the distance, and Mason looked up, pausing long enough to wipe the sweat from his forehead with a handkerchief from his pocket. He was getting older; that much was obvious. He didn't have the stamina that he once had, and every victim took longer to dispose of.

At last, the pit was big enough, and he stared at his work before glancing to the garbage bags beside him. He climbed out of the pit, kicked the bags containing the body inside, and started to cover them over with dirt. Sweat covered him in an unpleasant sheen, and he thought of his shower and bed longingly.

He was tired and achy, his adrenaline dropping rapidly and the fear that he was going to be seen rising. He wanted to get away from this girl as quickly as possible. While that had been true of all his victims, it was especially pertinent in this case. This one had given him the worst scare of his life. His heart still pounded at the sound of her piercing scream bouncing around the city street and the distinct sound of a man shouting, "*Hey!*" from the distance.

Whoever the man had been, he was close enough to see Mason grab the girl, which meant he was close enough to see *him*. He could give details to the police, details that could lead to a police sketch, and that could turn into an arrest. Mason could've shrugged that off—he looked like an everyday, average joe with his receding hairline, bulging stomach, and height that let him blend into the crowd—but the fact that he had been close enough to read Mason's license plate when he drove away worried him.

What if he had taken a picture?

What if, what if, what if… The questions swirled inside his mind like a mantra that he didn't want to adopt. He could torture himself for days with his own anxiety.

Pushing it away was a battle he would not win, so he tried to think one step ahead. Once the plastic was covered and the dirt evened out, Mason made it out of the woods and back to his truck. The drive home was a bit more serene, though he still kept his eyes on the rearview mirror, paranoid a cop would appear at any minute, see his plates, and pull him over.

When he got home, he drove his truck to the backyard and got out. He rummaged through the toolbox he kept in the back, retrieving a screwdriver to pry the damning plate off. Wrapping it up in some plastic sheets from his trunk, he tossed it into his trashcan with a thump. With any luck, it would be transported away to the dump with no one being any wiser. He turned back to his truck, screwing on a new plate from the pile he kept on hand at all times. From the very first kill, he had been wary of something like tonight happening, so he was glad he had the foresight to buy them. It wasn't much in the way of peace of mind, but it would lay the foundation for it. The new plate on the truck, Mason let his tired feet lead the way inside and directly to the kitchen, desperate to drown himself in alcohol. He had a shelf dedicated to his habit covered in bottles of varying volume but none of them left untouched. Mason selected his half-empty bottle of scotch, tipping it down his throat greedily. He was successful in getting himself buzzed, dumping more than his usual amount of the burning liquid down his throat as he settled on the couch.

He was on the brink of dozing off when a scream echoed through his mind, the wail of the woman from earlier, and he was jolted out of his state of semi-sleep, heart hammering in his chest. When his surroundings became clear, he relaxed a bit. He was at home. He was safe.

How true would that be the next time he had to go hunting?

His skin crawled at the thought of even stepping outside of

his house for the next few days, let alone doing anything else. Like a bolt from the blue, an idea came to him, a new way to reel in victims that might be a little less risky than casing out a place and picking one up off the street. The internet offered all sorts of new opportunities for people of every lifestyle. What if he placed an ad? People had all sorts of fetishes; maybe someone out there had a fantasy about being murdered.

Crazier things had happened, right?

It can be tracked, he reminded himself, the hope dying out as quickly as it had blossomed.

Maybe on the normal internet, that would be the case, but the Dark Web was a place where chaos was free to roam. Police scoped it out all the time, but the odds of them being able to trace something were slim to none. Thousands of people got away with things on the Dark Web every day. Mason himself had done some things he wasn't particularly proud of with people he had met there.

In his drunken stupor, he was overjoyed with his idea. He stood up, massive frame wobbling, before he crossed the house, scooping up his laptop from where he had left it on the table beside his bed. He carried it into his work room, setting it down on the desk before he settled himself into the chair. The wooden frame creaked under his weight, but he hardly noticed as he set up TOR—a program to keep his browsing anonymous—to navigate to the Dark Web.

Maybe this was an idiotic idea, but if anyone knew the odds of him pulling this off successfully, it would be these people. They might have tips, be able to point him in the right direction of breaking the law. After all, a few of them operated legal red rooms and got away with it all because of the way they worded their contracts. And yes, they had *contracts.* Hiding in plain sight? It was a beautiful concept. One he was surprised he hadn't tried to exploit sooner.

Mason breathed out slowly, trying to gather his thoughts before typing anything out. English had never been his best subject, but he knew what he wanted, and that was what fueled him to push through all the nagging worries. At last, he had the ideal website and ad in mind.

He paused then, tapping a chubby finger on the wooden desk. A huge appeal of the victims he chose was their innocence. Would he really be able to find that in anyone browsing through the Dark Web?

It's worth a try, he told himself as he pulled up the website.

He didn't know of a website where serial killers could post what they were looking for, but he did know of one that was similar to what he needed, a sex trafficking ring, known for kidnapping people as requested by users. He'd write his post directed at his potential audience instead.

For the sake of anonymity, I'm not going to post my name. I will go by the name of X. I am seeking out the perfect person to fulfill a certain urge of mine. In order to apply, this person must fit the following criteria:

~Lost their zest for life

~Be female between the ages of 20 and 25

~Brown hair preferred but not required

~Must be a willing participant who will not try to escape

If you meet these criteria, and don't mind the fact that you will not be walking away from the encounter, you are encouraged to seek me out. If it sweetens the deal at all, I can arrange a payment to next of kin to at least cover funeral expenses.

~X

At the bottom, he added an encrypted email link where anyone reading the ad could message him. He did his best to ensure it couldn't be tracked back to him. The last thing he wanted was for someone on the Dark Web to hack it and get his information. There was no telling what they'd do with it.

The cursor hovered over the post button as Mason reread his work. Satisfied, he sat back, clicked the button, and watched as the screen loaded. In a weird way, he was proud of himself. He had never been a sharp thinker, but as far as he could tell, this was a good idea. Would that still be the case when morning—and sobriety—came? There was no way to know until tomorrow. He stood up, his vision spotted with black circles, before feeling unbalanced and sitting back down, finally passing out onto his desk.

2

WHEN MASON WOKE up, the first thing he did was groan from the immense pain building up in the front of his skull and the back of his neck. When he sat up, his stomach sloshed with a similar protest, and he froze, wondering if he would puke up everything in his stomach if he tried to move another inch. Hangovers didn't bother him in his twenties. When he hit thirty, they started to get rougher, but now that he was in his forties, they felt like they could be fatal. He told himself that at any time, he could stop subjecting himself to this anguish, but as far as he was concerned, the only cure was more alcohol.

It was a vicious cycle.

His stomach gurgled, and he thought longingly about drinking some water as he reached up to wipe the drool from under his mouth with his sleeve. He had fallen asleep in front of his computer, the keyboard leaving marks on his face and his lower spine protesting from its time pressed against the hard back of the chair. He felt awful all over, worse as reality crept through the migraine, reminding him about everything he had tried to repress. The memories came first as flashes of victim six's face surged through his mind, and then it was followed by the close call and his not-so-bright idea.

He blinked, tapping his laptop to bring it back to life. His ad stared at him from the black background, and he screwed up his face as he reread it.

"What was I thinking?" he asked out loud as he stared at it.

The writing was coherent enough, but it was a ridiculous plan through and through. The last thing he needed to do was call attention to himself. He tried to maneuver to the settings, desperate to delete it. It would get no responses, he was sure. After all, no one *wanted* to be murdered.

Drunk me is even dumber than sober me, he lamented.

If anyone responded, it would most likely be the kidnappers on the site offering their assistance or their anger for him clogging up their feed. In the daylight, the stupidity of his drunken brain was enough to make him laugh so hard, his stomach started to protest again. Serial killers were supposed to be smart, weren't they?

"Ugh," he groaned, wiping his hand down his face as the screen loaded.

Thankfully, the ad was deleted with success. After refreshing to double check that it was really gone, he maneuvered to the encrypted email, not expecting anything to greet him. There was a "new mail" icon. He had a message. Mason blinked rapidly as he stared at it. He didn't want to open it, worried it would be a hacker from the Dark Web trying to send him malware, and thought about deleting it without reading it.

After all, the beast within him would be quenched for at least a week or so before the urge to kill would come back. All of this was just extracurricular.

But this could be a willing victim, he thought as the cursor hovered over the button.

Puffing his cheeks, he clicked on it with one ill-timed press of the button, and the message was before him.

X,

It's nice to meet you, I think. I read your ad, and I am interested in the service you are providing. I'm twenty, and I haven't seen the upside of life for a while. The thought of dying doesn't frighten me. I'd be perfectly happy with being your next victim, and I won't require any monetary gain, either. Let me know the time and place to meet you at, and I'll be there.

—Y

Mason was elated on the first read, but during the reread, the suspicion began to sink in. What kind of person would willingly walk to their death without even trying to get money out of it for the ones they were leaving behind? She sounded too upbeat, too enthusiastic, and Mason scoffed.

This has to be the police, he thought. *This is like one of those 20/20 busts.*

The thought made him uneasy all over again, and he wished he wouldn't have put out the ad. It seemed all he had done was put himself directly on the police's radar and if not the police's then *someone's.* In a flush of bitterness, he deleted the email.

Forcing himself to stand up, he went to the kitchen and made breakfast. The smell of the cooking eggs had his stomach sloshing all over again, but he tried to tell himself that food would help. That something other than staring at the screen of failures would do him good. The menial task of cooking didn't help. Y was at the front of his mind the entire time as he made a plate and sat at the table. The scent flooded his nostrils, making his mouth water with a sickening mix of hunger and nausea. He dropped the fork with a clatter.

Y.

Considering she could've put anything, it was an interesting choice for a signature.

That's what they want you to think, he scolded himself.

Gritting his teeth, he gave up on breakfast, dumping the entirety of his food into the trash before tossing his plate in the sink. He went to the bathroom, puked, and got himself ready for work. He felt better now that some of the alcohol was out of his system.

A glance at the mirror revealed he looked even worse today than he did on average.

It didn't matter, though. His job at the local butcher shop didn't require him to look glamorous anyway. Mason avoided the computer as he passed back through the living room to go about his day. He left his house, walking to his truck. All he wanted to do was forget about last night, but the drive to work had him wracked with fear that his fake plates would be called out for being such. They weren't, though, and he made it without incident. Thanks to his appearance, people thought he was unfriendly and unsocial, so he was left alone at work. He was grateful for that fact since the headache still throbbed at his temples. He tried to use it to his advantage to distract himself as he worked himself to the point of exhaustion, barely able to keep his eyes open by the time the end of his shift came.

His boss dismissed him, and Mason was once again faced with a nerve-racking ride in his truck. Once he made it home, he stepped into the living room, and his eyes went instantly to his work room and computer. As he stripped off his shoes and coat, he tried to tell himself to go past it, to go to bed, but his curiosity was piqued at the thought of the morning's email.

He groaned and looked around the living room, desperate for anything to distract him, but it didn't work. She was all he could think about. Sighing, he plopped down at his desk and opened his email. The blinking icon indicated a brand new message.

X,

I don't mean to pry if you've already found someone, but this isn't the police if that's what you're thinking. I'm in no way affiliated with them or anyone really. I'm just ready to go and too much of a coward to do it myself. Please consider responding. I'm patient. I'll wait for whenever you're ready.

—Y

Mason hadn't realized he had broken out into a smile until he finished reading. He had spent all day trying to tell himself that the perfect girl didn't exist, that this was a trap, but this email felt real. Some part of his intuition said he could trust this because he could recognize the desperation seeping through the computer. There were times he had felt just like this. Predator senses tapped like a shark drawn to blood, he couldn't stop himself from taking the bait. Bad idea or not, he hit reply.

3

ON A NORMAL hunt, Mason always considered the cleanup and disposal part of his process to be the most difficult step. On this one, though? The grabbing was going to be tough, and that was ironic since the entire point of this idea had been to make it easier. Getting ready to go out, his heart skipped wildly, torn between the desire for this to truly be happening and the fear that it was all a set up and he was about to get himself sent to jail for the rest of his life.

Y had given a description of herself—thin with long brown hair, blue eyes, and a slight limp to her walk from an accident in her teenage years. To him, she sounded exactly like the other girls he had mangled, and that only further fueled his belief that this was the police. They kept track of things like that, similarities in victims, and based on his ad, it would be too easy to assume who the poster was.

Mason plotted about the best way to handle this entire situation. It was too late to back out now, and even if he could, he didn't want to. Whoever Y was, he wanted to meet her, wanted to see what twenty-year-old would willingly throw her life away. He didn't want to give out his address, fearing that it would only result in a raid. Eventually, he gave her the address of an abandoned house at the corner of the street. It was close to his house, which he knew police would also take into consideration when comparing her to the other cases, but he didn't want to go out far. The more distance he had to travel with her in tow, the higher the chances were that he would be seen.

And that didn't need to happen again. Address sent, he gave her the instructions to show up alone at midnight. She would go inside and wait for him there.

Thirty minutes till midnight, readiness prickled at his skin. He wanted to be out the door, to be there when she arrived, but he had to remind himself that wasn't a good idea. If he wanted to get away with this, he needed to be smart, to study every detail, because it might be important later on. So, he bided his time. About ten minutes before midnight, he slipped out his back door, pulling his hood up as he traveled down the sidewalk.

The lights in the neighbors' houses were all dark. The only benefit of living in a neighborhood of older residents was the fact that they all had early bedtimes. It made it easier for him to travel unnoticed, on his own street at least. As he approached the lot with the house, he ducked into the shadows of the nearby yard, scanning the areas that he could see from his hiding place.

Midnight arrived, and every part of him wanted to leap into action, but he had to quell the instinct until his surveillance was done. There were no cars milling about in the street that he didn't recognize. There were two visible from the building, both of them belonging to his neighbors. Mason glanced up toward the building, the empty lot of land around it adding to its creepy aesthetic. He hadn't seen Y appear yet, and he wondered if she was going to back out. The thought caused him to frown, but he didn't dare step out of the shadows. He moved along the bushes, creeping around the lot as he scanned for anything out of place.

"Huh," he whispered to himself when he found nothing.

A new sight caught his eye near the street. A woman appeared from the shadows, the darkness a shocking contrast to the paleness of her skin. Her waist-length golden brown hair swung with her every step, more visible against her bright red coat, and Mason's jaw dropped open. By far, she was the most beautiful of any of the others, and he wondered if there was some kind of mistake. Surely, a woman like *this* wouldn't want to die.

She stood on the sidewalk, eyes scanning her surroundings, and he wondered what she was looking for. A second later, she started to cross the lot, the dilapidated old building in the distance not daunting to her in the least. She stepped up onto the tiny, stone porch and pulled the door open. From where Mason crouched, he could see the heavy darkness inside, but it didn't slow her down. She stepped through it, letting the door close behind her. Mason's heart started to pound with the familiar thrill of the hunt. His favorite part was watching his victim when they didn't know. Now that he had actually *seen* her, he wanted this so much more.

So much, in fact, that it was getting harder to focus. He breathed through the excitement, doing another scope of the perimeter to check for any pairs of watchful eyes. There were still none. As far as he could tell, she had come alone, just as he had instructed. Uneasiness still ate at him. Usually, if something seemed too good to be true, it was. Except this time seemed to be the exception. Or he hoped it was, anyway. On instinct, he stuck to the shadows as he approached the building, contemplating what kind of an entrance he wanted to make.

This is stupid, he thought. What did it matter?

He never spent so much time thinking about first impressions when he grabbed his victims off the street. It wasn't something that factored in, so Y should be no different. Steeling himself, he barged inside, unsure of what he would see. She was sitting in the middle of the room, Indian style, the light from a nearby window trickling over her. Her eyes were closed, her hands resting on her knees, and he had to hold back his surprise. He didn't know what he had expected her to be doing, but it certainly wasn't *meditating.*

The door slammed behind him, and her eyes opened. In the dark, he couldn't tell what color they were, but they were large, exaggerated by the shadows, and he noted how small the rest of her face looked in comparison. In a way, she reminded him of an anime character, and he didn't know what to do with that information.

"X?" she asked in a soft, musical voice.

Mason resisted the urge to mutter out something stupid and replied with a similar question. "Y?"

She nodded and climbed to her feet. "Okay, so how does this work? What's your process?"

Mason drew his eyebrows together as he stared at her. How could someone be so *upbeat* about their own demise? It made his skin crawl. She blinked at him, plump lips curving into a smile as she waited for his response. She actually wanted to know what he was going to do to her, but he didn't want to explain it. For some reason, that made it somehow perverse, *wrong,* and he didn't want anything to make him mess up this kill. She was his perfect victim after all.

"Am I asking too many questions?" she asked, smile drooping after the silence extended into a full minute.

"Just come with me," he said in a gruff voice, two octaves lower than his usual tone. His uncertainties were dangerously close to coming out, and he wanted to hide them deep down where they would never see the light of day.

"Okay," she said, allowing him to lead the way out of the building.

Despite her limp, she was able to keep up with him well. He cut her a sideways glance as she walked at his side and frowned. He had wanted to intimidate her, to stop her from smiling, but as she moved at his side, she didn't change in demeanor. Even though there wasn't a fully happy expression on her face, the slightly upturned corners of her lips suggested it was still positive in nature. He couldn't understand it.

Wary of any witnesses, he pulled the hood up even more around his face. Y made no such gesture. He looked at her from the corner of his eye again, thinking how distinctive her hair was, even in the dim light.

So many risks.

Again, he let out a little prayer of gratitude that his elderly neighbors were asleep. Y was the kind of girl they would've asked him questions about later. Once they were inside and the door closed behind them, Mason wasn't sure how to proceed again. He looked to her, and even though she was a good foot shorter than him, she didn't look afraid. Y didn't even flinch under his gaze. She stood toe to toe with him, waiting expectantly for what he had promised, but it was awkward now.

With the other girls, this was the part where he dragged them kicking and screaming to the basement, the sounds of their terror ramping up the monster inside him. The predator was piqued, of course, but it was more with morbid curiosity than the desire to fill a need. He looked into her eyes for a fraction of a second but had to pull his gaze away. There was electricity when he stared into them, as if he could feel the soul he was about to steal. Desperate to stir up the beast inside of him, he grabbed her wrist, harder than necessary, but she didn't even make a noise of protest. Her arm went slack, and she walked with him as he led the way down the stairs.

Their footsteps clattered into the dark, and when they reached the base, he flicked on the light, illuminating his own personal Red Room. There was a silver table in the middle, brown patches still spilled across it from Six. The stains extended down to the floor, and he frowned, only then realizing that he had been so swept up in his fear and idea for his next victim that he hadn't taken the time to properly clean up. The myriad of tools on the tiny tray beside the table were in the same state.

I'm getting sloppy. That sent a shock of fear down his spine. If he could've forgotten about something as important as cleaning up the blood, what else had he forgotten about?

He expected some sort of reaction to it all, but Y had none. Her huge eyes swept over every inch of the room before she looked over her shoulder at him and smiled. "You should really invest in some plastic wrap," she said and turned away toward the table. "Clothes on or off?"

Mason blinked, but before he could respond, she was already stripping the layers to the floor. Her coat went first followed by the white dress she had worn underneath. Pale skin exposed, she took her place on the table, not flinching when the congealed blood smeared off onto her arms as she stared up at the ceiling.

Mason stared at *her*. For everything he had ever seen in his life, this was, perhaps, the strangest moment he had ever encountered. He couldn't keep his eyes from running from her head down to her feet and back again. She turned her wide eyes at him, blinking expectantly. Without screams and cries, the basement was silent, and he wasn't used to that. There was no fear in her eyes, and he wasn't used to that, either. He stared at the straps hanging limply at the sides of the table.

He didn't even need them.

"Whenever you're ready," Y said and moved her eyes back to

the ceiling.

Mason started to wonder if he was still drunk and all of this was some sort of dream that he couldn't wake up from. It was too perfect and too wrong all at the same time. In a daze, he moved to the tray, picking up a bloody scalpel, before he turned toward the table. As he approached, she looked up at him through her lashes, and he wavered, fingers clenching around the tool.

"Why?" he demanded, swinging his hand so hard that the scalpel pinged off the edge of the table.

"Huh?" she asked, blinking her overly large eyes.

"Why are you here, so *ready* for your death?" he asked. "How are you not scared? I'm so used to listening to people pleading for their lives that this is…is…"

Y jutted her bottom lip out into a pout. "Do you want me to beg? Will that make it better for you?"

Mason flared his nostrils, feeling angry for a reason he couldn't understand. "No. I just can't imagine what would drive someone like you to make this decision."

Y shrugged. "I didn't think it mattered *why* I was here. I thought it just mattered that I *was* here. I could ask you plenty of questions, too, you know? I could demand to know what makes a person like you want to do this to someone else. I could ask you why you like girls with brown hair. I could ask you how many others you've killed. But I won't, because it's simply not my place."

Mason pursed his lips. She was right. Just because she was here didn't mean she owed him an explanation. The deal was that she show up, and she had done that. Now it was his turn to fulfill his end of the agreement.

4

MASON WOULDN'T ADMIT out loud just how hard it was for him to lower the scalpel to the skin over her stomach, but when he did, he smiled with pleasure at the first slice. Part of him had been so convinced that she wouldn't react to this either after how emotionless she had been so far, but as soon as the metal sunk into her skin, she screamed.

The familiar sound echoed off the walls and mixed with the metallic odor of her blood, and his smile grew. The monster inside of him was beginning to feel right at home. Gash after gash freed blood from the girl, and slowly, her screams started to taper off. He stopped, studying her, and her face turned toward him.

"Don't…stop," she wheezed.

Her skin, which had started off a shade of porcelain tinted pinkish with life, was now ghost-like. Mason paused to watch as the first drop of blood slipped from the table to join in with the muck already gathered on the floor. The devastation was bad, but her chest continued to rise and fall, and he couldn't contain his surprise. The fact she had survived *this* long was nothing short of a miracle. She had made it far longer than any of the other victims, and he didn't want this moment to end. He felt powerful, in control, and almost considered keeping the girl alive just to extend this feeling to another day.

The blood made the scalpel slippery, and he stepped away to wipe it off before approaching her again, staring at her. If he could feel anything close to human emotions, this would be what happiness was like. He hoped she could *feel* his gratitude for giving him this opportunity. By the time he went to lower the scalpel again, she took a massive breath and exhaled slowly, head lolling to the side with her huge eyes stuck wide open.

Sighing, Mason lowered the scalpel to his side before tossing it onto the tray. His eyes ran over his work, and he gave her a tiny nod before turning away, searching for his roll of trash bags. He thought about leaving her overnight. After all, if she had willingly come here, then she most likely wouldn't be looked for. Or at least he hoped she had taken the time to make the arrangements.

A gasp of breath made him whisk around. Y moved her head, blinked once, and her chest began to rise and fall with shallow breaths. Drawing his eyebrows together, Mason picked up the scalpel again, approaching her with an eyebrow raised.

"You were dead," he said.

A rugged gasp tore through Y's chest as she looked up at him, but she said nothing.

Mason breathed out a gust of air and lowered the scalpel to her, cutting a line along the bottom of her ribs. The new cut didn't bleed like the others had, and he tried to push it in deeper until the metal scraped against the bone with an unpleasantly shrill noise. Y made no reaction, and he frowned, lifting the scalpel. Before his eyes, the wound started to heal, a fading of the red at the corners, before it closed to a slit and disappeared. He blinked, and more of her wounds started to heal, leaving her perfect porcelain skin behind.

She moaned, and Mason was angry. Frustrated. How could this be happening? What *was* this girl? In a fit of fury, he slashed out again and again and again, meeting the same result every single time. At last, his energy started to dwindle, and he had to stop to take a break. As he watched, every wound healed completely once again. It was as if someone had pressed rewind on their session, taking them back to the moment Y had lain down on the table.

"I don't understand," he said, gasping to catch his breath, though if he was talking to her or himself, he wasn't sure.

She sighed then and sat up, legs swishing over the edge of the table. Her fresh blood smeared onto her skin along with the congealed blood from the previous girl, number six. With a quick look down her body, she frowned and looked back up at him. "Look, I appreciate you trying."

Mason's mind was blown beyond the point of coming up with a coherent response. "What?"

"This? I was hoping it would work. You seemed like a sure-fire thing, but I guess this just wasn't the answer I needed," she said and hopped off the table. She didn't slide in the blood and her feet made no sound as she bent over to scoop up her clothes.

"What answer?" Mason asked, tipping his head to try and catch her eye. Without it, he felt as if she were dismissing him, pushing him away, and he hated it.

Y tipped her head to the side as she looked back at him. "Oh, my. You look so confused," she said and pulled her dress on. She put her coat overtop, her long brown hair sleek and shiny as she tossed it over her shoulder.

He stared at it, yearning to give it a hard yank just to feel as if he were back in control of the situation.

After straightening out her coat, she said, "Don't feel bad, okay? Here's the deal. I'm already dead."

"You're…*dead?*" Mason asked, feeling as if he had lost all ability to create his own words. All he could do was echo her.

She bobbed her head. "Mmhmm. I was murdered years ago. They never figured out who did it, and I've been stuck here ever since. Not too long after it all happened, I ran into someone, a man. He told me the gist of my situation, told me that I was here for a reason, and if I wanted to move on, I needed to deal with what had happened to me. Now, I've heard about ghosts being stuck because of a tragedy, and I figured my case wasn't going to be solved anytime soon, so I thought maybe if I *accepted* my death, I could finally move on. Guess not."

"You replied to my ad," he stated stupidly.

"Yes."

"How? If you're dead, how could you do that? How could you *bleed?*" He blinked and tilted his head to look up at her again. "How could I touch you?"

"Something to think about, isn't it?" she asked and thrust her hands into her pockets. She smacked her lips before twisting them into a smile. "Truth is, the man never really told me *why* I was like this, and I figured it had something to do with my mission. I went through a period where I thought if I avenged myself—if I put down the men who did this—it would free me. I killed two men that I thought were the ones, but I'm still here. That means that I was either wrong in my choice or that there were others involved."

Mason blinked, staring into her eyes. The more he looked at her, the more familiar she looked, and he tried to keep his fear off his face. It had been a long time since number one had died, so long ago that he wasn't sure exactly how it had happened. It had been an accident, though, a drunken hit and run that had resulted in him burying a body in the middle of the night before anyone could realize he was responsible.

"Thanks for your time. It was nice meeting you," Y said and stepped delicately through the mess to peck him on the cheek.

She made a move for the door when Mason's voice stopped her. "When did you say you died?"

"Oh, I don't know. A few years ago?" she said and tipped her head. "Why do you ask?"

A few years ago, he thought, mind flashing through the images of the drive through the dark, the thump of her body, the long brown hair matted with blood.

Her piercing eyes searched his face, catching every change in emotion. Slowly, she turned away from the door, creeping toward him. Mason was so lost in his thoughts that he didn't notice when she slid the scalpel from his fingers. When he finally looked at her, she stabbed the blade into the side of his neck. Pain flooded through him at once, and he reached up, blood pooling around his fingers as he collapsed to his knees.

Y took a step backward as he choked and gasped for air. "You were the one," she whispered, her voice an ethereal growl instead of the lilting tone she had used so far.

"I-I'm sorry," he choked out. "I-it was…an *accident.*"

Y closed her eyes before she dropped to her knees beside him. Her stare didn't leave his as she pulled out the scalpel and stabbed him directly through the heart. Mason's peripheral vision darkened as the life slowly seeped out of him. Before his consciousness left him forever, an image of a black-hooded man escorting Y away caught his eye, and then his vision folded upon itself and faded to black.

DEAD AND BURIED

Matthew A. Clarke

MARK WESTON DIED THE DAY he put his daughter into the ground. He was reborn the day he heard her voice again.

The hole appeared on a record-setting Saturday in late October. It was the warmest day in England since they started keeping records, but the events that followed would go down in history for horrors far greater than the sweltering heat.

"We encourage all viewers to stay indoors, keep your curtains closed, and stay well hydrated. In other news, several large sink—"

Mark placed the remote on the coffee table in front of him and ran a hand across his saturated, gleaming scalp. It came away glistening with sweat, and with a flick of his wrist, he shook the runoff to the thick, pile carpet before drying his hand off on the arm of the sofa. It was too hot for TV. It was too hot for everything. He couldn't remember another day in his life that he had felt this damn uncomfortable; he could practically feel the blood simmering inside his veins.

The dusty air conditioning unit sputtered away in the corner of the room, fighting a losing battle against the forces of hell. Mark stood and shuffled toward it. He imagined he now understood how a rat must feel when trapped under a metal bowl with constant heat applied to it and no way out.

A thin pocket of air immediately in front the freestanding unit was still slightly cooler than the rest of the room, and Mark groaned as he got to his knees and pressed his face up against it, tasting and sucking it deep into his lungs, imagining it filling his entire body.

It was the kind of day that could make a muscular, middle-aged man do such things.

Mark stayed that way for a few moments longer, rolling his bald head around in the merciful breeze, then stripped off his saturated *Iron Maiden* t-shirt, tossed it to the floor, and collapsed back onto the sofa.

When he awoke a few hours later, it took him a moment to realize he had drifted off. The heat was unbearable, and his throat was so dry, he felt as if he'd been forced to drink a bottle of sand in his sleep. He pulled himself from the sofa and drew back the curtains from the bay windows that overlooked the front street.

The sun was now low in the sky. It cast a rich, golden glow that permeated the clouds and gave them a regal quality as they drifted lazily overhead. Mark peered up and down the street and was unsurprised to find it desolate. Water vapor rose from the cooling tarmac in ghostly sheets. A discarded action figure lay on the cracked pavement across the road, its face distorted from a day in the uninhabitable rays; bulging eyes had left it looking like a creature straight out of an Edward Lee novel. Dead flowers littered neighbors' lawns, wilting dismally amid a sea of brittle grass, crying out for water.

Water, he thought, instinctively rubbing at his stubble-studded throat.

He turned his back to the window and walked down the hall and into the kitchen at the back of the house.

The pint glass almost slipped from his grasp as he picked it up from the worktop; everything he touched became coated in human lubricant. Mark drank the first glass without stopping for a breath. Mid-way through the second, he reached for the plastic pull-chain to raise the blinds above the sink, expecting to see his own garden in a similar state of ruin as his neighbor's.

It was.

But there was something even more peculiar than a burnt-out flowerbed in late October: at the back, right corner of the garden, right in front of the shed, was what looked like a hole.

Mark unlocked the back door and strolled toward it, barefoot; the crisp grass felt good on the soles of his feet, and the soil was a comfortable temperature.

As he got closer, he noted that it was almost a perfect circle and that the grass around the rim was burnt completely black.

It wasn't particularly wide, and after a little further investigation, he found that his forearm slid in with ease. His bicep, however, did not.

He pulled his arm back out and put his face closer to it, squinting, shielding his eyes against the low sunlight with one hand while using the other to take his weight.

It looked deep. *Very* deep.

Mark returned to the kitchen, dug out his Maglite from the drawer beneath the microwave, and went back outside. Back on his hands and knees, he twisted the torch and pointed it into the opening as it flared to life. The powerful beam sliced through the darkness with the ease of a scalpel across the chest of a cadaver, illuminating the earthy walls of the shaft as far down as the eye could see, but it still didn't seem to reach the bottom. A fat, pink worm wriggled blindly, half its body dangling from one side of the muddy shaft. Mark watched as it squirmed its way free of the mud and fell down into oblivion. It gave him an idea.

By the time Mark returned to the garden, hands laden with an array of items to be sacrificed, the great fireball in the sky had retired for the day, and the temperature had started to drop a little. A distant, pale moon sat low in dark clouds, watching his every move.

Mark sat on the grass, next to the waiting mouth. He laid out the items for his little experiment in a neat line next to him.

First, he dropped coins. He started with a penny and worked his way up to a fifty pence piece. He would first drop the coin, then lean over the hole and shine the powerful ray of the torch down after it. One at a time, the coins were devoured by the earth. Despite straining with his ear to the hole and using his free hand to cover the other, he still couldn't hear any of them hit the bottom.

Next, he dropped a handful of glass marbles that had belonged to his daughter, Darla. He watched the colorful globes clatter against each other as they were swallowed by the shadows and then heard nothing else.

Lastly, he picked up the bottle of water. He took a small swig before screwing the cap on tight and releasing it into the hole. Even this didn't seem to reach the bottom.

Mark wiped the sweat out of his eyes with the back of his hand, huffed, and went back inside for a shower.

THE NEXT EVENING, after another day of brutal heat, Mark was laying on the sunbaked grass in his back garden, his left ear pressed to the hole. He had just sacrificed a large apple. This time, after a long moment of freefall, there was a faint sound, barely audible, like a bullet passing through soft flesh.

Then, a whisper. It sounded like…whispering. The longer he listened, the more he was sure of it.

Pushing up onto his elbows, he peered inside. "Hello?"

No answer. Of course, there wasn't going to be an answer. He was half naked, laying face-down on the brittle grass in his back garden, talking to a hole. Heat stroke. Had to be.

But then, as he was starting to back away before a neighbor

saw him, a small, distant voice said, "Daddy? Is that really you?"

Mark was now certain he was suffering from a heat-induced delusion. But he couldn't help himself, real or not he was hearing his daughter's voice. "*Darla?!*"

The heavens chose that moment to open, the marble gates in the sky finally crumbling, super-heated from the hellish temperatures of the last forty-eight hours. The rain didn't fall so much as it was thrown with deadly intent.

But Mark didn't notice. Thick droplets exploded across his skull, washing away the salty stickiness that had been plaguing the country without mercy.

"Oh Daddy, it really is you!" the little voice said. And then, after a moment, "I've been so lonely."

Mark's eyes began to melt tears that were washed away instantly by the lashings of the spontaneous downpour.

"Hang on, Sweetie, Daddy's gunna get you out of there." He began to get up—his rusty shovel sat in the tool shed only a few paces away.

"*No!*" the voice screamed. "You can't do that, Daddy. You *can't!*"

"What do you mean? I've got to get you out of there." He fell back to his knees, tears now streaming down his dark, stubbled cheeks and plummeting into the depths of the pit.

"I'm okay, Daddy. I just need you to talk to me. Maybe do a couple of things for me to help me get out of here."

"Anything, Sweetie. Just say it." A niggling voice—the voice of reason—in the back of Mark's mind told him that he couldn't possibly be talking to his daughter. He'd stood by her grave as she was lowered into the ground six months ago. But the less logical, desperate side of his brain told him that it was her. It *had* to be her. And she needed his help.

MARK STAYED WITH Darla in the punishing rain for the rest of the night, eventually falling asleep stomach-down on the waterlogged grass. They'd reminisced about Darla's mother, about the time she'd dropped the cake at Darla's seventh birthday. Mark sung her lullabies, as he used to do when she was very little. When Darla asked where she had been and why it was so dark, her father would carefully change the subject and reassure her she was going to be okay.

When Mark asked his daughter if she remembered anything of the day they had gone to the travelling fun-fair—the day she had died—she became evasive. He thought it better not to press further. Something was clearly going on that was beyond either of their comprehension.

It took everything he had in him not to go for his shovel and start digging, despite his daughter's pleas against it.

On the morning of the third day, a Monday, Mark awoke and let out a groan as he rolled onto his back, soaked through and shivering. A wet clump of mud slid from his chin as he moved.

The downpour had petered out sometime in the night, and the sun, although still low on the horizon, was working hard to dry out the evidence of the storm the day before.

Suddenly, a sharpened spear shot through Mark's stomach as he remembered he had been speaking to his little girl. Warily turning over once more, he said, "Good morning?"

Relief, warmer than the rising sun, washed over him when she answered his call. Relief that he hadn't just been having a fever dream. Relief that she was coming home.

Mark picked himself up and stumbled inside, peeling off his wet shorts and boxers at the door. He used the phone in the front room to call his office. Sarah Tilling answered on the third ring. He told her he had an upset stomach, and she told him to rest up and get better soon.

He was feeling groggy from spending the night outside in the rain, and sleeping face-down in the mud hadn't done him any favors, either.

Mark set the phone back in the receiver and went upstairs to put on a fresh t-shirt and shorts before going back to the kitchen and taking a swig of orange juice straight from the carton, swilling it around his mouth to remove the fuzz from his tongue and teeth. Brushing them didn't seem all that important right now. He went back out of the kitchen door to the garden.

As he approached the hole, he paused. It looked wider; he thought he could probably fit both arms inside it now. A strange scuttling noise was coming from somewhere within it, and small nuggets of dirt appeared to be breaking away from the rim, plunging into the depths.

Panicked, he threw himself to the ground and called out his daughter's name.

The noise stopped. The crumbling stopped.

"I'm here, Daddy." Her breathing sounded harsh and labored, but her voice was clearer now, which could only be a good thing.

Mark allowed himself to take a breath, suddenly aware he had been holding it. "Are you okay? I thought I heard something down there."

"Well, I *do* feel a little weak. I think I need to ask you for something now."

"Go ahead, sweetie."

The requests started simple—a loaf of bread, a bottle of water. Each time an item was dropped down the hole, Mark would follow the descent with the powerful beam of the Maglite until it disappeared completely. Occasionally he would hear the scratching, scuttling noise, and something he'd buried at the back of his mind would scream out in terror. He did his best to ignore it.

Two days later, the weather having relaxed and lapsed into more typical greys and browns, Mark had called the office once more and changed his illness from a bad stomach to full-blown flu.

Darla had asked for something that made him question his sanity once again.

"Please, Daddy. It doesn't have to be a cat, just some kind of small animal. I need something…alive if I'm ever going to get out of here."

Mark pictured her down there in the dark, looking up with wide eyes, rubbing her hands together gently as she would often do when she was nervous. His daughter sounded almost as upset to ask for it as he was to hear her asking.

"I don't understand, Darla. I'd do anything for you, but that…" He trailed off.

After a moment, he continued, "Why don't I just get the shovel—"

"No! Why won't you listen to me?" She began to cry.

"Well, why don't you help me understand why you're asking for this? I want to help you in any way I can, but I'm starting to wonder why I didn't just dig you out of there in the first place."

Darla stopped sniffling and sighed. "I'm not entirely *me*. I mean, I'm still me, but I'm not completely me. The only way I'll be me again and be able to survive up there is if I get better before I come out."

"Sweetie, there's a hospital five minutes away. We can rush you straight there."

"It won't work like that, Daddy. Did you forget that I died?"

So, she did remember. It really was his little girl trapped down there in the dark. Was he really going to do this? What would Darla's mother do if she were still here? He stood, putting a hand on each hip, leaning back to stretch out his spine.

Abigail would do whatever it took to get their little girl back.

PATCHES—A MANGY tabby cat that lived next door and had been shitting in Mark's garden for years—was the perfect candidate.

After leaving a heaping plate of tuna laced with crushed-up

sleeping tablets by his back door, he didn't have to wait long for his prey. Mark watched carefully from the kitchen window as the scruffy animal devoured the offering swiftly, as if it hadn't eaten in weeks, before skulking off to lay behind the dead rose bush against the back fence, belly full and ready for a nap.

By the time Mark had done what had to be done, the sky had transformed from a soft blue to black velvet, littered with glitter.

He removed a wad of tissue from his pocket, held it against his wrist, and watched the red slowly seep across it (although the animal had been woozy from the drugs, it still wasn't willing to be dropped down a dark pit without a fight and had thoughtfully given him a deep gash as a parting gift) while trying to tune out the disturbing noises coming from his daughter.

Then: silence.

"Daddy?" came her soft voice.

Mark lowered his face to the hole once more, "You okay, Darla?"

"Yes, thank you. Much better. I think I might be able to get out soon."

"I can't wait, sweetie. Would you like anything else? A drink?"

"No thanks. I think I'll have a nap now." She yawned.

"I'll be right here when you wake up," Mark replied.

"Daddy?"

"Yes?"

"I love you," she said, dragging out the last syllable.

His heart lurched and started pounding against the walls of his ribcage before settling down as suddenly as it had started. The last six months had been the worst of his life. Hearing his daughter say those words again was more than he could ever have wished for.

"I love you, too, Darla."

Mark went inside, washed his wrist in the kitchen sink, and winced as he lathered it in a generous amount of antiseptic. He then made himself a ham and cheese sandwich, retrieved the paperback from his bedside table, and went back to the kitchen.

Flicking the switch next to the back door to power the outdoor lights, he opened up the shed and dragged a wooden chair out next to the hole, which appeared to have widened once again.

Mark sat on the folding chair at the edge of the blanket of light cast from the garden lamps, eating his sandwich and reading his book, relishing in the feeling of having something to live for again.

Something he thought he'd never feel again.

MARK JOLTED AWAKE. It was still dark, and the exterior lights that had been comforting before he fell asleep now felt intrusive, unwelcome. He rubbed his eyes with both hands as he came to his senses.

That scratching, scuttling noise again. Something about it just seemed incredibly...unnatural.

"Daddy? Are you up there?" The voice, once faint, now sounded even closer.

"I'm here."

The noise stopped.

"Oh, okay. I was scared," she said, her voice almost a whisper.

"I'll never leave you. Are you okay?" Mark leaned forward in his chair, aimed his Maglite down the hole, and clicked the powerful beam on.

Something was down there. Barely visible, the end of the torch-light's beam gently licking at it.

"Darla?" Whatever it was, it didn't move. Mark squinted, trying to see better, but it was still too far down. All he could make out was something rounded and black. It had a slight sheen to it.

"Turn the light off! Are you trying to hurt me?!"

Whatever it was that Mark had seen sank lower, out of sight.

He frantically clicked off the light and said, "What? Of course not!"

"I can't be seen until I'm ready to be seen. I told you I'll be out soon. Please, just listen to me or it could be bad for both of us."

Mark's brow furrowed. "Okay. I didn't mean to scare you."

"That's okay...I need something else now, Daddy. If you can do this for me, I think I'll be able to come home tomorrow." She paused as if waiting for a response.

"What is it?" Mark said, now completely awake.

"This is going to sound a little weird, okay, and I don't quite know how to explain it to you. I just need you to trust me."

"Darla, honey, this *whole thing* is *a little weird*. But of course I trust you. I'll do whatever it takes to get you back to me."

"I need blood. Four pints at least. Maybe five."

Mark moved his watch into the light. It was just around two-fifteen in the morning.

"Where am I supposed to get four pints of blood from at this time of night?"

It didn't faze him that something would have to get hurt in order to fulfil her request; after Patches, it was as if something inside him, some type of moral compass, had been switched off. He'd subconsciously decided that he was seeing this through to the end no matter what.

"I need it Daddy, *please*. You could check down at the old foundry, offer one of the homeless people a bed?"

"A *person*?"

"Uh-huh." For just a moment, a chittering noise rose from the hole.

Mark ignored it. "Can't I just get you another cat or something?"

"No, that won't work. I won't ask for anything else after this, I promise."

As he sat back and thought it over (not if he could go through with it, but how he would go about it without getting caught), a trio of lights skimmed across the night sky. He looked up to the jet and was suddenly up there, sitting in it with his daughter, watching the world pass by below them as they set off to somewhere warm and magical.

A curtain twitched next door. Someone had been watching him.

"I'll be back in ten minutes," he said.

FIFTEEN MINUTES LATER, having just decanted several jugs of fresh blood down the hole, a satisfied belch echoed up from the darkness. The rim of the pit was wet and sticky, and Mark took great care not to lean on it as he got to his feet.

It had been even easier than he'd expected. Margaret Hawkins, the elderly spinster living next door, had answered her door in a stained off-white dressing gown, her withered eyes squinting against the porch light and an ancient rolling pin clutched in her right hand. Although it was the middle of the night, she still smelled like she'd just taken a bath in a bottle of floral perfume, and Mark had to resist the urge to cover his mouth with the sleeve of his jacket.

All it took was the mention of Patches' name and Margaret slipped her shoes on, following him over with no further questions.

"That's a nasty-looking nick you've got there, Mark. I hope my Patches didn't do that to you," she said, pointing a clawed finger at his wrist.

"It's not as bad as it looks," he said with a forced smile as he led her up to his front door. After a quick glance over his shoulder, he turned the key in the lock and ushered her over the threshold.

No turning back now.

"I had to close Patches in the bathroom to keep him from running away," Mark explained. He led her upstairs and opened the bathroom door.

He stepped aside and extended his good arm to allow Margaret to shuffle inside. "Patches?" she said, looking to her left, then to her right.

The old woman moved toward the bath and pulled back the shower curtain, and then she was dead.

The kitchen knife Mark had been concealing in his jacket parted the thin skin around her throat so smoothly that he thought he'd missed her completely. But the steady patter of blood on linoleum told him he'd connected and saved her from a second, unnecessary wound.

Mark shoved Margaret between the shoulder blades with his free hand, causing her knees to collide with the bathtub. She doubled over and fell forward, landing hard on the rim of the smooth porcelain, breaking several ribs. Her upper body hung limp over the tub and began to drain as a coppery odor obliterated her heavy floral perfume.

Mark stepped back to clean off his hands and the knife in the sink as his neighbor bled out next to him.

Thankfully, the wet spluttering noises Margaret seemed so intent on making didn't last for long, but he was still pretty sure they would haunt him for the rest of his life.

"If you get thirsty later, I have plenty more, sweetie," Mark cooed into the pit.

There was no reply at first, just a light crackling sound that went on for several minutes.

Finally, Darla said, "That was yummy, but I think that's enough for now. I don't want to be a greedy Gus!" A small giggle followed.

"Well, I'd better get back inside and clean up. If you're going to be home soon, we're going to need a functioning bathroom." Mark had already worked everything out. It was the perfect crime, really. Once his daughter had emerged from wherever she was, he would wait for the cover of night, take Margaret Hawkins's stiff corpse out to the garden, and drop her down into the pit. Then he'd dispose of the knife and the clothes he'd been wearing in the same fashion. All that would be left would be the (hopefully) simple task of filling the hole in. There was a garden center just down the road with plenty of compost for sale.

"Can't you stay with me until morning, Daddy? It's real lonely out here at night. I can help you clean up when I get out of here."

Mark thought for a moment. He was damn exhausted, but Margaret wasn't going to clean herself up. *Ah, screw it. She'll still be there in the morning*, he thought. He settled in for another night in the wooden chair and called, "Night, Darla."

"Night, Dad."

Her small voice sounded incredibly close this time.

"MARK? MARK, WAKE UP."

A gentle hand took him by the shoulder. Mark slowly opened his eyes. A silhouette stood over him against a grey backdrop that looked like rain again. The figure came into focus as his eyes cleared.

"Sarah? What're you doing here?"

Sarah Tilling, Mark's co-worker and only *real* friend in the office, stood next to him. She wore a tight black pencil skirt and white button-down blouse. A pen protruded from the tight, golden bun that was tied at the back of her head.

"You didn't call in to the office this morning. Everyone's been worried about you. I told Ron that I was meeting a client for a late breakfast, then came straight over. I did knock, but when I didn't hear anything inside, I peeked over the fence and saw you just sitting there with your eyes closed and your mouth open…" She stopped herself, seeming to notice she had been rambling. Genuine concern surfaced in her eyes.

Of course, he knew what "everyone's been worried" meant;

it meant Sarah had been worried. Nobody else would give a crap if he never came back, and he knew it.

He used to be one of True Print's best salesmen, outselling his peers three-to-one, with his charismatic charm and rugged good looks. But now, he was pretty sure he was well on the road to dismissal—he hadn't made a sale in weeks. After losing his wife, Abigail, to breast cancer, then his only child to pneumonia a few years later, the Mark everyone had known and loved was gone. He couldn't stand being around most people any longer. Even the ones that promised to be there for him, he had managed to push away eventually. Whether it was intentional or not, he wasn't sure. The one person that hadn't given up on him, yet, was Sarah Tilling.

"Thanks for your concern, but I'm fine. If you wouldn't mind, I'd like to get back to bed now."

He stood and gave her a dismissive wave with his left hand, noticed the dried blood that had crusted around his nails and discolored his skin, and quickly withdrew it again, but he wasn't fast enough. He wasn't the only one who had noticed it.

"Cut myself chopping onions," he said, showing Sarah the wound on his wrist. It was still hot to the touch and had started to seep a clear fluid.

"Right…okay. Well, let's get you inside. You need to get that cleaned up."

"I can manage, thanks."

Sarah's attention suddenly became focused on something behind them. "Oh, cool! You got one, too?"

"I'm sorry?"

"A pit!" She hurried behind him, toward the hole that would soon birth his daughter.

"Oh, that? That's nothing. Just a little hole."

"Haven't you been watching the news? These things have been popping up all over the country! My mother has a pit, too, and she swears that my dad is living in it, talking to her when I'm not around, but Dad's been dead for *years*. I'm worried she might be getting dementia," she said, circling the hole at a safe distance and peering down into it. Her nose wrinkled as she appeared to notice a patch of dried blood. She brushed at it with the tip of her work heels.

"That *is* strange. Old age, huh? Now, why don't you head on back to the office? Tell them I'll be back next week, would you?" Mark took Sarah gently by the arm and tried to lead her away.

She pulled against his grip. "Wait, did you see that? I think something just moved down there, Mark. Something *big*." She took a hesitant step back.

Mark froze. How would he explain his daughter suddenly climbing out of there? Sarah had been at the funeral, after all. She had driven Mark home afterward, bought him flowers, and did his shopping when he was at his worst.

Mark knew Sarah had a thing for him—she had for years. There was nothing wrong with her, but Mark wasn't interested; the thought of letting anyone else get close to him, only to lose them again, was too much to handle.

The aperture of the pit still wasn't particularly wide, but it was certainly enough to accommodate a child. "Hold on a minute. What *is* that?"

Before Mark could stop her, Sarah had pulled free of his grip and was on her knees, peering down into the earth.

Mark almost missed it. If he'd been looking elsewhere at that precise moment, he wouldn't have seen the thin, barbed appendage that shot up and impaled her through the stomach, pulling her down with incredible speed, her spine snapping in half as she folded in two.

He could've missed that.

But he couldn't have missed the loud crunch that accompanied her delicate frame closing in on itself like a mousetrap snapping shut or the fountain of gore that sprayed up afterward like something straight out of an eighties' slasher movie, raining blood and chunks of hot flesh down all around him.

"Sarah!" Mark's knees gave way. The color drained from his face as he crawled closer. "Darla?"

A crown of curly blonde hair, streaked with red, was now flush with the top of the pit. Mark moved back as it slowly breached the surface.

Darla's face looked up at him, her green eyes wide and frantic. "Daddy, help!"

"Darla!" Mark reached forward and began to paw away the loose earth around her face, impervious to the small hunks of flint that peeled away his fingernails and sliced open his hands.

Two long, dirty appendages appeared from the ground and rose high above her head. They lowered to the grass on either side of where Mark sat, the sharp tips burying themselves in the earth with ease as they hauled the rest of her body out.

Mark fell backward in horror as screams and shouting rang out in unison throughout the neighborhood, but nothing could penetrate the deafening bubble of the terror that had encapsulated him.

What towered over him was not his daughter. It had his daughter's face, but it wasn't the same Darla he had laid to rest.

Eight glistening, hairy limbs supported a bulbous, pulsating abdomen. A monstrous black spider with his daughter's head.

It beamed at him. "Daddy!"

THE "SPIDERPOCALYPSE" WAS what the news reporters were calling it, and although Mark found that to be disrespectful of the dead, he had to admit that an onslaught of bloodthirsty spider-people did kind of warrant the title.

Conspiracy theorists suggested that it was the result of a government experiment gone wrong or that it was caused by understaffed hospitals dumping their hazardous waste into the water supply, causing the graveyards to become contaminated through underground reservoirs, creating mutants. Of course, the rumors were completely unsubstantiated and were systematically debunked by the government, who appeared to be entirely transparent on the subject; the Prime Minister's husband had reportedly come back as a spider-being, too, and she put him straight back in the dirt with his old hunting rifle. You'd have to be crazy to *want* that to happen.

There was one thing that everyone could agree on, though; the day the pits had appeared across the country—the first day of the blood-boiling heat—something had happened that was not of this world. It was as if hell itself had opened its gates and sent forth a select few to divide and conquer.

The news reporter's voice climbed the stairs and droned on in the background. It was all they'd been talking about for weeks now; Spider pits had appeared across Spain, Australia, and most of North America, but people were better prepared now, and most of them were filled with concrete as soon as they appeared. Many of the pits in England had suddenly closed up as fast as they'd appeared, and things seemed to be returning to normal, for the most part.

MARK REACHED THE door to the spare bedroom and put his shoulder against it. It gave a fair bit of resistance, but he was getting used to that. He picked up the wooden broom that was propped against the wall in the hallway, brushed the thick cobwebs from the doorframe, then dragged the fresh corpse inside.

"Yay, dinner!"

Darla dropped from the ceiling and began her feast.

UNTIL THAT DAY ARRIVES

RJ Roles

2020

THE YEAR 1933 WAS THE worst one in Benny Grossman's life. And that was saying a lot considering the things he'd seen. He thought back on the events that led up to this moment in his life, having stormed the beach at Normandy during World War II. He remembered seeing the ocean's water roll in on crimson waves. By the end of the day, Benny had lost three of his close friends that he had gone through boot camp with. To this day, Benny would wake in the dead of night and see the haunting look on his dead friends' faces after they left the war—a war that was still to be fought by the living.

Even still, Benny had witnessed other horrific events through history: multiple nuclear plant meltdowns. Countless and, to him, senseless other wars around the world that were a constant reminder of the cruelty of mankind. He even had a front-row seat the day the world held its breath, watching as hijackers ripped the lives of nearly three thousand people out of this world in a single day. Yet 1933 was where his mind went when he was alone at night, trying to sleep. Ever since that year, it seemed to Benny that death had a way of following him around yet always passing him over.

Their faces. He could still see their faces. Nearly a century later and it was as if he were seeing them anew for the first time. Benny coughed into his pillow—leaving it spotted with blood—as he struggled to gain his breath. *Not long*, he thought to himself. That place. Those people. Something within him changed during his time there. Benny laid his head down and thought back to another time. Another place.

1933

AS THE YEAR 1932 clicked over to 1933, and while the rest of the world celebrated, Benny Grossman's life came crashing down around him. He sat shivering on a hard, wooden chair in the police chief's office. Others talked in hushed tones in an adjacent room, the people that would determine what was to become of him.

He was still in shock from the news that both his parents had been killed in an automobile accident. He had just seen them a few hours earlier. His mother appeared full of life and joyful; his father's eyes lit up the room, a contagious trait that Benny hoped he'd inherit. They both had kissed Benny goodnight before leaving for a party at one of their friends' houses.

Benny—left in the care of the family's live-in maid, Trudy— went to sleep that night with thoughts of what the new year would hold in store for them.

After being shaken awake by Trudy, Benny rubbed the sleep from his eyes and followed the woman as she led him down to the foyer. Waiting with a hat in his hand and grim-looking eyes— certainly not his father's—Police Chief Harkins informed Benny of the accident and told him he'd need to go down to the precinct to identify the bodies and then they'd need to contact Benny's next of kin to establish a transfer of custody.

The next couple of hours were a blur as Benny went to his

room to dress. He vaguely remembered riding in the chief's car, watching houses drift by. What he did recall were his parents' still faces and how he thought they couldn't possibly be the same people. Not these two…lifeless bodies. His mother and father were alive, were life incarnate, everything good and beautiful in the world. At least through Benny's eyes.

Now, while sitting in the uncomfortable chair, Benny read the golden plaque on the chief's desk; "Harold Harkins," it said. Chief Harkins and a few other people were talking in an office, the words barely audible to Benny. He'd caught a few sentences here and there.

"No, it seems the boy has no other relatives close by."

"He'll have to be sent to an orphanage. Unless maybe a family will foster him?"

"…not even an aunt or uncle to take him in?"

"The driver of the other vehicle lived. Had apparently been drinking at a New Year's celebration."

It was all a jumble in Benny's head. His body felt fatigued and his mind numb. He wished he'd been wise enough to have grabbed a jacket before leaving home but made do with the corduroy shirt he was wearing.

"Benny, son," the chief said after opening the office door. "I'm going to take you back home for the night and then come back around in the morning to pick you up."

"Pick me up? Where am I going, Mr. Harkins? I mean Chief Harkins."

"I'll tell you more about that in the morning. For now, let's move out, so you can get some sleep."

Without another word, Benny was on his feet and following the big man to his car. When they arrived back at the Grossman home, Chief Harkins wished him a peaceful sleep. While he traipsed up the stairs to his bedroom, Benny saw Trudy and the chief huddled in deep conversation, no doubt filling her in on what he himself would find out soon enough.

SLEEP NEVER CAME, and he laid in bed listening to the birds outside welcome dawn's first light. *It is my first day as an orphan*, Benny thought. And with that, he was finally able to allow his emotions to come flooding out. After, he dressed for the day ahead and sat on the edge of his bed until Trudy came to retrieve him.

Chief Harkins stood in the same spot that Benny had last seen him the night before. The man looked nervous, and Benny wondered what was to become of himself.

"How are you doing there, son? Get much sleep?"

"Only a little," Benny lied.

Harkins motioned with his arm for them all to sit on the sofa in the parlor.

"Well, I'm going to be blunt but honest with you. You don't have much in the way of family around these parts. Closest we can find is an aunt on your mother's side, but we've been unable to get in contact with her. I'll be sending her a letter in the mail explaining the situation, but I don't want you to get your hopes up." Benny could tell the chief was searching for any sign of emotion.

"Furthermore, as you have no living relatives within the area to take you in, you are now a ward of the state until you reach the age of seventeen. Therein, you'll have full access to any properties and assets your parents have left behind."

"Sir?" Benny said meekly.

"What is it, son?"

"Where will I live now?"

Benny watched Harkins' head bob up and down, his eyes flickering between him and the maid.

"You'll be rendered into the care of FrostOak Orphanage until a family member comes forward and offers to foster you or you come of age." His tone was somber.

"What about Trudy? What will become of her?" Benny

looked at the maid, who was avoiding his gaze.

"Oh, I'm sure she'll have no problem finding work with another family. You would vouch for her, wouldn't you?"

"Yes, I would." At Benny's words, Trudy smiled at the boy.

The chief beamed at him. "Benny, I need you to pack a suitcase. Just one. Bring clothes and anything you want to take with you. But everything needs to fit within the suitcase. Trudy will spend the next week seeing that the house and its contents are sufficiently stowed away."

Benny nodded and left the room to pack. An hour later, he'd gone through his dressers and belongings twice over. Satisfied that he was ready to go back downstairs, Benny closed the suitcase and latched it shut.

Before leaving the second floor, he stepped into his parents' room one last time. His mother's vanity sat close to the doorway, and he caught a scent of her favorite perfume. He could smell her. His eyes filled with tears when he looked at his father's hat and tie rack. Benny saw the fedora that he'd always beg to wear when his father came home from work for the day. Wiping his eyes dry, he left before he drowned in sentiment.

"Okay, I'm all packed," Benny announced as he reentered the parlor.

Trudy approached him, and he could tell the dam behind her eyes was ready to burst. "You be a good boy!" He felt her body shake in silent sobs as she drew him into a tight embrace. Releasing him, she mussed his hair before walking away.

Benny looked at Harkins, who gave a curt nod. "Shall we depart? We have quite a way to go before nightfall."

He nodded back and left the house that used to be his home.

CHIEF HARKINS WASN'T *lying*, Benny thought as the two traveled along a seemingly never-ending dirt road. Progress was slow, and it felt like they had been traveling to a higher elevation for most of the journey.

"Where exactly is this…orphanage?" Benny asked.

"Just outside of a town called Willow Hill. High in the Appalachian Mountains. Beautiful country, just a bit away from the modern civilization and the hustle and bustle of the city."

"Why here? Why bring me here instead of another place?"

He watched as Harkins looked at him and could tell the man didn't want to lie.

"Sadly, any such establishments like this that are closer to where you lived are already at max capacity. Not FrostOak, though. It's a large home with sprawling grounds that you'll be able to explore during nicer weather," Harkins explained.

Benny noticed the higher in elevation that they traveled, the lower the temperature dropped. Now, the sky was overcast with slate-gray clouds, and snowflakes drifted on the chilled wind. He watched as his breath came out in small puffs, dissipating just as quickly.

The terrain leveled out, and the whine of the car's engine lightened. Before the pair of weary travelers sat a large wrought-iron gate attached to a high fence of the same metal, which lined the perimeter of the orphanage. Beyond the gate, the outline of a large building—similar to a hospital, Benny thought—sat veiled by the falling snow.

"Well, we've arrived," Harkins announced.

Benny straightened up in his seat, straining his eyes for any and every detail he could absorb.

The car came to rest ten yards from the front entrance. A pair of double doors opened, and a woman appeared from within. Benny's instant reaction was to flee. Of course, he didn't want to meet this person. He wanted nothing more than to make the journey back home where, in his mind, his parents would be sitting by a cozy fire, waiting for him with warm embraces and gentle kisses.

"Are you ready, son?" Harkins' voice drew him from the daydream.

"Um, yes, sir." Benny felt embarrassed about his wandering mind.

They left the comfort of the cab. Harkins grabbed his suitcase for him, while Benny stood under the gaze of the woman on the stoop. Harkins walked around the car and stood behind Benny.

"Good afternoon, Madame Cass. I hope you are well." Harkins nudged Benny forward with the suitcase.

"As well as can be expected, Harkins. Is this…the boy?"

Benny stopped and looked up at the woman who towered over him. She looked down her nose at him, her face blank of emotion.

"Indeed, indeed. This is Benny Grossman." Chief Harkins set the suitcase on the ground next to where Benny stood.

"Benny, yes. I recall you telling me his name over the telephone. And is Benny Grossman a good boy?" she asked.

After a moment of silence, Benny realized she was waiting for *him* to answer.

"Y-yes." He watched as she squinted her eyes at him. "Ma'am."

"We shall see," she said in a cold, even tone.

Harkins stepped closer to the woman, rifling through his pockets for something.

"Ah, here it is." He handed her an envelope. "Your copies are inside. Just fill out the others and mail them to the state office."

Benny watched her take it and wondered what was inside. Harkins turned and said, "Well, I hope that you adjust well, son. Remember, Madame Cass wants nothing more than to help you along and for you to have a long, fruitful life. Mind her well." Harkins' hand gripped Benny's shoulder—as if to reassure him—before climbing into the car.

Benny watched as the car's lights faded away in the distance, as snow still fell in silence. The sun—barely visible in the sky, just about to dip behind the horizon—did little to warm the coldness

Benny felt inside.

"Follow."

Benny turned and found the woman already walking into the building. He grabbed his suitcase and trotted to catch up. Inside, candles flickered in their sconces on the wall. The lighting was dim, and Benny struggled to see as his eyes adjusted.

"The first floor is for administration and kitchen purposes only. It is not for frolicking and running about. The second floor is where children are quartered." She turned to face him. "And the basement is off-limits to all. Is this understood?" Madame Cass said in a stern voice.

"Yes, ma'am," Benny answered and swallowed hard.

"Daily classes are mandatory for reading, writing, and basic arithmetic. You will then have a set number of chores that are to be completed post-haste. Are there any questions?"

Benny shook his head and was filled with instant regret when Madame Cass's eyes flashed menacingly. "N-no, ma'am."

Her eyes narrowed into slits before she turned and walked toward the staircase. After lugging his suitcase to the top, Benny's arms were aching, wishing he'd decided against packing his dress shoes. On the landing, he saw that a long corridor stretched off in both directions.

"Children stay in the east wing. West wing is for adults," Madame Cass said as she continued to walk.

"Lights out at ten every night. No exceptions. You will be in bed by then or suffer the consequences." Benny trailed behind her, attempting to listen while lugging his suitcase.

"Here." She pointed at one of only two doors that he could see.

Pushing the door open, Benny walked into a large, open room. Beds lined the far wall—a few of them were occupied.

"Children. Children, attention!" Madame Cass's voice called out.

Squeaky bedsprings and the shuffling of feet echoed throughout the room as five kids lined up, as if for an inspection.

"Where is William?" Madame Cass asked with a snap.

Benny watched as the five shifted and fidgeted where they stood, all avoiding eye contact with their formidable overseer.

"Speak! You there, girl. Where is he?" She pointed to a meek-looking girl with blonde pigtails. The girl's eyes went wide with fear before she lowered her head and tucked it into her shoulder.

Madame Cass took a step forward before someone at the far end of the room spoke. "I'm here." William slid from the bed he'd been lying on and lined up with the others.

"You know the rules. You are to line up when attention is called." Benny looked up and could see she was shooting daggers at the defiant one.

"I just got caught up in my reading. Sorry, Madame Cass." When she looked away, William shot Benny a quick wink.

"Children, this is Benny Grossman. He will be staying with us for the foreseeable future. Just like any of you, he will be a resident of FrostOak until fostered to a family or he comes of age. I trust that you will all welcome him and inform him of our ways."

"Yes, Madame Cass," they all said in unison.

With a curt nod, the woman left the room, leaving Benny standing there feeling awkward.

The littlest of the children—a boy, Benny thought—ran away the second Madame Cass left. William also went back and fell onto the bed he'd been laying on. That left the blonde-haired girl with pigtails and a taller girl wearing a plaid dress—and a pretty face, Benny thought—with black hair, as well as a boy with smudges of dirt on his face and a runny nose, and a small girl—also with smudges on her face—whose hair had been closely cropped to her scalp.

"Hello, I-I'm Benny." He gave the others a small wave.

The pigtailed girl ran off to her bed without a word. The smudged-faced boy looked Benny over before leaving the room, with the smudge-faced girl quickly in tow. Benny watched before turning to face the tall girl in the plaid dress. His mouth went dry, and he found it hard to swallow when she smiled at him.

"Hello, I'm Heather. The two that just left are Jack and Sally." Heather pointed. "That lump back there is Willie. That one there," she pointed in the other direction at a wall where someone had knocked a hole in it, "is Rat. Not his real name, of course. But it's the only one he'll answer to."

"Oh, and the girl with pigtails?" Benny asked.

"That's Rose; she's very bashful. But once she takes a liking to you, she'll be more friendly." Benny blushed.

"This one here," Heather said as she walked to a nearby bed, "is yours."

Benny followed and dropped his suitcase on the floor in front of the steel frame bed. The mattress looked thin and was a ruddy shade of red.

"Thanks. Are there sheets? And a blanket?" he asked.

"In the box there." She pointed.

Benny opened the box and found everything he'd need to make his bed—including the saddest-looking pillow he'd ever seen in his life.

With his bed made, Benny started to stow his clothes and other belongings in the chest that he assumed doubled as a nightstand. The room was quiet; the other kids seemed to be occupied in their own worlds. When he pulled out the pocket watch that his father had given him the previous week, he saw that it was nearly ten p.m.

His belly growled—reminding him it had been a long time since he had eaten—but he ignored it, because his bladder was screaming louder for release.

"Hey, um, Jack? Where is the bathroom?"

Jack and Sally had come back soon after Benny was done making his bed, and Benny learned who his new neighbor was.

"Only working ones are down on the bottom floor. Just use the pail," Jack told him and waved his hand toward the far corner.

Pail? Benny thought.

He approached where Jack had motioned, and the smell hit his nose before his eyes saw it. An old, rusty ash bucket sat just behind a curtain draped over a line that ran from wall to wall. Benny was appalled at the sight. Looking over, he saw the little boy—Heather had called him Rat—watching from the hole in the wall. Benny shivered as necessity drew him behind the curtain, and he relieved his bladder—breathing through his mouth as much as possible.

Back in bed, he laid there staring up at the ceiling. He felt as if he was living someone else's nightmare and couldn't wake up. Just then, the lights winked out. *Must be ten,* he thought. The groaning of springs from the others shifting on their beds told him it was time to get some sleep. Tomorrow, he'd have a lot to learn. And remember.

DAWN BROKE, AND with it came the chirping of birds. Benny smiled in his sleep, imagining himself back home in his own bed. Reality came crashing down around him when a klaxon sounded from somewhere in the corridor.

"What's going on?" Benny asked through a fog of sleep.

"Rise and shine, lazy bones," Willie said as he kicked the frame of Benny's bed.

Benny opened his eyes and watched as the others stirred in their beds before bustling from the room. He slid from underneath his blanket and sat on the edge of his mattress, gathering his thoughts. He'd slept in his clothes from the previous day and felt they would do for another wearing today. After lacing up his shoes, he left the room.

He could hear footsteps descending the staircase, and he followed. On the ground floor, Benny was unsure where everyone had gone. He picked a direction and started wandering down the corridor. To his surprise, he'd chosen the correct direction and found the other children in a small room, each sitting next to one another at a long table. No one spoke as they dug into their bowls of whatever it was. *Gruel?* Benny thought when he saw the food.

When he found an empty seat, Benny sat for a minute before pulling a large bowl toward him and spooning some of the sludge into his own dish. His stomach growled with greed in spite of itself, so Benny wasted no time shoveling the food into his mouth. To his surprise, it tasted fairly decent.

With their bellies full, everyone helped to clear the dishes—Benny watching close, learning the routine—and then left for their morning class.

The lesson consisted mostly of learning letters and writing sentences. Madame Cass herself was the teacher, keeping her cold demeanor the entire time. During the last part of class, everyone took turns reading from an old, battered copy of a Jules Verne novel that Benny had already read.

After a noontime meal of beans and a slice of bread, chores were doled out. Benny watched as the others stood in line—quiet and behaved—before running off with their assignment.

Being the last in line, he read the list of jobs and found the only one not checked off said *Kitchen*. Others on the list—and more appealing to him—were *Grounds, Feed, Administration, Maintenance, Shadower,* and *Free*. Benny took the piece of chalk and checked off *Kitchen*. He made a mental note to learn what exactly *Shadower* meant.

Back in the room where everyone had eaten their meals, Benny shuffled through a door into an adjoining room that turned out to be the kitchen. A small woman was busy cutting vegetables and didn't notice him. He cleared his throat to get her attention.

"Well, don't just stand there; get to choppin'," she told him.

"Yes, ma'am."

"No ma'ams here. Just call me Gran."

Benny thought the name appropriate; stepping closer to the woman, he thought she looked ancient. He stood next to Gran and did as she did, slicing carrots, onions, and potatoes into chunks.

He watched the woman swipe the chunked vegetables into a

bowl.

"Here, add these in with the meat," Gran told him and nodded toward a large pot on the stove. "And give it a good stir."

Benny did as he was told and dumped the bowl into the boiling pot. He picked up a nearby ladle and began stirring. It was mind-numbing work, watching the contents swirl around inside. His arm was starting to ache, and when he looked down, he saw something looking back at him.

"Ahhh!" Benny yelped, backing away from the pot, dropping the ladle in the process.

"What's gotten into you?" Gran scowled at him.

"T-there…in the pot. An eyeball!" He pointed.

Gran walked over and looked inside, shaking her head.

"Are you some kinda idiot? Not all there?" She tapped a finger to her head.

"No, ma'a—I mean Gran. I know it was there." He walked over and looked inside, only seeing the vegetables swirling around.

"All right then, I'm through with ya for the day. Just run along and wash up for supper."

Later that evening, Benny sat staring into his bowl. Everyone around him was slurping and scooping huge spoonful's of soup into their mouths. He took his spoon and sloshed his own soup around. *No eyeball, just vegetables and chunks of meat,* he thought. A shiver ran up his spine, and for the second time in two days, Benny went to bed hungry.

The rest of the week went as well as Benny could've hoped. He was able to pull grounds duty and feed duty—both being outside in the cold January air. It was hard labor, and each night after, Benny fell into bed in utter exhaustion and slept through the night.

Benny had taken a liking to Heather and Rose—when she would talk to him—while the others he would only speak to in passing. Rat was the only one that seemed to never speak to anyone. Jack and Sally—always arm in arm—would skip to wherever they were going, singing songs in a language he'd never heard. Although he didn't know why, it never failed to leave him with a sense of dread after hearing them sing.

It was the first Saturday since Benny's arrival, which meant everyone could spend the day as they pleased. Benny thought it would be a good idea to learn more of the terrain within the gates of FrostOak Orphanage, so he bundled up and set out on his wandering.

After walking the front lawns and meeting a strange man by the name of Bob, who was busy trimming a tree, Benny found himself near the chicken coops out back. He watched as the animals pecked around on the ground for any scraps they could find.

He was just about to call it a day when a well-worn path leading into the nearby forest caught his attention. Benny decided to take a quick look before going back inside to where it was warm.

The skeletal trees raked against one another; Benny thought it sounded like someone rattling a bag of bones but brushed off the thought as he continued deeper into the woods.

He heard the giggling first before finding some of the other children were also out in the woods. Jack and Sally, Rose, and even Rat were all bending over looking at something on the ground.

"Hello," Benny called to them.

He heard Jack hush the others before turning and narrowing his eyes at Benny. The others quieted and turned to face Benny as well.

"Hey, new boy," Sally said. "What are you doing out here?"

"Oh, I don't know. I was just learning the lay of the land. I saw a trail and decided to check it out. What are you all up to?" Benny asked as he approached them.

"Not really your concern, is it?" Jack snapped.

Walking up, Benny could see the group was huddled around a rabbit laying on the ground. One of its legs was bent at an odd angle, and it was thrashing around. He could see a stick in Jack's hand and knew he'd been poking at it.

"You should put it out of its misery. It's suffering," Benny said.

"Yeah? To live is to suffer. What makes this thing special?" Jack asked.

Before anyone else could say anything, Rose scooped up the rabbit and walked back toward the orphanage, Rat following close behind.

"You'll want to watch yourself, new boy," Sally said and sneered.

Benny turned to Sally. "Why's that?"

"The weak, they never last long. Not here." She and Jack laughed before leaving Benny standing there in complete befuddlement.

After having a bath, Benny laid in bed until drifting off to sleep. He dreamt of dead birds, the other children laughing at him, and a strange chanting which he was unable to understand. He woke in the middle of the night, soaked in sweat. After changing his nightclothes, Benny got back in bed, waiting for the sun to rise and cast away the sense of despair he felt.

MONDAY ARRIVED, AND Benny was able to draw administration duty for the first time. Had he known he would have had to work directly with Madame Cass, he would not have been so eager to take the post.

"Sit straighter. You must not slouch!" she snapped at him.

Benny corrected his posture and continued to copy the documents she had given him. Each page was written in another language, but he knew it was Latin from some of the books his father kept in his study.

"Yes, ma'am," he said.

Madame Cass was busy binding the pages together with twine before adding them to the stack that was stored in a crate in the corner.

"Madame Cass?"

"Speak."

"What is this?" Benny asked, curiosity getting the best of him.

"It is not for us to ask such questions. We are but servants in this life, and even that pales in comparison to what we should strive to achieve in his name."

He thought her words didn't make much sense but assumed she referred to something having to do with religion. He himself didn't know much—both of his parents told him he was free to make up his own mind on such things—but he'd always been intrigued by Bible stories when he heard them.

SNAP SNAP SNAP

Benny's attention was brought back to the present when she snapped her fingers at him.

"Back to work," she said in her signature cold tone.

After dinner, Benny was sitting on his bed, half reading, half watching Rat in his hole, wondering why he was like that, when he saw Madame Cass step into the room.

"Children, attention."

Squeaks and groans and the shuffling of feet echoed around the room until everyone was standing in line, all eyes on the woman.

"We have a visit tomorrow. I expect you all to be bathed and presentable before the noon meal. Is this understood?" Everyone nodded in reply.

Benny watched Madame Cass leave before he approached Heather.

"What does that mean, a visit?" Benny asked in a hushed tone.

"It just means that a potential foster family will be coming here. Don't get your hopes up, though. No one ever leaves." Benny thought she looked mournful.

"Why do you say that, 'No one leaves?'" he asked.

"As long as I've lived here, no one has been fostered or

adopted."

"How long *have* you lived here, Heather?"

She yawned before saying, "I'm really tired, Benny. Lights out soon, so we should get ready for bed." She smiled at him before patting his shoulder and left him more confused than he was when he asked her his initial question.

Benny's night was a restless one. In his dreams, all the other children stood in a circle around him. He was lying on the cold ground, and they all held sticks and took turns poking him. Even Rat participated, a high, wheezy laugh coming from the boy every time it was his turn. Benny started crying from the abuse. Heather knelt beside him and wiped away his tears. She bent close and whispered in his ear, "Nothing is as it seems when you only see with your eyes. Look beyond and see the truth." She then reached behind her back. Her hand returned with a knife, which she drove into his eye.

"NOOOoo!" Benny jolted upright in bed, yelling and swinging his arms over his face.

Sunlight filtered through the grimy windows, and he saw that the others were already awake and getting dressed for the day. He decided he might as well get ready—bath and all—hoping to put his best appearance forward for the potential foster parents.

Even after the lukewarm bath and the usual gruel for breakfast, Benny felt sluggish by the time the couple arrived. All the children had to line up in a room he'd never been in before. The room was on the ground floor and was lavishly furnished. Benny stood marveling at all the expensive-looking knickknacks when Madame Cass escorted the young-looking couple into the room.

In an instant, Benny saw the faces of the others light up—as if being told they would receive an ice cream cone for producing the biggest smile. To Benny, everyone seemed to stand straighter while trying to present false happiness.

The couple also wore their own facade—each one had a toothy smile. He watched as they paused before each child, silently judging them as if they were a painting in a museum.

When it was Benny's turn, he stood and looked at them and held their gaze. From man to woman and then back again. He felt like some prized animal up for auction, like he'd seen at the county fair two years ago. Judged on appearance alone without getting to know the person within.

The couple spoke a few words to Rose but continued on down the line of children. They ended up leaving the same way they'd arrived. Heather had been correct.

With window shopping over, Madame Cass told everyone they were to do chores early, and afterward, the day would be theirs to do as they wanted.

Benny had grounds duty—which he found to be the most pleasant—and was able to finish at a record pace. He reentered through the main entrance and found the building vacant. He made the decision to snoop around and learn what was behind the doors on the ground floor. He knew where the kitchen, administration, and bathrooms were. Now he would know what the other rooms contained.

The first door he opened turned out to be a janitorial closet—one of the last duties he hadn't yet been assigned. The next was an empty room that had a thick layer of dust covering the floor. *Why has no one cleaned it?* he thought. The hinges squealed when he closed the door, and his heart hammered in his chest, listening for someone to come and catch him out of bounds. When no one came, he moved on to the next.

The final door he came to had the words "Do Not Enter" scrolled across it. Benny looked down the corridor in both directions before turning the door handle. The door did not budge. He bumped it with his shoulder, but to no avail. Shrugging, he left it as he found it, closed.

Later that night, Benny woke with the overwhelming urge to relieve his bladder. He stepped behind the sheet but quickly backpedaled. Someone had done a nasty business, and the smell was terrible. With no other options, he made his way to the lavatories on the ground floor, making it just in time to save himself from embarrassment.

With an empty bladder, Benny headed for the staircase and back to bed. He was just about to ascend when a light far down the corridor caught his attention. As he came closer to its source, he saw it was a shade of murky green and undulated in movement.

Benny read the words "Do Not Enter" on the door that was partly open, and he peeked inside. The light shone through a massive tank of water, and the contents were sloshing around. He stood transfixed by the motion of it. Hypnotized. As the sloshing began to shimmer, the hair on the back of Benny's neck stood on end while he watched Madame Cass step out of the tank, naked as the day she was born.

Benny could see something wrapped around her body. Something he thought was moving on its own accord. He watched as she disappeared from his limited point of view and heard her start to gasp. Afraid of what he would see, but too curious not to look, he slipped his head in the gap of the doorway to see.

Benny had seen a few women nude before—either bathing or in between undressing and dressing—but he had never seen one like this. Madame Cass was laying on a bed, writhing back and forth. Whatever had been wrapped around her body was now moving over it, rippling in waves. Long, sickly looking tentacles slid up and down before converging somewhere between her legs—all while she gasped and moaned.

For the second time that night, it was a photo finish for Benny as he made it to the toilet just in time to lose his meager dinner.

Back in bed, he now thought—since the first time he arrived—that there was something unnatural about this place. About these people.

A MONTH PASSED, and Benny grew accustomed to the workings of FrostOak Orphanage. Two more couples had come, and still, everyone remained a resident. And even though he'd been here for over a month, Benny still felt as if he was an outsider. Heather was nice, and even Rose was talking to him more now, but the others treated him like a piece of furniture they had to step around to get to where they were going.

While Benny sat peeling potatoes, he reflected on the little boy they called Rat. He tried to have a conversation with him on the rare occasions when everyone else was busy with chores. Rat never replied to any of Benny's questions; he just sat and listened. *Very ambivalent*, Benny thought.

His mind switched tracks, and Benny thought about all the strange happenings that he'd experienced since the night he'd stumbled onto Madame Cass and whatever it was she had been doing.

In another instance, the man everyone called Groundskeeper Bob was hacking up an animal when Benny went to feed the chickens one day. He waved at Bob, but the man just sneered until Benny moved on to the coops. It still made him shiver when he thought about the pieces of the animal spread out on the ground at the man's feet.

The first time Benny pulled administration duty since seeing Madame Cass nude had been awkward. It was the usual copying of Latin from old pages, but he found it difficult to concentrate on the task while the woman hovered over his shoulder to inspect his work. A few times, Benny swore he saw a tentacle appear from beneath her dress, and he struggled to keep the food he'd eaten in his stomach.

Aside from those events, Benny thought he'd seen the other children's eyes appear as solid white spheres a handful of times. When he looked away and then back, they would be their normal dull gray, blue, or green that he was accustomed to.

The strangest—and most concerning—event that still kept Benny from getting a decent night's sleep was when he'd apparently been sleepwalking one night. He'd been tired from working the grounds that day and fell into a deep sleep as soon as his head hit his pillow. Hours later, Benny woke from a deep thrumming sound that he felt throughout his body. When he opened his eyes, he found himself just outside the door that led to the basement. He looked around and found he was alone, but the wet spot on the front of his pants let him know that he'd peed on himself at some point. The thrumming continued behind the door, and when he tried the handle, he found it locked tight.

Benny filed the incident away as trying to get to the lavatory but not being able to make it in time. As far as the sound, he had no clue as to what it was but also explained it away as something to do with the boiler.

With the potatoes peeled, and the onions cut up, Benny was done with his kitchen duties and left before Gran could find something else for him to do.

When he woke the next morning, it was the first time he'd looked at his own complexion in the cracked mirror everyone shared. Dark circles encompassed his eyes, and his skin looked pale and made him think of the character Dracula from one of his favorite books. Rose's shouts of, "Willie! Willie! Where is he?" drew his attention away from the mirror.

Benny joined the other children that were crowding around the missing boy's bed and was shocked to find it completely bare of anything Willie had owned. Before anyone could say anything, Rat whimpered and went running, jumping back into his hole in the wall.

"What happened to him? He was here last night before lights out," Benny asked.

A long silence followed his question before Heather spoke. "He must've run away during the night."

All of the others seemed to accept her answer, but it didn't feel right to Benny. He knew Willie was about to come of age, so why would he run away now? Benny sat on the edge of his bed, trying to figure it out.

From then on, the rest of the day became stranger with each passing hour. During breakfast, no one seemed to want to talk—which wasn't unusual, but given recent events, he thought it was just a bit strange. Benny looked at the twins—who normally chittered on about something—and saw that both stared into their bowls.

After their daily lesson, he'd tried to talk with Heather, but she told him she wasn't really in the mood for conversation. Rose had given him almost the exact same reply, as if instructed or rehearsed.

He held no hope of talking with Rat, since the young boy had never spoken to him since Benny had arrived at the orphanage. And talking with Jack and Sally just seemed more trouble than it would be worth, so Benny—drawing *Feed* as his duty for the day—bundled up and went outside.

He grabbed a pail and threw two scoops of chicken feed in it before he walked to the coops at a leisurely pace. An eerie silence, normally broken by clucks and crowing sounds, caused Benny to halt in his progress.

The flock of twenty or so birds were nowhere to be found. Not one single chicken. Not one single rooster. He searched the coops high and low and never found so much as a feather.

Panic crept up his spine, and after dropping the feed pail, Benny rushed to find someone. He found Groundskeeper Bob first. He worked to catch his breath before blurting out his discovery in one long sentence.

Benny thought the look on Bob's face—one eye cocked higher than the other and his mouth hanging half-open—was one of irritation more than anything. When Benny reiterated his story with more urgency and asked the man to confirm it, Bob started to grin and then laugh in a high-pitched cackle that turned Benny's blood into ice.

Benny left the laughing man—covering his ears until he was far enough to not hear him anymore—and entered the orphanage. Wasting no time, he rushed into the room he knew Madame Cass would be.

After throwing the door open, Benny froze in shock. The room where he normally copied the Latin pages was dark, aside from a few candles that were burning. Rose sat at the desk, and although it could have been the poor lighting, Benny swore it looked like blood on the pages instead of the ink he used.

Madame Cass had been kneeling next to the desk, chanting something that chilled Benny, before she rose and shouted at him.

"Uninitiated, you are not worthy! Out! Out I said!" She shoved him back into the corridor before slamming the door shut.

Benny's chest stung where her hands had pushed him. Lost as to what to do—the chickens gone—and his mind still trying to process what he'd just seen, he went to the second floor to lay down.

"Benny."

Benny opened his eyes to find Rat standing next to his bed. The boy had his arms wrapped around himself in a mock embrace.

"Um, hello, Rat…" Benny said, feeling terrible about calling him that.

"You need to leave."

"Why do you say that?"

"Just do it, before it's too late."

Benny shifted and sat up to face him. "I don't understand. Why do I need to leave? And where would I go?"

"Doesn't matter, just go. Now. Don't wait." Rat hung his head and walked back to his hole and climbed in.

Benny felt discombobulated by his first interaction with Rat. He rolled the little boy's words around in his head. He looked at his dad's pocket watch and saw that it was nearly time for dinner.

When the evening meal came, Benny was starting to think Rat was right. All throughout the meal, he would look up from his plate and find a different person staring at him. The tension in the air was palpable, and his sense to flee was growing with every passing moment.

About the time he'd decided to heed Rat's words and walk to

the nearest town—weather be damned—Benny's head started to dip down, lulling from side to side. His eyes grew extremely heavy. His head drooped so low that his chin dipped into the food on his plate, jolting his eyes open for a brief moment. Dread filled his senses when he saw every person in the room was looking at him. Even Gran, Bob, and Madame Cass had joined the others. Benny tried to rise from his seat when his vision blurred and he slipped into unconsciousness.

BENNY HELD HIS mother's hand while they waited for his father to come back with something everyone was infatuated with: they called it cotton candy. The three of them were having the perfect day. Benny and his father rode the Ferris wheel half a dozen times, while he and his mother had ridden the carousel.

Now Benny walked along—flanked by both of his parents— and ate his cotton candy, while each of his parents placed a hand on his shoulders. His mother suggested a walk in the nearby park. As they approached a pond nestled in the center, Benny felt the urge to turn away, to run as far from this place as quick as he could.

When he gave in to the urge and attempted to turn away, his parents' hands held firm on his shoulders and continued to push him toward the murky water. He dropped his cotton candy and started to struggle. Benny called his parents' names, and when he looked up into their faces, a gaping void looked back at him.

Nearing the water's edge, he cried out in pain when their hands clamped down, their fingers biting into his flesh. Others in the park all stood and watched as everything went down. Benny pleaded for someone to help him, but when he looked at the gawkers, he saw a black void in place of their faces as well.

It was when he felt his feet leave the ground that Benny truly panicked. Never slowing in momentum, the things posing as his parents hoisted him high—with ungodly strength—and flung him into the center of the pond.

BENNY GASPED WHEN the water splashed over his face. The shock of the freezing water stole his breath, leaving him paralyzed. It wasn't until he tried to wipe the water from his eyes that he realized his arms were actually being restrained. Through blurred vision, he tried to make out the person that was standing closest to him.

Squeezing his eyes shut a few times, he was able to clear away the water and saw that it was Jack standing there holding a bucket. Past the boy, Benny looked at the room they were in—feeling awestruck by its sheer size, but it was the skeletons that lined the walls that caused his blood to run cold.

Torches above the skeletons provided poor lighting, but Benny could see that everyone he'd met since arriving at the orphanage was in the room—even the recently displaced Willie, who was tied to a stake with his arms stretched above his head, his feet barely able to reach the ground.

A pool of water lay behind where Willie was staked, green light filtering from within and casting an undulating image on the ceiling. Benny watched it move around and thought it looked like a mass of snakes weaving in and out of one another. It caused his stomach to seize, and he turned his head and puked out his dinner from earlier.

He heard Jack laugh before the boy turned away and joined the others. They made up two lines on either side of Willie. From somewhere behind, Benny heard the chiming of a bell. The sound grew closer, finally sounding on the spot where Benny was restrained. He saw that the bell crier was Madame Cass. Again, she lacked clothing, exhibiting stark nakedness and what looked to be blood coating her entire body. From her other hand, she tossed out feathers, and Benny realized where the chickens had gone.

She continued forward, and as she passed the others, they began to chant something too low for Benny to hear. Madame Cass knelt before Willie, bringing the bell above her head every so often, causing it to ring and echo around the cavernous room.

Benny struggled against his bonds but was unable to budge them. His mind soon started to wander to things and people from his past. Times and events he had no business remembering at the moment.

The chanting continued.

His head grew heavier and heavier by the minute. His eyes soon started to droop. Benny felt as if he'd been awake for the past week, and he wanted nothing more than to lie down and sleep.

The chanting continued.

Finally, after what he felt had been hours, or was it only minutes—Benny couldn't decide which—he watched the naked woman stand and point at him.

"The boy is ready," Madame Cass said.

Through half-opened eyes, Benny could see Groundskeeper Bob step in front of him and cut whatever was keeping him restrained to the wooden planks. With his sudden freedom, he was shocked to find that his feet started to move on their own accord—driving him forward, even though his mind was screaming at them to move in the opposite direction.

Step by step, he moved forward, unable to control any part of his body—aside from where his eyes were able to look; he felt like he was being manipulated like some macabre marionette. Benny drew close to where the other children were lined up and heard the words they were chanting.

"Ph'nglui mglw'nafh Cthulhu R'lyeh wgah'nagl fhtagn"

He had no clue what the words meant. Or even if they were actual words. They sounded more like guttural beast-like sounds. Benny's heart pounded against his ribcage, and still, his feet kept their pace.

Benny watched as Rose stepped out of line and stood facing

him. Those chanting lowered their tone, and Benny's feet stopped moving. Rose walked forward and presented Benny with a wicked-looking blade. The knife radiated its age—Benny felt it deep within, knowing it held power beyond his understanding.

He watched as his hand reached to take the blade from her. Fighting with every fiber of his being, Benny was able to stall it in its progress. The chanting ramped up again and boomed in his ears.

"Ph'nglui mglw'nafh Cthulhu R'lyeh wgah'nagl fhtagn"

His hand wrapped around the handle and took it from her. Rose backed away and rejoined the others—starting to chant as well.

Benny looked at Willie, noticing now that his mouth was gagged. Willie's eyes were wide with fear. Benny instructed his arm to sling the blade away, toss it into the water and help Willie, but his body wasn't his own. Not anymore. It was being controlled and guided by some cosmic force.

Madame Cass stepped into the pool, and the familiar tentacles reached out and wrapped themselves around her body. She moaned, and Benny heard her above the children's chants on either side of him. A sickening, bulbous head appeared on her shoulder—beady black eyes fixed on him—and she raised her hand, motioning in a "come hither" gesture.

"Ph'nglui mglw'nafh Cthulhu R'lyeh wgah'nagl fhtagn"

Willie started to grow larger in his view before Benny realized his feet were moving on their own once again. Tears started to stream down Benny's face as hopelessness settled in his heart. Willie's head started to whip from side to side; his bare toes scraped against the ground.

Both of Benny's hands were wrapped around the knife's handle, and his arms rose above his head. He screamed and told his body to obey him. When it did not, he squeezed his eyes shut until he felt his hands swing and come to a sudden stop. When he opened them, he saw the blade—hilt deep—sticking out of Willie's chest.

"Ph'nglui mglw'nafh Cthulhu R'lyeh wgah'nagl fhtagn"

The chanting grew louder.

Madame Cass's voice drew Benny's attention when she yelled, "Do it now!"

Benny looked as the groundskeeper came rushing in with a large mallet in his hands. Drawing back, the man brought it down hard and fast, smashing it into the base of the stake Willie was tethered to. Benny watched it teeter for a moment before falling back into the pool of water where Madame Cass waited.

The water splashed, and Willie sank deep into the water. Benny looked up as the green shimmer turned dark. He looked down at the pool and saw Willie's blood spread throughout the water. Madame Cass—who had been submerged in the water—surfaced and stepped out of the pool.

Benny tried to run, but his legs stood firm, planting him in place. He watched her take the creature from her shoulder, turning it in her hands to reveal a sucking maw underneath. Benny's pleas—both to Madame Cass and to the other children—fell on deaf ears.

His cries were finally silenced when the woman pushed the creature over Benny's face. In the time he remained conscious, Benny saw his life. Past, present, and future all blended into a single moment. He saw the earth—as it was now, and what it would become—and begged for a swift death in that moment. Benny looked at the stars and everything beyond them. Just before he fell from all knowing, he saw an ancient entity sitting on its massive throne. Once again, his body reacted without his knowing and bowed to one knee in praise of the great Old One.

Benny heard a loud pop, the rushing of water, and his mind knew the world no more.

"Son? Son, are you all right?"

Benny didn't hear the stranger talking to him.

"Please, stop. Get in the car and…my god, look at your feet."

The man's words finally brought Benny's mind back into the present. He looked down at his bare feet and saw that they were cracked open and bleeding. He then realized how cold it was and that he was only wearing pants and a shirt. When he opened his shaking hands, he saw that he was clutching his father's pocket watch; the metal was frozen to his skin.

A snowflake touched his nose, and he shivered. Looking back, Benny saw the trail of bloody footprints he'd left.

Nodding to finally acknowledge the man's offer, Benny asked, "W-where am I?"

The man looked forlorn before saying, "A long way from anywhere."

The man opened the car door, and Benny attempted to climb in but found he was too weak to do so. With the stranger's assistance, he was able to sit in the cab and felt its warmth wash over him.

After arriving at the nearest police precinct—and after a doctor tended to him—Benny was only able to tell the police that the last thing he remembered was arriving at an orphanage called FrostOak after his parents died.

The surprise Benny saw on everyone's face at the mention of the orphanage wasn't reassuring, and it was only after they told him about the place—formerly an Asylum for criminally insane prisoners that had burned to the ground near the turn of the century—that he fainted.

Anytime the subject was brought up from then on, Benny would withdraw into himself and stay quiet.

It was later deemed by the authorities that, if she was willing, the Grossman family maid, Trudy, would be allowed to assume custody of Benny. She told them that she was more than willing to do so, and the two would be able to live in Benny's family home.

2020

OVER THE YEARS, bits and pieces of what happened that night in the bowels of FrostOak Orphanage came back to him, but nothing that he felt explained the true nature of the events that unfolded there. He saw some of the other children during his ninety-nine years on earth, whether it was a flash of Rose's face when he'd be sitting at a restaurant eating dinner or when he'd been hunkered down in a foxhole, suppressed by German gunfire and saw Jack and Sally skipping by, their arms interlocked and both wearing smiles on their faces. Rat was almost a constant companion when something terrible was about to happen. An omen that Benny learned to never ignore.

Benny held no fear in life. Not of the living, nor the dead. He felt no emotion toward it one way or the other, not after that night.

Lying in bed, Benny knew that his life was waning—could actually feel it as his life slipped away—like sand in an hourglass. And he could just make out Rat's outline from the shadows in the corner of his room.

He'd lived a long life. *Unnaturally long for someone that's seen as much horror as I have*, Benny thought. But now, he felt age seep into his bones and welcomed death—and whatever awaited beyond.

Benny coughed again, leaving more specks of blood on his pillow as he turned over on his back. His hand clutched his father's pocket watch, hoping to one day return it to its rightful owner. That hope was something Benny kept in his heart when times were bad, but he suspected he was destined for something else.

He lay still as his breath rattled in his chest. He closed his eyes…

…and when he opened them, he was looking at the wide, expansive grounds of FrostOak Orphanage. Benny was twelve years old again. Milling around the grounds were hundreds of children, most of which he'd never met before.

He saw Jack and Sally climbing a tree in the distance. Rat was already there in the limbs of the tree and waved when he saw Benny. Some of the children were playing baseball, and when Benny heard the crack of the bat, he looked to see Willie running the bases. Something sinister hung over the place like a raincloud.

It wasn't until Heather stepped beside him and took his hand in hers that the dread in Benny's heart dissipated. A smaller hand slid into his other, and he looked to see Rose smiling at him. No one spoke—no one had to. With a simple look, all shared an understanding.

The three of them walked hand in hand toward the main entrance of the orphanage. Madame Cass stood by the door wearing her usual grim scowl. The woman motioned her hand, and the doors opened. Benny thought he saw her lips curl upward into a grin before she said, "Welcome home."

HARVEST OF TRUTH

L.K. Pinaire

A ROOSTER CROWED, A RAVEN squawked, and I arose from bed to the unfolding mystery of my past. Still wedged into the purgatory between sleep and wakefulness, the dark man from last night's dream reached out to pull me back. I jerked away to the light of an early dawn, chest hurting and ribs aching. I regained my breath and reason. Ailionora, for whom I'd abandoned my monastic life and vows, opened her eyes and kissed me.

"Another bad night?" she said.

I nodded and faced my son, Abernethy, still asleep in his crib, a few blankets over straw inside a frame. I decided to let him rest.

"I'll be back in three days before the sun sets," I whispered to Ailionora, having filled the bin with firewood and stocked the springhouse with food for a week.

"Watch yourself, Seamus. Be done with this foolish searching. I pray you might rid yourself of these dreams."

I slipped into my clothes and boots. "I will, my sweet. I'll think of you each night before I retire."

Under cool, gray morning skies that promised rain, I grabbed my hat and walked from the centuries-old structure where I lived and taught school. I had converted the old structure after I left the monastery. Beneath the shadow of its two stone wings connected at right angles by a rectangular watchtower, I opened the stable door, stepped inside, and glanced to see my fellow travelers.

I had saved enough from the nine silver English groats I made each month to travel to the nearest village. From there, I hoped to learn about my mother and father, who'd abandoned me to the church. I hoped then the nightmares about them might end. For the next few days, the monks would run the school in my absence.

Another traveler who had arrived before me, a dirty man in a leather hat and coat, mounted his horse. I tied my bags to the Abbot's horse and climbed on. When our armed guide joined us, we rode off into the morning, past harvested fields and tall, wooded hills toward the village of Kilbeggan.

Behind us, Tullamore, the school, a two-storied inn, and a handful of farms disappeared in the dust from our horses. I prayed for our safe passage. Danger always accompanied travelers beyond the Pale.

The other traveler drew close. He had a ruddy complexion and matching beard. "Morning." The man nodded, and smoke from his pipe blew off into the cool sky. "My name is Anamcha. I'm from Kilbeggan."

"God to you, Anamcha. I'm Seamus Hartlidge. I teach at the school for my lord, the local abbot."

"Seamus, you are a fortunate, indeed. I've never before come across an educated man outside the monastery. You have been blessed, indeed."

"The monks raised me there, and I studied many years to become one of them." No need to tell him I'd served two years as a cleric before giving up my vows.

Our hired escort, the third member of our group who carried a long knife, was a worn, old man, who rode to our side. He scowled and wiped his face with his filthy léine. His eyes were bloodshot, and he stank of ale. He squinted at the sun as he rode past us, taking the lead. Could he even protect himself?

"Are you stopping at Kilbeggan?" Anamcha spat.

"I am. I have a bit of business there, a family matter, and I'll return in a few days."

"I don't recall anyone named Hartlidge there."

Though I hadn't planned to share this search with anyone, perhaps this man could help. "I'm searching for my mother and father, the family I've never met."

"I might be able to help you."

"I would appreciate that. Thank you."

Our horses kicked up a foul-tasting cloud of dirt. I kept my mouth closed and rode in silence for hours. By the time we passed the road to St. Colmcille's Well, my soreness had grown into blisters.

Anamcha rode through the flying dust. "Did you know the well is famous for being magical? Years ago, the monks recovered the Book of Kells in a nearby field after thieves stole it and removed the bejeweled cover. It's been said that someone placed a curse on the entire area."

"I don't believe in magic, but spells are another matter. My friend, Martin, the senior monk at Tullamore, taught us that spells are nothing but lies."

"Is that right?" Anamcha laughed and coaxed his steed to increase the distance between us.

We passed the church at Durrow and later my old monastery atop the steep hill to our left, but after that, the countryside flattened with small farmers' huts dotting the landscape. Time crept at its own slow pace, and I thought again of my parents. Had Father been a criminal or Mother a local trollop, or had both fallen to Black Death or perhaps something worse?

Anamcha brought his horse close again. "What do you know about your parents?"

"The monks gave me the name." I pointed back to the hills

where I had studied. "They told me my mother died during my birth. That is all I know."

Anamcha rubbed his chin. "We can talk after we arrive and clean the dirt from our bodies." He guided his horse away so we could both breathe.

The road wound between green rolling pastures, and after hours of riding, Kilbeggan grew with our approach, an inn with a stable and a church all surrounded by thatch-covered huts. My muscles hurt. Under usual circumstances, a twenty-five mile trip wouldn't have been worth the misery to reach a place with fifty people.

We stopped at the stable behind the inn, where the guard and I boarded our horses, and then he walked to the inn without a word.

"I'll be back tomorrow." Anamcha's brow furrowed, and his eyes turned to the side. "I can show you around then if you like."

"I would. Thank you."

"As young as you appear and based on your age, I may have known your mother. Have you heard the name O'Neill?"

"I can't say I have."

"I'll meet you here tomorrow morning and show you what I can, but now I must get some rest." He tipped his hat and rode north from the village.

I brushed the dust from my clothes and carried my bags inside the two-story inn to arrange for a stay. I settled in a second floor room, and after a bath, I went downstairs for dinner and some ale.

By the time I finished dinner, night had fallen, and I returned to my room, passing two overfed friars on the stairs. I went to bed and prayed for my family. Sleep came, but, as usual, I found no peace.

I staggered, disoriented, through a dark field. The ground writhed and shook as hissing creatures approached my feet, the grasses twisting as they came. Bitter wind blew, and I shivered. Turning to flee, I came to face the dark man from other dreams. He blocked me. "Stop, son." Behind him stood a woman, head bowed. She looked up with tear-filled eyes. Beyond her, a man lay chest-down on a stone, headless and bleeding. A child sobbed in the darkness. These dreams all felt the same.

Morning brought cloudy skies and a cacophony from the nearby fields: dogs, sheep, and roosters. Kilbeggan smelled of manure, more like a farm than a village. After breakfast, Anamcha awaited me outside the inn.

"I'd like to show you a graveyard two miles past the village's north edge."

I agreed, and we walked down the dirt road, anticipation growing within me. My breath rose in small patches like mist. We approached the parish church and its graveyard under a dark blanket of clouds reminiscent of my dreams with tendrils twisting down ready to snatch birds from the sky. Distant, unintelligible murmurs and whispers drifted in the breeze. The hair on my neck stood up. These nightmares proved that my imagination had never been a friend.

Since childhood, I'd been preoccupied with the past, the mystery of my parents and heritage, but the prospect of learning the truth loomed. For a moment, I wanted to return home, forget this madness, but I had to stop these dreams. "So, you remember my mother?"

"Anna O'Neill was young and fair. She died bearing a son raised in the monastery."

"That sounds like me. Did you know the father?"

"I remember him, an older man, maybe thirty, worked as a laborer, never came to the inn. He didn't live here long."

I considered Anamcha's words. The monks had taught me to seek all truth and warned of how difficult the undertaking might be, but could they have been wrong? Might some knowledge be profane? I sometimes questioned the wisdom of my search.

Please, Lord, help me to find my parents, if they are still living, and allow these foul dreams to end.

Instead of gaining hope, a sense of dread crept through me. Above, dark clouds formed nefarious shapes. I shivered.

Anamcha stepped ahead, and I followed him through a field of gravestones. While dark clouds swam above, I conjured unseen monsters from dark, forgotten dreams. Ethereal fingertips disturbed the fine hairs growing from the bumps on my arms and back. He led me to one of the newer markers. In the face of this gloom, my chest tightened.

"I believe this is your mother's stone. The dates fit."

I knelt and read "Anna Patrick O'Neill 1393 – 1412." *Might be my mother.* She died the year of my birth.

I pictured my mother, the sad one from my dreams, and a sense of peace settled over me. "Did you know her well?"

"Her parents both died. The family moved to the village before she met your father. I remember seeing her a few times helping in the fields. They had raised her to become a God-fearing woman with a good heart."

As I stood there, my stomach grew tight. An empty longing swept me up, and I grieved for her. "Thank you very much." In spite of the relief of what I had learned, I was not done. "Now if I can only find my father."

"Can't help you there. I told you. He hasn't been seen in years."

My chest tightened. The wind blew my hair across my shoulders, and oh, I'd heard him, but my hopes had been so high. I kicked away the weeds from around Mother's gravestone. *Thank you, Lord, for the blessing of finding her.*

"One of the villagers might know where he went."

"You can search, but I doubt you will find anyone who can help you." He hesitated. "Most of the other young men didn't like him."

I didn't intend to give up yet. We walked back toward Kilbeggan before the sun reached its zenith. Outside the village, Anamcha pointed to a one-room stone hut. "Your father boarded there, working the fields a while for another family before he married your mother. He came from north of here, I believe."

They'd been married. The small abode, once covered by thatch, stood in ruins. The interior had disintegrated into heaps of rotting wood.

"Seamus, I can see your disappointment." He led me to another home in no better condition than the first. "Your mother died here." Anamcha folded his hands together. "I had hoped not to have to say this, but your father always brought trouble with him wherever he went, and you wouldn't want to find him if you could. If you take nothing more from today, listen to my warning. Go home and forget about your father! He left years ago."

If Anamcha couldn't or wouldn't help me further, perhaps one of the other locals could. We walked back to the village, and Anamcha rode off.

I walked the street, disillusioned. Stopping at the wooden church, I spoke with a young priest, and he knew nothing. Then I visited the local residents.

During dinner at the inn and afterward, I spoke with other guests about my parents. I asked an old man, a farmer who'd lived all his life in the village, then I sat down with a young man who worked in the stable. Neither knew my father. The older one remembered Mother, but not well.

I returned to my room, prayed, and retired early. Sleep came easily.

In a field of grass to my knees, I trembled in the face of the dark man with palms held out to push me back.

"Go!" The dark man's angry tone shook me.

As though someone was pulling ropes toward him through the grass, the stalks moved. I turned to get away. A hundred pair of beady eyes peered up from my feet.

The dark man waved his arms and shook his hands. "Go home! Go back to Tullamore!"

I awoke, drenched in perspiration. In this dream, I had seen my father but not my mother. Perhaps I had made progress. Feeling weak, I collected myself and proceeded downstairs for some food and ale. After hours of trying to suppress the desire to go searching, I succumbed, wrapped leftover bread in a cloth, and poked it in a pocket for later. Walking the next half hour down the moonlit road, I returned to Mother's cemetery.

I still entertained hope of learning more about my father, probably some sot who'd left Mother with child and slipped away, but I suspected Anamcha knew more than he'd let on. He had seemed overly interested.

The sky darkened as clouds rolled in, and a crow cawed overhead. I jumped, heart pounding to the rhythm of fluttering wings. I struggled to see, and the chill from a coming storm settled on me. The icy air reminded me of winter, not autumn.

The wind blew cold, and leaves circled in the air. Some creature howled, and lightning flashed behind the old crypt I'd seen earlier.

I took shelter there beneath a stone ledge and closed my eyes against the coming storm. Sheets of wind-driven rain fell and washed over me. A flash of light turned the sky bright as day. Darkness returned with thunder and more cold rain.

Nothing I knew of could have driven me to return to the inn in such weather, so I sat with my back to the sealed door. With the help of the ale I'd consumed earlier, I rested my eyes and slipped into another dream.

Martin's hand weighed on my shoulder, warning me about visions. He shook his head and pointed toward the dark man. Martin turned to face all the naked people marching into hell. Lava poured from a cliff to fill a glowing pool. These men and women strode into the boiling magma, and before they could scream, their flesh dissolved and fire consumed what remained. The stench turned my stomach.

A faint, chittering voice woke me. I heard the noise again, a tiny child or some distant spirit up from the underworld. Another nightmare? I searched for the source.

The storm had stopped, and a foot-tall woman covered in feathers stood on the nearby steps. She had horns on her forehead and wings the size of my hands that fluttered as she spoke Gaelic. "I might be able to help."

I gasped and jumped back, shivering in wet clothes, cold as

ice. Was I still dreaming while wide awake? Might this be madness? I stood, took a deep breath, and smiled to dampen my fear. "How can *you*...help...*me*?"

The tiny, feather-covered woman turned. She was beautiful though diminutive. "For a small gift, perhaps a bit of bread, and a promise, I can tell you more about your father."

She had come to me surrounded in mystery. Was she a demon or an illusion sent by the Devil's whim? I wanted to know so badly. Should I turn her away? "What promise?"

"You must return home and never come back."

How could I leave before learning more? Yet I had heard all the Kilbeggan villagers would willingly say. "Okay, I promise to return home the next morrow." This was the truth if I'd ever told it. I removed the bread from my pocket and placed it near her feet. "Will this do?"

The tiny woman picked it up and nodded. "This will suffice."

A brilliant light flashed around her hands. The bread transformed into a puff of white smoke.

"Well, what is your name, and what do you know about my family?"

"I am called Sien."

I leaned over to see this fantastic visitor.

Blonde hair hung to her miniature waist, and she seemed mature and thin with tiny wrinkles on her face. "Like your mother, your father, Conor Byrne, died years ago, but he's not buried here. Angry villagers murdered him before your birth."

My head dropped. "Please tell me more."

The little creature shrugged. "I cannot say, except you must remember and abide by your promise or you *will* regret your decision."

She vanished in another flash of light and puff of smoke.

Had I made a promise in a dream?

Sien's voice came from all around me, a whisper muffled by the wind. "Return to Tullamore and cast the dead behind you. I have told you what I can."

"But…"

The flutter of wings broke the cool darkness and filled me with unexpected calmness. For a while, I stood there against the roaring wind while distant thunder crackled.

THE STORM PASSED, and occasional bursts of moonlight broke through the clouds, lighting the way back. My boots sloshed in the mud, and the air smelled like acrid fire.

Reaching my room, I collapsed on the bed, exhausted, but the myriad of ideas and questions raging inside me kept sleep away. When I calmed and slipped into slumber, *the dark man stood before me. He waved his arms to the sky, thunder struck, and the wind howled.*

When dawn lit the room, I awakened in a cold sweat, shaking. I went downstairs for breakfast, intending to arrange for the ride home. The tired-looking woman who ran the inn took my order. I should have told her I was leaving but didn't. She brought my bread and eggs, but before she returned to the kitchen, I asked if she'd lived there long.

When she frowned, her brow furrowed. Years of hardship gazed at me through dull, unflinching eyes. "Too long." She made no pretense at a smile. "All my life, the last fifty years."

"I hope you don't mind my asking. I've been searching the cemetery behind the church for my father's grave, but I couldn't find his marker. Did you know Conor Byrne or could you tell me about him?"

She crossed her arms. "He doesn't live here anymore." Then she rubbed her chin. "He might have been murdered, but you really should be more careful what questions you ask around these parts."

"Can you suggest another place nearby where he might be buried?"

She nodded. "I know of a graveyard eight miles north of the one by the church. It's near the road…"

While the old woman traced a map of the road over ale spillage on the table, my mind returned for a moment to the promise.

"Here." She touched a place by the road and north of where she marked Mother's graveyard. "…or he might be buried up near the creek by the old parish ruins." She moved her finger farther along the road, where she drew a bridge at a bend in the road and shuddered.

"If he's there—" She shuddered again. "Stay away. It's dangerous. Something took place there years ago, and the whole parish fled. I've heard stories, a monster wandering the countryside day and night. Don't go there." She crossed herself and mumbled a prayer.

"Thank you." I finished my food, wrapping up a bit in case I got hungry later, and I left two coppers for payment.

I shook my head, unsure what to make of this woman's story, then I remembered the promise. I needed to honor my word, but what if I could find my father's grave? Without seeing his resting place to be certain of his fate, how could I end the dreams? I had one more day to return my master's horse, and I could leave the morrow's morning. What difference could a few more hours make? The shaking from last night returned, but I stepped outside anyway.

The temperature had fallen since yesterday, and dark clouds hid the sky. Another storm. The warmth evaporated from my body, and the threat of these dreams seeping into my waking life made me choke back a scream.

I walked to the stable, spoke with the keeper, and rode my master's horse north over the hardened mud. Well past Mother's cemetery, I found the Old North Road Graveyard surrounded by a low stone wall and simple markers.

I searched for the name, Conor Byrne, but by mid-afternoon, I hadn't found it. If they'd buried him there, he had no stone, which made sense in the light of Sien's explanation. The situation felt hopeless.

The wind and whirling, white flakes brought back images from Last January. Snow in October? I rested and finished the bread, concerned about the ride home and the approaching night. Having come so far, I couldn't turn back yet, not without finding the abandoned church.

I loosed the horse from the tree and climbed on. Down the road, I searched for the old parish graveyard. In my mind, Anamcha rode alongside me, his red hair blowing like a mane. The vision passed, and I wondered what he knew about my father that he wouldn't say. I galloped past barking dogs and fields picked clean of grain.

The promise to the winged woman hung in my mind, but I'd come so far to get this close. How could a little bit of truth hurt me now? Even though my body still trembled, I couldn't stop. Not yet.

Farther and farther from Kilbeggan village, I grew fearless and rode on. I'd become oblivious to my surroundings, driven by obsession until the impoverished landscape around me grew distracting, populated with dark huts, perhaps two rooms, a shed with broken down fences.

Beyond the next field, a stone bridge marked a turn. The barmaid's words and map returned. "Don't go. It's not safe." This had to be the one.

At the stream, I let my mount drink. Then I followed the brook about a mile, searching for the last graveyard until evening approached. Snowflakes fell harder, but an hour later, the sun hung on the horizon with no old church in sight. God, how I wanted to leave this place and return to the inn, but the nightmares and questions might never stop.

A building wall came into view, the remnants of another church. This one had two graveyards, one within a low stone barrier and a second off in the distance in the shadow of a tall limestone outcropping. A number of small markers stood near the church against a backdrop of dark sky. Some leaned, others had broken, and a few had crumbled to dust.

It took perhaps an hour to conclude that my father didn't have a marker by the church. I turned to the distant graveyard where some terrible wind might have thrown and scattered the stones. I remembered the promise and all the warnings. Anamcha, the little winged woman, and the barmaid had told me to give up. Even my dreams had warned me.

Lord, allow me to find my father or his stone and safely return to the inn.

I hadn't meant to lie to the little winged creature but merely needed more time. I rode through the fallen snow, approaching the graves near the limestone protrusion.

The Abbot's horse dug her front hooves into the ground and refused to go farther.

"Come on, girl." She ignored me while snowflakes and strong wind hammered us, flattening the tall grasses at her hooves.

With no cover or protection, I tied her to a tree and patted her neck. "I won't be long, girl." The pressure from unseen fingers wrapped around the base of my neck. I wanted to scream. When I turned to see…

Nothing.

I tightened my wool léine at the neck and stepped forward under the waning sun. Searching the stones, I studied the names, while an icy feeling grew in my gut.

The fog should have blown away but, instead, obscured the stones. As I stepped toward the outcropping, a wagon wheel squeaked from the mists. I stopped, paralyzed with dread. Movement in the distance caught my eye. I jumped. A hooded man in black came forward, his head turning left and right. He reeked of dead animals. I should have run, but my body wouldn't obey.

I struggled to breathe. How could anyone else be here? The barmaid's words came back, haunting me, her warning. What in the name of Hell had I done?

Lord in Heaven, protect me.

The man's skeletal face grimaced. His black, eyeless sockets oozed dark liquid. He pointed at the distant road. "Go back." His voice rattled like a tree, splitting. "Leave this place forever."

My sight narrowed. Ripples moved through the fog at my knees, circling me like ink in water. I raised both trembling hands, took deep breaths, wanting to run. I spoke instead. "I'm searching for my father's stone."

"Your father isn't buried here." The man raised both hands to the sky. "Go!" His rattling voice grew to a shout and echoed.

Anger kept me there, trembling. "You don't know me. How can you make such a statement?"

As though in response to my words, lightning flashed and thunder pounded. I'd never seen such a bitter storm. The snow and fog at my feet roiled with writhing snakes, and the cold... Still shaking, I wanted to leave, but how could I run from a demon? Besides, my body refused. "Who are you? Why did you come here? With no horse, you'll die in this storm."

He shook his head. "Never mind me. I died before your birth." This dark man's hood fell back, and now his face had flesh. "Though I sometimes come and go, I have been here a long, long time."

"Anamcha! It's you!"

Before the words left my mouth, the man transformed, not like a caterpillar to a butterfly but more the way water takes the shape of its container. He shrank into the little feathered woman from Mother's graveyard and stood at my feet. The tiny winged woman looked up with Anamcha's face and piercing eyes. My fingers moved to my parted lips, and I shuffled back a couple of steps.

"You didn't listen. I warned you, but you still came. Why didn't you go home? I tried to stop you at every turn."

An inkling of understanding crept into my unsuspecting mind. Before I caught my breath from the startling revelation, Sien grew into the dark man from my dreams. A fog lifted from my mind, and I recognized them all to be the same.

"Seamus Hartlidge, can't you see? I'm your father."

My God! How could I be both so blessed to find my father and so cursed that he be like this? I drew air in raspy breaths, and my whole body trembled. An unholy beast had been hiding within my dreams, a real creature and not imagined…a monster I had to face. I had come too far to turn back, so I gathered what strength I could from my years of instruction at the monastery.

"How can a man be twenty years dead and still walk the earth? Did you not even die?"

"I am both dead and twice cursed. I pray the same is not true for you."

I failed to understand. "How can this be?"

"Well…first, my ancestry was cursed long before my birth. My grandfather, my father, myself, and probably you—whether you know it or not—were born shape shifters. Later, as the result of my death, I received the curse of becoming the parish Ankou."

"Ankou?"

"I'm telling you these things because they might affect you. As the parish Ankou, I must guard these graveyards until another is selected. If you don't leave here, you might be the one to take my place."

I stood as tall as I could, trying not to lose my bladder. How could a man change shape at will? Could this really be my father? This surely could not be my fate!

"You broke your promise and came here. Why?"

"I was searching for you."

"Your decision may cost you dearly."

I crossed my arms. "This whole day seems like madness."

"Because I can take the shape of any creature I can imagine, the world has turned against me. God has forsaken me."

I leaned back and reminded myself to breathe.

"A couple of years before my death, I met and fell in love with your mother. One of the young villagers must have learned about my true nature. They dragged me out here and murdered me to put an end to my kind. As the last to die here that year, and as the curse goes, I became the parish Ankou, and I must remain until another person dies here and takes my place. Unfortunately, the whole parish ran away."

For a moment, I remembered my mentor and teacher, Martin, and his words about the devil marching people into hell. "Can I do nothing to help you?"

"When I learned your plans to travel here from whispers carried by the wind, I tried to appease you, send you back before you learned the truth about me. I am ashamed of what I've become. And worse, if you die here, you will take my place."

I shivered at the idea.

"You have what you came for. Go home!" His words faded in the growing wind, blowing across the graveyard. I rubbed the back of my neck and rocked back and forth in despair for my father's misfortune. What had he done to deserve this fate?

Conor pointed to my horse. "If you do not leave, you might not survive. This will be a terrible storm."

Without warning, lightning struck the ground and thunder followed, sending me to my knees. My horse whinnied and rose on her hind legs. She broke free.

I choked out the words, "No, no, no," stood, and rushed to steady her, but she reared and knocked me down. She snorted, whinnied again, and came down hard, leaving a cloud of dust flying behind her as she headed back toward the road...without me. My chin lowered to my chest, and my hands dropped.

Conor opened his mouth to speak...but nothing came out. He didn't need to. I stood twelve miles from the inn in a rain-soaked graveyard, and when I examined the area around me for firewood, glistening ice had begun to form on the ground. Nothing here would burn.

"What if you transformed into a great bird and carried me back?"

"Son, I have exhausted my time away from here. You still must leave; walk as far as you can. You might make it back. This parish ends at the road. Above all things, you must not die here."

"Father, I'm so cold. Is there some shelter that I don't see?"

"Yes, but you cannot stay here. I will take a moment and show you why you must not stay. You must not."

He steered me to the karst where the outcropping met the ground and a small tunnel led down. We moved into the darkness, and I pushed my palms out to protect my face.

"If you are my father and intended me no harm, why didn't you introduce yourself? Why did you wait?"

"I should have. I'm so ashamed that I let you come this far. I thought you'd be better off not knowing."

From somewhere I couldn't see, a faint light enabled my vision and—Oh no!

The large chamber offered shelter from the wind and storm. Someone had lined up a row of knee-high stone slabs perpendicular to a vertical wall like graves side-by-side. Wind whistled through an opening that allowed the grey light of dusk to enter.

Some person or creature had positioned the remains of a headless carcass on hands and knees onto each slab. The spines of those corpses all pointed forward toward their skulls, stored in a series of little cubbyholes in the opposing wall.

"That one…" The dark man pointed to the skeleton next to the empty slab. The remains appeared different, perhaps that of a man from the shoulders to the waist, but from there down, the bones of a dog.

"Those bones belong to me. When my murderers attacked me, I had begun a transformation to a hound so I could flee but not in time. As my disembodied predecessor's last act, he removed my head from my body and placed me there. The other skeletons are the men who came before me. Nothing at this church has changed since before your birth." He pointed to the remaining foundation. "Because no one lives here, I've suffered this scourge for thirty years. In a community with sufficient parishioners, my curse would have been to serve one year."

I bowed my head and prayed for my father. My thoughts

turned to Ailionora and Abernethy. How would they fare if I failed to return home? People disappeared beyond the Pale all the time. Unless…

I wondered if God might show some bit of forgiveness for the spirit of a man who'd been double-cursed, and Brother Martin's words came back. "All curses are lies."

Perhaps from the revelation of truth, some hope of releasing my father from his burdens might arise. I remembered an old prayer from my studies at the monastery and knelt.

"Oh Lord, I ask according to Your law, destroy all the words and works of sorcery or demonic-evil influences here. Steal away the strength and power of thoughts or spoken words which have burdened this man, my father, Conor Byrne, since before his death. Lord, I ask You to destroy Words from people, spirits of people, and spirits of the kingdom of darkness, all unrighteous agreements, lies, Words of God spoken with wrong intent of heart twisted around for a selfish purpose, misuse of God's authority. Release the evil hold on this man and free him from these unrighteous curses. Set him free, Lord. Set him free."

I repeated the prayer as best I could remember it through the depths of the long night. While the wind still blew and the ground outside covered white, I rested and continued to pray. Meanwhile, my father paced the ground. I couldn't be sure, but for a moment, I thought I saw him kneel and pray. The storm raged, the night progressed, and I leaned back, exhausted from the day.

The sun had long ago set, and I shivered in the darkness. Resting within the shelter of this place, I had fallen asleep and awakened sometime later from no dream at all.

"Father," I called out. "I forgot to tell you. I have a wife and a son."

He did not answer. When I looked around, he was gone. Perhaps my presence here and the truth about our curses had allowed him to move on.

Oh, Lord, thank you for all your help in my quest, for finding my mother's grave and freeing my father or for helping me try. Thank you, my

Lord, for the hope of returning home and leaving my nightmares behind.

Outside, the storm had broken. The sun should warm the coming day.

Oh, Lord, please have mercy and allow me to survive this night. By God's grace, I might make my way to the road and walk back to Kilbeggan.

Oh, please, Lord, grant me the blessing of returning to Ailionora.

Now a warmer breeze entered the chamber, and I would have to wait and see.

Please Lord, remove the shape-shifting petulance just now awakening within me, the same one, which will develop within my son, Abernethy, when he matures, the one we have inherited from my father. Allow me to return home and make amends for his sake, if not for mine.

I sat and waited, my fate in the Good Lord's hands, preparing for whatever might come. Only God's mercy could save me. I must have slept longer than I'd thought, because a hint of crimson had burst from low into the eastern sky. The storm I had feared so greatly had passed the parish, and a warm breeze soothed me.

I returned to the crypt where Father's bones had been the last added to the collection. I had broken the chain of the Ankou curse. Moisture filled my eyes. By the mercy of God, I might see Ailionora and Abernethy again.

I began the long walk to Kilbeggan, glancing around for the Abbot's horse. As I passed the parish graveyard, I whistled "Mirie it is while sumer ilast" and thanked God for his blessings. His truth had freed me from these evil curses. I reached the road, turned left, and crossed the bridge on my way to the inn. The rising sun warmed my face, rendering me helpless to fend off my emerging smile.

KUNK

Alan Derosby

ELLY SANBORN SAT AT HER desk, holding the envelope in her hand. Many times in the past year, she had questioned herself, asking why she didn't heed the warning. It all made perfect sense now, her own tale mirroring the one before her. Now, as she flipped through the cover letter and the story of dread, Kelly awaited her own fate.

Dear Ms. Sanborn,

I have attempted to pen this letter many times throughout the past few days. I write, erase, and write again, never completely certain with what I have down. Things do not seem to come out in a way that would help you fully comprehend the gravity of what I am asking you to do, to not listen to my child when, eventually, she is sent to your office. Have a conversation, act interested, and move on. Do not attempt to solve the problem. The results will be truly horrifying, I promise you that.

What I've decided to do is to write my thoughts down, outlining how

things unfolded. Your duty is to my child, as her school counselor,
and the letter attached hopefully gives you some understanding.

Thank you for your time. I sincerely hope, for my sake, that you do
the right thing and burn these letters once you have read through them.

Tracy Vincent

I guess the best thing to do would be to start at the beginning.
Now, I am frightened, although it all started out so small…so
innocent. Much like you, Ms. Sanborn, I am a guidance counselor
at an elementary school, though my path was quite unorthodox. I
spent years studying child psychology, in hopes of owning my own
practice. Bills and life have a way of changing things, and an
unplanned pregnancy and college debt required me to find a way
to support myself. I lost the child soon after I started my
employment at a school half an hour from my home, but I was
entrenched. Ten years later, I'm still here.

Things have changed for me, which is the reason I wrote this.
I married, had a child of my own, and divorced soon after. It hasn't
been easy raising a daughter on my own, with only promises of
support from a father who'd rather party with co-workers than
spend time with his little girl. Many nights, I stayed awake with
Charlotte, explaining to her why her dad didn't pick her up like he
was supposed to. I lied so many times, not to hide his penchant for
being a total asshole, but for her sake. These were her formative
years, where she developed positive relationships with both male
and female role models. How would she observe men if her first
real memory was of one that was absent from her life? But that
isn't your problem, and I want to avoid going off on tangents of
my own misfortunes.

I went to work on a Monday that started out like most every
other Monday during the school year. Of course, the ones after
vacation are much worse. Kids' habits—the ones the teachers try
to break—have returned, after spending a week away with bad
influences. Most Monday mornings are busy. Weekend emails need

to be answered; questions from DHS about any issues that have occurred have to be handled. Concerns over nutrition, diet, and poor hygiene are brought to my attention. It can come down to lack of care by parents, but most times, it turns out to be a financial issue. Those are my usual mornings, but the email I received from a colleague with concern over a particular student is one I wished I never answered. That does sound bad for me to admit, that I'd rather not help someone in need, especially someone that was just five years old, but it is the truth.

Her name was Autumn Hall. I hadn't known her prior to the email I received from her teacher, asking that I speak with the student. I assume I was the one that registered the young girl into the school database, but the name didn't ring a bell. Even looking at her picture on the profile page elicited no memory of ever speaking to this child.

The email was a fairly common one I often receive from faculty members, especially ones working with kids of a younger age. Change in behavior causes concern. Some kids lash out; others act in ways out of the norm. With Autumn, it was neither. She was very even keeled, a little hard worker who was never a nuisance. She was never too loud or out of control. But lately, whether it was in class or during recess, she had become particularly withdrawn. Miss Marshall didn't overreact, giving the situation a few days. Children, much like everyone else, can go through periods of elation and sadness. Behaviors can vary from week to week. But Autumn's demeanor had transformed over the past few weeks and had gotten to a point where her friends—only five years old themselves—voiced their concern to the teacher.

"She refuses to talk at all," Miss Marshall said, at first through email and then over the phone. "And it wasn't overnight. This has been going on for some time. Initially, it was just less conversation with friends. But this past week, it's been weird. On the playground, she'll go off by herself and stand against the fence, staring out toward the woods."

I asked tons of questions, attempting to really gauge the

problem. Had Autumn complained of things at home? Divorce was the one constant I could count on to really create chaos. Parents that married too early, of which I was one, caused children to be stuck in the middle of a battle for finances, homes, and even them. As a result, abnormal behavior developed, and kids did things that kids normally don't do. I received no information that truly concerned me but decided to ease the mind of a fellow co-worker by calling the girl in. It was a mistake I will forever regret.

Autumn was at my door before lunch that day. She stood no more than four feet tall, with scraggly blond locks of hair that hid blue eyes. From the moment I saw her, I could tell something was off. Her head was lowered, looking down at her hands, which were locked in what was assumed to be prayer. Her body appeared worn down, dragging herself against the door. Rarely did she make eye contact, and only for a few seconds, as if any real kind of connection would cause her to burst into tears. Her fingernails, worn down, were caused from what I assumed to be her chewing on them, probably to relieve stress.

"Autumn Hall, come on in," I said, standing up and ushering her into my office. I closed the door slowly behind her, but even the click of the door handle as it hinged shut caused the girl to jump a bit.

"It's all right. It's safe in here. Come sit." I pointed to a chair placed across from my desk. I always had a variety of toys and objects for students to play with, perhaps to keep them busy as well as give them things to explain feelings. These sat on a small table next to my desk and in very close proximity to the child. Many times, a stress ball being squeezed would indicate repressed feelings of anger. Autumn took the seat but did not reach out for anything, keeping her hands locked together.

I could see this would not be an easy task. Oftentimes, kids were sieves, sharing anything and everything. Information might not come immediately, but it eventually did. This felt different, as if a thick black cloud entered the room with her.

"So, Autumn, do you mind if we talk? I'd love to just get to know you a little bit." I didn't want to come out and let her know people were worried about her. More quality information came out when kids felt comfortable. Putting her on the defensive would do nothing but keep her quiet.

The child said nothing, staring down at her hands. Occasionally, her eyes would lift to scan her surroundings.

"Okay, I'll start. My favorite food is ice cream, though I can't eat as much as I used to." I wanted to break the ice with something she might relate to.

Autumn lifted her eyes up, and for a brief moment, I thought I had something. Her mouth moved slightly, wanting to smile. Then nothing. She wouldn't take to any of my other silly questions, either. I might get that quick glance, but that was all.

"Can I ask you something? I mean, if you don't want to answer, I'm assuming you won't. But I'd love to hear your voice at least once." I needed to make some headway, and this behavior was disturbing. This child wasn't just depressed; she was shut down. I did receive a nod in answer to my question, though I wasn't all that certain I'd receive a response.

"What's making you sad? I'm good at seeing when people aren't happy." I believed coming out with the question was better than dancing around it.

"Kunk." A tiny voice whispered a word I had never heard of.

"What?" I asked, hoping the child would provide clarification.

"Kunk," Autumn said, this time a bit louder.

"What's a kunk?" I'd never heard this term before. Perhaps it was merely a word being mispronounced, like spaghetti or cinnamon.

"He's my friend," Autumn said. This time, she looked up at me, and I saw those tears in her eyes. It might have been an unorthodox way to find information, but we were getting somewhere. I'd have this problem solved by noon, or so I thought.

"Ah ha. And this friend of yours, he's the one that is making you sad?" Ways a man could make a young girl feel sad or afraid went through my mind. Was this merely a case of a mean boy down the street or an abusive neighbor? I had the Department of Human Services on speed dial, just in case of emergencies. This could quickly become one.

"Yep," Autumn said, this time slightly bubblier. I realized later that the burden of carrying this secret was far too great for a child. Even letting one other person know his name helped.

"What does he do to you? Does he hurt you?" I needed to know.

"No. But he won't leave me alone." Autumn was opening up a bit. Her hands were now in her lap, the tight grip gone for the moment.

I should have called in more help and handed this entire case over. Perhaps I was too confident in my own abilities. I might have to call in extra guidance, but I would make sure this child was safe.

"That's not fun. So how old is he? Is he a kid like you or more like a dad?" I needed to know if an adult was abusing her or not. I wasn't all that sure Autumn had a father in the picture, but surely she had friends or family that might be.

"I need to go," Autumn said abruptly. "Kunk doesn't like when I talk about him." Her hands went back together, her fingers becoming red from the grip. Her head lowered, and that was the end of the conversation. She refused to talk.

I sent the child back to class after trying to pry any additional information out of her. She might not be productive, but it was better than sending her into an environment that was bad for her. When she was gone, I placed a call to her mother. I wanted to avoid asking for help before I talked to family. This could clearly be miscommunication, and bringing in the state would change everything. Again, my arrogance at feeling I could personally solve this problem led me here.

"Good afternoon," said the voice on the other end of the phone.

"Hello, Ms. Hall. This is Tracy Vincent. I'm Autumn's counselor. I am hoping this conversation stays between us and

Autumn never even knows I've called. That can hurt our chances of her opening up if she ever needs to."

"Okay. Makes sense. What's this call about?" Ms. Hall sounded curious but not concerned.

"She was sent to me due to a few concerns over recent behaviors, and through discussions, the name of 'Kunk' was mentioned. I was wondering if you could shed some light on this man."

"Kunk? Kunk is imaginary, Ms. Vincent." Autumn's mother was clearly frustrated her daughter had brought it to anyone's attention.

"He's not a real man?" I asked her. I had never even considered it. It could mean several things, however, from overactive imagination to delusions of a deranged mind. Nothing was off the table.

"No more real than Bigfoot or the Chupacabra," Ms. Hall said. She wanted to be off the phone, that much was certain, but I knew she was playing it safe to avoid anyone coming into her home.

"Phew, that's a relief. The things that went through my…" I was stopped mid-sentence.

"Unless you feel this conversation has to go further, I will excuse myself. I promise you there's no one abusing or harming my daughter, except her imagination. Good day." The mother hung up the phone before I could say thank you.

"Bitch." I said, loud enough for the lead secretary to hear me. We both had a good laugh at Kunk and Ms. Hall's reaction. It was a poor decision on my part. I did not understand what I was doing. The rest of the day went on, without me ever thinking about the incident another moment.

The next morning, I saw Autumn walking to the lunchroom. Instead of me initiating conversation, she waved and bounded toward me. I waved off Ms. Marshall to let her know the girl was fine with me and met her in the middle of the hallway.

"Hi," Autumn said, a large grin on her face.

"Hey to you, too. Things better than yesterday?" I asked, assuming they were. Sometimes, kids need an adult to show they are concerned. If I asked about our previous conversation, the child would assume I was invested in her problems.

"Yep, yep," Autumn said, a bounce in her step. Whatever had been getting her down was no longer there.

"Perfect. Well, go eat lunch while you still have time." I attempted to usher her down the hall. Instead, she stood there, and the smile faded from her face.

"But Kunk isn't happy. He's mad at you. You shouldn't have called Mom." Autumn stared at me and then spoke again. "Okay, bye." The little girl's disposition changed, like a light switch going off. Before I could ask her anything, she ran down the hall.

I stood in complete shock, anger welling up inside me. I had specifically asked Ms. Hall NOT to mention our conversation to her daughter. That could only lead to problems, and I felt I was clear with her. As soon as I got back into my office, I picked up the phone to call her. I should have discussed the situation with a colleague or administrator first. Either could have talked me off the ledge. But alone, without the guidance of others, I was seeing red.

"Hello?" the woman on the other end of the line said, picking up on the first ring.

"Ms. Hall, I thought we came to an agreement yesterday. I was a bit shocked, to say the least, when I found that wasn't the case." I jumped right in, unable and unwilling to hold back my frustration. I worried that now Autumn would avoid sharing anything with me and this could hamper the relationship.

"Ahh, hello, Ms. Vincent. Let me stop you before you go on any more of a rant. I did not tell my daughter a word. I didn't question her on anything or act differently. Your accusations are baseless, to say the least." There was to be no backing down on either side.

"That can't be possible. Autumn made it a point to approach me and mention it." I was not believing a word this parent was saying.

"Listen, I don't know what to tell you, but I'm a bit busy. So, unless there's a specific reason to contact me, please don't." Ms. Hall hung up the phone, ending any chance at negotiation.

That conversation bothered me the rest of the day and into the next morning. I thought about all the ways that both of us could be correct. Perhaps Autumn's mother had recorded the conversation and the child found it. Maybe a series of questions designed to see if her daughter was all right was enough to alert the girl that something was off. Either way, my quest to prove I was on the right side of this argument was the worst decision I could have made.

"Autumn, thanks for coming to see me. Want something to drink?" I had called the girl into my office after lunch, letting her teacher know I needed a good amount of time. In reality, the issue was over with. The child freely took a juice box from my mini fridge, sucking it down as she chatted away about what she was doing in art. Her stained hands clearly showed she was a master painter. It was more my curiosity that brought the child to my office.

"So, yesterday, you told me your friend was mad?" I asked, getting right to the point. I needed to find out where this "friend" came from. I could see from the child's file that her parents were divorced. Oftentimes, in situations where a child sees only fighting, they will create something in their mind to divert the attention, such as an imaginary friend.

"Kunk. Yep, he was mad," she said, crushing the juice box in her hand and tossing it into the trash.

"Oh no. I don't want to make Kunk mad." I tried not to come off as sarcastic and condescending, though anyone over the age of ten would have picked up on it.

"Did he tell you why?" I asked.

"Kunk said he didn't like that you called Mommy and talked about him. He was mad at me for talking to you about him, and now he doesn't like you," Autumn said, her face stoic.

"Interesting. And how does he know I called?" I now was fairly certain that this anger was not by an imaginary being, but by a child who felt betrayed that I ratted on her. The thing that shocked me was the child wasn't closed up or acting distrustful.

"Kunk lives there. He hears everything. He said you called Mommy and blamed her for his actions. Mommy was so mad. She kept talking out loud about me and Kunk. She doesn't think he's real," Autumn said, now showing the nervousness of our first encounter.

"He lives in your house. Like he has a room?" I asked, without even thinking.

"Yes. He lives in the attic." She pointed to the ceiling of my office, just in case I didn't know what an attic was. It made me smile. She didn't return the gesture.

"Hmm, can I ask you something, Autumn? It is a very serious question. Can you answer a serious question for me?" I wondered if I should even be continuing this conversation with her. I knew it might upset the mother and the child.

"When did you first meet Kunk?" I wanted to nail down the time. Perhaps it was after her father left for good, never to be seen again in her life. Maybe Mom was too busy fixing her own life to worry about her daughter's. Imaginary friends were self-soothing in times of sadness or loneliness. This was clearly the case.

"Kunk knocked on the front door. I opened it, and he was standing there. He asked if he could come in," Autumn said.

"Was this a time that you were mad at your mom or dad?"

"Nope. He just came. I'm not supposed to talk to strangers, but he looked nice, so I said yes. Now he lives there." Autumn looked to be about done with the conversation, her demeanor changing. She was clearly uncomfortable talking to me about her friend.

"Can I tell you a secret, Autumn? I had an imaginary friend as well. His name was Gooey, and he was this green blob that followed me around my house. We'd play games and have tea parties together. He'd always listen to my problems, like when my dad died. I could cry and talk to him, and he'd just sit and listen. I liked that about Gooey. He always made me feel better. Does Kunk do that? Does Kunk listen to you when you're sad?" I figured if I lied a bit, I could get to the heart of the issue without saying it outright.

"No, Kunk tells me not to complain. There are different ways to take care of problems. That's what he says to me." Autumn stood up. "I don't want to talk about this anymore. He's going to be super mad at me."

"If you keep it a secret, so will I. Kunk will never know we talked." I was not one to talk kids into keeping quiet, but it would put her mind at ease a bit, which was important.

"He'll know. He always does." Autumn clearly wasn't calm anymore.

"Then blame me. Tell him it's my fault. I'm not worried," I said defiantly.

"Okay," Autumn said. She went back to her class soon afterward, leaving me alone with my thoughts.

I wanted to reach out to the mother again, to find out what happened. It was clearly a case of a child needing attention that wasn't being offered at home. It was obvious that Ms. Hall had no desire to converse with me again, partly due to the way I handled the last discussion. My decision was to wait a few days and then perhaps reach out with an olive branch. Together, we could help Autumn recover from whatever was bottled up inside her. I didn't have to wait long.

The child was back in my office the following day, sent down by her teacher. Autumn was barely able to keep her eyes open, falling asleep several times.

"What's going on?" I asked her. I could tell she was beyond tired.

"I can't tell you. It gets bad when I do," Autumn said, yawning. I had never seen fear and lethargy at the same time, but this was it. The child's eyes said it all.

"Autumn, if something is happening, I want to know. I can

help you," I begged. This girl was clearly in need of assistance, and it might be time to call in bigger guns.

"No, you can't. You can't help, and Mommy can't help. No one can." Autumn was crying now.

"But wouldn't it be better if we tried? Maybe I could talk to Kunk for you?" I asked.

"NO!!!" Autumn screamed. "You can't talk to him."

"Okay, okay. I won't talk to him. What if I talked to your mom about finding ways to help you instead? It won't be about Kunk at all. Would that be okay?" I was grasping at straws. She agreed and, after a quick nap in the nurse's office, went back to class. I waited until after lunch to call her mother again, apologizing even though I wasn't at fault. I had realized the importance of this child's delusions and the demons she was fighting. It was clear her anger and sadness had created this figment of her imagination. While we didn't care for one another, it was obvious to Autumn's mother there was an issue with her child that we needed to discuss.

In our lives, we make decisions that have long-term ramifications, lasting much longer than one can imagine. Think of someone that attempts to steal from another person. The accused is captured, tried, and imprisoned for many years, depending on the severity. It was never the criminal's intent to spend many years locked away in exchange for material goods. The momentary lapse in judgement leads to a lifetime of regret. Mine was when I agreed to go to the Halls' home after dinner to have an open conversation, in hopes of solving Autumn's problem.

That evening, I left my daughter with my parents, picked up a bottle of wine, and headed to the house. The address was several miles out of town, so it gave me time to decide what I wanted to say. It was clear that things were bothering the child. When I knocked on the door, Autumn answered. She was already in her pajamas, showered and ready for sleep, which wouldn't come easily.

"Hey kid, is your mom home?" I asked, winking.

"You shouldn't have come. He is so angry," Autumn said.

She left the room to get her mother, leaving me alone by the front door. To the left of me was a living room, a series of furniture surrounding a fireplace. The television was mounted high on the wall, with family pictures around it. Directly in front of me was a series of wooden steps leading to a second floor. I looked up, impressed with the craftsmanship of the handrail. It slightly curved as it made its way up the steps. It was just then, out of the corner of my eye, I saw something at the top and to the right side of the stairs. It was slight, and at first, I doubted it was anything at all. It almost looked as though someone was peeking down at me.

"Hello, Ms. Vincent. I'm glad you came." Ms. Hall walked to me with her daughter directly behind, sticking out her hand, hiding the fact that she loathed me. She ushered me in, offering me a seat on the couch. "And wine. Let me go grab some glasses."

I sat there, my eyes taking in the surroundings, wondering if I could pick up on any small hints. Autumn sat in a chair next to mine, staring at me. It was an uncomfortable look, one not usually given by children.

"Kunk doesn't like you. He hates you are here," Autumn said, breaking her silence.

"Dear, that isn't true. Why would he hate me? I'm just concerned for you. If he is your friend, he will understand." I didn't want to tell the girl her friend was imaginary, so I danced around it the best I could.

As soon as I answered, I heard it: footsteps running across the second floor, almost above our heads. The child must have seen me glance up.

"I told you," the child said, grinning slightly.

"You told me you hear things upstairs. Do you have pets?" I was hoping that was the case.

"It was Kunk. He said you know it was him. He even let you see him just enough to prove you wrong." Autumn looked out toward the kitchen, just to make sure her mother didn't hear our discussion.

"Now you know he is real, you need to let it go. He said

things will get worse if you don't." Autumn stood up and went into the kitchen. Both Halls returned with a plate of crackers and cheese and wine glasses.

The conversation was surprisingly positive, and I found that the mother and I had a lot in common. We both were raising a child on our own without any help. She was as concerned with her daughter as I was, although we had different beliefs about this "friend." While I only heard bits and pieces containing veiled threats, Autumn's mom had a much different experience. She talked of uneasy feelings around the home, as if someone or something was watching her. When the discussion of the first phone call came up, neither she nor I could figure out how Autumn found out.

We capped off the bottle of wine, and after the young girl was taken up to bed, we enjoyed some tea and more conversation. She was more concerned than I about her daughter's behavior. Mom remembered the first time she heard of Kunk. She was in the kitchen making lunch when her daughter called to her. She wanted a friend to come in, but upon opening the door, no one was there.

"I told her it was okay for her friend to play if they were good. I was merely humoring her. Since her dad left, it's been rough. She's always been shy but at least would play with the neighborhood kids. It's been harder to get her to connect with kids her own age. Lately, she would rather be inside her room alone than outside." Miss Hall wiped some tears away, as if sharing about this was difficult for her. Her daughter was struggling, and it hurt to see it.

"At first, she wouldn't talk of Kunk. I'd ask her who she was playing with and she'd say a friend. You want to know something? And this might make me crazy, but there are times I hear two voices upstairs. I'll check, but most times she's playing."

The rest of the night went without a hitch. We talked about getting together again—which unfortunately never happened— and steps we could take to help Autumn out. We decided to support her and give the child the opportunity to talk about anything necessary. Her mom and I would keep in contact through text, so no one could hear our conversations. When I left, I even received a hug and a thank you. It wasn't until I left that I once again felt uneasy. As I looked back at the house before driving away, I saw something in an upstairs window, the full shadow of a man watching me. I blew this off as nothing more than nerves and an illusion. It was not.

The next morning, I noticed that Autumn was on our absentee list. That wasn't all that unusual, as kids of that age seemed to come down with many different ailments. I sent off a text to her mother, both thanking her for the prior evening as well as checking in on Autumn. I didn't expect to receive an *immediate* reply, but by the afternoon, when I still hadn't heard back, I made the decision to call. The phone rang and rang before finally going to voicemail. I left a message, hoping between it and the text she would respond. I heard nothing that evening and on the second day saw the child's name on the absentee list yet again. This time, I went down to the office to see if the mother had called in to let the school know Autumn was sick. She had not. I again left a text, coming to the decision that I would swing by after school if I hadn't heard back. I called my mom to see if she'd pick up Charlotte from day care, and as soon as the clock struck three, I hopped into my car to drive to the Hall residence.

The first thing I did upon pulling into the driveway was to look up at the window where I had seen the black, shadowy figure. Nothing was there except drawn curtains. The family car was still in the driveway, the same place it was when I last visited. Without hesitation, I walked up the front porch and knocked on the door. I believed I'd established enough rapport with the mother to simply stop by. I knocked once and then a second time, much harder. I waited, listening for any footsteps on the other side.

"Ms. Hall? Are you home?" I yelled as I tried knocking once again. When I still received no reply, I grabbed the door handle and turned. It opened immediately into a darkened and eerily quiet home. I yelled out, looking to see if anyone was around, but heard nothing.

"Autumn? Are you home?" I called for the young girl. Nothing. It was like everyone had disappeared.

"KUNK! Are you here?" I don't know why I called out to something I didn't believe in. In all honesty, I doomed myself. At the time, though, I was merely looking for answers.

Unlike the others, Kunk answered. I could hear footsteps above me, starting as quiet knocks. Then, whatever was above me broke into a run across the second floor.

BANG!!! A door upstairs slammed shut, as if what was there was attempting to hide. I was frightened, almost unwilling to check the upstairs. Instead, I walked into the living area. I tried the light switch, but nothing worked. All the furniture was where it had been two nights prior, a chair pulled back with the television remotes on the armrest. It was when I got into the kitchen that I knew something was very wrong. I first noticed a handprint on the top of the island that sat in the middle of the room. Since I had little light, I took out my cell phone and flashed it toward the mark. It was blood. Only then did I notice a trail of the same substance at my feet, leading to a room with the door closed. I should have run from the house and called the police without going farther. I now think that wouldn't have mattered, not sure if I would have even been allowed to. Instead, I walked toward the door, gripping the handle.

"Ms. Hall? You all right?" I said, pushing the door open. Immediately, the smell hit me, and even though I had never been near a dead body, I knew this was the scent of one. All the shades had been drawn and the lights were off, but I could still make out the silhouette on the bed. With the light on my phone, I flashed it toward the bed. Ms. Hall lay on her back, her throat slit. Her white shirt was stained with a deep red blood. Stab wounds were covering her entire body; her hands positioned with both palms up revealed defense wounds, as if to stop an attacker. I covered my mouth to avoid screaming.

"Autumn!" I said loudly, hoping the child was not dead. I again should have called the cops to let them know what I found.

It could have ended right there. As soon as I called her name, the bedroom door shut on me, locking me in. I screamed, trying to open what seemed to be a locked door. I could hear breathing coming from the other side. I wanted out of this bedroom, but I also didn't want to know what was keeping me in. Though my mind was playing tricks, I thought I heard the body behind me rise. It was as if I could smell her leaning over my shoulder. I pulled harder, not wanting to turn around, finally yanking the door open. I rushed out, closing the body inside.

I screamed for the child now, running out of the kitchen and to the steps that led to the second floor. Grabbing the rail, I slowly made my way up. I had never been in this part of the home but only knew Autumn's bedroom was here somewhere. To the left of the steps was an open loft, with children's toys covering the floor. Close to it was a bathroom, door open, revealing nothing. It was the closed door at the end of the hall, light coming from beneath the crack, that caught my attention. Did it even cross my mind that it was the only light working in the home? Not at the time. I could hear the music coming from beyond it and the chatter of tiny voices. All I knew was that someone was in there, and my hope was it was the young girl.

"Autumn?" I said, knocking on the door.

"Come in, please," the voice I recognized as belonging to Autumn Hall said.

I pushed the door slowly, peeking in. The girl was sitting in the center of the floor of her bedroom, smiling at me. It made me uncomfortable.

"Kunk said you were here. At first, he didn't want you to come. But he's glad now. And I'm so glad, too." Autumn stood up, walking toward me. Her hands were behind her back, holding something. A quick turn let me see enough to realize it was a knife.

"Autumn, baby, drop that, please. We can leave here once you do." I wanted to scream. I knew what she had done. I saw her mother. This girl needed serious help.

"My mommy is sick, isn't she?" Autumn was still walking

toward me.

"Honey, you have to put the knife down. It's dangerous."

Just then, the girl stopped. She stared at me then turned behind her, as if someone was talking to her.

"No, I don't want to do that," Autumn said.

"Autumn, come here. Let's go. We can leave," I begged her, even with the knife in her hand. I could knock it out if necessary.

"You sure it won't hurt?" the girl asked the nothingness behind her.

"Autumn…COME HERE, NOW!!!" I couldn't get her attention. She was in a zone, talking to the voices that were in her head.

"Okay. I know you wouldn't lie to me, Kunk," Autumn said. She turned to face me, a blank look across her face. Without saying another word, she took the knife and jammed it into her own neck. She tried to scream in pain but could only gurgle as blood filled her throat and mouth. I couldn't even help her. I felt a pressure on my chest push me back, tossing me to the floor. Before I got up, the bedroom door slammed. I pounded on it, screaming the girl's name, hoping what I saw was not real. Eventually, I gathered my wits, ran to my car, and called the police. I had some explaining to do as to why I was there, but the child's fingerprints and DNA were all over the murder scene. I did mention the voices she was hearing, still not fully accepting the belief there was something else in the room with us.

That night, I went home and made sure to hug my daughter extra tight. To see a child go through the pain like Autumn did, suffering from severe mental illness, made me want to stay closer to home and be present for my daughter, through all her own struggles. Months turned into a year, and still I dreamed nightly of that event. To even get a wink of sleep, I took to drinking and pills. But when I woke up, the image was still there. Eventually, time does move on, and as my own daughter turned five, I sometimes could go a day without thinking of Autumn. One day it all came back, which is why I wrote this to you, so you don't make the same mistake.

It happened two months ago. Winter had come early, and we already had several tiny snowstorms. I was in the kitchen, baking cookies for my little girl, who had a slight sniffle. She had been bundled under a pile of blankets and pillows, watching movies to keep herself entertained. At first, I was uncertain if what I heard was the television or not.

"Let me ask," I heard Charlotte's voice whisper before coming into the kitchen, a big smile on her face.

"Mommy, can he come in?" Charlotte asked.

My entire body froze in fear. It was as if all those stories from years ago flushed back to me. "What did you say?" I ran to the front door, which was wide open.

"Can the man come in? He wants to play with me," Charlotte said, pointing at nothing.

And even though no one was standing in front of me, I looked down to see large footprints in the snow. Kunk was here.

Ms. Sanborn,

PS…

Please understand that I know this story sounds crazy. It's not. None of it is. Perhaps when my daughter, Charlotte, looks out of sorts or sad, you'll pull her in to discuss her feelings. Maybe you will think that there's something wrong at home and I'm deflecting attention away from a worse abuse. I'm not. Save yourself and your family. Stay far away and my hope is you have no children for Kunk to play with.

Tracy Vincent

WITHERED

Cassandra Angler

IAM SAT WITH HIS BACK against the brick wall of the school's auditorium as conversation and excited chatter filled the room. The pep rally left everyone energized and excitable. He took his headphones from his pockets and plugged them into his phone, cranking up the volume to drown out his peers. Groups of girls giggled at each other, one of them making eye contact with him, but only long enough to sneer. He shut his eyes and laid his head back against the wall with a sigh, his long black hair falling down around his shoulders. The bell rang, and everyone started filing out of the room, headed for their buses or the pick-up lane just outside the front doors. Liam waited until half of the crowd had left before leaving himself, his hands tucked in his pockets.

Taking his seat on the bus, he rested the side of his head against the window and watched as the rest of the students pushed through the doors, eager to get home to their families. As the bus started to move, wads of paper hit Liam in the back of the head, followed by laughter from the back of the bus. He slumped down into his seat, trying to ignore them, as he watched the street signs and buildings pass by. The bus stopped, and he stood, making his way to the front and down the steps. He wasn't surprised to see his case worker standing in front of the house, stuffing trash bags filled with his belongings into the trunk of her car. Her brown hair, which was tucked up in a bun, bobbed as she pushed the bags down into the overflowing space.

"Moving day already, Evelyn?" he asked, pulling the headphones from his ears.

"I'm glad you find this so amusing. This is the third foster home in less than six months." She slammed the trunk lid shut and stood with her hands on her hips, scolding him with her eyes. Liam noticed the way her grey pantsuit did nothing for her body shape but decided against mentioning it.

"I didn't even do anything!" he said, climbing into the backseat and slamming the door shut behind him.

"You must be doing something. They didn't even want to see you before you left." Evelyn sighed. "You have to start letting people in, Liam. You're almost eighteen years old. If you want to be adopted before you graduate, you have to start being cooperative. Do you not want a family?"

"I really don't care. No one is ever going to want a bastard like me, and I've accepted it. Maybe you should, too," Liam grumbled, slumping his thin frame down into the seat.

Evelyn looked at him through the rearview mirror. He glanced up and saw her staring. It was obvious that his words wounded her; her eyes were glassy and wide. They rode in silence the rest of the drive, parking in front of a large white house with purple shutters. The front porch was wide, boasting a table and an array of potted plants. Liam groaned and pulled his belongings from the trunk. He dragged the bags behind him as he climbed the front steps. Evelyn stood in front of the door, waiting until he was standing beside her before knocking. Liam stood, staring at the ground as the door opened.

"Well, hello! You must be Liam." The woman's voice was

excited, an octave too high.

"That's me," he said, not lifting his eyes from the porch.

"Come on in. I've got coffee made if you'd like some."

Evelyn smiled. "I wish I could, but I have another case to go check on before my shift's up. Maybe next time." She turned to Liam and lifted his chin, making him meet her eyes. "Please, buddy, behave."

She squeezed his arm and jogged back down the steps as Liam was ushered inside.

"It's really nice to meet you, Liam," the woman said, holding out her hand. "My name is Abigail. Can I help you with your bags?"

Liam dropped the tied end of one of the bags into Abigail's open hand and lifted his gaze to meet hers. She was surprisingly pretty, he thought. Her eyes were a bright green, and her curly black hair stopped halfway down her back. She smiled, exposing a set of bright white teeth.

"My husband, Caleb, will be home from work here soon to meet you, but for now, let me show you your room."

They climbed the stairs, the walls of the stairwell lined with canvas paintings of trees and landscapes.

"Did you do these?" Liam asked, pointing to a painting of a black tree, its red leaves littering the ground as a little girl in a ponytail looked up at it.

"I did. Do you like them?"

He nodded and ran his hand over the painting, fascinated.

"Maybe we can put that one in your room," she suggested. "Or I can make you a custom one. Anything your heart desires."

They climbed the rest of the stairs and walked to the back of the hall, into a large bedroom. The walls were bare, the bed sheetless and the dresser empty.

"Our last foster aged out over a year ago, so it's a little dusty. I apologize. Would you like some help unpacking?"

Liam set the bags down on the floor and sat down at the edge of the bed. "I won't be here long anyway, so no use in pulling anything out of the bags."

Abigail sat down beside him and rubbed her hand up and down his back. "I wouldn't be so sure," she said, breaking the silence. "We've never returned a foster."

Liam looked up at her, his expression asking his question for him.

"We usually take in the older kids. That's why there are no other children here. They've all grown and gone," she said with a smile.

He nodded and looked around the room. *Maybe this is it*, he thought to himself. Abigail stood and left the room, returning a few minutes later with clean sheets and a pillow, which she set at the end of the bed.

"I'd appreciate if you would make your bed while I get supper started," she said with a smile. "Afterward, you're more than welcome to give yourself a tour of the house."

She walked through the doorway, pulling the door shut behind her. Liam made the bed and riffled through his bags. He pulled a notebook from the bottom of one and scratched out the names of his former foster parents.

"Another one bites the dust," he said with a chuckle.

Liam rubbed his hands up and down his face and made the bed. Afterward, he decided to take Abigail up on her invitation to explore the house, deciding it would be better than sitting there, bored. He stood up to walk out of the room but paused when he heard the sound of scratching coming from above him. He tilted his head and listened. It stopped after a minute or two, and Liam shrugged. *Probably a mouse.*

Walking down the hallway, he could see three other bedrooms, one of which belonged to his new foster parents. Everything was immaculate. The bed was made neatly, and there wasn't a speck of dirt anywhere that he could see. Farther down the hallway was an office, the walls lined with full bookshelves. He walked the length of the room, skimming the titles adorning the shelves. They were mostly horror with a few fantasy and non-fiction titles scattered throughout, not in any particular order. Liam noted the smell the old books gave off and grinned to himself.

At the top of the steps, a rope hung down from the ceiling. The attic, Liam assumed, as he reached up and tugged. The stairs groaned loudly as they unfolded. He had just started to climb them when Abigail came bounding back up the stairs.

"No, no, no!" she yelled. "That's off limits!"

Liam flinched at the scolding and stepped back down. "I'm sorry," he said, digging the toe of his tennis shoe into the carpet.

"It's okay," she said, pushing the stairs back into the ceiling. "I should have told you that beforehand. My fault."

As the attic door slammed shut, dust particles fell down on top of them. Abigail quickly grabbed a vacuum from the upstairs closet and swept the area where the dust had fallen. The sound of the front door shutting drew Liam's attention. He craned his neck toward the stairwell to see Caleb slipping his shoes off and placing them on the shoe rack beside the door. Caleb was larger than Liam had expected. Caleb's wide shoulders made his dress shirt look sheer at the top, a tattoo visible between his shoulder blades. His blonde hair was slicked back with hair gel. For the first time Liam could remember, he felt intimidated.

Caleb felt the boy's stare and turned to face the steps, meeting him with a toothy grin. "You must be Liam."

Liam nodded and gulped, swallowing the lump that had formed in his throat as he descended the stairs, meeting Caleb at the bottom. Caleb slapped the boy on the back with a fat-palmed hand and pulled him in for a hug. Liam grunted as the strength behind the hug forced the air out of him.

"It's nice to meet you."

"Thanks, you too," Liam said, forcing a smile.

Abigail walked down the stairs with her hands on her hips.

"Where's mine?" she asked playfully.

Caleb laughed and wrapped his arms around her. He kissed her and lifted her up off the ground, giving her a spin before setting her back down.

"Dinner smells amazing."

"Stir fry," Abigail said. "And it's about finished."

Caleb set the table as Abigail brought the food into the dining room, placing it in the center of the table. They sat in awkward silence as Abigail filled their plates and took a seat next to Caleb, squeezing his hand before draping a napkin across her lap. Liam picked at his plate and pushed the food around. He could feel Caleb's eyes watching him but refused to look up from his dinner.

"So, tell us a little about yourself, Liam," Caleb said finally.

"There isn't much to tell," Liam muttered, stabbing a few green beans with his fork and finally shoving them into his mouth.

"Do you have any hobbies? Any friends?" Abigail pressed.

"No friends," Liam said, his mouth full. "I like to read and listen to music. I guess those are my hobbies."

Caleb and Abigail shared a look, their eyes transferring a message between them that Liam couldn't decipher. *Maybe they're already thinking about shipping me off to another home.* He laughed internally as the thought crossed his mind before stuffing another fork full of food into his mouth.

"We've decided that homeschooling for the rest of the year is probably for the best. You've only got a couple of months before you graduate, and I thought it would be easier than transferring to a new school." Abigail watched him, gauging his reaction. "What do you think?"

"Works for me," he said with a shrug.

"Just a few more things," Caleb said, his eyes hard and serious. "You'll be expected to do chores throughout the day, when your lessons are done, and once it's dark, you are to remain in your bedroom. No exceptions."

"Why?"

"Those are the rules." Caleb's voice took on a hard edge, warning the boy not to press the issue.

Liam held up his hands in mock surrender. "All right. Jeez."

They finished eating, all three of them working together to clear the table. Abigail rinsed the dishes in the sink, handing each one to Liam to load into the dishwasher. Caleb stood in the doorway, watching them as they worked.

"I've got some work to finish up in the office," he said.

He kissed Abigail on the forehead and gave Liam a salute. "I'll see you in the morning, Liam."

Caleb left the room, his heavy footsteps thumping against the stairs. Abigail dried her hands with a towel and tossed it onto the counter, sighing.

"You should probably go get cleaned up and make yourself comfortable upstairs."

"But it's barely six," Liam protested. "Can't I watch some television?"

"We'll see about getting you a TV for your bedroom. I'm sure there is an extra one in the basement. Not tonight, though." Abigail pointed out the window at the sun, which was beginning to hide behind the tree line.

"Fine," Liam huffed as he turned on his heels and exited the kitchen.

He didn't understand this new set of rules, and it pissed him off. No one else had ever had any problem with him being in the family room or anywhere else in the house after dark. He grumbled under his breath as he climbed the stairs, annoyed, walking through the upstairs hallway. The light from Caleb's office seeped from under the closed door. The light shifted from movement within the room, and Liam stopped in front of the door, straining his hearing to listen, his curiosity getting the better of him.

Caleb was on the phone—he could tell that much—but Liam couldn't make out the context of the conversation. Caleb spoke in fast, hushed tones. Liam inched closer to the door, and the floor creaked under his weight. He froze. Caleb went quiet, then the phone beeped. Caleb had ended his call. Liam heard Caleb walking toward the door and quick stepped down the hallway into the bathroom, flipping the light on. He was fussing with the towels when Caleb stepped through the bathroom doorway, arms crossed.

"What's up?" Liam asked.

Caleb ran his fingers through his hair and let his arms drop.

"Heard something outside my door. Just wanted to make sure you didn't need anything."

"Nope. Nope, I'm good." Liam forced a smile and laid a towel on the edge of the sink.

Liam squeezed himself between Caleb and the doorframe, out into the hallway and into his room. Once the door shut behind him, he let out a sigh of relief.

"Holy shit, that guy's scary," he mumbled to himself as he sifted through his clothes.

LIAM LAID IN bed, staring up at the ceiling. The scent of the newly laundered sheets mixed with the dust that had settled in the room conflicted and made his nose itchy, making it hard for him to fall asleep. He tossed and turned, listening to the house settling around him. He started to doze off but was jolted awake when he heard scratching from above him. It was the same sound he heard earlier in the day, but louder. Now alert, Liam focused on the noise, noticing that it didn't carry a pattern the way footsteps did.

The click of a door opening down the hall made Liam jump. He covered himself completely with the blanket and lay still, listening to footsteps approach his bedroom door. It opened with a creak, and Liam felt eyes on him as he lay there, trying to stay as still as possible. He waited until he heard the door latch shut again before sitting up. He stood, concentrating on the weight of his steps as he made his way to the bedroom door and pressed his ear against it.

Abigail and Caleb spoke in whispers, making their conversation difficult to hear. A creaking filled the silence, followed by a thump. *The attic.*

He heard them climb the steps, their footfalls loud against the thin attic floor. Liam cracked the door just enough to look into the hallway, and when the stench hit him, he gagged. The smell of rotten fruit and feces wafted in through the door's opening. He covered his mouth, muffling the sound of his coughing, and quickly closed the door again. Liam remained still, terrified to move at the risk of being heard.

"We don't have much time left, Abby," he heard Caleb say.

"We'll get everything together. Don't worry."

An agonizing moan pierced the air as the scratching grew increasingly louder. The sound gave Liam goosebumps.

"Shhh, now," Abigail cooed. "It's going to be okay."

The house went quiet until the sound of footsteps climbing back down the steps carried into the hallway. Liam jumped back into bed and covered himself up the way he had been when they checked on him before. He was surprised when they didn't come back into the room, certain they had heard him jump into the bed.

As he concentrated on every noise, he heard the shower turn on in the bathroom beside his room, and he tried to stop his body from shaking. Maybe there was a trapped animal up there that they had to take care of. That would explain the smell and the noises. He talked himself down with halfhearted explanations. His body aching from the tension, Liam let his mind relax and eventually, he drifted off while listening to the water run in the next room.

THE SMELL OF bacon roused Liam the following morning, causing his stomach to growl. Leaping out of bed, he dressed quickly and absent-mindedly reached to grab his phone off the top of the dresser. When he couldn't find it where he was sure he had left it the night before, he pulled the dresser from the wall and looked behind it. He only found cobwebs and dust. Frustrated, he shoved the dresser back into place. He stomped down the steps, his fists clenched at his side.

Abigail sat at the table, still in her pajamas, a plate of eggs and bacon in front of her. She had already made him a plate and placed it across the table from her before Liam stormed into the room.

"Where is it?" he growled.

"Where is what?" She didn't look up from her plate.

"You know what. My phone! Give me back my phone!"

"You'll get it back once I'm sure there isn't any harmful material on it."

Abigail stood and took her plate to the sink and washed her hands.

"Please. There isn't anything on it besides my music. It doesn't even have service, but I paid for it myself, and it's special to me. Please give it back," Liam begged, now almost in tears.

"What's the pin to unlock it?"

He paused. "1498."

Liam watched as Abigail pulled the phone from the pocket of her robe and punched the numbers in. He clenched his jaw until it hurt, his eyes never leaving her as she searched every application downloaded on the phone. Once she was finished, she stuck the phone back into her robe pocket.

"You can have it back once your chores for the day are finished. I made a list for you and pinned it to the fridge. I have to run to the grocery store, and once I'm back, I'll boot up the computer for your lessons."

She stormed off to get dressed, leaving Liam to collect himself. He took several deep breaths and went into the kitchen to review the list Abigail had left for him. First on the list was to move the TV from the basement to the bedroom, followed by putting the dishes away, taking out the trash, and dusting the bedroom.

He sighed as he pulled the list from the fridge and folded it up, placing it in his pocket. He sat down to eat his breakfast as Abigail was coming back down the stairs wearing a pair of black leggings and an oversized sweatshirt, her long hair pulled back into a ponytail.

"I'll be back after a bit." She didn't wait for a response before picking up her purse and walking out the door, locking it behind her.

Liam finished eating and emptied the dishwasher after taking a few minutes to figure out where everything went. He opened each door in the kitchen, assuming one of them had to be the basement. He found the right one and flipped the light on. As he thumped down the stairs, he kicked up dust as he went. In the far corner, on top of the work bench, was an old fat-back TV. Liam groaned at the sight of it, knowing it was going to be a pain to carry up both flights of stairs.

Noticing something covered in a tarp against the wall beside the bench, he peeked underneath, lifting the edge to keep from disturbing its placement. A white crib wrapped in plastic sat underneath. Liam shrugged his shoulders and lifted the TV up off the bench. He waddled toward the stairs, his pants creeping down his rear end. He made it halfway up the steps before having to stop and catch his breath.

By the time he made it to his bedroom, Liam's legs were wobbly and tired. He set the TV on top of the dresser and flopped down onto the bed. Laying back and shutting his eyes, he debated on whether he could fit in a nap before Abigail got back from the store.

A thump from above shook Liam from his dozing. He sat up with a start, his heart beating against his rib cage. Another thump, this time louder and more deliberate.

"Hello?" Liam called, his voice shaking. "Abigail?"

He walked out into the hallway and to the top of the stairs before calling out again.

"Abigail? Is that you? Caleb?"

He stood there, waiting for an answer, but the house remained silent. A series of loud pounding coming from the attic broke the silence, making Liam jump.

He reached a shaking hand up, grasped the rope that dangled from the ceiling, and pulled down the stairs. The smell of rot was overpowering as he forced himself to ascend the small steps.

Apprehensive, he stuck his head up through the attic door and looked around.

The floor was littered with blocks, rattles, and baby dolls, as well as a small fort that stood at the far end, partially hidden in the darkness. He pulled himself completely up into the creepy space and stepped toward the darkened corner. A loud moan raised the hairs on his arms as he continued forward.

"Hello?" he called.

The sound of something scooting across the floor made Liam want to run, but he stayed in place, frozen in fear. A figure appeared from the darkness, pulling itself along the dusty floor with disfigured limbs. It was thin, skin stretched across bone. Its elbows bent the wrong way, spider like and lanky. Its fingers were long and ended in sharp points. As it crawled forward, small, boneless legs dragged eerily against the floor behind it.

A scream raised up into Liam's throat as the thing looked up at him, its eyes sunken in their sockets, emanating an unnatural red glow.

"Hun…gry," it moaned.

Liam turned to run, a scream still stuck in his throat, when he slammed face-first into something solid. He fell back onto his butt with an "oof" and looked up, wide eyed.

"I see you've found the baby," Abigail said. "You found my Elvin."

"What? Baby?" Liam looked from the figure to Abigail, still trying to make sense of everything.

"I told you this space was off limits, yet here you are."

"I…I heard banging. I just wanted to check!" Liam excitedly tried to explain, backing away as Abigail walked toward him.

"Disobedient little shit," Abigail spat as she dug through her purse.

She pulled out a small plastic bag and opened it. Abigail quickly retrieved a rag from inside and leapt forward. Liam stood, making a run for the attic door. Jumping onto the boy's back, Abigail screamed as she tried to press the rag to Liam's face. They fell to the floor, wrestling as they rolled. The mangled figure, which seemed to be conjured up from the depths of hell, continued to pull itself closer to them as they fought.

"Momma…Hun…gry. Please, Momma," it begged.

Abigail rolled on top of Liam, her lips pulled back into a wild sneer as she overpowered him and pressed the rag hard against his face. Liam screamed and flailed as he saw the figure close in, its lips unnaturally slack and sagging away from its face, a low moan emitting from its rancid mouth as it swayed. It was so close, Liam could feel its breath, right before his vision went black.

LIAM WOKE TO pounding inside his head. He looked around the room, unable to tell where he was in the darkness. He reached to scratch his face, but his hand was met with resistance.

"What the fuck?" He tried to swallow his anxiety as he tested his bindings.

Liam craned his head, trying to make out shapes in the darkness. He kicked his feet and found they were also bound. He thrashed again, and something fell over with a loud clatter. Looking down, Liam saw white bars glowing against the darkness.

Basement. I'm in the basement. Despite the ache behind his eyes, Liam thrust and kicked against the rope.

"LET ME OUT OF HERE! HELP!" he screamed, rocking the work bench back and forth.

The basement light switched on, and two sets of hurried footsteps came down the stairs.

"Let. Me. Out!" Liam ordered.

"No can do, man," Caleb said, coming into view.

"I won't tell anyone. I'll run off and never come back. Please!"

"You're right about one thing," Abigail said from the bottom of the basement steps. "You won't tell anyone."

She carried Elvin, cradled in her arms. His lifeless legs hung over the crook of her elbow. Whimpering, he chewed on the bones that were his fingers with toothless gums.

"Wh...what is that?" Liam asked, nodding his head toward Elvin.

Caleb's brow creased. "That's our son."

"When Elvin was born, he died before we got to bring him home from the hospital. Complications, they said." Abigail explained the tragedy, bouncing Elvin as she spoke. "We pulled his body from the casket before burial and brought him home with us. We made a deal with the powers that be. They gave us Elvin back, the cost being our mortal souls."

"Except Elvin didn't come back the way we thought he would. He needs human blood and flesh to stay alive," Caleb interrupted. "We've tried substituting animal meat, and it just doesn't work. Our growing boy needs the suffering of the human soul laced in his meals."

Liam's eyes widened in fear.

"That's why you're here. It works best if death is prolonged. So don't worry; you're not going to die just yet."

Abigail leaned forward, holding Elvin out toward Liam. Elvin sucked his sagging lip in between his gums and vibrated with excitement as he got closer to Liam's wiggling fingers. Under the light of the basement's fluorescent bulbs, Elvin's clay-like complexion was more distinguishable.

Liam screamed as Elvin bit down on one of his fingers, his sharp gums severing it from his right hand. Warm wetness ran down the back of Liam's hand as he tugged at his restraints frantically, desperate to get loose.

Abigail pulled Elvin back against her bosom as he chewed and sucked happily on the finger in his mouth, blood running down his chin.

"We'll feed him what you can live without first. Fingers, toes, arms, and legs. Once those are gone, you'll have to die so that he can eat your organs and flesh," Caleb said nonchalantly.

"You people are insane," Liam hissed.

Caleb and Abigail shared a smile, and they nodded. Without another word, Abigail sat Elvin on the floor and sat on Liam's chest. Though she didn't weigh much, the pressure of panic and added weight made it hard for Liam to breathe. Caleb untied Liam's left hand and fought to keep it still as the boy flailed frantically. Caleb held a meat cleaver above his head and in one swift motion sliced the hand off at the wrist.

Liam screamed, the pain immense. The smell of cooked meat filled the room as Caleb cauterized the wound with a heated iron.

Sweat ran down the side of Liam's face as he lay there, exhausted from the exertion. Abigail hopped off his chest, scooping Elvin back into her arms. He had eaten the severed finger down to the bone, now sucking the marrow from the center noisily.

Liam sat up as much as the restraints allowed and threw up, most of it caking the front of Caleb's pants.

Caleb jumped back, cursing under his breath. "Are you sure we can't just kill him? He's pissing me off."

"Honey, you know we can't," Abigail scolded. To Liam, she said, "We'll be back after a while with some water for you. I hope you know this is nothing personal."

Liam spat at her, missing her and hitting the floor. She looked at the puddle of spit and shook her head before walking back up the stairs. Liam heard the basement door lock and began to cry. They hadn't secured his mutilated arm before leaving, and Liam wondered if that was intentional or not as he looked at the stump where his hand used to be.

"I've got to get out of here," he whispered to himself.

He curled his remaining hand into a fist and clenched it, despite the pain from his missing finger, as he tried to loosen the ropes. After two attempts, they loosened some, but it hurt too much to continue. Liam sighed and wiggled his hips, rocking the table underneath him.

He took a deep breath and prepared for impact before

throwing all his weight over to one side of the work bench, tossing it onto its side with a bang. The bench leg broke when it landed, freeing his hand. Liam ignored the pain in his ribs and hip as he undid the rope around his ankles and jumped to his feet.

He searched the area, hoping Caleb had forgotten something he could use as a weapon. He found nothing of use except the broken bench leg. Liam grabbed it and hid under the stairs just as Abigail and Caleb came running back down the steps to investigate.

Liam watched as they inspected the destroyed bench, anger etched across both their faces. Raising the wooden club above his head, he charged Caleb and slammed it down on the back of his head. Caleb fell to the floor, face first, with a thud.

"You asshole!" Abigail screamed.

Liam ran up the basement steps, stumbling as he made it to the top. Elvin lay on the living room floor, watching a movie that played on the television. Candles flickered on the coffee table. Abigail screamed as she scrambled up the basement steps behind him. Liam watched as Elvin tore flesh away from what once was his hand, chewing happily as cartoons lit up the television screen behind him. Before Liam knew it, Abigail had caught up to him, pushing him forward, slamming him into the coffee table. The candles spilled across the living room floor in different directions.

Abigail wrapped her hands around Liam's throat and squeezed, her thumbnails painfully digging into his neck. Her eyes bulged, bloodshot with rage as she worked to cut off his air supply. Liam swung his fist, landing a punch to her face. Her head snapped back from the blow, but she didn't let go. When she looked back down at Liam, blood began seeping from her nose.

Elvin, who was making his way toward them, screamed in terror at the sight of his mother's blood. The floor of the house began to shake and the cabinets in the kitchen opened and slammed shut on their own. Pictures flew off the walls, the glass shattering as they fell to the floor. Flames made their way across the carpet and up the side of the wooden entertainment center.

Abigail, distracted by the chaos around them, turned to calm

Elvin. Liam took the opportunity to twist his hips and pull himself out from under her, scrambling backward on his elbows. She grabbed and clawed at his leg as Liam made a break for the front door, pulling him back down to his knees. He kicked as hard as he could, his frantic movements causing him to miss several times before his heel landed a blow against her temple with a sickening crack. Abigail's eyes rolled into the back of her head as she fell to the floor. Her blank eyes, still open, stared up at him.

Elvin screamed, a sound so shrill and powerful that Liam thought his eardrums would burst. He covered his ears as the ceiling fell down around them.

The flames engulfed the couch and crept up the curtains, which curled under the heat like paper, bits of the fabric floating through the air. The heat was unbearable as smoke filled the crumbling house. Elvin's screams turned to growls as he grabbed Liam's legs with a powerful grip and quickly climbed his way up Liam's chest until they were face to face.

Liam, frozen by fear, could only gape as the creature spoke.

"You killed Momma…" it said, biting its own pointed index finger.

A small stream of glowing liquid flowed from the wound. He shoved it into Liam's open mouth and forced his lips closed around it. "You will suffer, as I have suffered. You will know my hunger; you will know my pain."

The room shook as a warmth spread through Liam. It felt like his veins were vibrating, alive beneath his skin. Panicked, Liam shoved Elvin off of him. Elvin's screams shattered the living room windows as flames engulfed his small frame. Liam turned and threw the front door open. The sunlight was blinding as he crossed the threshold. He could hear sirens as a set of powerful arms wrapped around his waist and pulled him back inside, a plume of smoke escaping as the door shut again.

CARRIE WATCHED FROM her office window as a man sat in the driver's seat of his car, his hand pressed against his chest as he leaned back in the seat. The sun had set, and the rest of the office was already empty. She grabbed her bag from underneath the desk and shut off the lights before locking the door and making her way outside.

From the stairs, she could hear the man gasping for air.

"Help me," he pleaded. His broad shoulders heaved in distress.

She searched the parking lot and saw no one else around. An uneasy feeling settled over her, but her concern won over.

"What's going on?" Her heels clicked against the pavement as she approached.

"I think I'm having a heart attack," he gasped.

As she got closer, she could see that he was heavily scarred, purple and pink overlapping peach-colored skin.

She stopped just outside his open car door. "Okay, hold on."

Carrie looked down and started to dig through her purse, searching for her phone.

Caleb jumped from his seat, a chloroform-soaked rag in hand, and grabbed Carrie by the arm, yanking her toward him. He pressed the rag against her face with force as the woman thrashed in his arms. Finally, she stilled, slumping against him. Caleb dragged her to the back of the car and unlocked the trunk. The burns on his upper body—which were still healing—ached as he threw Carrie into the trunk and slammed it shut, leaving her in darkness.

THE CABIN WAS dark when Caleb pulled into the driveway, gravel crunching beneath the tires. He looked around the campground, making sure he was alone before lifting Carrie from the trunk.

She groaned as he walked up the stairs, her arms dangling limply at her sides. Through clouded vision, she watched Caleb fumble with the keys and push the front door open.

The air was heavy as they entered the cabin; the smell of rotten food and copper overwhelmed her. Carrie coughed, and Caleb looked down at her.

"Oh good, you're awake," he said with a smile.

"If you're going to rape me, please kill me first," she begged, her voice a hoarse whisper.

"Don't flatter yourself." He laid her down on the floor and started to back away. "You serve a different purpose."

The sound of something being dragged across the floor behind her caught Carrie's attention. She turned her head, fighting to keep her eyes open. Crawling from the other side of the room was a boy, withered, skin and bone. Its eyes glowed against the darkness as it crawled toward her.

"Hu…ngry," Liam moaned as he grabbed Carrie's foot and pulled her shoe off.

Caleb sat cross-legged on the floor, listening to Carrie scream as Liam bit away her toes one by one.

"That's it, my boy. Eat up."

IT HAPPENED ON STATE STREET

Peter Rocha

HERE IS A STORY FLOATING around that I killed someone. Never mind the rumors about the parish priest at St. Charles and something about past misdeeds. Never mind the suddenly pregnant daughter of the Evangelical couple down the street or the actual, provable arrest of the sheriff's boy for aggravated burglary of the Braum's on Highway 66. I myself am aware of a little old lady, sweet as a honey badger, who carries around a duffle bag in lieu of a purse, filled with rope, bottled water, a lighter, and, of all things, a queen of hearts—not exactly the items one would need at church bingo. Okay, so she's my aunt on my mother's side, but that's a story I won't be telling.

Instead, all eyes are on me. This unwanted scrutiny started with, of all things, a bus ride. Yes, a bus ride.

I HADN'T RIDDEN the bus since grade school. Not much had changed in twenty years. The predawn March morning was wet and depressing. In addition to my POS car dying with a whimper last Saturday, I hadn't bothered to purchase an umbrella. Thus, my wet jacket, my wet hair, my Neanderthal odor and increasingly foul mood, and my need to utilize public transportation on this glorious Monday morning.

"Can I have ice cream, Mommy?"

Ice cream. Jesus.

The little voice came from a girl dressed in a pink jacket and blue jeans, a pink hood over her blond bangs. She looked eight or ten, but her blue eyes were zoned on me with an unsettling adult look. She seemed to be scanning me. She sat next to a faded woman, whom I assumed was her mother.

"Mommy, ice cream?"

"Yes, dear," the timid voice replied. The mother wore a black lace shawl over her gray head and sunken shoulders. She stared through vacant eyes at the opposite window, seemingly deadened by her own reflection.

As odd as the pair seemed, nobody out of the dozen or so occupants of the #1015 bus paid much attention to them.

"Look, he's holding a newspaper, Mommy." The little girl giggled. "He must not have internet."

Great. I'm being roasted by a ten-year-old girl.

The mother only appeared alive when the little girl—finally a little girl again—spoke.

"I'm glad I brought my parasol. Isn't it stupid not to have a parasol on a rainy day, Mommy?" She was glaring at me through the side of her eyes.

"Yes, dear."

A bag lady and a young man got off near the public library, and I was inclined to follow them.

"Mommy. Even though I had ice cream yesterday?"

"Yes, Nona."

"I hate that name." The little girl Nona growled the words.

She noticed I was startled by the suddenly unnatural sound of her voice. "You know I won't be too mad if you say no to ice cream." The little girl Nona feigned an innocent look, as if trying to prove that she was a good girl.

The mother looked down at her daughter and crossed herself.

"Mother, please don't." A gray filtered through Nona's face, and then she noticed me again. "Go ahead, Mommy. Do your thing."

The mother pulled the cord, and the little girl Nona stood in front of her and offered her hand. The two rose, the little girl leading them off the bus to God-knows-where.

I, for one, felt as if I had encountered a Dr. Seuss version of *The Exorcist*.

"IN THE NAME of the Father, and of the Son, and of the Holy Spirit—"

"—AMEN."

The thunder and rain seemed to answer along with the congregants of St. Charles Catholic Church. The torrential downpour proved an eerie soundtrack to the ancient Catholic rituals being performed. I always thought this church odd, with its circular construction and a hippie, risen Christ in lieu of the more traditional crucifix just behind the altar.

But who was I to pass judgment? I was what you might call a part-time Catholic, keeping one foot on base, so to speak, while many of the faithful ran around beating their brains trying to cross every "t" and dot every "i." I didn't always follow all the rules. Who could? But it was the religion of my elders, and I always seemed to rebound back toward what I knew. Here's hoping I'd be in one of my rebound cycles on my last, final day on earth.

I sat in the last of the pews that circled around the very rear of the church and along the aisle, trying to be as inconspicuous as possible. A few metal chairs lined the back wall on either side of the main entrance for those stragglers and late-comers or for those mothers blessed with uncooperative children.

We had gotten to the point in the ceremony of the "Sign of Peace," where one greeted those around with a "peace be with you." A growl from behind startled me. I instinctively looked for a wandering dog or puppy in the aisle. A wolf would have been a more welcome sight than the pair that I saw on the metal chairs instead: Nona, in a pink dress, with her faded mother.

I tried as best I could to concentrate on the Mass, but I could feel the steely-blue stare and the vacant gaze winding around the music, inserting itself between the responses. Between "amens" and "hallelujahs," Nona would grunt and even once squawked like a blue jay.

No one seemed to notice. No one turned a shoulder or raised a quizzical eyebrow.

At communion, the strange pair stayed behind, against the wall, while I followed the procession to the altar. Nona's eyes were like two blue stars burning on my shoulder blades. I searched for any kind of recognition of the situation from the priest as I approached for communion, but he seemed as blissfully nonchalant as the rest of the congregation.

"The Body of Christ, Max," Father Moran said as he placed the wafer on my palm.

"Amen."

When I returned to my pew, the mother was handing Nona her pink jacket and the parasol. The rain had not relented, nor had my uneasiness. For a moment, the mother met my eyes with hers. For a moment, she actually saw me, in my eyes, and for a brief second, her eyes pleaded with mine. Then it was gone, and the vacant stare returned.

After the last sign of the cross, signaling the end of the mass, mother and child followed the circular concourse around the inside of the church to the back entrance. While the congregation erupted in holy hymns, I noticed a folded piece of paper in the corner of the pew. I unfolded it. "Help" was written in a frantic font. I felt compelled to follow the pair. It was still raining heavily. I raised my umbrella (I finally wised up and bought one) and could see them heading east across the large parking lot, through a muddy patch between two sheds or garages, and finally through the back door of a two-story house.

I hesitated for a moment but followed behind, weaving through the cars of the parishioners. I reached the muddy patch and tried to leap from left to right, but my shoes became engulfed in mud, leaving deep tracks. I finally reached a sidewalk and stepped up the three stairs, rapping on the back door, which opened immediately. The mother, haggard and terrified, shoved a heavy paper bag into my midsection.

"Take your things. We don't want it," she whispered and slammed the door.

I knocked again, but all I could hear was a voice from inside: "We don't want it."

I THREW THE bag on the couch once I reached my apartment a few blocks away. I changed clothes and dried off. I was afraid of what was inside the bag. As irrational as it sounded, I kept picturing the end of the movie *Se7en*, when Brad Pitt's character was torn between looking or not looking in the box. It felt heavy enough to be a human head, although I couldn't say that I ever held one by itself.

I sat on the couch, and with a forceful jerk, I shook the contents loose from the bag. A very large hardback book bounced onto the couch. It appeared to be a library book of sorts, maybe retired from circulation. It had white tags around the lower part of the binding and the cover was slightly dog-eared. On the front, large words: *Codex Gigas*, and in parenthesis, "The Giant Book."

I set it on my lap. It was thick, six to eight inches at least, and large, twenty-four by twelve. The cover and binding was embossed in gold, and the pages were illustrated like the old medieval texts. The words were all in English, which seemed oddly out of place, considering the apparent age of the tome. It was the Bible, a translation thereof, but filled throughout and on nearly every page with ornate framing and calligraphic font. Gorgeous paintings from the Old and New Testaments littered the text. I thumbed through the book, looking for anything unusual, as if the book wasn't unusual in itself. I had never seen such imagery, even in Fantasy literature. These didn't have the fantastic realism of Dore wood engravings, nor quite the surrealism of a Dali, but something in between. I could picture a hermit or a monk, someone totally dedicated to the task at hand, forging by candlelight, this thing of beauty that survived the ages, just like the stories depicted: Genesis, the Psalms, the Maccabees, the Gospels.

I noticed that burn marks seemed to embrace the edges of a few of the final pages, so I turned to those to investigate. One page, in particular, seemed to have burn marks or black streaks radiating from the center of a blank illustration. Now by blank, I meant that the page was still ornately embroidered, but the thing that it embroidered was missing.

The *Codex Gigas*. Of course, my cell was dead, so no quick internet search. Nothing in my bookshelf touched on the matter, although I had plenty of books on medieval paintings, Chaucer criticisms, and various histories related to the Dark and Middle Ages. There was nothing in Aquinas or Origen to describe what I was more convinced was a haunted tome. Obviously, the book was a copy, probably purchased at a library book sale, among the many James Patterson and Nora Roberts paperbacks. If only the haggard mother from the church had bought a cookbook instead.

I stood at the sliding door of my second-story apartment. The rain was still heavy, and I could barely see the high school across the field behind my building. This was none of my business, this woman, this strange little girl, this Nona. It was made my business. Still, I could bury the book. I could leave it for some random high school kid to find, which could lead to an interesting horror story that didn't include me. I didn't want it. I had to get rid of it.

I noticed my cellphone had finally charged to a point where I could use it. Still, the browser wouldn't connect to the internet. So, I made a call instead.

"St. Charles rectory," an elderly woman answered.

"Yes, ma'am, I'd like to speak to Father Moran, please."

"Let me see if he's around. He usually goes to breakfast in between masses. Can I take a message? I can always make an appointment for you."

Damn it. "I could…but it's really important."

"Hold on a sec, okay?"

I expected elevator music, or a Gregorian chant while I was waiting. Two minutes felt like a year.

A gruff voice spoke: "Father Moran speaking."

"Father, this is Maximus Milliner, one of your parishioners."

"Yes, I remember you. Welcome back."

"I have a strange question for you."

"I may not have time for strange, Max. I have the basketball score for you, though." He laughed. "I do have another mass here in a few."

I blurted out before he could dismiss me. "Have you ever heard of a book called *Codex Gigas*?"

"*Codex…Gigas*? No. No, I don't believe I have. What is it—a novel? Dan Brown? James Rollins?"

Damn it. "No, it's a bible, of sorts. With embellished borders and ancient illustrations. Something like medieval script, like the monks used to make."

"Oh, yes, yes."

"Well, I've come into a copy of this book, and it all seems a bit strange, just the pictures or, in one instance, the lack thereof…"

"Why don't we make an appointment…"

"…I'm really in a quandary with this thing, Father." I swore

I could hear him shake his head.

"Mr. Milliner, let's make an appointment so we can discuss in more detail, okay? I don't see Doris around here, so call back and she'll arrange for a time on my calendar, okay?"

"Just one more thing, Father."

"Quickly, son."

"There's two parishioners I've never seen before. I know, I know. I've skipped mass the last few years, but last Sunday I saw a mother and her daughter at the back of the church."

"You must mean Ms. Porta and her daughter."

"The one who makes noises during mass."

"They're harmless, Mr. Milliner. We kinda let them do their thing."

I RECALL A theme running through the movie *Jumanji*, where one can hear the beating of the drums, which are a precursor to the supernatural events to come. The *Codex Gigas* had to go. The drums, so to speak, were beating in my head. On cue, the thunder rumbled across the afternoon sky and the rain seemed to come down harder than before. Nature was trying to leave me trapped in the apartment with super-nature.

I could always burn the book in the tub, but no doubt the seventh level of hell would rise up and swallow me whole, with Dante Alighieri clapping on the sideline. Besides, I had to know why this Miss Porta would give the book to me. What was wrong with it? And with her? I knew what I had to do. I rewrapped the book, grabbed my jacket and umbrella, and entered the elements.

At approximately two o'clock on this March Sunday afternoon, I entered the elements with the purpose of murdering a book, not a person. My apartment was across Fiftieth Street, just north of the St. Charles Church complex, which was situated between Grove Avenue on the west and State Street on the east. The rectory sat on the northwest corner of the complex, the circular church just behind it, and the long, L-shaped parochial school framed the south end. To the east of the Church was the large parking lot that served both the school and the church-goers. East, past the parking lot, stood the two-story house facing State Street. This was my destination.

I jaywalked across Fiftieth and headed south on State, a row of small homes to my left and an oblong grove of spruce on my right. The streetlights already glowed, a melancholic glow, and seemed to struggle against the feigned twilight of the heavy rain and the mountain range of dark clouds. The imaginary drums beat in my head, and I found myself mumbling gibberish about ghosts and goblins and the End of All Things. I also reminded myself not to renew my library card if I survived this strange ordeal.

The white house faced east on State Street, with two windows lit like yellow eyes in the rain. A front porch ran the width of the house, with a black railing and stone steps rising on the right-hand side. I took the steps, dropped my umbrella to the side, and beat the excess water from my jacket and pants with my hands.

I knocked.

The mother with long, gray hair and gray eyes answered the door.

I tried to remain calm. I really wanted to toss the book through the doorway like a grenade and run.

"Miss Porta? I believe I have something of yours."

From inside, I heard a man's voice: "Who the hell is it?"

"Is this a bad time?" I asked.

Miss Porta opened the door wider and motioned me in. I tried to hand her the parcel on my way in, but she turned away.

"You wouldn't mind putting your shoes in the corner there?" She pointed at a plastic mat with three or four pairs of shoes lined in a row. None seemed to be men's shoes. "And your coat on the coatrack, if you'd like."

I was standing in the living room. Ahead, I could see a well-lit, narrow kitchenette and a long, dark back room that led straight to the same back door that I had encountered earlier. A couch ran along the north wall of the living room with a lamplight on each side. Opposite the couch, two recliners and a coffee table stood, with a little blonde girl sitting on the chair closest to me. She wore a pink nightgown and pink slippers.

"Well, well, who brought the milliner? Have you wares to sell, milliner?" The innocent pitch of her voice contrasted with the sarcasm dripping from her words. It was the same adult look that had made me so uneasy on the bus.

"How do you know my name?" I asked.

"Have you come to do my mother, milliner? She sooooo needs to be done, and properly."

"Nona!" For once, the mother's face showed color.

The girl held out her hands and shrugged. "Fine, I'm going to my room. You two do your thing." Nona disappeared down a hallway to the left of the recliner.

"I'm sorry about that," the mother said. "All I can do is apologize. She really is a sweet little girl." She shook her head, and I could feel the grief emanating from her soul. "I need to show you something."

"Miss Porta…"

"My first name is Porta, Mister…?"

"Milliner. Max Milliner."

"Oh, okay, that's what Nona meant."

"How did she know my name?" I asked.

"She didn't, Mr. Milliner. She's making fun. Making a pun. A milliner is a man from the Middle Ages who made coverings for women's hair, especially for church-goers."

"Okay," I said, still puzzled. "Why would she know what a milliner is?"

"She loves books. She loves to read. Or it could be the demon with its ancient knowledge."

I didn't know how to answer, but she did notice the look of incredulity on my face.

"I need to show you something, Mr. Milliner," she continued. "Bring your shoes."

How about taking this damn book first?

I followed her through the narrow kitchen, to the back room, and out the back door. The torrents had finally slowed to a sputtering. A floodlight attached high up on the second story lit the small sidewalk and the massive patch of mud. Across the mud, I could see the parking lot and, in the distance, the back of the church.

I followed to the end of the walk, about fifty feet from the house, and she stopped and pointed at a spot in the center of the mud.

"Do you see that?"

"Yes."

"Tell me that's not a hoof print."

"A hoof print?"

"Yes. A single hoof print. Not four. Not two. One print."

The marking was in the center of a fifteen-yard circumference of smooth, shiny mud. I could see no other markings leading to or from the print.

"Now, Mr. Milliner," she said, almost in a whisper, "this is the same mud that we tracked through when we came home from church this morning, the same mud that you tracked when you followed us."

This made no sense.

"It's here, Mr. Milliner. He's here."

"Who, Miss…Porta?"

"Satan, of course, Mr. Milliner."

Lightning split the sky, and thunder like a thousand diesels rumbled over us. I squinted to get a better look at the print. Sure enough, it looked like a goat print, a cloven clue of God-knows-what.

"We need to talk about the book, Mr. Milliner."

Finally.

"Let's get inside before the sky falls," I said, and to me, at that moment, this was a literal fear. I followed her back into the house, and she offered me a seat in the living room.

"Have you plugged her yet?" growled a man's voice from the other room.

Porta shook her head, tears welling up in her eyes. "I don't know how much more I can take, Mr. Milliner."

"Is there a Mr. Porta back there? Are you in danger? Do I need to call someone?"

"There is no 'Mr. Porta.' Porta is my first name, Mr. Milliner. And there is no man in the other room. That voice you hear is Nona."

THE LIVING ROOM was decorated like a Catholic church. In one corner, by the front window, a two-or three-foot statue of the Virgin Mary, hands folded at her breast and pointing to the heavens, stood watch over the room. A vase of fresh white lilies stood before the statue and contrasted sharply with the dark ambience I felt enclosing on me. On the wall above the recliners were framed pictures of the Sacred Heart of Jesus and Our Lady of Mount Carmel. The coffee table was covered with pamphlets on confession and a book concerning the Three Days of Darkness. Holy votive candles flickered in every corner, on every end table. A tall bookshelf, filled with old volumes of hagiography, anchored the wall next to the kitchen doorway. No TV, no radio, no computer, none that were visible anyway.

"I'd like to leave," I said. I was calm. I didn't stand up suddenly or make any abrupt movements. It was a statement of fact. "I'd like to give this book back to you and leave."

"I need your help, Mr. Milliner." Her eyes pleaded. She wrung her fragile hands together, so tightly that I thought her fingers would snap like twigs.

On cue, the clouds opened up, and the rain sounded like bullets on the roof. At this point, getting shot seemed preferable.

"I need your help. Nona needs your help."

"Ma'am, I'm not a priest. It looks like you may need a priest."

"I know."

"I don't know what you think I can do. I'm not trained in these matters."

"You are a Catholic, Mr. Milliner? I saw you at mass."

"Yes, I am, but that doesn't mean…"

"It means you might have some sort of understanding of what's going on here," she said. "You might have some acknowledgement that these things can happen."

"These things?"

"Possession, Mr. Milliner."

"Possession. Have you talked to Father Moran about this?"

Porta laughed, and it made me uncomfortable. Laughter didn't suit her.

"Have you ever talked to Father Moran, Mr. Milliner? Does he seem concerned about anything other than Sooners' basketball or football?"

She had a point. I rose and retrieved the paper parcel that I had left leaning against the wall by the front door. I sat down again and pulled the heavy tome from the bag.

"Tell me," I said, "what this is."

"Woman," a voice growled from the other room. "I'm hungry."

"Mommy, Mommy, we're hungry," this time in Nona's little girl voice.

"She's going to kill me, Mr. Milliner," Porta said as she made her way to the kitchen. She opened a cabinet and pulled out a sleeve of butter crackers. "I'll be back."

I followed her, without her permission, down the hallway and into Nona's bedroom. Porta was reaching the crackers up the wall, where Nona was inexplicably sitting, her legs crossed, no support, her back leaning on the upper wall as if she were hanging on a hook.

"Oh no," Nona snarled. "We mustn't scare the innocent little milliner out of his wits now, should we?" She floated down, her bare feet finally touching the floor. "You like my posters? Gabe?"

Nona had her walls plastered with posters of cartoons, animated trolls, kids' movies, all hung upside down, as if I were standing on the ceiling.

"You like what we've done with the place, Mr. President?" she asked in her most innocent voice. "Is it your birthday?"

Porta responded as if this were a typical day. "Nona, I brought crackers."

"Thank you, Mommy. What a good mommy, bringing me crackers and a man. I love snacks. Such a good mommy."

I retreated into the living room, and every instinct I possessed urged me to run.

Porta soon followed, her face ashen, her skinny frame slumped in resignation. For all the empathy I felt for her, she was as much a mystery to me as the demon-child in the next room. What had she exposed her child to? What had she exposed herself to that infiltrated her little girl? She sat on the couch, crossed her legs, and folded her bony hands in the lap of her long skirt. I sat in one of the recliners, keeping constant eye contact with her. We sat in silence for a few moments.

"She's my little girl, Mr. Milliner," she finally said. "I'd do anything for her."

"Why me, Porta?" I said. "I'm not a priest. And I am far, far from a saint."

"But you saw us. I mean you really saw us. Everyone silently acknowledges that Nona has a problem, but no one wants to help. No one can help."

"Including me." I rose, slipped on my shoes and my jacket, and walked out the front door.

THE RAIN WAS the forty-days-and-forty-nights variety. I stood on the front porch on State Street and tried to process what had happened in the last few hours. I was rid of the book, finally. Finally. I could return to my normal life. But my normal life of what? Part-time Catholicism? Daily jogs around the lake? Ogling sun-bathers? My normal life of movie-watching and failed attempts at journal-writing?

A scream from inside the house interrupted my thoughts. I rushed back in. Nona was on the floor, on her back, and Porta was kneeling over her, sobbing heavily. I scooped up the little girl and laid her on the couch.

"Porta, what happened?"

"She walked in and saw it," she said. I didn't understand. "She saw it." She nodded toward the recliner I had been sitting on, the *Codex Gigas* leaning against its legs.

"She saw the book?" I asked. "This made her faint?" The idea of the growling, man-like yet girl-like Nona fainting was ludicrous to me.

Porta retreated to the kitchen, presumably for a cool, damp rag, while I lifted the book to my lap and thumbed through the pages until I reached the second to the last page—the missing illustration.

The page didn't seem to fit with the rest of the book. The burn marks looked like spider webs around the edges, like something had burned its way off the paper. Like something was burning its way into my soul.

"Well, well," Nona said.

"Sit up, child," Porta said. "I brought a damp cloth and a cup of water. Here, this will help."

Nona sat up and sipped the water. I searched her eyes, hoping to identify which personality would manifest itself. I would soon find out.

"Ah, the mule is here," she hissed. "For more muling, I suppose. Are you here to mule, muling milliner?"

She studied me, outlining me with her eyes, as if trying to find a weakness, an opening. Her mouth curled into a snicker.

"You're afraid to die. I can tell," she said.

"Why do you say that?"

"Oh, the running, the screaming."

"I wasn't screaming, and I wasn't running," I said.

"You were. In your soul. The sweet, sweet music of the scared soul." Nona turned to her mother. "Sit down, woman."

Porta hesitated.

Nona growled: "I said SIT DOWN, WOMAN."

The sudden manliness of the little girl startled Porta, even at this point, so she sat in the recliner next to me and pulled a rosary from deep within her skirt. She started whispering the ancient prayers to herself.

"You're no priest, milliner...you're no priest, milliner, milliner..."

"I never said I was a priest. I'm just a guy."

Nona shook her head slowly. "Oh, just a guy, just a guy. I don't think you're just a guy. You don't think that, do you? Guy?"

"Who are you?"

An innocent voice: "I'm Nona."

"Who are you, really?"

"You can't pronounce it." Thunder rolled across the sky. "You hear that? That is my name." She pointed toward her mother. "You smell that? That fear? That smell is my name." Nona opened her mouth, and a cackle rose from her throat, from deep inside her diaphragm, rippling through the house. "You see that, milliner? Guy? Non-priest? I know what's in your heart."

"You know nothing of me, little girl."

"Nona, Nina, Nana, Nona isn't speaking to you. 'Blessed are the pure of heart, for they shall see God.' That isn't you, is it...guy? You're seeing something different altogether, now, aren't you…guy?"

Anger started rising inside me, and I tried to suppress it, suppress the memories of my past deeds, all those seedy moments in the dark. I tried to make sense of the situation before me. *She's a little girl. Something is in her. This isn't her.*

"Oh, you dirty, dirty milliner," Nona continued. "Have you done her yet? Why haven't you done her? Can't you see she needs it, you selfish, dirty guy? Whatever happened to charity? What ever happened to treating others as you treat yourself? And you have treated yourself, haven't you? Much, too much self-treating for you."

Before I could reply, Nona redirected toward her mother.

"Mommy, can I have ice cream?" in her most innocent voice.

"Talk to me," I told her firmly.

"Fuck you," she growled at me, and then her voice flipped again. "Mommy, ice cream?"

"Not right now, honey." Porta's voice was weak. "Talk to Mr. Milliner."

"I hate you, Mommy," in a little girl inflection, almost singing. "I hate you. I hate you. I hate you."

Porta continued with her whispered prayers. Nona, or the thing inside her, glared at the frail woman.

"Mumbling," Nona said. "Always mumbling. Why do you mumble, Mumbles? You know those petty little words don't help you or me or anyone else. Mumbles mumbling and mules muling. I think I'll call you Mumbles instead of Mother. Always mumbling. Would you like to see a trick, non-priest? She's right there. Her name is Mumbles."

"Nona!" I yelled. "STOP."

"Oh, I see. I see…guy." Nona's voice became timid. "Not the trick you want? You have your dirty eyes on sweet little Nona?"

I balled my fists.

"Well, well. You going to strike me, milliner? You going to strike me and take me? Is that your thing? That's your thing, isn't it? To slap me in my sweet little mouth. You want to see a trick?"

Nona stood on the couch and leaned her back flush against the wall. Slowly, like a snake, she slid up the wall, facing us, and stopped just before her head touched the ceiling. She slid her nightgown down her body and tossed it toward me, leaving her in her underwear. She crossed her bare feet, one over the other, and extended her arms against the wall.

"Who am I?" she said. "Who am I? Mumbles, you should know this one. Non-priest, you ought to know this one, too."

"Nona, please come down from there!" Porta rushed to her daughter in a frenzy and stood on the couch, reaching at Nona's bare legs and trying in vain to pull her from the wall. Nona kicked with both feet and knocked Porta off the couch. The back of the frail mother's head slammed into the coffee table, scattering the holy literature across the room, and she went limp on the floor.

Nona's cackle filled the living room. She kicked her feet against the wall.

I could contain my anger no longer. This was no little girl. I grabbed the *Codex Gigas*, the largest item I could use as a weapon, and approached Nona. She saw the book, and her demeanor suddenly transformed into a sniveling little girl.

"No, not that book! I thought that book was destroyed." She slid down the wall and attempted to flee through the kitchen. "Porta, you bitch! You said you got rid of it! Porta, you..."

I caught up to her and swung the book as hard as I could. I felt the book slam into the frame of the kitchen doorway, the force of the swing lifting me off my feet and onto the kitchen tile. I rolled over onto my stomach and looked for the girl. She was gone. I had seen the book as it was about to contact her right ear. But no girl. I could see a large divot in the doorframe where my swing had landed. The *Codex Gigas* was on the floor, opened to the second to the last page of the book. But the empty illustration wasn't empty anymore. Nona was there, with her blonde hair and impossibly blue eyes, two horns on her head, her forked tongue reaching out like a snake's, her lower body morphed into a single goat's leg with a single goat's hoof, covered in mud.

THE POLICE DIDN'T believe my story. Who, in their right mind, would? Porta was dead. The fall against the coffee table saw to that. There was no proof that I had anything to do with her death, except for the fact that I was there when she died—excuse me— was murdered. The police knew this.

They pried me about the missing girl. I told them the truth. Open the book. Open the book. But don't leave it open too long. Let her do her thing. And don't let the demon child crawl out and into your life.

NEVER HAVE I EVER

Red Lagoe

AN APP APPEARED ON MERCEDES' phone that she'd never seen before. It was an image of a finger pressed to red lips.

"What the hell is this?" she asked. "Tara, did you download an app to my phone?"

Her daughter Tara paused on the stairway, glancing over her shoulder from behind long red hair, a buried history emblazoned in those fiery strands. "Really? Why would I download an app to your phone?"

Mercedes forged a smile for her two book club friends who were by the kitchen island, well within earshot of her daughter.

"All right, Sweetheart. Just checking." A brown curl dangled over Mercedes' eyebrow. She tucked it neatly back into place behind a bobby pin. Tara kept her course upstairs.

Smooth red wine touched Mercedes' lips as she pulled a sip from her crystal stemware. "Does your daughter still give you attitude like this?" she asked Kim.

Kim flipped a page in *Tales of Karma*, this month's book club selection. Typical of Kim to come unprepared for the book club discussion. She carefully plumped her thick black curls, which were held back from her face with a wide blue band. "Hell yes. Why do you think I drink so damn much? Kids." She huffed. "You'd think growing up and going away to college would make them appreciate their parents a little more, but no. Sadie is still a hormonal little bitch."

Mercedes gave a polite chuckle, disgusted with Kim's blatant belligerence toward her own daughter. Social etiquette wasn't something Kim seemed to understand all too well.

Kim sipped her Syrah. "At least she got over that Wiccan phase, or whatever that was."

Mercedes nodded with approval, swiping her eyebrow again for a lock of hair she was certain had fallen, but every strand was in place. "Ridiculous…all that witchcraft nonsense. Good thing it was just a phase."

"So much sage." Kim laughed. "The house stunk of it for two years. Spell books and such… So, Tara is done with all that witchy stuff, too?"

"Absolutely," Mercedes said. But the truth—conversations with Tara were scarce since the accident. After Mike died, Tara graduated high school, spent the summer sulking in her bedroom with her herbs and crystals and whatever she thought would bring back her dad. She barely spoke a word to Mercedes. She needed space. Time to process. Before Mercedes knew it, Tara was gone—moved into the dorms. Tara had been avoiding the house, likely because she couldn't handle her father's absence.

The big, suburban, loving home transformed into a cold, empty nest in which Mercedes spent far too much time alone with her thoughts. Book club was a nice break from the horrific silence. Today was the first time she'd seen Tara in months. Most college co-eds were out partying with friends for spring break, but Mercedes found hope in the fact that her daughter chose to come home. Back to Mom, where she belonged.

The lights over the kitchen island dimmed, muting the

carefully selected colors of the charcuterie board. Mercedes had scoured Pinterest for the most visually stunning, yet simple, arrangements of meats and cheeses for her book club meeting. The island became an oasis of Havarti and Camembert, summer sausage, prosciutto, fruits, and wines. Mercedes would force a sense of normalcy back into her home through Martha-Stewart-approved entertaining. After Mike's death, she owed it to herself. And to her daughter.

The bulbs in the shabby-chic overhead lights fought to return to their warm, bright glow.

"Was that a brown out?" Janelle, a forty-year-old blonde bombshell, clutched her gold cross. It dangled in the cleavage of her proudly showcased new breasts. Breasts that she kept concealed beneath a conservative blouse when she volunteered full-time with the children's hospital. But every other moment of the day, she had them oiled and displayed like trophies.

White light flashed through the windows, lighting up Janelle's porcelain-pale skin. A second later, a sharp crack of thunder.

Janelle's shriek rolled into laughter. "Sweet Baby Jesus, that scared me."

Another explosive bang pierced the night, shaking the house. Janelle kept her hand tight against her chest as if the rumble might bounce her breasts right off her body.

"I think a transformer blew." Mercedes glared out the window. Streetlamps snuffed out. Torrential rain hammered at the glass while the lights in Mercedes' home dimmed again. "I don't think anyone else is coming out in this weather. It might just be the three of us."

"I didn't know it was going to storm," Janelle said.

A vibration alerted Mercedes back to her phone. The mysterious new app icon blinked. Mercedes clicked, and the screen went black. "Shoot," she said underneath her breath.

"What's wrong?" Kim hovered her plump fingers above the charcuterie board like an alien craft carefully selecting its abductee. Manicured, long purple nails descended for a mini sausage link.

Mercedes set down her wine. "There's a weird app on my phone and when I clicked it—"

"Don't click it!" Kim said. "It could be a virus or something."

"Too late." Mercedes shook her phone, and the blackened screen lit up with red letters reading: Never Have I Ever...a Game of Truth & Consequence.

Janelle lingered over Mercedes' shoulder, reading the title aloud. "Ooh, I remember that game."

"Never Have I Ever?" Kim nearly blushed. "That drinking game fucks me up."

Janelle pursed her lips. "Well, if you weren't such a slut, it wouldn't."

Kim's passion pink lips slid into a slippery smile. "Those days are over. I'm a married woman now. A happily married woman."

Happily, my ass. Mercedes had invited Kim's spouse to book club countless times, but Kim never brought her. Kim claimed her wife didn't enjoy reading, but Mercedes—and everyone, for that matter—knew it was because Kim loved being away from her. Every chance Kim would get to take a conference trip out of town, she was there, leaving her wife of eight years at home.

"Oh, you know I'm just kidding about the slut thing," Janelle said. "Golly, I haven't played that game in about twenty years."

"Golly." Kim rolled her eyes.

Janelle raised her eyebrows. "But it's not really a drinking game, you know. You hold up ten fingers." Janelle's French manicured nails all went up. "If you've committed the never-have-I-ever act, then you drop a finger. First one out of fingers loses—"

"Or wins." Kim looked to Mercedes. "Our girls used to play like that. With fingers instead of booze."

"Shall we start book club with just the three of us?" Mercedes asked.

"I kind of want to play Never Have I Ever," Kim said.

Janelle nodded, blushing. "We really don't know each other all that well, now do we? This could be fun."

Mercedes' screen bled from a black background into a deep ocean blue. White lettering appeared. RULES:

"Are you serious?" Mercedes let out a sigh and grabbed her glass of wine, caving to her guests' request. "Let's go sit in the den."

Once the charcuterie board and wine had been moved to the coffee table, Mercedes cozied into the worn-leather Lazy-Boy. She hated the thing but couldn't bring herself to get rid of it, even if it reminded her of her beloved husband. Sometimes when she sat there, it was as if she could still feel his presence. And that was enough for her to be certain that he had forgiven her for what she had done.

Janelle and Kim sat side by side on the sofa. Seasonal pillows with a daffodil design accented the white Italian leather.

Mercedes read the rules from the screen aloud: "Never Have I Ever is a game of truth and consequences. You'd rather die than reveal your most guarded truths…"

Mercedes tensed, as if the game had outed her. She would rather die than tell anyone about the things she had done. Lights flickered, and the windows went black. A baritone groan—like the sound of a massive sinking ship—seemed to squeeze the walls of the house.

It fell silent.

"Was that thunder?" Janelle asked.

Mercedes maintained her posture and shrugged. She looked back to the screen.

"…so, you must allow the other players to reveal your truths. If you do not, you lose."

"What the hell does that mean?" Kim asked.

"Maybe if you lie, you're out of the game?" Janelle's face twisted in confusion.

"Each player starts with ten counters. On a player's turn, the player states, 'Never have I ever…' and then a statement that is true for the player. If the statement is false for any of the other players, the player for whom the statement is false will lose a counter. The game ends when a player is out of counters OR when all players' most guarded secrets have been revealed."

"How do we know if our most guarded secrets have been revealed?" Janelle asked.

"Who cares?" Kim sat forward on the couch. "It's obvious some preteen made this game and didn't think it through. Let's just play. Fuck the point system, though. This needs to be a drinking game."

Mercedes shook her head. "I haven't played a drinking game since college."

"Me neither!" Kim rubbed her hands together. "Let's do this."

"With a thirty-dollar bottle of Syrah?" Mercedes asked.

A play button appeared on the screen. Mercedes tapped it, and three vertically stacked profile photos replaced it—the social media profile pictures for each of the women. Kim's on top, followed by Mercedes, then Janelle on the bottom.

"What the hell?" Mercedes set the phone on the coffee table and slid it toward her friends. "I think I've been hacked or something. How does it have our pictures?"

Janelle shrugged. "That's how these apps work nowadays. You agree to play, and they get access to your social media stuff. No biggie."

Kim shook her head. "How the hell did it know we are playing?" She pointed a thumb between herself and Janelle.

"Hey, Tara!" Mercedes shouted over her shoulder toward the foyer, hoping her daughter would hear and come downstairs. If anyone would know, it'd be her. That kid loved computers. She did advanced coursework in high school, which allowed her to graduate with certification in cyber security. Even went on to study it in college. "Tara, sweetheart! Can you help us with something?"

"Technology is crazy," Kim said. "Alexa is always listening. These apps get info that way, I bet."

"Maybe." Mercedes was not entirely convinced. It didn't make sense that the app was on her phone at all. How the hell did it get there?

"Look! My picture is glowing." Kim twisted the phone to get a better look. Below her avatar were the words "Never have I ever..." "Never have I ever..." Kim licked her lips and looked to the ceiling as if the perfect statement would materialize up there. "...finished reading any of the books for book club."

"So, anyone who has finished the books for book club..." Janelle shifted her eyes and held up all her fingers, "...must drop a finger."

"Put your damn hands down, Janelle," Kim said. "This is the drinking game version. If you've finished a book for book club, then take a drink. If you haven't finished a book, then you're safe."

Mercedes lifted the glass of red to her lips and sipped. "Neither of you have ever finished a book for book club? Shame on you." How was Mercedes supposed to host the monthly book club and admit that she had not finished reading the selected material? Kim and Janelle may have had the personalities to get away with that kind of behavior, but not Mercedes. She had an image to uphold.

On the phone, alongside each picture, were ten counters. Vertical lines—five to the left and five to the right of each woman's avatar. Mercedes clicked on a line, but nothing happened. "How do I make a counter go away?"

Janelle scooted to the edge of the couch to get a better look. "Whatever. We'll just keep track on our fingers."

"We're not playing with our fingers, Janelle. Or the counters." Kim's irritation bled through. "Mercedes, you're up."

"Okay. Let's step it up a notch, eh?" Mercedes eyed her opponents as her avatar's glow pulsed. "Never have I ever...had a one night stand."

"What?" Kim laughed. "You've never had a one-night stand?"

The statement was true. Mercedes met Mike when she was in college. She'd had other partners prior to Mike, but never for only one night. "I was with Mike for twenty years."

"There's no way you—" A chunk of summer sausage

dropped from Kim's hand to the floor.

The prospect of the grease staining the carpet had Mercedes on her knees in a fraction of a second.

A shrill screech. Kim cradled her right hand. Blood pooled in her left palm. It overflowed to the floor, seeped into the carpet's white fibers. Between Kim's feet, instead of a fallen sausage, laid a plump, severed finger with purple nails. Kim's finger.

Janelle's shrieks joined Kim's. Mercedes leapt to her feet, knocking against the coffee table and spilling her wine.

There goes the carpet. She pushed the shallow thought out of her head while she rushed to the kitchen for a hand towel.

A cacophony of screams echoed off the walls. Mercedes charged into the den and threw a blue and white checkered hand towel onto Kim's hands. Before the towel concealed the gore, Mercedes caught a glimpse of what appeared to be a surgically precise excision through the pointer finger, right above the knuckle.

Kim's eyes were wide and desperate, confused as hell, as Mercedes pressed the towel against her hand.

"What happened?" Mercedes squeezed.

Kim's face drained of color into a pallid, sickly blue. Her scream turned to a stuttering sob as her lungs emptied.

"Stay with me, Kim," Mercedes said.

Janelle backed toward the kitchen, each step in rhythm with her pulsating screams.

"Shut up and dial 911, Janelle!" Mercedes stood over Kim, applying pressure while blood dripped to the floor.

Kim's eyes crossed. Losing consciousness, she collapsed to her side, head thumping against the arm of the couch.

"It doesn't make sense. What happened?"

Janelle dug into her purse for a phone. Tears dragged black mascara down her cheeks. "Maybe there was something sharp in the meat platter. The knife?" Janelle tapped at her phone.

"That little cheese knife?" Mercedes kept a hand on Kim. Warm blood soaked through the towel and contacted Mercedes' skin. She cringed.

On the charcuterie board sat a two-inch dull blade, marred only by remnant smears of soft cheeses. No blood. Even if she had sliced her finger with it, there was no way it could lop off the entire digit.

A million medical conditions flew through Mercedes mind, from gangrene to leprosy to diabetes—people could lose their legs with diabetes, right? It was all outrageous. Nothing about this was medically explicable.

Janelle tapped at her phone with violent urgency. "I can't call out. The emergency thing isn't even working."

"Go get help, then!" Mercedes folded up the corners of the hand towel to add extra layers to the makeshift bandage. With her other hand, she gripped Kim's wrist as tight as she could to reduce blood flow. "Tara!"

No response.

Mercedes' heart thrashed wildly within her ribcage as Janelle ran from one end of the house to the other.

"What the hell are you doing?"

"I can't get out. The door won't open." Janelle dashed through the kitchen toward the back door, heels clicking across tiled floor. "Everything is black out there. It's all black!"

Moron. Mercedes released her hand from tourniquet-duty on Kim's wrist and reached for her phone on the coffee table. With one hand still applying pressure to Kim's towel, she tried to exit the game. The screen wouldn't diminish. A yellow glow around Janelle's avatar undulated to the beat of Kim's weakening pulse.

"Kim?" Mercedes whispered. "Please wake up."

Eyes as blank as a deer in headlights, Janelle ran back into the den.

"Grab another towel. In the kitchen. The stack of cheesecloths," Mercedes said.

Janelle did as instructed and brought a clean cloth.

"Go in the bathroom. Under the sink, there's a first-aid kit. Get it." Mercedes forced herself to remain as collected as possible.

Blood oozed from Kim's nub as Mercedes replaced the blood-soaked hand towel with the fresh white cloth. Gauze and medical tape held it in place. The bleeding gradually slowed.

She released Kim's hand and checked her pulse—slow, but strong. Mercedes dropped to her knees beside the couch. A blood-drained severed finger sat at the edge of a massive crimson stain. The thing was so damn surreal laying on the floor. Like an anatomical model of a finger had been stolen right out of a doctor's office and dropped into Mercedes' perfect home. Bone and skin cut with impossibly clean edges. Without even a splinter of bone jutting out or a jagged tear of skin. Sawed through with surgical precision.

The carpet was drenched with blood, clots clinging to the fibers. Reminiscent of the day Mercedes so often tried not to think about. She'd been young and dumb. Blood and placenta had seeped into the linoleum cracks of the RV's floor. Tears poured down her face. A newborn baby screamed in the bed, while another baby lay stillborn in her arms. She had been wretched in pain so horrific she wished death would come swoop her away. Mercedes raked the memory out of her mind, swept it beneath the blood-soaked carpet where she didn't have to see it.

While bagging Kim's finger and putting it on ice (that's what you're supposed to do, right?), she tried restarting her phone. The screen defied her.

"Tara!" Mercedes ran to the base of the steps in the foyer. Instead of a pale grey wall with photographs leading up a stairway to the second floor, there was a blackness. An impossible, dark chasm. With trepidation, she edged up the steps, but where the light stopped, she couldn't get through. A black wall of nothingness blocked her path.

"What is happening?" she whispered through dry lips. Mercedes yelled for her daughter, but her voice echoed off the black barrier and pushed Mercedes back down the stairs.

The house was shut tight. Windows blackened. The doors jammed. Beyond the exits was that black nothingness holding her hostage.

"What the fuck is happening?" Mercedes smashed a chair into the foyer window, but it bounced back. Trapped.

"Mercedes! Kim is waking up." Janelle sat with Kim on the couch, fingers rubbing her cross pendant.

Once Kim woke, Mercedes dosed her with some Vicodin to help with the pain. She explained everything. How they couldn't reach the outside world. How they couldn't get upstairs to reach Tara. How they couldn't make a phone call out.

"I don't even know if my daughter is all right up there." Mercedes' eyes filled with tears. "I don't know what to do...I always know what to do."

Her phone buzzed on the table. The screen flashed blue with a countdown clock ticking away in the upper right corner above their avatars.

A pop-up message warned, "The clock is ticking. All truths must be revealed before time is up or game over."

Twenty-eight minutes remained, and one of the vertical lines to the right of Kim's avatar had disappeared.

A wave of nausea slid through Mercedes. All three of the women stared at the phone as she set it on the coffee table. A collective realization.

"That's not possible," Janelle said.

"No shit." Mercedes topped off a glass of Syrah. "She lost a counter. Kim's fucking finger." Mercedes steadied her shaking body and handed Kim the glass. "For the pain."

Kim accepted it, trembling.

Mercedes brushed her curl off her face and back beneath the bobby pin.

"So that means Kim had a one-night stand?" Janelle asked.

"Jesus, you're fucking dim," Kim snapped. "Not exactly something we need to discuss."

Janelle hung her head. "Well, how come nothing happened to Mercedes when you said the thing about finishing the book?"

"Because I lied." Mercedes crossed her arms. "I've always

hated this game."

Janelle let out a deep sigh. "Never have I ever—"

"Whoa!" Mercedes held out her hands. "What are you doing?"

"We have to finish or game over," Janelle said.

"What does game over mean?" Kim's face drooped, her eyelids heavy.

"Never have I ever," Janelle continued, "gone to the moon."

Mercedes released a held breath. "Nice, Janelle. But we need a plan. We can't just ask questions until time runs out, can we?"

"Why not?" Janelle asked.

"We need to know where this came from. We need Tara."

"Mom, what's going on down here?" Tara asked from the foyer, looking into the den.

TARA EXPLAINED THAT she had passed through from upstairs without noticing the barrier. But she couldn't get back to the second floor, nor could she get out of the house, like the rest of them. Perhaps whatever was keeping them in was only a one-way barrier. Which meant emergency workers could get inside, potentially, if Mercedes could find a way to get contact to the outside world. Maybe there was hope. Mercedes filled Tara in as quickly as possible about the app. About the finger. As insane as it sounded, her daughter listened intently.

The game wouldn't shut off, not even when Tara pulled the battery out of the back of the phone. That little countdown clock kept ticking away. Twenty minutes remained.

"You guys keep playing…just in case." Tara opened a laptop at the kitchen island and went to work on trying to get a connection to the outside world.

"Keep playing? In case of what?" Kim set down her wine

glass, her hand shaking violently.

"So, we play with ridiculous 'gone to the moon' statements until Tara can call for help?" Mercedes said.

A terrible plan, but it was the best plan they had.

Kim's avatar glowed. "Okay. Something safe. Something impossible." Kim shrugged. "Never have I ever…murdered someone."

Mercedes' heart plummeted to her gut. Of all the fucking things to say.

She sprinted to the kitchen sink, locking her fingers together. A sharp sting to her left ring finger. A papercut kind of pain that grew deep—deeper than any cut she'd ever had. Blood seeped from the indentation of where her wedding band used to sit.

Last year, she had removed her ring. Intentionally dropped it over the wooden beam barrier at the cliff's edge. Mike had gone over the fence to fetch it when she asked him.

She grabbed her ring finger and closed her eyes. The digit slid out of place, slippery against a bloody nub. Mercedes' let out a yowl—an animalistic sound that reminded her of her husband's scream when she had pushed him over the edge of the bluff.

Throbbing swells of sharp, grueling pain over-powered her memory and brought her back to the present. She refused to look over her shoulder to see what was certain to be the shocked and terrified expressions on her friends' faces. More than anything, she couldn't face Tara.

Mercedes pressed a cheesecloth against her hand and screamed as the excruciating pain intensified. Her vision tunneled. The ring finger fell into the sink with the thud of a fallen chicken wing. She slid to the floor with her back against the counter and focused on her breathing so as not to pass out.

WHEN MERCEDES WOKE, she was on the couch beside Kim, hand bandaged and throbbing.

Tara sat in the La-Z-Boy, her stony face cold and unforgiving. "Do you have something to tell me, Mom?"

Janelle's arms were crossed over her body as she rocked to and fro, clutching her cross and murmuring what sounded like a prayer.

Kim side-eyed Mercedes.

"Don't look at me like that," Mercedes said. "You have no idea what he was going to do."

"What was he going to do, Mom? What was he going to tell me?" Tara asked, without a hint of emotion in her voice.

"What are you talking about, sweetheart?" Mercedes' cold lips went dry.

"Dad said he needed to talk to me about something important, and then he mysteriously fell off a cliff?" She reeled her rising excitement back in. "What was he going to tell me?"

Tears welled in Mercedes' eyes. "Your father was going to do something terrible."

"Lies!" Tara stood up. "Clock's ticking, ladies." She plucked a chunk of Havarti from the meat tray and moved to the kitchen.

"You did this?" Kim gasped. "Of course! You little fucking witchcraft whore!"

Tara turned to face them. Lights behind her—the shabby-chic overheads in the kitchen—hummed to an intense glow then dimmed. "I'm not the one living with lies."

"You can fix it, can't you?" Janelle asked.

"You have fourteen minutes." Tara popped the cheese into her mouth and spoke with her mouth full. "Trust me, you don't want the game to end without revealing your most guarded secrets." She slid her finger across her throat and shrugged.

"Tara…" Mercedes barely recognized her girl.

"I'm going to fucking kill her!" Kim stood, but she wobbled from the blood loss and sat back on the couch.

"How the hell did you do it?" Mercedes asked. "A cursed

game? A cursed app? How is that possible?"

"You wanna spend time talking about it? Okay…well, the barrier was the hardest part, actually. Took years of practice…I had been studying it for a while but never really had a reason to attempt it. It's kind of dangerous." Tara leaned against the counter in the kitchen, glaring into the den toward the phone—the clock counting down to their demise.

Mercedes let out a sigh. She'd drag the game out until the end before revealing anything else. "Never have I ever time-traveled."

Janelle broke into a sob. "I can't take this anymore!"

"You're just wasting time," Tara said. "You have to reveal your truths."

"Never have I ever…" It was Janelle's turn. She sucked in three sharp breaths as tears streamed her face. "I don't want to lose a finger. I quit. I give up." Her tremulous lips could barely get the words out. "I embezzled money from CHKD for my boob job!" Janelle kept her eyes closed and let out a steady breath. "That's it. That's my deepest darkest secr—" Janelle collapsed to the floor.

Mercedes rushed to her side. No pulse. Not breathing.

Tara gingerly approached. "Is she…" Tara held her hands over her mouth.

Mercedes pulled away. "You killed her."

"No way." Tara dropped to the floor and rolled Janelle to her back. She started CPR. Eyes full of tears, Tara thrust full-force against Janelle's chest. "I didn't mean for this to happen. I didn't really think it would work."

"You knew exactly what you were doing, you selfish little cunt," Kim said.

"Hey!" Mercedes held out a hand to Kim. "Watch what you say to her. You didn't know, right, Tara?"

Tara pounded on Janelle's heart, but with each passing second, Janelle became more cyanotic. "Please," Tara hissed under her breath. She turned to Mercedes. "Hurry up and finish the game!"

"Turn the game off," Kim said, holding out the phone.

"I can't. It doesn't work that way."

"How does it work, Tara?" Mercedes tried to keep her tone calm.

"I don't really know. It was kind of experimental. Just finish the game! Reveal each other's secrets!"

Mercedes and Kim stared at each other, willing information from the other. There was no way Mercedes would tell her other secret. She'd lose every damn one of her fingers before she'd put that kind of pain on Tara. It's why Mike had to die. Telling Tara the truth would hurt her more than keeping the secret. And she could never hurt her daughter.

Tara gave up on Janelle. Genuine tears fell from her eyes. She edged toward the phone on the coffee table. Janelle's avatar was marked with a bold, red "X." Both Mercedes and Kim's were down to nine counters. Eight minutes remained.

"I don't want to lose another finger," Kim said, trembling.

"Then I better reveal your most guarded secret," Mercedes said.

Kim's brow furrowed. "You're still in the game. Why isn't it game over for you? You murdered your husband. Is that not your biggest secret?"

"You shut up about that. I had more than a good enough reason." Mercedes crossed her arms.

"Come on, girl." Kim changed her tone. "Your daughter knows something anyway. No secrets anymore. Give me a clue."

"No fucking way."

"I think we all know, anyway. I mean, look at Tara's hair… Mike wasn't a redhead. Neither are you."

"That doesn't mean anything. Genetics are tricky." A lump in Mercedes' throat swelled. How could this be happening now, after all these years? She and Mike were so careful with the birth certificate.

"Never have I ever…" Kim's voice shook. "…adopted a child."

Mercedes released a breath, pressing her bloodied, bandaged

hand into her belly. "Tara is mine. That's ridiculous." Mercedes turned toward Tara. "I gave birth to you in an RV in Oregon. We were traveling the countryside when you came. I have medical records to prove I was pregnant with you. This is absurd. Stop this stupid game!"

Tara wiped her tears away and stood firm. She shook her head. "You told that story so many times, but it's not true, is it?"

"Mercedes," Kim said, "it's your turn. You have to figure out my secret."

"Give me a clue," she said.

"No way. I'm not ending up dead." Kim stared Mercedes down with a ferocious glare then looked to her left hand where she used her thumb to wiggle the band around on her finger. A clue? Of course.

"Never have I ever," Mercedes said, noting only six minutes remained on the clock, "...cheated on my spouse."

A smile jumped onto Kim's face. "Yes!" She let out a sigh of relief that was quickly engulfed by agonizing cries. Holding out her bandaged hand, she gripped her wrist and fell to her knees. "No!"

Somewhere within that bulbous mass of cheesecloth and bandage, another one of Kim's fingers had fallen off.

On the phone, Kim's avatar turned blue. A text box popped up to the left:

"Your biggest secret has been revealed. Congratulations on coming to terms with your truths. Please continue to play until all players' secrets are revealed."

Fresh blood seeped through Kim's bandage. She squeezed her right wrist to cut off circulation. Nostrils flared as Kim fought through the pain to speak. "I have to keep playing?"

Tara edged closer, tears in her eyes. "Time's almost up, Mom. I worry that you'll both die if she doesn't figure it out."

"What the fuck?" Kim's eyes went heavy as she whimpered, fetal position on the couch.

Mercedes tucked her bandaged hand under her arm, chin quivering. "I would rather die…"

"Mom!" Tara shook her head, then sprinted to the foyer closet.

"Mercedes." Kim lowered her tone. "Give it up, babe." Her gaze steady, watery. "It can't be that bad."

Tara returned with a faded manila envelope in her hand and dropped it onto Kim's lap.

"What is that?" Mercedes asked.

"Dad gave it to me before you killed him." Tara's eyes dug daggers into Mercedes' soul. "He wanted to tell me something, but you wouldn't let him."

"He was supposed to burn that!" Mercedes lunged toward Kim, but Tara held her back.

Tara's grip on Mercedes' bandaged hand sent her to her knees in pain.

"You already know?" Mercedes asked. "You already know and still you put me through this? Why?"

Tara released her and held her chin up high. Her breath hitched. "I needed to hear it from you. You needed to realize your truth and stop living this lie."

Kim shuffled through the papers in the file. Inside, Mercedes knew there to be medical files from Mercedes' pregnancy, which would indicate her baby died in the womb a month before she was due. Also, there would be newspaper clippings from nineteen years ago, from a town in New Hampshire. Kim's hand fell limp on the pile of papers, and she glanced at the phone.

Two minutes remained.

"Never have I ever," Kim's upper lip curled, "stolen a baby?" Her eyes met with Mercedes'.

"You have no idea how much I wanted a child…" Mercedes looked away and collapsed to the floor. She tucked her knees to her chest as she awaited the inevitable. The bite of another severed finger ripped through her nerves. Within her bandage, her pinky finger fell loose, rubbing against blood-wet skin. But the sting of revealing her secret hurt more than any lost limb. She wished she'd just drop dead like Janelle instead.

The phone buzzed on the table, but Mercedes didn't care to look.

"It's over," Kim said. She backed out of the den toward the foyer. "I can see outside again. That dark wall thing is gone." Kim grabbed her purse from the coat rack and ran from the house.

Tara, with her head held high, towered above. "I'm sorry about Janelle. She didn't deserve to die. And Kim didn't deserve to lose fingers over an affair." Tara shook her head, wiping away tears that wouldn't quit.

Mercedes' heart folded in on itself, more so than the day she learned her baby was dead in the womb. Without her baby, she was nothing. Without a baby—any baby—how could she live? Mike understood her pain all those years ago and let her keep the newborn infant she had snatched from the stroller of an inattentive teen mom in New Hampshire. That girl had no right having a child. Mike understood Mercedes' pain and let her keep Tara. They went on the run across the country in an RV and waited for her body to give birth to the stillborn, so they could replace her with Tara.

Mike went along with it, but guilt ate away at him over time.

Tara dragged a suitcase from the hall and stopped in the foyer. She held up a newspaper clipping and read the headline from nineteen years ago. "'Search is on for a Baby Kidnapped from Stroller in Manchester.' That's me, right?"

Mercedes lay destroyed and helpless on the floor. She couldn't manage to look her daughter in the eye.

"The parents' names are in the article," Tara said. "I'm going out to the East Coast for a while." She tucked the newspaper clipping back into the file under her arm. Tara wiped her face and looked at the family portrait at the base of the stairs. "Was everything a lie?"

"I love you." It was the sincerest truth Mercedes could tell.

Tara brushed her red hair out of her face and looked around her childhood home one last time. She took a step over the threshold and, without looking back, said, "But you love your lies more."

KILLER RADIO

R.E. Sargent

WEDNESDAY, SEPTEMBER 28TH, 1983
COTTONWOOD, ARIZONA

RICKY JEPSON YANKED THE CARTRIDGE out of the deck and replaced it with one for the upcoming song. The current song was halfway over, and he grabbed a bottle of water off the counter in the small studio and took a chug, moistening his throat before he had to speak again.

Ricky keyed up his microphone and waited for the last couple seconds of the song before he cut to a live feed.

"That was 'Photograph' by Def Leppard, and *Pyromania* is still tearing up the charts after eight months!" Ricky hit the backlit button under the player, and the opening chords of "Shout at the Devil" by Mötley Crüe cut into the broadcast through his headphones. "Now for the most requested song of the night. Hell, the week! Ever since this song hit the airwaves a couple of days ago, the phones have been lighting up! We got what you want here at 102.9 F.M., K-L-L-R, Killer radio! Rock on, metalheads!"

After cutting the mic, Ricky took off his headphones, pulled out the Def Leppard cartridge—which the DJ's referred to as "carts"—and cued up the reel-to-reel player that was ready to play six songs with a commercial in the middle. He pressed the button that would auto-play the tape on the reels when the previous song ended before he headed back to the dinky bathroom that contained a toilet and a sink. As he relieved himself, he listened to the heavy guitar riffs that were playing through the small station, which could be heard everywhere except the soundproofed booth.

After washing his hands and running his wet fingers through his long brown hair, he stooped down and looked in the mirror. He had not felt this relaxed in years, and even though he worked long hours, he could still see contentment lining his face through the three-day growth that adorned his stubborn chin. He looked at his thin frame in the mirror, knowing he fit the rock-and-roll image, confident he had made the right decision by buying the station. Outside, he propped the back door of the station open with a chair and lit up a Marlboro, taking a deep drag off the cigarette.

Ricky smiled to himself as he listened to the hardcore music wafting through the open door. It was a great time for music, and "hair bands" were coming out of the woodwork. Although he had always been a lover of rock music, it was an exciting decade where the music got heavier and the outfits outrageous. Bands such as KISS and AC/DC had paved the way through the late seventies, and the sounds had morphed from power chords to wailing guitar licks and solos. Ricky loved what he did and was excited for the future.

KLLR radio was born ten months earlier when the previous station—an FM country station—shuttered its windows. Ricky, a thirty-two-year-old DJ at an easy listening station in the nearby town of Flagstaff, Arizona, had heard through the grapevine that the country station had closed. On his next day off, he convinced his wife to jump into their 1975 Toyota Corolla and trek the sixty-four miles with him to the small town of Cottonwood, Arizona, where the empty shell of the station sat.

He recalled how surprised he was by the size of the building.

It was small, like a construction trailer, but was made from brick with an asphalt shingled roof. The single red door was the only opening on the front of the building—there were no windows. The chain-link fence topped with barbed wire surrounded the station, as well as the land around it. The steel-latticed mast that sported the transmitting antenna—which was anchored to the ground and secured by guy-wires—appeared to be over five-hundred feet tall. While his wife, Amy, hadn't quite seen his vision, she eventually gave in to his pleas, and after selling their house, which gave them a nice down payment for the station, they moved into a rental house in Cottonwood and Ricky got to work rebranding the station and taking it live, with the new rock and metal format.

Now, while lighting up his second cigarette, Ricky looked out at the still night air that surrounded the station. As owner of a startup station, advertisers were not quite in abundance yet, and Ricky cut corners whenever he could. He had hired a talented morning DJ for the morning show, which brought in many listeners, as well as an afternoon and evening jockey that were well received; however, he preferred to work the late nights and overnights himself. Not only did it save on salaries, but he could also get away with going for long periods of time without talking in between songs. The later it got, the more he used automation, which allowed him to focus on other station-related tasks. After ten months, the station was doing well, but he still wasn't in a position where he could hire another DJ or two. His long-term plan was to get out of the booth himself and, eventually, add as much automation as he could to minimize the need for overnight DJs as well as create efficiencies within the station. He could still hear his dad's advice in his head from when he had been a kid. *Work smarter, not harder.*

Ricky's thoughts shifted to the letter the station had received the week before. It was the third one in the past six months, and he smiled at the hatred that seethed through the words. The anonymous author was apparently sickened by the "music of Satan" that the new station was playing, and the letters demanded the station change their format. The last letter was…well, different. It felt more hostile. More disturbing. Ricky hated people trying to censor what they played, and no one was going to tell him what the people in the area should listen to. When the new Mötley Crüe album came out, he didn't waste any time getting it in rotation, hoping to piss off his oppressors.

As the last song on the reel played, Ricky finished his third cigarette, snuffed it out against the brick wall of the building, threw it in the Folger's can that sat by the back door, and yanked the door shut behind him.

Back in the booth, Ricky added another reel of tape to the other player—this time a longer one—got on the mic to give the station information, and introduced the next song before he moved to a desk in the corner where he started going through the day's mail. As he shuffled through the envelopes, he came to the letter he had received a few days prior, which was hanging out on the bottom of the pile. There was no return address, and the address was written in angry-looking block letters. He smiled again and paused for a few seconds before tossing the entire envelope, letter and all, in the trash can below the desk.

"Eat shit," he mumbled.

Throughout the night, Ricky switched back and forth between the booth and other duties around the station. He cleaned up the mini break room area. He refreshed the paper towels in the bathroom. As owner, he took care of everything that he couldn't afford to hire out and didn't expect the DJs to do. The night rolled into Thursday early morning, and sometime after two a.m., he found some time to get into his tiny office and file away a few papers and organize his desk. "Metal Health" by Quiet Riot pumped through the cramped space, and Ricky couldn't help but scream the lyrics as Kevin Dubrow belted them on the title track of the album. Although he heard nothing over the music, the smell of smoke pulled his attention away from the tasks at hand and alerted him that something was wrong.

Panicked, Ricky ran to the back door and turned the handle,

anxious to see what could possibly be on fire outside. The door would not budge. Eyes wide, he took quick, shallow breaths and ran toward the front door of the station. He noticed the smoke more now, and his mind tried to conjure up any plausible explanation for it, knowing that the station was surrounded by a wide-open space. He focused on getting out of the building where the air was fresh and crisp. Once outside, this would all make sense, and knowing what the situation really was, he would know what to do.

"Please, please, please!" he muttered under his breath. There was no reason the back door shouldn't have opened, but he was positive the front one would, yet it was stuck like a Ford truck in a mud-bog.

Turning the handle of the front door, Ricky pushed. It did not move. Trying again, he threw his shoulder at it. Still nothing. Ricky started hacking as he realized he was in deep trouble. The smoke had overcome the top third of the building, and Ricky could hear crackling coming from the roof. A moment later, a shower of sparks and flaming debris fell in on the back side of the station, covering the floor in front of the back door.

Unsure how stuck the back door was, Ricky pulled his t-shirt up over his nose and mouth and ran to the broom closet, grabbing a push broom out of it. He ran to the pile of flaming material and pushed it away from the door and into the open bathroom. Looking up, Ricky saw the flames burning through the roof. It looked like the fire had started from above and was burning its way down into the station.

As his eyes burned, Ricky tried the back door again. When it didn't give, he ran at it and tried to kick it open. The middle of the door dented out, but the door remained unwavering, almost as if it was one with the steel frame that surrounded it.

Wildly looking around, Ricky ran through the station and surveyed every crack and crevice for a vulnerability. He found none. The front and back doors were the only means of escape, each acting as the emergency exit should the other be blocked.

Taking a step back, Ricky blinked rapidly and covered his mouth with his hand. His panic rescinded, and he knew. This would be the end of the road.

Running into the studio, Ricky closed the door and realized there was less smoke hanging in this space. *Maybe if help can get here quickly…* His thoughts trailed off as he picked up the phone and dialed 911.

"Nine-one-one. What's your emergency?"

"This is K-L-L-R, the radio station. The studio is on fire, and I'm stuck inside." Ricky was shocked at how calm he actually sounded.

"We are sending units right now. What's your name?"

"Ricky Jepson."

"Stay on the line with me, Ricky. Units are rolling as we speak."

"They'll never make it in time."

"Just hang tight. We will get to you. Can you get to one of the doors?"

"Yes. Both. Neither will open."

"Have you tried breaking them down?"

"Yes. They are metal and won't budge."

"Either of them?"

"Correct."

"Can you bust out a window?"

Ricky watched through the studio window as more burning debris crashed down on the other side of the wall by the back door. The smoke was getting so thick that he could barely make out the space. The window started to blacken, and he knew it was only a matter of time before it imploded on him.

"There are no outside windows here," Ricky answered solemnly.

"No windows?" the dispatcher repeated.

"None."

"Oh."

If Ricky had not already resolved himself to the fact that he was a dead man, he would have been angered at the helplessness of the single word.

"Hang tight, Mr. Jepson. Try to stay as far away from the flames and smoke as you can. Stay close to the floor and cover your mouth with a wet rag if possible."

Ricky set the phone down on the desk, ripped a sleeve off his T-shirt and poured half his water bottle onto the thin material. He placed it to his mouth and breathed through it, noticing a little improvement. He looked around, watching as flames licked up the interior walls, writhing in angst as they tried to meet up with the flaming roof. His dream was over. He had put everything into the station, and now it was gone—and he would soon follow.

Snapping back to the inferno around him, Ricky noticed the music had stopped. The wires had probably been burned through. He turned to his equipment and was surprised to find the lights still lit. The reel had simply finished playing, and he had not queued up the next one. He was actually broadcasting dead air. Could the listeners still be tuned in? Could they hear him if he turned on the mic?

Knowing this was his final chance to broadcast, Ricky frantically looked through the cartridges that lined the wall, finally found the one he wanted, and loaded it into the player. Keying up the mic, he spoke.

"This is Ricky Jepson, and you are listening to K-L-L-R, 102.9, Killer Radio. Tragically, this will be our final broadcast. Thank you from the bottom of our hearts for the last ten months here at K-L-L-R. You guys kick ass! Oh, and Amy, if you're listening, I love you, babe. Thanks for letting me live the dream!"

Ricky pressed the button on the player, and the sounds of Megadeth's "Countdown to Extinction" filtered through the popping and cracking of the fire. Ricky reached for the dial and turned it up as loud as the speakers would handle without distortion. He glanced over and noticed all the lines for the station had lit up. Evidently, the listeners were still receiving the broadcast. Closing his eyes, he pushed back in his chair and listened to the lyrics, taking them in. When the song ended, radio silence returned, but Ricky was no longer aware as the window imploded, and the flames devoured the studio.

TUESDAY, AUGUST 28TH, 2018
PORTLAND, OREGON

BRITTANY STEPHENS HONKED at the blue Prius in front of her as she tried to navigate around him. She had unknowingly been biting the inside of her cheek for the last few miles as the car repeatedly sped up and slowed down for no apparent reason. Now, she was definitely going to be late for work for the third time this month, and her boss, a narcissistic asshole who thought the world revolved around him, had already warned her about her tardiness.

Finally around the erratic driver, she praised herself for not flipping him off as she got on the I-5 onramp and headed toward Portland. She was thankful that the rain hadn't kicked in yet for the year, which would only have delayed her further. She had fifteen minutes to get to the time clock on the third floor of the office building she worked in, yet she knew it would take her longer than that just to turn into the parking lot.

Pressing down the gas pedal and getting into the left-hand lane, Brittany pulled her long blonde hair out of her face, pressed the power button on the stereo, and her iPhone connected, kicking on the last song she was listening to when getting ready. Five Finger Death Punch filled the small cabin of her Toyota Matrix as she weaved in and out of traffic, trying to gain a few minutes on the drive. Halfway through "When the Seasons Change," the iPhone cut out, and the source changed over to FM radio. The numbers of the stations rapidly counted through the entire spectrum over and over and suddenly stopped on 102.9.

"What the fu—"

Brittany was cut off when background music started broadcasting over the station. A voice—harsh and raspy—cut through the music in the background, and she could make out some static in the broadcast.

"This is 102.9, K-L-L-R, Killer Radio, and I am going to draw one lucky listener's name right now. The winner will receive a tour of our station, after which we will whisk you away by limousine to a private concert by the band Six Feet Below, which will be held at a private eighty-five acre estate in the area. You will join seven other very lucky listeners for an extremely private event. You will also have backstage access to meet the band, check out their tour bus, and party your ass off with them after the show."

Brittany tried to change the source of her stereo back to her iPhone, but the controls did not respond. The voice continued.

"Our winner for today...Brittany Stephens of Portland, Oregon."

Brittany stopped fiddling with the controls, a frown taking over her face as she scratched her cheek. She thought she had heard her name, but she had never listened to this station before, and she certainly hadn't entered her name into any contests. The concert ticket piqued her interest, though, and she turned the radio up. The volume knob responded.

"Brittany Stephens, if you're listening, go to www.102.9 KLLR-Radio.com and claim your prize within the next forty-eight hours. Now for a little taste, here is 'Better Off Dead' by Six Feet Below."

The DJ's voice cut out, and a song started, a guitar riff blasting through her speakers. She turned the radio down a little and tried to get her iPhone to reconnect, but she was unsuccessful. Bewildered, she pushed the gas pedal down again and listened to the song as she drove. Given her taste of music, it was right up her alley, although a little old school, but she had never heard of this band before.

I'd have to live tomorrow
Like I had to live today
It'd bring me too much sorrow,
And I'd have to go away
In the end I can't portray that
Things I've done were ever right

Will it end with sprouting wings,
Or a far more sinister plight
There's no reason to stay,
I'm better off dead, better off dead,
I'm burning borrowed days,
I'm better off dead, better off dead
There's no reason to stay,
I'm better off dead, better off dead,
I'm burning borrowed days,
I'm better off dead, better off dead

Brittany shivered at the lyrics as she pulled into the parking lot, parked, jumped out of her car, and ran toward the entrance. She actually had made up some time and had a minute to clock in. As she ran, she pressed the key fob to lock her car, making a mental note to check out the website after work and see if it was her that had really won.

TUESDAY, AUGUST 28TH, 2018
CHICAGO, ILLINOIS

SETH PETERSON GOT out of his work truck, wiped his dirty hands on his jeans, and went to the front door. When he opened it, the smell of whatever was cooking for dinner assaulted his nostrils in a good way. He tossed his keys on the side table and shut the door behind him.

"Honey, I'm home!" he yelled.

"I'm in the kitchen. Dinner will be ready in twenty minutes."

Seth walked down the hall and entered the dining area while trying to make out what the aroma was.

"What are we having?" he asked his wife Zoey, who was bent over the oven, checking on its contents.

"None of your business!" she warned him, standing up and abruptly shutting the oven door. She turned around to face him and noticed him staring. "Were you just checking out my ass?" she joked.

"Busted!"

"Thanks for noticing," Zoey said, looking down at her breasts before winking at Seth.

"Someone is on ten today," Seth teased.

"And that's different from when?" she bantered. Zoey eyed Seth up and down. "Damn, you're filthy today. Did that boss of yours actually make you work?"

"Can you believe the nerve? I was playing around in the dirt all day."

"Well, you have just enough time to take a shower and get your ass back down here to set the table."

"My thoughts exactly!"

Seth leaned over and gave Zoey a kiss and left the kitchen, heading upstairs to the master bedroom. Their home was a modest three-bedroom, but Seth was proud of what they had achieved, and they were both still under twenty-five. With no children yet, they were both concentrating on building their life together and getting established.

Twenty minutes later, Seth went back to the kitchen wearing a tank top and a pair of basketball shorts. Zoey left the stove and went over to him, ran her fingers through his thick, dirty blonde hair, and kissed him passionately. He wrapped his arms around her thin waist and kissed her back. When they finally separated, Seth took a deep breath.

"What was that for?" Seth asked.

"Well, you clean up so good, I thought I'd have myself a sample," Zoey teased.

"Damn. Can't wait for dessert. What's the occasion?"

"I got my bonus at work today."

"That's awesome. I thought it was going to take another week."

"Me, too. Anyway, set the table, and dinner will be ready in a few."

Seth grabbed the plates and utensils and put them on the table and then grabbed two glasses. A few minutes later, Zoey opened the oven and pulled out a roast, placing it on potholders on the counter. After she served the meat and vegetables, they sat down and started to eat, making small talk about their day. As they were finishing up, Zoey bolted upright in her seat.

"OH! I forgot to tell you. Something weird happened today."

"What's that?" Seth asked, his attention piqued.

"Were you listening to the radio today on the job site?"

"Yeah, we were. Why?"

"Did you hear anything strange?"

Seth thought for a minute. "No, not really."

"Well, we listen to the same station, so I thought…" Her voice trailed off.

"What happened?" Seth prodded.

"A Dire Straits song was playing, and in the middle of it, the broadcast cut to some Megadeth song."

"Oh! Is that what you mean? I remember some metal song came on in the middle, and one of the guys turned it off."

"Then you missed the good part."

"What's good about a Megadeth song?"

"They announced a contest winner. It was you. Or at least someone with your name."

"Wasn't me. I haven't entered any contests. What was the prize?"

"A private VIP concert for a band named Six Feet Below."

"Damn. I've never heard of the band, but a private VIP concert sounds like a blast."

"I wrote down the website where you can claim your prize."

Seth pushed his plate away. "Let's check it out!"

Seth went to the bedroom and grabbed his laptop and brought it back to the table. Zoey handed him a Post-it note with the website address, and he entered it into the address bar. The site came up. Seth's eyebrows furrowed.

"What's wrong, babe?" Zoey asked.

"It says here that the radio station sponsoring this contest is in a town called Cottonwood, Arizona. The concert is nearby in the same town."

"Must be a different Seth Peterson, then."

"You would think, but it lists Chicago. Should I click the link?"

"How could we possibly have been listening to a radio station from Arizona? It's not like it was satellite."

"Exactly."

"What should I do?"

"Click it! I want to figure out what the hell is going on."

Seth clicked the link as Zoey watched, and the site came up.

Zoey pointed. "Look! That's your name right there...Seth Peterson, Chicago, Illinois."

"So weird."

"Click the button at the bottom to claim your prize," she suggested. "What can it hurt?"

Seth exhaled sharply and followed Zoey's lead; the site prompted for an email address. Seth entered it, and the site instructed him to look for an email and click the verification link. He brought up his account, found the email, and followed the directions. It returned him back to the site.

"Holy shit!" he gasped, his hand covering his mouth.

"They have our address listed!"

"Yup. I don't understand. This has to be some mistake."

"Seems like it. Why don't you claim the tickets and maybe we can go on a mini vacation?"

"To Arizona?"

"It would be nice to get away."

Seth frowned. "It says here it's just one ticket."

Zoey sighed. "What kind of shit is that...one ticket? Figures. Well maybe you could sell it. Or...we could still go, and I'll hang at the hotel."

"So, should I claim it?"

"Do it! What do we have to lose?"

WEDNESDAY, AUGUST 29TH, 2018

DALLAS, TEXAS

"SO, YOU ARE really doing this?" Jonathan Hunter's mother, Melanie, asked.

"Yeah! The ticket showed up in my email this morning," Jonathan informed her.

"Did you say it's in Arizona?"

Jonathan ran his fingers through his short hair and looked up. "Mom, I'm nineteen."

"I know, but that doesn't mean I just stop worrying about you, you know. Arizona's a long way away."

"It'll be good for me."

"The house will be quiet without you. I'm not ready to live alone."

"It's only four days, Mom."

"Don't you have to work?"

"The boss said I could take those days off."

"Well, can you take a friend with you?"

"I only won one ticket."

"What was the name of the band again?"

"Six Feet Below."

"Sounds morbid. I've never heard of them."

"Me neither. I Googled them but couldn't find anything. Still, they sound bad ass."

"Language, Jonathan."

"Sorry, Mom."

"When was this concert again?"

"September 28th."

"Mark it on the calendar, will you?"

"You got it, Mom. Speaking of work, I gotta go. See you tonight."

Jonathan gave Melanie a hug, went out the front door, and got in his '97 Honda Civic. As he drove off, he cranked up the stereo, looking forward to four days of independence and a wild night of rock and roll.

WEDNESDAY, AUGUST 29TH, 2018
FARGO, MINNESOTA

CALVIN HAWKINS NAVIGATED to a travel website, put in his preferred dates, and brought up the results. It appeared from his research that the nearest major airport was in Phoenix, Arizona, which looked like it would be a couple hour drive once he landed.

He chose to fly a week early since he wasn't currently working, and he would stay at a Phoenix hotel until the day of the concert, then stay at the hotel the radio station had booked for the night after the concert.

Calvin was still confused over the events from the previous day. At fifty-three, Calvin still had a vinyl collection from the days before cassette tapes, then CDs took over. A rocker at heart, Calvin was listening to *Diary of a Madmen* by Ozzy Osbourne when the player had stopped in the middle of the record, followed by the radio turning on. The stereo he had in the living room was old school and had the turntable built into the top of the unit, which also contained eight-track and cassette players. The radio dial was a manual one and required someone to turn a knob to change the station, but as soon as the record had stopped—it hadn't slowed to a halt, it had immediately ceased turning—he could hear the unit flipping through different stations until it landed on a station, which Calvin later noticed was 102.9. He knew there wasn't a local radio station on that frequency, yet the station came through ultra-clear. When he tried to turn off the radio and turn back on the turntable, the controls would not function. It was then he heard the contest winner announcement and his name.

Floored, Calvin immediately went to the website and verified he was a winner of a contest he hadn't even known existed. He was paying so much attention to the website that he didn't even notice when the record had started playing again.

After he had found his name on the website, he tried to find a number for the radio station that was hosting the contest. There was no contact information listed. No matter how many Google searches he did, KLLR did not come up. He hoped to find a phone number for the station as he had so many questions. Finally, as a last-ditch effort, he called information; however, that was another dead end.

After his futile efforts, he decided to click the link and fill out the form. He was surprised to see his name and address on the website. More surprising was the concert ticket that was emailed to him after he registered. Calvin studied the email, hoping it would have contact information. It didn't.

Back at his computer, Calvin finalized his travel plans and paid for the trip. With his airline ticket, rental car, and Phoenix hotel paid for, Calvin went to the kitchen and poured himself a glass of orange juice. As he sat at his small table that overlooked the back yard, he watched as a bird landed on the fence and took off again. He thought about the trip and was excited, not for the concert, because he didn't know if it was real or not, but for the time away. Divorced for the past ten years, he lived alone. The only thing left, his job, had kept him getting out of bed each day with something to look forward to, but when the accident happened, he wasn't able to work for a year, and they couldn't afford to keep him on the payroll. They had paid his medical bills and a very nice severance package, but he missed the human interaction. He hadn't gotten out—really gotten out—in a very long time. He was going to enjoy this vacation and the mild September Phoenix climate, concert or not. A rock-n-roll vacation was just what the doctor ordered.

TUESDAY, SEPTEMBER 11TH, 2018
TOPEKA, KANSAS

PRESTON RHODES PULLED into the garage and unloaded the suitcase from the trunk. After hitting the button to lower the door, he went into the house, rolling the empty suitcase behind him. He paused when he saw his wife sitting on the couch, watching one of the many crime shows she indulged in throughout the day. Her eyes went from him to the suitcase and back.

"What's with the suitcase?"

"Jesus, Mary, we discussed this."

"Yes, we did, and I said I didn't want you going."

"And I agreed to shut you up, but when I passed the suitcases at Walmart, I decided to buy one. Oh…and I'm going."

"Seriously? You're going to traipse off to some other state to go to some stupid-ass concert for a band you've never heard of? How are we going to afford it?"

"I'll figure it out."

"Like you've figured out how to pay the bills? The water gets shut off in ten days if we don't come up with the seventy-nine dollars."

"I'll pay the damn water bill. I'll come up with the money for the friggin' ticket. I'm tired of never having any fun. I'm going. End of discussion."

"Well, you better have fun, cause I don't know if I'll be here waiting when you get back. I hope it'll be worth it."

"I should be so lucky," Preston mumbled under his breath.

"What did you just say?"

"Nothing."

"I can leave right now if you'd like. Just say the word and I will go back to my mother's house. At least *her* water isn't going to be turned off."

"Do what you want, Mary. I'll do the same. Maybe it's better that way."

Preston tried to stomp off toward the master bedroom; however, the suitcase he pulled behind him hindered his tantrum march, and he stumbled and almost lost his footing, looking like an idiot in the process. Stowing the suitcase in the corner of the room, he went back out to the garage and started puttering with the lawnmower, not wanting to be around his wife. Both in their mid-thirties, they had only been married for a few years, but the romance had definitely been gone for the last half of the short marriage. He wasn't sure why they argued so much, but he knew some of it was financially induced. They were always short of money since she quit her job after six months of marriage, and although she made plenty of promises, she would never get off her ass to go look. To add insult to injury, she gained almost seventy-five pounds because of it and no longer felt like having sex. Their sham of a marriage was a freight train rolling toward a brick wall. He didn't know how much longer he could handle things with her. He needed a break, and he needed this concert.

He thought about how he would feel if she left while he was gone. He was shocked when the first word that came to mind was "relieved." It was then he realized that the marriage had been over for a long time. It wasn't just the loss of income—which Preston desperately tried to make up for; it was also the way she treated him. She was all over his ass about everything, and no matter what he did, it didn't seem to be good enough.

Preston thought about life before marriage. He had been single a long time. He attributed it to his looks. At six-foot-two and one hundred twenty pounds, he was a string-bean of a man. He resembled an awkward teenager with stringy brown hair, and he even still had the occasional pimple on his face, but he was far from a teenager and a few years from forty. If Mary left, would he spend the rest of his life being alone? If so, did it matter to him? He was alone before her, and truth be told, he didn't marry her for her looks anyway. He married her because he was lonely and she was willing. The grass had looked greener from the other side, but of course now, he realized that wasn't the case.

His mind in torment, Preston wiped a spot of grease off his bird-like leg and counted the days in his head until the concert. Two and a half weeks and he would be gone, whether Mary liked it or not. He hoped she made good on her threat. It would be easier that way.

THURSDAY, SEPTEMBER 20TH, 2018
NORFOLK, VIRGINIA

AROUND THREE A.M., Roxanne Lowe finished up with her last lap dance, grabbed her top, and made her way to the ladies' lounge. Earlier, she had finished dancing both the main stage and the secondary stage before she worked the crowd for lap dances. Luckily, she ended the night on a great note, and one of her regulars, who seemed to be a really nice guy, kept her busy for the last hour of her shift, pulling out twenty after twenty to keep her there. Hell, she hadn't even had to perform lap dances for him for half the songs. He just enjoyed her company, and they usually just sat there and talked when he came in. As long as he was paying, she would hang out with him all night, when she wasn't needed on stage, which she had to do on rotation. She didn't mind the shower of dollar bills she received while on the stage, but the lap dances were where the money was.

Back in the lounge, she stripped out of her G-string and got dressed in her street clothes, consisting of a pair of tight jeans, a tighter t-shirt that accented her fake breasts, and a pair of boots. After touching up her makeup in the mirror, she pulled her long blonde hair into a ponytail and pulled it through the back of a baseball cap.

"Are you ready to go, Jasmine?" another dancer asked her. The dancers typically called each other by their stage names, and Roxanne went by Jasmine while at work.

"I am! Let's get out of here."

Roxanne pulled her leather jacket out of her locker and slipped it on, meeting four other girls at the door that led out back. Luckily, the girls didn't have to leave by the front door, where some of the creeps hung out, hoping to catch their favorite stripper after hours where they could hit on them more aggressively.

As they left as a group, not only because there was safety in numbers, but because they typically went out for breakfast every Thursday morning, Roxanne peeled off from the rest and climbed into her red Infinity. She watched and made sure the other girls got into their cars safely before pulling out of the lot.

A mile down the street, Roxanne pulled into the IHOP

parking lot, went inside, and grabbed the usual table. The girls filtered in within minutes of each other and slid into the booth. The topic turned to their plans for each girl's next day off.

"What do you got going on, Jasmine?" a brunette that went by the name of Mercy asked.

"I'm actually working straight through until Wednesday, and then I'm taking a few days off."

"You doing anything fun?" Brandy, another brunette, asked.

"I'm actually going to Arizona."

"What are you doing in Arizona?" Mercy asked. "I'd love me a little Arizona weather right about now. It's getting chilly."

Roxanne told them about the concert and the strange event that led up to her getting chosen as a contest winner.

Cherry, a bottled redhead who had been sitting there, quietly joined in. "Trippy! How does that happen? We're pretty much on the other side of the world over here."

Roxanne held up her hands. "I know, right? It doesn't make sense, yet I got the ticket through email, and it promises to be an elite event. I actually have an uncle that lives not too far from there, in Sedona, so I'm hoping to see him while I'm there."

"Does he know you're a stripper?" Cherry asked, laughing.

"Hardly," Roxanne said, smiling. "He thinks I'm a waitress. None of my family lives on this side of the States, so I doubt anyone would ever find out otherwise."

"So why are you all the way out here?" Mercy asked. "So far from home."

"That was the idea," Roxanne answered. "I moved here to get as far away from my train-wreck of a mom as possible."

"Are you going to see her when you go back?" Brandy asked.

"She actually passed a month ago, so no."

"Oh my God, I'm so sorry!" Mercy offered, the other girls offering similar sentiments.

"Don't be. I haven't talked to her in forever, and we didn't really have a relationship. I didn't even go back for the service."

The subject got changed quickly, and the girls finished their breakfast and talked about everything from the strange concert to bikini waxing. By the time the sun peeked up over the horizon, the girls were getting up to leave, exchanging hugs all around.

"Jasmine, make sure you post video of the concert on Facebook. I can't wait to live vicariously through you!" Cherry demanded.

"You got it, Cherry. Just keep the pole warm for me. I'll be back soon."

WEDNESDAY, SEPTEMBER 26TH, 2018
CHARLESTON, WEST VIRGINIA

REGGIE REEVES PLACED his carry-on luggage on the belt and slipped off his cowboy boots. Checking his pockets for the last time, he placed the boots, his belt, and his cap in the gray bin and walked toward the body image scanner. He wasn't used to being without his hat, and he ran his hand through his smooshed-down brown hair, then through his shaggy beard.

In the machine, he held his hands above his head, and when he was cleared to proceed, he gathered his things at the other end of the belt, put everything back on, and proceeded to the gate. He was extremely early, and the gate only had a few other occupants, two of them laying across the hard seats, trying to get some much-needed sleep. Reggie picked a seat that overlooked the tarmac and watched the activity through the floor-to-ceiling windows. Life in West Virginia had been hard on him, and for the past month, he had been couch-surfing, staying at whatever friend's house he was allowed to until he wore out his welcome. Almost out of options, a strange situation with his friend's car radio had him boarding a plane to Arizona. Everything he owned was packed into the one suitcase that would soon rest lazily in the belly of the aircraft. Although he had no idea what he would do after he landed in Phoenix and caught a bus to the city where the concert was, he knew one thing: he would not be coming back to West Virginia.

THURSDAY, SEPTEMBER 27TH, 2018
HOUSTON, TEXAS

KERRY KELLEY DRAPED the blanket over her father and made sure he was comfortable, then gave him a kiss on the forehead.

"Great to see you again, Daddy. I'll see you again next week."

"Thanks for coming to see me, baby. I love you. Please be safe."

"I will, Daddy. I'll only be gone five days."

After giving him one last hug, Kerry left the bedroom and found her mother in the kitchen.

"It's hard seeing him like this, Mom."

"I know, honey. The chemo is kicking his ass. He is tired all of the time."

"Please let me know what I can do to help you guys. I'm only a half hour away."

"I know, but Bill and the boys need you. Don't you worry about your father. He's a tough old goat."

"I'm still coming over at least once a week, Mom. Just let me know if you need anything. It's not just him I worry about. I'm sure it's taking its toll on you as well. You look tired."

"Is that your way of telling me I have bags under my eyes?" her mom asked, smiling weakly.

"Those words never left my lips!" Kerry said, smiling back, but she couldn't help notice the dark circles that had become more prominent under her mother's eyes.

At thirty-nine, Kerry had her own responsibilities taking care of her husband, Bill, their two sons, William Jr. and Timothy, as well as working a full-time job as an escrow officer at one of the local title agencies. Her dad getting sick was not supposed to happen, and none of them were ready for it, but cancer had a funny way of doing whatever the hell it wanted.

With all of her responsibilities, Kerry quickly blew off the winning VIP concert ticket that came her way. She didn't understand it, nor did she have time to think about it. She had people that relied on her, and she was needed right where she was.

When she had told Bill about her strange experience while listening to hold music on the phone at her job, both of them had a good laugh about it, but when Kerry had pulled up the website for—as she described—shits and giggles, it all seemed too real. She and Bill fussed over it for the evening, but by the next day, after seeing her dad, working a full shift, and fixing dinner for the family, she had forgotten about it.

Now, it was the day before the concert and her Uber was eight minutes out. Kerry had been raised on rock and roll, and when she and Bill had first started dating—they were high school sweethearts—they started a trend of seeing as many concerts together as they could. Life revolved around music for both of them, which was evident by her ticket collection, which was probably an inch thick. It was the day prior that Bill had presented her with an airline ticket and urged her to go. He had labeled it, using air quotes, as "the chance of a lifetime." After calling her boss and arranging last-minute coverage, she had packed her things and got to bed as early as she could.

Now, at her parents' house, slipping in a quick visit before her flight, she gave her mother a hug and promised to come straight over from the airport when she returned. To make sure she kept her promise, she was leaving her car parked in her parent's driveway.

"Have a great time, honey. That man of yours...he is something else."

"Tell me about it, Mom. He made all the arrangements to make sure he and the kids will be fine without me. I'm trying not to think about the fact that they will probably be eating pizza for dinner every night."

"And if they do? Is that such a bad thing? Stop worrying, Kerry. They'll be fine. You do everything for everyone. It's time you do something for yourself."

"Thanks, Mom. I love you."

Kerry gave her mother a hug and noticed the Uber pull into

the driveway.

"I better go. See you soon." Kerry grabbed her suitcase and started toward the front door.

"I love you, baby. Be safe."

FRIDAY, SEPTEMBER 28TH, 2018
CAMP VERDE, ARIZONA

SETH PETERSON ENTERED the lobby for Cliff Castle Casino and approached the front desk. The information he had received was to show up, check in, get ready, and be in the lobby at six o'clock p.m. He looked at his Seiko and noticed it was 12:30 in the afternoon. He would have time to get a nap in before the concert.

As he waited in line, he noticed a thin blonde girl at the counter in front of him. She seemed out of place wearing what looked like a sun dress. Another hotel employee came up to the counter and motioned for him to approach.

"Checking in?"

"Yes, sir," Seth answered, handing over his driver's license.

"Ahh, Mr. Peterson. Thanks for coming. It looks like you are in one of our suites on the top floor. Are you here for the concert?"

Seth felt flushed and noticed out of the corner of his eye that the blonde was looking at him.

"Yes, I'm here for the—"

"Ohmygawd, me too!" Brittany interrupted.

Seth turned toward the girl and looked at her, noticing for the first time that she was attractive. "Awesome. I'm glad to meet someone else going to this thing. I thought maybe I was the only one." He reached out and shook her hand. "I'm Seth."

"I'm Brittany."

"So, Brittany, what can you tell me about this concert? I know nothing about it."

"Then we're in the same boat."

Seth turned toward the person that was coding his room key. "You seem to know about the concert. What can you tell me and my new friend Brittany here?"

"I'm afraid you know everything I know. We have eight rooms reserved for eight winners that won tickets to a very secret concert. We don't know who or where, only that you are all to be well taken care of and that we should remind everyone to meet in the lobby at six."

"I wonder why the big shroud of secrecy?" Brittany asked.

"I don't know, but it's kind of exciting, don't you think?" Seth answered.

"Hell yes. That's why I'm here. That and any excuse to get away from my asshole boss."

"Yeah, those are no fun," Seth sympathized. As the employee handed back his ID, Seth asked, "Has anyone else that's here for the concert checked in yet?"

The man checked the computer. "Not yet. You two are the first."

Seth turned to Brittany. "Want to get a drink?"

"I'm so down," she agreed, smiling.

Seth looked at the employee's name badge. "Doug, is there a bar here?"

"Yes, sir. You'll enjoy our Cliff Dweller's Bar. If you want to drop your bags in your rooms first, you can get there by following this route." Doug pulled out a site map and drew a red line down the path they should take. "Your rooms are on the same floor."

"Thanks, Doug. We appreciate it," Seth told him, taking his room key and the map. "Will you do us a favor? Will you tell anyone else that shows up for the concert that some of us are drinking in the bar?"

"Will do."

"Thanks again, Doug!"

Brittany had already finished checking in, and together, they made their way to the elevator, discussing the concert like they had known each other for years. When they got off the elevator on the top floor, Brittany spotted her room and went to the door and opened it.

"So, Seth, will I see you in the bar?"

"Thirty minutes?"

"Perfect. Gives me time to change and freshen up."

"See you then," he confirmed, and they both made their way to their rooms.

SETH ENTERED THE bar and spotted Brittany talking to a guy with a shaggy beard and a ball cap. Guessing that it was some random local trying to pick up on her, Seth made his way to the table to play the hero and protect her.

Brittany spotted him coming, and a smile lit up her face. "Seth! Glad you're here! I want you to meet Reggie. He's from West Virginia and will be joining us tonight."

Seth was caught off guard for a minute and then remembered they had invited others to join them. "Oh," he said, "you're here for the concert?"

"Yup! Same as you."

"All the way from West Virginia?"

"Yeah…long way. What about you, Seth? Where are you from?"

"Chicago."

Brittany's eyebrows arched. "Holy crap. Oregon here. What are a bunch of random people from all over the United States doing in some small Podunk town for a concert?"

"Hopefully a question that will be answered later," Seth responded. "How did you find out you won?"

"Some radio station cut in when I was listening to my iPhone. It was so freaking weird. Some rock and roll station that is supposedly near here."

"Almost the same thing for me," Seth told them. "What about you, Reggie?"

"Same concept. But how is some local radio station broadcasting all around the United States?" Reggie asked.

Brittany jumped back into the conversation. "You know what's weird? No matter what I did, I was never able to pick up that station again. It says it's 102.9, but I tried that station in Portland, and it's a completely different station. I also tried it in my rental car when I got to the hotel. There is no such station here."

"The mysteries are just piling up," Seth admitted.

A stranger approached. "Sorry to interrupt. Are you guys going to the concert?"

They all turned toward him, and Brittany answered. "We are! I'm Brittany from Oregon. Who are you?"

"Hi, Brittany. I'm Calvin from Minnesota. Nice to meet you."

Seth extended his hand. "I'm Seth."

Reggie did the same. "And I'm Reggie."

"Nice to meet all of you," Calvin told them. "I see I'm the token old guy in the group." He laughed, and the ice being broken, they all followed suit.

"So, Calvin," Seth said, "any idea what this is all about?"

"I'm guessing you guys know as much as I do, which is nothing except we are supposed to be going to a concert tonight."

"That's about where we're at," Brittany said. "I guess we will all find out soon."

The four of them continued to get acquainted and ordered food. As they ate, the last four attendees came into the bar, one at a time, and joined them, each one curious to meet the others and find out any more information. They pulled two tables together, and the newcomers all ordered food and drinks. Because there was no other information available regarding the concert, they all chatted and got to know each other.

"So, Jonathan, I see you ordered a Coke. Do you not drink?" Roxanne asked.

"I do but can't here. I'm only nineteen."

"Ah, that explains it," Roxanne said.

"Well, you win the honor of youngest, and I apparently am

the oldest, so we have something in common," Calvin joked.

"You aren't that much older, Calvin," Kerry told him. "I'm almost forty, and Preston over there looks about my age."

"Close," Preston answered. "But it looks so much better on you."

Kerry smiled and turned to Roxanne. "So where are you from?"

"Virginia," Roxanne answered. "You?"

"Texas. Have you ever been here before?"

"Unfortunately, yes. My uncle lives in the next town over, and I used to live in the area before…well…a long time ago. I moved to Norfolk to get away."

"What's in Norfolk?"

"Just my job. I actually found an online ad for a cheap guesthouse and decided that was as good of a place to live as any. I hopped a plane the next day."

"You must have really hated it here."

"I didn't hate *where* I lived…more the people I lived *with*."

"Your uncle?"

"No, I love my uncle. In fact, he's coming by to say hi soon. It was actually my mom I had to get away from. She was evil."

"So sorry you had to deal with that."

"It's all good. I don't let it define me."

The group continued to talk and get to know each other as they ate and drank. Sometime during the get-together, the waitress came to their tables and announced their host was picking up the tab. She wasn't surprised by the barrage of additional food and drink orders she received immediately following her announcement.

Around five o'clock, the group watched as Roxanne jumped up out of her seat and ran to meet a man that had entered the bar. He looked to be pushing sixty. As they embraced each other, Reggie turned toward Calvin.

"Sorry, Calvin. Looks like you're not the oldest any longer."

"It's about damn time," Calvin said, laughing.

Roxanne brought the man to the table and introduced him to her new friends.

"Uncle Joe, I'd like you to meet my new friends. I'll go around the table." She pointed at the group. "You guys correct me if I screw this up, okay? Starting over here on the left, we have Jonathan from Dallas, Texas, then we have Brittany—isn't she pretty Uncle Joe?—she's from Oregon. Reggie over there is from West Virginia, I think. Is that right, Reggie?"

"I was. I'm going to probably stay here now."

"Oh, that's right. Then we have Kerry, and she is also from Texas—I think Houston." Kerry nodded. "In the middle there is Preston from Kansas, who is probably leaving his wife when he gets back, next to him is Seth from Chicago, and next to him, Calvin from Minnesota. I think that covers it. Everyone, this is my uncle Joe, who is my mother's brother. He lives in Sedona, which is close by."

Joe greeted everyone at the table, and they pulled a free chair from a nearby table and offered him a seat.

"So, what do you do, Joe?" Calvin asked.

"I'm semi-retired, but I drive a cab part-time for a privately owned taxi company in Cottonwood."

"How long have you lived here?" Kerry asked.

"Most of my life. My parents moved to this area when I was five. I never left. I like it most days," Joe said, grinning.

"So, do you know anything about this concert?" Seth chimed in. "Any local buzz?"

Joe scratched his head, causing his silver hair to dance around. "I haven't heard a peep. And this is a pretty small community. Can't seem to take a shit around here without someone knowing about it. Fill me in on what you all are doing here. Maybe it might jog something in my memory."

Roxanne explained to him how they had all been contest winners for a private concert in the area. She also explained the strange circumstances around the radio breakthroughs and the fact that not a single one of them had entered any type of contest.

"Any idea who's playing at the concert?" Joe asked.

The group looked at each other, and finally, Jonathan piped up. "I remember. It's Six Feet Below."

Joe squinted. "Never heard of them. Are they new?"

"Not sure," Roxanne told him. "I couldn't find anything out about them. Anyone else know?"

They all looked at each other and shook their heads.

"So, you all know nothing about this concert, how you got entered, why, or who the band even is and yet you all traipsed from all over America to see it? Wow. That's crazy."

Preston spoke. "I think we all have our different reasons for coming. Personally, I needed to get away. The mystery surrounding this was one that I couldn't pass up on."

Others at the table murmured in agreement. Joe turned to Roxanne. "So, knowing how much you hate this place, why did you come back?"

"Cause you're here and it's been years. It was a good excuse to come back, and now with Mom gone, I figured why not?"

"I'm so glad to see you, sweetheart. I missed you."

"Hey, Joe, do you know anything about the radio station that is sponsoring this thing?" Calvin asked.

"I'm sure I would. Nothing gets by me here. Which one is it?"

The conversation at the table ceased as everyone turned to hear Joe's answer to the question.

"K-L-L-R. Some sort of rock/metal station. Have you heard of it?" Calvin asked.

Joe blinked rapidly and glanced around the table. Finally, he spoke.

"I think you must be mistaken. K-L-L-R hasn't been around for a very long time."

Roxanne touched his arm. "Yeah, all the years I lived here, I don't remember it, either."

"That's because you were born in ninety. The station was...er...gone...in 1983," Preston managed to say, clearly shaken.

"What do you mean 'gone?'" Brittany asked. "I have the email right here." She held up her hand with the email and printed ticket in it. "It says 102.9, K-L-L-R. Killer radio. How can it be gone?"

"That doesn't make any sense," Joe said, shaking his head. "I think it's best if I tell you all what happened. This is craziness. I think someone is playing a prank on you. I seriously doubt there is a concert."

"What do you mean?" Jonathan blurted. "I came all this way for nothing? I had to pay for my plane ticket all by myself."

"We all did," Brittany told him. "Chill for a second and let's hear what Joe has to say."

"Thanks, Brittany," Joe continued. "It was the early eighties, and hard rock and heavy metal were starting to take over the music scene. This area had a handful of radio stations, but not really any good rock stations. Some fellow by the name of Ricky…his last name was Jepson…bought an old country station that had shut down, and he rebranded it. When it went live, many of the townsfolk were shocked to find out it was a rock and roll station. Had it been older rock, things might have been different, but the way music was progressing, the station quickly grew a group of protesters that weren't very quiet about their disdain for the station and the music it played. I think they started speaking out in the media about it as 'devil music' or something to that effect. You get the gist.

"The station had a ton of listeners as well, and because of that, it was starting to bring in advertisers. The station had operated for less than a year and was doing well, much to the chagrin of its persecutors."

"Something tells me this story doesn't have a happy ending," Roxanne interrupted.

Joe looked down. "No, hun. No happy ending here. This town has all but forgotten the tragedy that happened on that night in September of 1983. That date will forever be etched into my memory. It was the 28th…your mother's birthday."

"Wait!" Calvin said, jumping into the conversation. "Are you saying that something happened to the station on September 28th, 1983?"

"I am," Joe said, nodding.

"That's today's date!" Calvin stated.

"Maybe they're celebrating a re-grand opening or something," Brittany offered.

Calvin's eyes rolled up in his head as he did the math. "Thirty-five years after whatever this event was—to the frickin' day—we were all invited here to attend a concert. That can't be a coincidence."

"That's some freaky shit," Reggie agreed.

Roxanne held up her hand. "Hold on, everyone. I think we need to hear what Uncle Joe—"

A man in a chauffeur's uniform approached the table as she was talking and interrupted the conversation. "Excuse me, everyone, I believe you are the group I'm picking up. It's time to get going. The agenda for the night, as I am told, is as follows. We are all going to climb in the limo, and I am to take you to the station for a tour and to meet the owner. After that, an hour later, I am to pick you all back up and take you to the concert location, where you will be wined and dined."

Everyone was unsure of what to do and looked at Joe, then Roxanne.

"Where is the concert?" Kerry asked.

"I apologize, but I haven't been given that information yet. I'm told it will be sent to me right before I pick you all up from the station."

"It can't be," Joe whispered. "The station is gone."

"Maybe they reopened it?" Jonathan suggested. "A thirty-fifth anniversary reopening that is to be kicked off by a kick-ass private concert. I don't know about you guys, but I'm going. I've come all this way, and I'm not chickening out now."

The table erupted in conversation, many of the concert-goers unsure. Finally, Jonathan stood up and joined the chauffeur. "I'm going. Who is joining me?"

The occupants of the table looked at each other. Finally, Brittany stood up. "I'm in."

Seth also stood up. "I'm in, too."

Slowly, the rest of the occupants all stood up, except for Roxanne, who looked at Joe.

"What should I do, Uncle Joe?" she whispered.

"Whatever you want to do, baby girl, but if you go, I'm going with you, as far as I can anyway."

"Deal. Let's go," she said, standing and grabbing his hand. "I can't miss this…I *won't* miss this."

THE MOOD IN the limo was a mix of excitement and nervousness. No one asked anything more about the tragedy that had befallen the radio station, and Joe decided to keep his mouth shut until they got there. He would either be proven right—that the station no longer existed—or be proven wrong, and it would be open and operating. None of these people knew him, so he decided to keep his comments to himself—for now.

More drinks were poured in the limo, and the group chattered idly for the twenty-minute trip into Cottonwood and then the additional ten minutes it took to travel the gravel road that led up the hill to the station. Dusk had approached, and the road was cloaked in shadows as they traveled over it; however, it was light enough to see the road in front of them clearly. As the limo crested the hill and rounded the final bend, Joe inhaled sharply. The station sat in front of them, exterior lights ablaze, looking like it did the day it was built. A lit sign atop the brick building advertised the station as KLLR, 102.9 F.M., Killer Radio. The chauffeur pulled in front of the building, stopped, got out, and came around to open the door closest to the station entrance.

"Okay, all out. I'll be back in an hour. Go on inside. The owner is expecting you."

As soon as all nine passengers were out of the vehicle, the driver shut the door, climbed in the front, and started down the gravel drive. They watched it depart and, when the taillights disappeared, turned toward the building.

"Now what?" Jonathan asked.

"Well," Calvin answered, "you wanted to see the station, so let's go in."

Amazed at the condition of the building, Joe reached over, pulled the front door open, and held it for the group as they all shuffled inside. When he entered the building himself, the door shut behind him, and he joined the rest of the group inside the entryway.

"Hello?" Seth called, looking around and not seeing anyone. Music spilled out of the speakers that were placed throughout the station.

"Is this that band where the girl crawls on the hood of the car in the video?" Preston asked.

"You mean Whitesnake?" Calvin asked. "Yes, and the girl is Tawny Kitaen."

"I love that video," Preston said. "That girl is hot."

"*That girl* is almost sixty now," Calvin said, laughing.

"Gross," Preston said. "Where is everyone anyway?"

"Maybe he's in the can?" Brittany suggested.

"That would be weird, considering he was expecting us," Roxanne said, concern etched into her brow.

The song ended, and the "On Air" light illuminated above the studio booth. A voice bellowed through the speakers.

"That was Whitesnake with 'Here I Go Again.' Thanks for joining us tonight at Killer Radio. 102.9 FM, K-L-L-R. I'm Ricky Jepson, and this is 'The Last in Line' by Dio. Rock on, Cottonwood!"

The sign above the booth went dark, and the song started.

Joe went to one of the windows of the booth, placed his face against it, shielded his eyes from the surrounding glare, and looked around.

"It's empty," Joe announced.

"Must have prerecorded this portion," Calvin offered. "Looks like it's on autopilot."

Kerry walked toward the back of the station and found three doors, all of them closed. She knocked on each one. "Hello? Is anyone here?" After a few seconds, there was no response, and she knocked again. There was still no answer.

"Open them," Reggie suggested.

Kerry opened the first door, which turned out to be a small office. It was unoccupied. The second door yielded a storage closet. The third door contained a toilet and a sink, but it was also unoccupied.

"Looks like this is a bust," Jonathan said. "We should get out of here. This place is creepy."

"Says the guy that was so damn gung-ho about coming here?" Roxanne said, her frustration making her come across harsher than she meant to.

"Well, I didn't know. Besides, you guys didn't have to come with me. That's on you."

"No need to argue, you guys," Brittany said. "The limo driver will be back in an hour. We can hang here until the owner gets back, or the limo shows up. Whichever comes first."

"Well, I'm going outside," Jonathan announced. "You guys can stay if you want."

Jonathan went to the door and pushed, but it didn't budge. He tried a second time with the same result. Joe went to the door, panic edging into his face. He tried to open it then rammed his shoulder against it, but it still didn't move.

The song finished, and AC/DC's "Highway to Hell" automatically started playing. Seth and Calvin went to the back door of the station and tried to open it, but it didn't budge.

"Okay, this shit isn't funny," Kerry said. "I have a sick parent

I left behind for this. My family is waiting for me. Someone get the door open."

Roxanne looked at Joe, her eyes wide with concern. When she noticed him standing still, staring at the ground, she knew something was extremely wrong.

"Uncle Joe. Uncle Joe! What's going on? What do you know?"

When he didn't respond, Roxanne touched his shoulder. He turned to look at her.

"Uncle Joe, what's going on?" She noticed a small tremor work through his body.

"I…you all…I think you need to hear the rest of my story."

EVERYONE GATHERED AROUND Joe to try and hear him over the AC/DC tune that was blasting over the speakers.

"On September 28th, 1983, this radio station burned to the ground. The owner, Ricky Jepson, was trapped in here when it started and couldn't get out. His body was so badly burned, they had to identify him by dental records."

Reggie interrupted. "Isn't that the name of the DJ that announced the Dio song a few minutes ago? Or at least the name used on the recording?"

Calvin nodded. "It was. I remember."

"So how do dead people talk?" Brittany asked.

"They don't," Seth answered, "but remember the voice was recorded."

"What? Thirty-five years ago?" Kerry asked incredulously.

Roxanne held up her hand. "Please!" she shouted. "If you remember, we're stuck in here. I think what Uncle Joe has to say is more important than the name on the recording!"

The other occupants of the room fell silent, and the song

ended, then kicked straight into "Fly to the Angels" by Slaughter. The song started off softly, and no one paid attention to the music.

Joe rubbed his right palm across his face and exhaled sharply. "Okay, there's more. Apparently, the owner made a final broadcast saying that K-L-L-R radio would be no more, thanking everybody, and then passing a message on to his wife. He knew he wasn't getting out, and he rode it out until he was gone."

"Why didn't he just leave?" Jonathan asked. "Maybe the doors were stuck. Oh wait, like now! Oh shit! We're all gonna die!"

"Jesus, Jonathan. Calm the hell down. We're not going to die," Brittany chastised him. "Let Joe finish."

"Thanks, Brittany," Joe said, once again resuming his story. "Anyway, there was a big investigation. Turns out that the fire was ruled an arson. Someone set that fire."

The occupants of the small station looked around at each other, shock on their face.

"Who, Uncle Joe? Do they know who set the fire?"

Joe glanced down at the floor, unable to meet Roxanne's eyes.

"Uncle Joe?"

Finally, he looked up and met her stare. His voice was barely a whisper. "No. They never figured out who did it, but I have an idea."

"Who? Who did it, Unc?"

Joe stood straight and took a deep breath. "Remember how I told you it happened on your mother's birthday?"

"Yes."

"She'd been blabbering for weeks about the station and how it was run by devil worshipers. She convinced many people she knew the same. They even got together weekly to discuss it, trying to formulate a plan to get the station shut down."

"No. You're not saying Mom had anything to do with this."

Ignoring her, he continued. "Anyway, the night leading into her birthday, she was celebrating and had a little too much to drink. She made me come pick her up from the bar and take her home.

She left her car there. Seems she had no way to get anywhere without her car. That played in her favor later. When the police questioned her, she was at home asleep with no car. The fire happened in the wee hours, the morning of her birthday. Here's the kicker. I had asked her a couple weeks earlier what she wanted for her birthday. She stared me straight in the eyes and said she wanted the station to be gone. It's way too much of a coincidence."

The other occupants of the station watched and listened to the conversation in horror.

"Why didn't you tell the cops, Uncle Joe? She got away with murdering someone and walked away, scot free?"

"I had no proof. Besides, she's my sister. I didn't know what to do, so I did nothing."

"So, on a scale of one to ten, how convinced are you that she did this?"

"Then? Maybe a three. Today? A ten. Absolutely a ten. Comments she has made over the years made me more convinced every day. And I don't think she was alone, either. I think her group of fanatics helped her. They blocked the doors from the outside, set the roof on fire, and let it burn. They murdered Ricky Jepson."

Reggie ran to the front door and tried to open it again and then started kicking it while Seth ran to the back door and tried to get it open again as well. Neither door budged. Defeated, they once again joined the rest of the group in the center.

"We have to get the hell out of here!" Seth yelled. "Something isn't right."

The song ended, and a cover of "Live and Let Die" by Guns and Roses filled the small space. Panic edged in on many of their faces as they realized they were trapped.

The panic ramped up to sheer terror when Calvin spoke. "Um…guys? Um…have you been paying attention to the songs that have been playing since we got here? 'Here I Go Again'…'The Last in Line'…'Highway to Hell'…Now it's 'Live and Let Die.' This is creepy. The station burned down thirty-five years ago today. The doors are locked. The music that is prerecorded is talking about death, and it's happening all over again. Someone needs to call 911 now!"

Those that had brought their phones with them reached for them, trying to call out. One by one, a look of defeat ensconced their faces.

"No signal," Kerry said, her lip quivering.

"Me neither," Brittany agreed.

"Uncle Joe, what is happening?" Roxanne yelled, wiping her clammy palms on her jeans.

"I don't know, honey. I don't know."

"Everyone, spread out and see if you can find another way out," Preston demanded, heading toward the studio and trying the door. It was locked, and he could not get inside, so as the others checked the other rooms, he did a visual inspection of the ceiling to see if there was any access to an attic or anything. He found nothing. The group all rejoined in the main room, and then as suddenly as he was there, Seth ran off into one of the smaller rooms, then came back a minute later.

"What was *that*, Seth?" Brittany asked.

"There was a phone in the office there. I didn't even think about trying it the first time I was in there. I just went back to check it. It's dead."

"Figures," Brittany responded.

The song ended, and the "On air" light lit over the booth. Ricky Jepson's voice boomed over the speakers. The group paused to listen, staring at the speakers.

"That was 'Live and Let Die' by Guns and Roses. This is Ricky Jepson with 102.9, Killer radio, and tonight is indeed a special night. Visiting our lovely little studio are eight contest winners, and we are so happy they are here. Oh, the night we have in store for them!"

Jonathan yelled, pulling everyone's attention to him, but when he tried to speak, the words wouldn't come out. Instead, he covered his mouth and pointed at the back corner of the building. Thick smoke pushed its way down from the roof.

"We want to thank all of our guests for joining us today. We've waited thirty-five years for this! We are 102.9, K-L-L-R...Killer radio and this is Queensryche, 'Take Hold of the Flame' from their album *The Warning*. Again, this is Ricky Jepson, and I bid you farewell."

The opening bars of the song started playing just as Kerry screamed. Flames started to lick through the ceiling in the back of the building, and the smoke started getting thick. Chaos ensued as everyone from the group started pounding on doors and kicking the walls, but the steel and brick were unrelenting. Flames burst through the roof over the studio portion of the building and started licking down the walls. Panic taking over, some cried, others stared in dumbfounded silence, and those that wouldn't give up hammered at the doors. Over the next few minutes, the entire roof was consumed in flames, and fiery chunks of wood rained down throughout the studio. The smoke was almost impossible to breathe through, and those that were still conscious had their shirts pressed against their mouth and nose.

Calvin and Joe were still trying to get the door open, using a fire extinguisher and an office chair as battering rams, but their strength was fading as the heat and smoke sucked the air out of the room. Joe looked down at the floor next to the door, where his beloved niece was unconscious. A tear slipped down his face, carving a pink line through the soot.

As Joe gave up and slipped to the floor beside his beautiful niece, the song ended, and Metallica's "Fade to Black" started playing. Joe glanced up at Calvin, and they both nodded at each other, knowing that this was the end. The song played on as the fire continued its path of destruction; however, besides the dancing flame and popping chunks of burning materials, there was no other movement.

AMY JEPSON SAT in the chair beside the hospital bed in the ICU, dabbing at her eyes with a tissue. There were tubes and wires everywhere, but the breathing tube that was forced down the throat of the bed's inhabitant was too much for her. Tenderly, she pushed the soiled blonde hair from the patient's face and tried to rub some of the overlooked soot from the patient's forehead.

Startled, Amy looked up as the nurse came into the room. "Hi, there," she greeted the nurse. "I just got here like fifteen minutes ago. Has she…Roxanne…regained consciousness at all since she's been here?"

The nurse set down her clipboard. "We have her in an induced coma. She's tried to wake up a couple times, but we want to keep her down for right now. She is going to be extremely miserable. Her lungs are heavily damaged, and we are worried about infection setting in. It may be another day before we bring her out. Are you family?"

"A friend of the family actually. I heard what happened and rushed down here to see her. I don't know if she has anyone else."

"Her emergency contact is her uncle, but he's admitted, too. Three rooms down, actually, in about the same shape."

Amy looked down at the ground, sniffled, and then turned her attention back to the nurse. "Did…uh…anyone else…you know?"

"Did they what?"

"Make it?"

The nurse walked over and placed her hand on Amy's shoulder. "These two aren't out of the woods yet, hun. It's very touch and go. There was one other victim that came in. He's down the hall. A total of three came in. Not sure how many didn't make it. By the way, does Roxanne have any…um…next of kin besides Joe Grimes?"

"I'm not sure. He's the only one I know of," she lied, having no idea, but not wanting to let on that she actually didn't know Roxanne at all.

"Okay, well, we will keep looking. In the meantime, feel free to stay, but she won't be waking up today. You'd be better off coming back tomorrow."

"Thank you, I'll do that."

Amy got up from the hard chair and tucked her purse under her arm, leaving the nurse to check on the patient. As she left, she glanced at the names on the charts that were beside each door and spotted the one with Joe Grimes' name on it. Peering in the door, she saw a man that was in his late fifties with short gray hair, the same tubes and wires attached. He also appeared to be either asleep or in a coma. Her emotions taking over again, she rubbed her eyes and headed to the elevator, then out to her car.

Inside her Hyundai Santa Fe, she started the engine, pushed aside her shoulder-length brown hair, and put on her seatbelt. She caught the reflection of her eyes in the mirror and gasped. She looked gaunt and lifeless. She rubbed the smeared mascara away from under her eyes and realized that her normally brown eyes looked almost black.

She thought back to that night thirty-five years ago. The night Ricky had died. The horror of the pictures, knowing her soulmate had been inside. One young daughter left without a father. It took her two years for the nightmares to subside…two long, horrifying years racked with dreams of fire, burning, and destruction. When the nightmares finally did stop, she continued to deal with the guilt, knowing if she had just told Ricky that she didn't want to— wouldn't even—leave Flagstaff, if she had never agreed to this crazy idea of opening his own station, he might still be with her now.

It took close to ten years and many sessions of therapy for her to be able to accept his death and move on in life, letting the guilt drain through the cracks of her broken life. Although no one had ever been arrested or charged for the fire—or his death—she finally was able to let go. That was until the year before.

Putting the car in reverse, Amy backed out of the spot, heading for home. Two minutes later, she broke down and started bawling.

THE NEXT DAY, Amy sat by the side of Roxanne's bed, holding her hand. Roxanne was still in the induced coma, but Amy had been informed that they were planning to bring her out a little later in the day.

Running her finger up and down Roxanne's arm, Amy thought about their daughter, Michelle. She would be turning thirty-nine soon, but Amy would not be celebrating the day with Michelle. In fact, Michelle had stopped talking to Amy the day she turned eighteen. Amy had never seen someone pack up and leave so quickly. Michelle had made it extremely apparent that she felt her father's death was Amy's fault. That event had sent Amy into another spiral for several years before she finally joined AA and stopped drinking, cold-turkey. She had been clean for eighteen years.

Roxanne, although younger, reminded Amy of Michelle, and Amy felt a connection with her, even though she had never met Roxanne before. Once again, she tried to hold back her tears as the guilt tore through her body. Life had been cruel to her, but this time, many more had been affected. If she had only known what the dreams had meant, maybe she could have stopped this.

"You're a pretty, young thing, aren't you?" she asked Roxanne, not expecting an answer. "Probably ten years younger than my Michelle. I'm so sorry. I didn't know. I'm so, so sorry," she repeated, tears slipping out of her eyes before she could stop them.

Grabbing a tissue, she dried the tears again, sniffled, and cleared her throat.

"You didn't deserve this. I promise, I didn't know. I didn't know what it meant."

The lights on the monitors continued to dance across the screen, but Roxanne did not move nor did she open her eyes.

"It was exactly a year ago. September 28th, 2017. I had woken up in the dead of night, drenched in sweat, screaming. It had been thirty-two years since I had nightmares like that. At first, I couldn't remember what it was about, but as I was changing the bed, I remembered. The fire. It was intense. I was there. In the station. I tried to get out but couldn't. That's when I woke up.

"I was confused as to why, after all those years, I would have dreams about the fire again. Brushing it off later that day, I forgot about it. That is until the second night. I had another dream. It was just as bad, but it wasn't about me that night. I saw other faces inside the fire. I didn't know what it meant but again hoped it would be the last one.

"That wasn't the case. For the entire last year, I've dreamed nightly. Always about the station. There was always a fire. Sometimes I was there. Sometimes Michelle. Many times, Ricky was there. He always told me that he would get even with those that had harmed him—killed him. On more than one occasion, I asked him who was to blame, but I never got an answer. The faces were always unfamiliar. Until now. Your face...I've seen it—younger, but familiar.

"It wasn't until the night of the fire—the one you were in—that the dreams clicked. An entire damn year of dreams ramping up to one grand finale—the final event. Ricky brought you all back to the station to make you pay. Thirty-five years after he was killed, he tried to get his revenge.

"I am so sorry I didn't get there sooner. The anniversary of Ricky's death has always been hard for me, but the feeling of dread that I had a couple of days ago was something I had never experienced before. I just knew something was wrong. That evening, I started to have a panic attack, and I felt a driving force. I knew I had to get to the station, even though it had been nothing but a burned-out brick skeleton for thirty-five years. As I got closer, I could see the smoke, and I called 911. They arrived and made me stand way back, but I watched as they cut the door open and started pulling out the bodies closest to the door."

Amy paused, trying to regain her composure again.

"If I had just figured it out sooner. The lady I saw in my dream, I think she may have been your mother. When she died a month or so ago, I think you were destined to take her place. The others? The paper published their names and their pictures. I was up all night researching…trying to make the connection. I made around half of them. I'm going to assume the remainder were there last night for the same reason as you were, and the others I researched.

"Calvin Hawkins is the only other survivor besides your uncle. He had an older brother that lived in Cottonwood for about a year—the same year as the fire. He passed away from heart failure around five years ago. Jonathan Hunter was only a kid, really. Nineteen. Lived in Dallas with his parents. Turns out his grandmother used to live in Cottonwood before moving to Sun City, Arizona. Preston Rhodes was thirty-five. He was born a month after the fire. His parents lived in Cottonwood at the time of the fire and then moved on to New Mexico immediately after, but they died in a freak accident five years later. Kerry Kelley was put up for adoption at birth, but I am thinking maybe her parents or another relative used to live here. I'm going to keep digging, but it all is adding up. Ricky's need for revenge didn't end when his murderers died. Instead, he went after those linked to them. Had I just figured it out sooner, the other six wouldn't have died."

The nurse entered the room. "We are going to cut off the Propofol now and let Roxanne come out of the coma slowly. I'd expect her to become conscious sometime a little later today."

"May I stay? I don't want her to be alone when she wakes up."

"Of course," the nurse answered, changing out the IV bag. "Will you please push the button when she wakes up? We will want to talk to her."

"Absolutely," Amy told her.

"Thank you," the nurse said and left the room.

"Can't wait to meet you," Amy whispered. "I'm here for you.

There has been enough loss and tragedy."

One Month Later

"How are those tacos?" Amy asked.

Roxanne smiled. "Delicious. Thanks for bringing me to this restaurant. The food is really good here."

"Happy to! How have you been feeling?"

"Better every day. Thanks for giving me a place to stay while I recovered. It was nice to get off of the oxygen, but I'm just now feeling like myself again."

"How does it feel to be back in town?"

"Weird. I've always hated it here, but I'm starting to think that was simply because my mother was here. This place is kinda growing on me now. I suppose I need to get back to Norfolk soon, though. My apartment is still there, and they're holding my job."

"Remind me why you moved to Norfolk again?"

"Because it was about as far away as I could get from here."

"I get it, but do you really want to go back to that job?" Roxanne had confided in Amy the week prior.

Roxanne sighed. "Well, it paid the bills. Honestly, I don't really want to go back, but I need money, and it's all I have right now."

"Well, why don't you stay here?"

"I appreciate it, Amy. You've been so kind to me. But you don't have to take care of me. This wasn't your fault. You couldn't have known."

"Well, what if I got you a job at one of the bars in Old Town? You certainly have the personality for it, and I bet you'd make the big bucks in tips."

"That actually sounds like fun, but I feel I'm imposing, staying with you. Plus, a girl needs her own space. Not sure slinging drinks will pay the rent."

"What if there is no rent?"

"What are you talking about?"

Amy slid a key across the table toward her. "Your uncle Joe asked me to give this to you. It was for your mother's house. She left it to Joe, but he wants you to have it. It's paid off, by the way."

Roxanne's mouth fell open. "No way."

"I'm serious. He wants you to meet him there after lunch. He has a contractor meeting you guys there as well. He said they can remodel it and make it seem like an entirely different home. You'd have no rent payment. Now what's your excuse?"

Roxanne was silent, trying to process the news. Finally, she spoke. "I'm sorry, Amy, but I have to go back to Norfolk."

"I was hoping you wouldn't say that," Amy said, her eyes tearing up. "We just became friends. I don't want you to go."

"Oh, didn't I tell you?" Roxanne asked.

"Tell me what?"

"I'll be back in a couple weeks! I'm just going to get my stuff and my car."

Amy leaned across the table and hugged her. "I'm so happy. You'll always have a home here."

"Best home I've ever had," Roxanne said, returning the hug and pulling Amy in tight.

EIGHT MONTHS LATER

ROXANNE STOOD UP from her seat at the wedding party table and held up her glass, tapping a spoon against it to get the guest's attention. When the room finally quieted down, she recited the speech she had committed to memory.

"Ten months ago, I almost died, along with this strapping man, my uncle Joe. Today, I am so pleased to be able to be here to share this day with him, and his beautiful bride, Amy, who in nine months has been more of a mother to me than I ever had in my entire life. She is a loving, kind, and caring soul and not only saved my life, as well as my uncle's life, but she was the only one that was there for me when I got out of the hospital. I love this lady so much, and although I can't really call her mom since she is marrying my uncle, I can certainly call her Aunt Amy. So, Uncle Joe and Aunt Amy, I wanted you both to know that I think you are perfect together, and I wish you nothing but happiness for the remainder of your days. I can't think of a better place to be than one town over from you guys. Congratulations, you two!"

The guests all clinked their glasses, and Joe and Amy gave each other a deep, passionate kiss. Roxanne had never felt so complete.

SEPTEMBER 28TH, 2019

CHARLES ETHAN MORGAN checked into the hotel and made his way up to the room. Inside, he unpacked his bag, excitement coursing through his veins.

His flight the day before from Vancouver, Canada, was fairly uneventful, but the long layover in Seattle had caused the day to be a long one, and he had spent the night in Phoenix before driving up to the hotel.

At thirty-two, he had lived in Canada most of his life with his mother and his adoptive father, even though his earlier memories were from when they had lived in England. Even though his dad wasn't his real father, he loved him like they were blood. Charlie felt no need to search for his birthfather, Calvin, who had decided he wasn't ready to be a father when he found out his girlfriend—Charlie's mom—was pregnant.

Although Charlie had never been to Arizona, the fact that he won a ticket to a VIP concert experience wasn't something he could pass up, even though he lived a long way away. He wasn't fazed by the fact he had never heard of the radio station, KLLR, before. He was going to have the time of his life.

ABOUT THE AUTHORS

STEVEN PAJAK is the author of novels such as the U.S. Marshal Jack Monroe series and the Mad Swine trilogy, as well as short stories and novellas. When not writing, Steven works as an administrator at a university. He continues to be an avid reader of Stephen King and Dean Koontz, John Saul, Richard Matheson, and many other favorite authors in the horror, suspense, thriller, and general fiction genres. Steven lives in the Chicagoland area with his wife and two teens. Find out more about Steven at www.stevenpajak.com.

GERALD DEAN RICE technically lives in Southeast Michigan but he only maintains that residence to satisfy the government. He typically moves from abandoned building to burnt out house to sewer network to stay ahead of them. Before he rests his head--wherever that may be—he bangs out a word or two and sends it by carrier donkey to publishers who fund the effort to overthrow whichever omega quadrant overlords are currently slurping the brains of what's left of the human masses. If you have no idea what any of this means, they are either at your door or on their way. He's also the author of Dead 'til Dawn, Part-time Zombie, and he edited the anthology, Anything but Zombies. He also has a rescue cat named Pedro. His new novella, The Devil's Gunt, is available on Amazon, Barnes & Noble, and everywhere books are sold. You can follow him here: http://bit.ly/GDRice.

JANE ALVEY HARRIS is the author of the award-winning YA psychological fantasy thriller series, the My Myth Trilogy. Book One, RIVEN, is optioned for a feature film. Jane loves to watch and study what makes us tick as humans. She's definitely a dreamer. Her favorite thing to do is use her wild imagination to weave together settings and stories for characters to live and learn in...herself included. Jane also enjoys writing short stories, which provides her the perfect opportunity to delve into her emotions and psyche in order to breathe life into the characters and scenes that beckon to her in her waking and sleeping dreams. Her shorts are published in several anthologies. When she isn't working on her own manuscripts, you can find Jane teaching private creative and academic writing classes, and narrating audiobooks. You might say she's a bit obsessed with the written word. Find out more about Jane at www.janealveyharris.com.

MIKE DUKE writes an eclectic mix of horror stories. He explores dark supernatural entities, cosmic terrors, and natural monstrosities. However, the wicked deeds the human heart can conceive and inflict on others as well as our capacity to act against such things pervades much of his work. According to Chris Hall, at DLS Reviews, Mike is "a master of utterly uncompromising hardboiled revenge-thrillers." He has a way of provoking a significant response from his readers—whether shock, terror, dread, an uneasy sense of empathy, Heebie Jeebie crawlies, or surprise at unexpected twists. Mike will make you feel while you read his words. As one reviewer said, when you read a Mike Duke book, you don't just read about an experience, you have an experience. Mike has published six novellas, three novels, and short stories in twelve different anthologies. Find out more about Mike at: facebook.com/mike.duke.author.

KAYLA KRANTZ is a proud author, responsible for a number of novels in the genres dark fantasy, psychological horror, and supernatural thriller. She is fascinated by the dark and macabre. Stephen King is her all-time inspiration, mixed in with some faint remnants of the works of Edgar Allen Poe. When she began writing, she started in horror, but somehow drifted into thriller and fantasy. She loves the 1988 movie Heathers. Kayla was born and raised in Michigan, but traveled across the country to where she currently resides, in Texas. Find out more about Kayla at: www.author kaylakrantz.com.

MATTHEW A. CLARKE is a rising name in the world of horror. He has many short stories published across multiple anthologies and is currently working on his debut novel. His obsession with horror began at a young age when he discovered Goosebumps books and scary movies on late-night television. Nowadays, his influences range from Jack Ketchum to Junji Ito. Matthew lives in the South of England with his fiancé, Issy, and a little dachshund called Frank. Find out more about Matthew at: www.matthewaclarkeauthor.co.uk.

RJ ROLES started his writing career in 2019 with his release *Girl's Best Friend*. RJ has been busy typing away on tales to bring excitement to the reader. Not wanting to restrict his writing, he does so under the banner of "Genre Fiction Author" and plans to dabble in all fields that interest him. You can find him on most social networks as RJ Roles or RJ Roles fiction. Find out more about RJ at:

L. K. PINAIRE Larry and his wife, Peg, of 36 years live in a wooded neighborhood in Southern Indiana. He is a retired quality manager. He writes science fiction and horror as well as substitute teaching in the local high schools. He has written five yet-unpublished science fiction novels and published numerous short stories. Larry loves gardening, IU basketball, and spending time with his family and has been an active member in Sertoma (International Speech and hearing group) since 1979. Find out more about Larry at his website: www.lkpinaire.com.

ALAN DEROSBY, a Maine native, has spent the past several years focusing on his passion: writing. Alan has created original and spooky short stories, having "The Ghost at Old Pier's Pub" published online as well as two in print anthologies, titled "Going Home" and "Full Moon." He has made it to the second round of the Amazon Breakthrough Novel awards with his young historical fiction novel Lost Souls of Purgatory. Last, but certainly not least, Alan's debut novel, Man of Clay, will be released in Spring 2021. When not writing, Alan is teaching history at Messalonskee High School in Oakland, Maine, spending time with his family, or watching the New York Mets suffer through another disappointing season. Contact Alan at: Alanderosby@gmail.com

CASSANDRA ANGLER is a lifelong resident of the buckeye state (Ohio) and a happily married mother of four. When she isn't corralling her four minions of darkness she is busy conjuring nightmares in literary form, reading and overall trying to better the world. Cassandra has always been a fan of all things horror and macabre. She has been featured in several anthologies, and her debut novel, Contaminated: Book 1 was released in October of 2020. Some of her influences include Eleanor Merry, Stephen King, Paige Dearth, and Brian Keene. Find out more about Cassandra at https://www.facebook.com/cassandra.anglerauthor.9.

PETER ROCHA is a writer from the Midwest who loves to dabble in poetry, playwriting, and short stories. His first excursion into the horror genre was "A Touch of Grace" which was included in the anthology "If I Die Before I Wake, Volume I." He often posts his poetry on his Facebook page. He is married with 3 children, two dogs, and a brain that won't stop. He can be contacted via Facebook or at peterrocha2010 @hotmail.com.

RED LAGOE grew up on 80's horror and carried her paranoia for slashers and sewer creatures into adulthood. When she's not spewing horror onto the page, she substitutes at an elementary school and dabbles in amateur astronomy. Red is a staff writer for Crystal Lake Publishing's Still Water Bay series. Several of her stories have been published by CLP, Dark Moon Digest, Sinister Smile Press, and more. Her horror collection, *Lucid Dreams*, released in February 2020. Find out more about Red at www.redlagoe.com.

R.E. SARGENT is the author of several novels, as well as a handful of novelettes. R.E.'s novels include *Relative Terror* and The Fury-Scorned series. At a young age, R.E. fell in love with books. While many of the other kids were playing sports, he was reading as many books as he could. He quickly got hooked on mysteries and suspense. It was his love of books and storytelling that led to his passion for writing. One of his biggest inspirations is Dean Koontz. R.E. currently lives in Oregon with his wife and their two fur-children, Riley and Mason. Riley is a Chocolate Lab and Mason is a Bernese Mountain Dog. Find out more about R.E. at www.resargent.com.

MORE FROM SINISTER SMILE PRESS

IF I DIE BEFORE I WAKE
VOLUME 3: TALES OF DEADLY WOMEN AND RETRIBUTION

Go ahead, run. Hide, even. No matter. There's no place you can go that she won't find you.

A woman scorned. The sanctity of her sanctuary threatened. The betrayal of trust...even loyalty. Don't ever tell her not to take it personally, because that's exactly what it is. Personal. Your first blunder was mistaking her kindness for weakness. Your second was betraying her. The third? Underestimating her. Don't say we didn't warn you. Take the plunge into these tales of deadly women who will stop at nothing until vengeance is theirs. Available now!

IF I DIE BEFORE I WAKE
VOLUME 4: TALES OF NIGHTMARE CREATURES

Your worst nightmares come true.

Razor-sharp teeth. Vicious claws. The soul-piercing eyes that stare you down right before it pounces. What will you do when it's you against a purveyor of pure evil? You think it's just a dream? Think again. These nightmare creatures have transcended the pages of the books they were written into, they've ripped their way from the silver screen, and now they are coming for you. There is nowhere to hide—they will find you. But the question remains. Do you have what it takes to conquer the beast or will you let it destroy you? Available February 28, 2021. Preorder now!

IF I DIE BEFORE I WAKE
VOLUME 5: TALES OF THE OTHERWORLDLY AND UNDEAD

Sometimes, the dead do come back. Sometimes, they crave your flesh...and sometimes, they desire your very soul, but they aren't the only thing you have to fear.

You don't believe in what you can't see, yet something is there, watching, waiting. You can feel its unholy intentions deep down in the marrow of your bones. You don't know where it came from, but you know with every fiber of your being that it is not from this earth, and as you feel its gaze searing through your skin, you know the end might just be near.

It took its last breath, you watched the dirt being shoveled onto its coffin, yet there it is, standing before you, staring you down like you're its next meal. It's vicious and it's evil and even though you know— you're absolutely positive—that the abomination before you should be dead, somehow it's not, and its ungodly eyes are focused on you.

The Otherworldly and Undead are out there and they are coming for you. When you run—and oh, will you run—you don't need to be the fastest...you only need to be faster than the person beside you—at least until there is no one else left. Join us for the most terrifying stories of Otherworldly and Undead beings as they stalk and torment the living, feeding off their souls and their flesh before recruiting them to eternal damnation. Available June 14, 2021. Preorder now!

A MESSAGE FROM SINISTER SMILE PRESS

Sinister Smile Press wishes health and happiness for all our readers during these very difficult times. We hope our books are keeping you wholeheartedly entertained, and we encourage you to check out our next publication, *Devil's Gulch*, coming November 16, 2020.

Sinister Smile Press is a publisher dedicated to the publication of anthologies and collaborative novels focusing on themes of horror, supernatural, karma and vengeance. Creating nightmares is our business...and business is good!

Sinister Smile Press

Horror Themed Anthologies
and Collaborative Novels

Creating Nightmares is our Business...
and business is *good!*